A Monstrous World Novel

# Ironling
## A Fantasy Monster Romance

## S. E. Wendel

*This is for everyone who's ever had a crush. Isn't it horrible? All the agony and longing!*

*But what if they'd felt the same?*
*What if everything went right . . .*

The Fish
Culdan
Larach
Shamago R.
Scarbo
Northpoint R.
Kilkarach
Bandaraugh R.
Granach
D
EIREA
Middlerun R.
Calcarr
Casholl
Rathcaran
Southford R.
Briggan
The Scales
Gray Knolls
Kinvar
FAELANDS
Griegen Mountains
Lune R.
FALLORIAN
Kaldebrak
Holdur
The Twins
ORCISH
BALMIRRA
TERRITORIES
Innrinho
DRAGON KINGDOM
The
MONSTROUS
WORLD
HIGHHOME
The Droplets

CALEDON
Glendown
INSLEY
The Gates
Bellbee
Intersea
GLEANNÁ
Larkspur
Adrigoll
Threepoints
Abbon R.
Kilgaran
R.
GOLD SEA
BORDERLANDS
LYCEA
Birrin
tone-Skin
Camp
PYRROS
Irynian
Delta
CONQUERED
CONFEDERATION
trait
2024

# Before You Begin...

I hope you're ready and excited for *Ironling!* A few quick notes before you begin:

This is book 2 of the Monstrous World series. The book stands on its own but will be best enjoyed after book 1, *Halfling*.

A few content/trigger warnings: our heroine Aislinn is neurodivergent and experiences fits/panic attacks, including in the Prologue. Our hero, Hakon, is partially deaf in one ear. Both of them have lost parents/grandparents. The book also includes a toxic sibling relationship, characters put in peril, intolerance, and fighting/battle/violence. So take care of yourself!

The book includes a glossary of people, places, pronunciation, orcish, and medieval terms in the back. Don't be afraid to flip back and forth, but don't spoil anything for yourself.

All righty, let's go! I hope you enjoy our return to the Monstrous World!

# What's Come Before . . .

Just a quick refresher for you before you begin! In the first book of the series, *Halfling*, a woman named Sorcha is betrayed to slavers, who kidnap her from her family's estate and sell her on to a splinter camp of orcs, the Stone-Skins. Orek, a half-orc whose own mother was a human slave purchased by the clan decades before, frees Sorcha and agrees to take her home. The two fall in love along the journey, and Orek joins Sorcha's large family.

Upon their arrival, they report what's happened to the liege lord of the land, Merrick Darrow. It is Merrick's son and heir, Jerrod, who sold Sorcha out to the slavers after she rejected his romantic advances. Merrick gives Sorcha the choice of what should happen to Jerrod. She decides he should be banished to the Ward, a castle converted into an infirmary, run by monk wardens. He is also stripped of his inheritance and position as heir, which is given to his older sister and Sorcha's friend Aislinn Darrow.

Sorcha and Orek settle into their new life, Jerrod is sent off to the Ward, and Aislinn is left to grapple with her new role and all the responsibility that comes with it.

# Prologue

"**W**hat are you doing in here?"

Aislinn threw open the door of her study to find her younger brother, Jerrod, toying with one of her new devices. Jerrod looked up guiltily, sticking out his bottom lip in a pout.

"I just wanted to see," he said by way of apology.

Aislinn scowled, looking from Jerrod to her new instrument. It was a delicate thing and had taken her days to assemble. The glass lenses set in tiers of metal rods were meant to help magnify old texts and anything else too small to see well.

She'd barely gotten to use it herself, and she certainly didn't want her eleven-year-old brother getting his sweaty fingers all over it. She didn't like him in her space, either.

Their father, Lord Merrick Darrow, had let Aislinn have the room for her study barely a year ago. Aislinn had spent that time filling it with her favorite things—books. She collected books and tomes and treatises on math, astronomy, architecture, and more. Anything she could, she gathered and read. The study had quickly become a haven of paper and ink, a little refuge from the busyness of Dundúran Castle.

And . . . since their mother had passed in childbirth, and their infant brother along with her, two years prior, Aislinn had found much comfort in the company of books and learning.

She didn't appreciate the intrusion, and Jerrod knew it. When she didn't immediately demand he leave, though, he dropped his guilty look and turned back to the device.

"Fine," she grumbled, "just don't touch anything."

Aislinn rounded her desk and sat down, keeping an eye on her brother. He was often careless, and many cups and plates and crystal had broken under his sloppy hand.

Taking up her quill, Aislinn got started sketching a new idea. She'd been talking with one of the senior gardeners, Morwen, about the castle gardens and orchard, and it got her thinking about irrigation. Morwen told her the last time the irrigation system had been worked on was under Aislinn's great-grandmother nearly ninety years ago.

She'd left her study for less than an hour to find a book on irrigation in her father's large library—and apparently hadn't locked the door behind her.

Aislinn glanced at the interloper. He had his hands folded behind his back as he inspected the device, at least.

She chewed her cheek, wishing she could tell him to leave, but the voice of Dundúran's chatelain, Brenna, echoed in her mind. *"Be kind to your brother, he's suffered so much."*

*Nothing more than I have; she was my mother, too,* she often grumbled, but only to herself, as such thoughts were selfish.

It was also selfish of Aislinn to resent that Brenna, who had come with their mother Lady Róisín when she married their father, favored Jerrod over her. Always Jerrod got away with his antics, while Aislinn was scolded, reminded that Lady Róisín wouldn't have done such a thing or acted in such a way.

*"Ladies don't have tantrums,"* Brenna was fond of telling her.

Aislinn wasn't a lady, though. Not really. Not like her mother.

She didn't like the things her elegant mother had and didn't think like her, either. Aislinn disliked attending court functions. She didn't like wearing fancy, stiff gowns and sitting for hours through speeches.

She dreaded the word play and games of politics. She loathed greeting guests and having people kiss her hand and holding her tongue when she'd rather just tell the truth about being bored.

While Róisín had lived, she'd helped Aislinn learn enough about courtly etiquette to survive. Her mother had understood Aislinn's difficulties and taught her as best she could, all to combat the roiling emotions that sometimes overwhelmed Aislinn.

Brenna called them tantrums or fits. Róisín had called it feeling too much.

Whatever it was, Aislinn hated her outbursts of emotions.

Without her mother to help her, she'd taken to avoiding things she disliked or that easily overwhelmed her. Aislinn spent her time reading and studying on her own, as tutors had little to teach her anymore, even if she was only fourteen.

Her father needed her, though. He'd made it his mission to root out the awful slave trade that took root in southern Eirea during the brutal wars of succession fifteen years past. Someone had to oversee Dundúran, and although Jerrod, as the son, was heir, Aislinn was older—and smarter.

Brenna as chatelain handled much of it, but Aislinn was growing up and more than capable, as her father put it. She wanted to make him proud. Anything to relieve the devastation in his eyes after losing Róisín.

Aislinn sighed, wishing for the hundred-thousandth time that her mother hadn't fallen pregnant, that she was still—

*Is that smoke?*

Looking up, Aislinn saw Jerrod angling the biggest lens of the device into a beam of sunlight from the window. A concentrated cone of light radiated down on an open book, a thin plume of smoke rising from the darkening paper.

"What are you doing?" Aislinn screeched.

Jerrod jerked up to stare at her wide-eyed, the lens left to bore into the paper. Within a moment, flames erupted from the pages.

Aislinn sprung up and raced across the study.

Jerrod yelped, smacking into the device. It went clattering to the floor, glass shattering.

Aislinn threw a spare blanket over the burning book, beating at it with her hands until the small flame was snuffed. Her hands smarted from the heat, and smoke filled her study.

Tears streaming down her flushed face, Aislinn turned on Jerrod. He gaped at her with his blue-gray eyes. Their mother's eyes.

They'd always looked wrong in his face. Too gentle, too warm, when Jerrod was neither.

"Sorry," he said.

He didn't mean it.

He never meant it.

Frustration boiled inside her, overwhelming and consuming. She burned hotter than the fire he'd almost set, her temper snapping.

Aislinn shoved him.

He stumbled backward, tears springing to his eyes, and yelped.

She filled her fists with his tunic and shook him, her rage poured out of her in tears and screams. She didn't know what she said—it didn't really matter.

How dare he come into her space, her refuge? How dare he ruin her device?

He always ruined everything.

*I hate him! I hate him I hate him Ihatehimhatehimhate—*

"Aislinn!"

She was yanked away from Jerrod, who was left sniveling in the corner. Aislinn clawed at the body trying to restrain her, kicking and yelping like a caught animal.

The air fled her lungs, and Aislinn screamed silently, thrashing to be free.

The someone holding her boxed her ears, stunning her.

Panting, Aislinn looked up into Brenna's horrified face.

"Stop this at once!" The chatelain delivered another smack to

Aislinn's face, not hard enough to hurt but enough to snap Aislinn's attention back into the study, away from her anger.

She held very still, not wanting to be slapped again.

Brenna waited a long moment before hurrying over to help Jerrod. She cooed and clucked over him, helping him stand.

Aislinn drew her arms around herself as she began to shake.

*What have I done? What have I done?*

Her stomach roiled with every pulsing ache in her palms from hitting Jerrod, and she balled her trembling hands into fists.

Aislinn detested violence. She never watched the knights at tourneys or in the practice field. She always hurried away when Jerrod tried to brawl with his friends, and she never laughed when jesters struck each other for cheap comedy.

*How could I do this?*

"What have you done?" Brenna demanded, cradling Jerrod to her.

"He broke my new device and set a fire. He could have burned the castle down," Aislinn argued, but without any true heat.

Brenna tutted. "I'm sure he didn't mean to."

"I said I was sorry," Jerrod sulked from the safety of Brenna's skirts.

The chatelain pinned Aislinn with a look of deep disapproval. "Ladies don't hit. If your fits become violent, I'm going to have to tell your father you need confining."

"No!" Aislinn dreaded that above all. While she didn't exactly enjoy most other people, she couldn't bear to be locked away.

She loved her home. Dundúran was beautiful, built of local blonde limestone and crowned in blue-gray slate roofs. Blue Darrow banners flapped on poles atop conical turret towers. Her mother's rose garden still bloomed, and the wisteria hung thick in the spring. The Shanago River meandered to the south, perfect for punting and shoreline strolls. She loved the castle and its staff. They were her friends.

"Then you mustn't behave like a wild animal," Brenna chided.

Aislinn's gaze skittered away. She couldn't look at Jerrod when she said, "I'm sorry."

A long moment passed in silence, finally drawing back Aislinn's reluctant gaze.

From his place at Brenna's side, Jerrod considered her shrewdly with those eyes that were and were not her mother's, a little smirk on his mouth.

"All right," he finally said.

"Good man," Brenna praised, rubbing his arm. "Now, clean this up, young lady. Then it's time to wash up for dinner."

Ushering Jerrod in front of her, Brenna walked them toward the study door.

"Oh, and I don't think there's any reason to tell your father about this," said Brenna. "Accidents happen."

Finally left alone in her study, Aislinn hugged herself tighter.

She couldn't bear to look at the broken device, all of its lenses shattered and its metal parts twisted. The room smelled of smoke and probably would for weeks.

Heavy tears splattered her chest. Another wave of emotion rose up her throat, and she quickly closed and locked the study door.

In the privacy of her refuge, she had another fit, screaming and crying. She pulled at her hair and beat her own chest, her rage overflowing. What she'd done, the threat of being confined, her broken device, all of it poured out of her in a maelstrom.

Thankfully, it was a smaller fit, most of her energy expended already, and Aislinn slumped to the ground when it was done, exhausted.

Surrounded by her books, Aislinn eventually dried her tears as best she could and then began to pick up the pieces.

# I

*Fifteen Years Later*

For all that Hakon's grandparents had done for him, gave him a loving home, taught him everything they knew at the forge and beyond, he couldn't bear to stay in their home more than a fortnight.

It hadn't been one thing but a series of little difficulties that felled his beloved grandmother—aching joints and a thick cough and a bitter rainstorm. Although already elderly, even for an orc, she was hearty and healthy—yet she'd quickly taken ill. She'd passed peacefully twelve days ago. It hadn't taken his grandfather long to follow, his own health fading as rain pattered against the slate roof.

Hakon had begged his grandfather not to go. Not yet. There was so much yet they had to do. He was all Hakon had.

His grandfather's gnarled green hand had risen to hang in the air, and Hakon hurried to grasp it. *"You have everything you need, vittarah,"* he said. He hadn't called Hakon *little hammer* in years. *"You don't need me anymore. But I need my mate."*

Hakon had sat beside his grandfather, weeping into the quiet night, as the old orc slipped away to his mate in the afterworld. Leaving Hakon behind.

That had been a week ago. A week was all he could bear in their quiet, cold house. No longer a home. The trinkets and tidbits of their life littered the house, their cold disuse burning him whenever he reached for one. What use was his grandmother's shawl or his grandfather's cane?

The life that had been lived in that house was over.

In his tide of grief, Hakon sometimes believed his own was, too.

After a week, he'd no intention of relighting his grandfather's forge. It sat ashen and dark, an empty mouth never to be fed again. He couldn't bring himself to stand there and work the bellows, bring life back into a place so well loved.

His grandparents' bodies were washed and prepared in the proper way, he saw to that. He and his aunt Sighíl said the rites and laid them upon the funeral bowers. Their pyres burned long into the night, scattering flames into the sky to be carried away by the wind to the afterworld, where together they would live again.

Without Hakon.

All he'd ever known in his thirty years was his grandparents and their home nestled into the Green-Fist clan's stronghold of Kaldebrak. After his human father perished in a hunting accident and his orcish mother disappeared into the wilderness with her grief soon after, his grandparents were his life. He whittled and set gemstones with his grandmother as they chatted with their hands; he worked the bellows and wielded the sledgehammer as his grandfather formed molten iron into fantastical shapes. Although the rest of the clan was ambivalent to him as a halfling, his grandparents had shown him nothing but kindness and love.

Ever since he was a youngling, Hakon had been hard of hearing in his right ear, just like his grandmother. She'd taught him to speak with his hands and read the lips of others. It made them good companions for a blacksmith, as many a smith lost their hearing over a lifetime of hammer strikes. Outside his grandparents' home, his ear was a vulnerability, one he worked to compensate for by being quick, strong, and observant.

Still, his grandparents couldn't help protecting him, even coddling him. It would be easy to live the life they built for him—safe, secure, a place he understood. They had left him the house, the forge, everything he needed. Except, as the cold, lonely days passed gloomily inside that very house, Hakon had come to the painful realization that his life was no longer here.

Chieftain Kennum would surely take him on as a blacksmith if he sought work—war might be coming, and there was a need for every available smith, even in a place like Kaldebrak that overflowed with them. He could earn respect and a living through his skills. But he didn't want a living, he wanted a life. Which wasn't to be found here.

He could honor his grandparents' sacrifice and gift, or . . . he could take the chance to be happy. Get away from his stifling grief and the life of little promise he'd have here and go find . . . something else.

Of course, this was all difficult to explain to his aunt Sighíl. Even now, she took up most of the front room of the modest home, fists on her hips, her frown imperious as she watched Hakon pack. She hadn't been quiet about her disdain for his plan to leave Kaldebrak—but then, his aunt wasn't quiet about most things. There was a reason his grandfather had taught him the trick of using the beeswax they put in their ears to dull loud hammering whenever Siggy came knocking.

As a grown male, Hakon realized now that Siggy was loud because she wanted to be heard in a family hard of hearing and hard of head, but it was also because she cared. Based on her current volume, she cared a great deal.

"I just don't see the point," she said for the third time, shaking the rafters. "You have everything you need here. *Manan* and *daron* left you the house. *Daron* his forge and tools. Everything you could need."

The guilt of those truths burned the back of his throat, but Hakon didn't stop his methodical folding. He wouldn't be bringing too much, just what he could carry on his back; clothes, a few treasured baubles, supplies for the journey, the gems he'd sold the house for, and some of his grandfather's smithing tools he couldn't bear to part with.

Oh, and the glorified rug currently snoring by the fire.

Like many in Kaldebrak, his grandparents had always been fond of dogs. They kept a pack of wolfhounds that trotted after them into the market and sat at the table to keep them company on rainy days. Most were gone now, either passed or taken in by Siggy and her two mates, who together ran another smithy specializing in silversmithing on the other side of Kaldebrak. The only one left was Wülf, a grumpy four-year-old hound who didn't really like anyone and was too stubborn to leave with his siblings and Siggy.

Hakon loved the mutt, and even if he wasn't the friendliest dog, his constant companionship was welcome over the last week. Hakon had no doubt that when he left tomorrow, Wülf would follow, even if he huffed and grumbled about it.

For now, the beast was content to lie there as a general nuisance and tripping hazard.

By contrast, Siggy stood across the room, her contained energy making her vibrate with impatience. If Hakon let her, she'd have him packed up and moved in with her, her mates, and her twins. While he loved visiting them, their home was already full to the brim—especially now with three more giant hounds.

And . . . the house was full of love. Siggy and Halstern were the loud, boisterous ones, and often their tempers and stubbornness got the better of them. Viggo was the peacemaker, soothing tempers and keeping the smithy orderly. Their lives were controlled chaos to Hakon, but it worked for them. He didn't want to upset the balance of their home.

Nor witness every day the thing he wanted most—a life, a family. Matehood. If he stayed, he feared his envy would grow into something even uglier.

He couldn't burden them. He couldn't stay in this empty house. He couldn't live a half-life, safe but hobbled. So away he must go.

His mind was made. *Now just to convince Siggy of that.*

"There's nothing for me here," he told her patiently.

"No, nothing, just your *family* and your *life*," she huffed.

He winced. Her barb wasn't meant to hurt, not truly; he knew Siggy, she was sharpest when she herself was hurting. He glanced up and finally *looked* at her.

Siggy stood there, arms crossed over her muscular chest and eyes gone glassy with dammed tears. In that moment, she looked much younger than she was, like the young orcess who'd already lost her elder sister and now her parents.

Siggy and his grandparents often remarked how much he resembled his mother Ingrid. Even though he had a more human face, with shorter ears and small tusks and a thinner nose, he'd lived his whole life being told he had Ingrid's eyes, Ingrid's countenance, Ingrid's good nature.

It'd taken Hakon a long while to outgrow his resentment over it. He didn't want to have parts of his mother—he wanted all of her. He wanted her to have stayed with him, that he'd been enough to keep her from falling down the pit of despair that came with losing a mate. But he hadn't. She hadn't.

Hakon, with his mother's eyes and good nature, was all his family had left of Ingrid, beloved sister and daughter. When Siggy looked at him, he wasn't sure she always saw him, Hakon.

He couldn't fault her for it. The aching maw of loss was ever-present in his heart at Ingrid's absence, and he'd hardly known her, young as he'd been. Siggy and his grandparents had had her for far longer.

Yet, Hakon wanted to be his own person. With his own life.

He wanted to be more than Ingrid's poor orphaned halfling.

He wanted out of this house, with its dark corners and cold hearth and heavy memories.

"You know what I mean," he admonished Siggy gently. "I know I can work *gadaron*'s forge, but that's not a life. I want what you have, Siggy."

Her lips thinned into a line between her tusks, capped with jeweled silver to show off her craft. Her leathers were soft and polished, no doubt thanks to Viggo, and her tunic and kirtle had been embroidered at the hems and cuffs with intricate designs of hammers and tongs. A double-layered torque lay around her neck, two gems winking on either side of her throat.

Hakon definitely wasn't jealous that Siggy had *two* mates when he had none. Definitely not.

Of course, he knew his aunt worked hard for the life she had, and she deserved every happiness. Hakon was determined to work just as hard to deserve the same.

Siggy huffed again, lifting a few strands of her dark mane from her brow. "There are more females in Kaldebrak than just Feeli."

Hakon's ears heated at the name, and he pointedly kept his gaze on his folding. Getting far away from Feeli and his old feelings for her were more reasons to leave.

He couldn't even blame his infatuation on being a foolish youth, for he'd pined after the orcess for far longer than that. Feeli had been the only orcess to show any interest in him, and even though she'd made clear she'd never accept a mate-bond with him, nor even be the only male she lay with at a time, for years Hakon held onto hope that she might change her mind.

Plenty of kin mated more than one other—Siggy, Halstern, and Viggo were easy proof of that. However, deep inside, Hakon had always been a jealous sort; covetous, desirous. He wanted all of someone for himself. It was an ugly sort of possessiveness, and he'd done his best to squash those feelings, as he knew, even in his deepest infatuation, that they were useless when it came to Feeli. The orcess had no interest in choosing just one bedfellow, and even if she did, it wouldn't be him.

In the end, they'd taken their pleasures with each other. Hakon learned how to please a female and Feeli discovered what it was like to lay with a halfling. There had been times when they stayed awake late into the night, lounging in bed and just talking, that Hakon thought perhaps it would turn into something more. But now he was wiser and perhaps a bit smarter. Feeli wasn't the female for him.

"None would have me," Hakon reminded his aunt. He was friends or acquaintances with plenty, having grown up with many other kin, but most only saw him at best as a brother, at worst a pity. *Poor Hakon the halfling, no kin, only one good ear*—what was there to recommend him?

"You don't know that," Siggy insisted.

"I do."

"And you think a human woman would accept you?"

Hakon's ears burned again.

*That's the hope, yes.*

"I've tried to find a mate here. It's time I search elsewhere," he said, quite diplomatically, he thought.

"But humans . . ." Siggy made a dismissive, rude gesture. "They're so . . ."

"My father was human."

"Yes, but Cormac was different. Strong. They aren't all like that, you know."

"Not all orcs are the same, either, Siggy."

She pointed a warning green finger at him. "Don't argue with me, nephew."

"Not arguing, just pointing out."

"You're doing it again."

"Doing what?"

Siggy made a disgusted sound before marching across the room. Hakon braced for a sisterly slap, but instead, Siggy laid her hand on his shoulder and squeezed.

"I've lost my sister and now my parents. I don't want to lose you, too, nephew."

Heart aching, Hakon dropped his folding to pull his aunt into a firm embrace. They were nearly the same size, Siggy slightly taller but Hakon with wider shoulders. He felt her love and her loss through her embrace—it almost convinced him to stay.

"I want you to be happy, I do. I just worry that your leaving is out of grief, not to find happiness."

Hakon pulled back to look up at her. "I will carry them with me wherever I go. And this isn't goodbye."

Siggy sighed deeply. "Where will you go?"

"Do you remember what the trackers who came last month said? About the human place accepting other folk?"

"The Darrowlands."

"Yes. Apparently, there are already halflings there." He'd be lying if he said he wasn't curious to meet one of his own kind, another who was both human and orc.

Stepping back, Siggy held him by the shoulders, assessing him with those deep-set brown eyes. The family all had such eyes, including Hakon. They were a mark that, even if he was only half, that half was theirs.

"Perhaps it's for the best," she finally said reluctantly. "There's talk that Vallek Far-Sight may come north, looking to recruit. Young smith like you would get taken, and I don't want that life for you. His talk of unity is all well and good, but war is ugly."

Hakon made a noise of agreement. Vallek Far-Sight was chief of chiefs, the closest thing the orcs had to a king. Ruling over the ancient stronghold of Balmirra, Vallek had taken up the banner of unifying the orc clans into something like a human kingdom. It wasn't the first time such a feat had been undertaken. The orcs had once held a vast region, far beyond the craggy reaches of the Griegen Mountains they currently dwelt in, but dragon and human conquests, as well dissent amongst the orcs themselves, had eaten away at orcish territory.

There were renewed whispers of threats to the east. Pyrros was again expanding its borders. Having spent centuries at war with the nomadic tribes across the southern plains, as well as the dragons in their desert and rocky islands, the Pyrrossi empire had consolidated its borders and was now looking west, at the mineral-rich Griegen Mountains. There was also talk of Eirean lords encroaching on the disputed borderlands to the north, more human villages sprouting in the forests and foothills.

Vallek wasn't the first leader to claim that the only safety was to band together and stand united against such outside threats. However, orc clans were unruly, and several had long since splintered away to live in the eastern foothills, far away from others the last time a Balmirra chief tried to fly a single banner. Perhaps the other chiefs wouldn't mind Vallek trying to subdue the cruel Stone-Skins and vicious Sharp-Tooths, but as for the other clans, the Broad-Backs and their own Green-Fists and the others, Hakon didn't know how well they would accept having their own power subjugated.

All of it smelled of coming war—and Siggy was right, he wanted no part of it.

Hakon wanted a good life, a small life. A mate, a family, work to be proud of. He'd no interest in politics nor war games. Give him a good woman, a hearty forge, and the chance to make something of himself and he'd be content.

His dreams weren't big or grand, but they were vivid—and his. His grandmother and Siggy often called him a dreamer, losing himself in his daydreams while working the forge.

Perhaps he was a dreamer. Perhaps he was foolish. All Hakon knew for certain was that he had to take this chance and get away.

Blowing out a loud breath, Siggy reached into her pocket to pull out a bulging sack. She pressed it to Hakon's chest, the jagged contents poking him even through the hide.

He took one look at the fistful of uncut gems and handed them right back.

"I can't take this."

"Oh yes you can," she retorted, pushing his hands and the sack back toward him. "We've got plenty. Use it to start this life of yours."

Hakon gripped the sack, the gems inside tinkling. Kaldebrak was a rich city built into a jagged eyetooth of a mountain deep within the Griegens. Uncut gems and geodes were almost a nuisance, sprouting like weeds out of the dirt. Behind the chief's seat in the great hall, a vein of gold thicker than Hakon's arm swirled in the rockfall.

The Griegens, and Kaldebrak in particular, was everything the Pyrrossi dreamed it was and more. It was why the orcs kept to themselves; such wealth would only bring trouble to their door if anyone knew.

"Thank you, auntie," Hakon said, throwing his arms around Siggy's neck.

His aunt huffed at the monicker and hugged him right back, a rib-cracking embrace that squeezed the air from his lungs.

"You'll come back," she said, not a question nor request. "When you find this woman of yours, you'll bring her back to meet us."

"Of course," he promised. "No matter where I go or how far, we're family, Siggy."

Eyes glittering with tears, Siggy nodded. "Good. Now, move over. Your folding is atrocious.

# 2

*Five Months Later*

Aislinn could only hide away in her study for so long. She knew this, and yet each day, she hoped she might have another half-hour of solitude before someone found her, needing her direction for this or her opinion for that. It was a fruitless hope, of course.

As heiress of the Darrowlands, one of the largest and richest demesnes in the kingdom of Eirea, her time was no longer her own.

That didn't mean Aislinn had come around to the new reality, though. In fact, as three crisp raps struck her study door in quick succession, a sure sign that it was the formidable chatelain Brenna who'd found her, her first thought was, *I need to find a new hideaway.*

Setting down her pen with a heavy sigh, Aislinn scrubbed her palms over her face, only remembering afterwards to check that they were free of ink.

"Come in," she called, although Brenna was already closing the door behind her.

A sturdy woman who brooked no nonsense, Brenna commanded the staff of Dundúran Castle with ruthless efficiency. All bowed to her will and worked hard in her wake. No one wanted to displease her, including Aislinn. Her dark hair was threaded with silver and scraped back into an unforgiving plait, and her starched, straight skirts hung stiffly as she crossed the room to Aislinn.

The chatelain's face was grave, but that wasn't necessarily cause for alarm. Brenna had come to Dundúran many years ago with Aislinn's mother, and since Lady Róisín's death when Aislinn was twelve, the woman seemed to find joy in nothing.

Aislinn could hardly blame her. The death of Lady Róisín had fractured the Darrow family in ways that were still felt even seventeen years later.

Brenna's eyes, gray like steel and just as sharp, assessed Aislinn at her desk, surrounded by her books and charts and drafting tools. Aislinn had long since given up trying to make Brenna understand her desire to engineer experiments and undertake projects, so she no longer felt the burn of embarrassment at having Brenna in her most sacred place. For her part, Brenna seemed to have given up on trying to mold Aislinn into the graceful image of a perfect Eirean noblewoman. In short, her mother.

At least, that was until several months past, when the honor and duty of being the Darrowlands' heiress passed to Aislinn.

She purposefully turned her thoughts away from that rutted path. She'd spent many hours already worrying herself sick over it—there was nothing for it now. The matter was settled, the deed done.

And . . . she knew better than to let her emotions get the better of her in front of Brenna.

The chatelain moved aside the heavy set of keys dangling from her girdle to reach into a deep pocket of her plain gray frock. She pulled out a folded parchment with a red wax seal to hand to Aislinn.

Aislinn always did appreciate Brenna's way of cutting straight through niceties to get to the point.

"From the Ward," Brenna said as explanation.

Heart jumping to her throat, Aislinn took the letter, turning it over in her hands. Indeed, she ran her fingertip over the official seal of the Ward, a pestle and mortar set within three rings.

It didn't look like the other letters from her brother Jerrod, but then, odious as he could be, her brother wasn't entirely stupid. He'd been known to change tactics when he recognized his strategy wasn't working toward getting him his aim.

Aislinn stood and pocketed the letter, feeling its weight in the folds of her well-worn cornflower blue kirtle.

Brenna's eyes lingered where the letter had disappeared. "It'll be from Jerrod," she said.

"Yes." Aislinn didn't wish to discuss it further, nor read it in front of Brenna. She'd never been close with her brother, but he was still her brother, and his actions, and consequences of them, had directly changed the course of Aislinn's life. It was a burden she was still unknotting in her own mind, so she didn't wish for an audience.

"Thank you for bringing it to me."

"The messenger arrived just now in a rush. Not the usual courier from the Ward, either. He insisted it be brought to your father immediately."

"He'll have made trouble, then," Aislinn grumbled. Even after everything he'd done and brought upon himself, Jerrod just couldn't help being an ass, apparently. "Thank you, Brenna. I'll see that my father gets this."

"Very good. In the meantime, Hugh wishes to go over the week's meals with you, four guild-masters have sent their tokens asking for an audience, and there are still arrangements to make to prepare for the vassals' arrival tomorrow for the council meeting."

Aislinn chewed her cheek, her annoyance threatening to get the better of her. There was never an end to the things that needed doing. Many of the domestic duties fell to Brenna, and Aislinn was grateful for it, as it meant Aislinn had some hope of keeping up with everything that required her attention.

Although Jerrod had been heir until his disgrace, he'd also been fairly useless. Aislinn had no choice but to act as the lady of the castle, for although she didn't take to the duties naturally, they still needed doing to ensure the wellbeing of all within Dundúran and the Darrowlands. With the official title of heiress came substantially more responsibility—especially since she intended to dedicate herself to it, unlike her brother.

"I'll attend to Hugh and the guild-masters' requests while I look for my father."

"And the preparations? The vassals will begin arriving tomorrow morning."

"See to what you can, I trust your judgment." When Brenna opened her mouth to protest, Aislinn said, "Bring me whatever definitely needs my attention at dinner."

That seemed to mollify the chatelain, and with a curt bob of her head, the older woman left.

Aislinn paced the length of her study, avoiding the piles of books and papers. She needed to organize the space, but she never had the time. Any who entered surely thought it utter chaos, a complete mess, but Aislinn knew where everything was.

Although alone again, she knew it was only a matter of time before someone else came knocking, needing her for something else. Legs restless, she took up her own set of keys and slipped out the door.

She looked both ways before silently taking a side stairwell that led straight down to the kitchen and gardens. The proximity to the little getaway was why she'd chosen the room for her study. It was far smaller than her father's study, and he often told her she should move to something larger, what with all her books and notes and models. Aislinn liked the little space, though, liked feeling surrounded by books.

The day was bright and clear, the heat of late summer ebbing into the pleasant temperance of early autumn. A few kitchen staff were out tending the garden or picking crops for the evening meal, and a handful of guards clanked in their mail as they made their rounds. Her blue skirts swished pleasantly against her ankles as she stole for a hideaway she knew no one would disturb.

Her mother's rose garden had sat fallow for over a decade. The plants had gone feral, the thorns and brambles overtaking most of the blooms. Aislinn had to fight to push the key into the lock of the little gate, pricking several fingers in her struggle.

The gate creaked vociferously as she opened it just enough to slide inside and wailed as it closed behind her.

Blowing a lock of blonde hair out of her face, Aislinn assessed the garden.

It was just as overgrown as she'd thought, the grass of the once neat lawn standing nearly knee-height, hiding the flagstone walkways and marble benches. Gopher holes dotted the space, forcing Aislinn to pick her steps carefully as she delved deeper inside. Her mother's prized roses, vivid red and satiny yellow and peachy orange, bloomed in a chaotic spattering, nearly choked by the foliage.

The air was thick inside the walls of the garden, and as Aislinn settled onto a weather-beaten stone bench, she breathed in the verdant green of it. Although warm and a bit hard to breathe, the air nevertheless carried a hint of roses and lush greenness that she always associated with her mother.

The memory tickled that old wound inside her, the grief of losing her mother so young an ever-present hollowness that nothing filled. She liked to pretend that her reading and learning and projects would somehow ease the ache, but they never did. At most, they distracted her.

Losing their mother so young had forever altered Aislinn and Jerrod. She'd been twelve, Jerrod nine. Before then, the siblings had gotten on, and the castle was full of bustle, the whole demesne gravitating to the beautiful young noble family and their lively court. It was a love match between her parents, their natures and minds complementing in a way that Aislinn still marveled over.

Lady Róisín had been the kind of noblewoman all aspired to be. Graceful, gracious, and beatific, she was a patron of the arts, a fierce negotiator, and funded schools throughout the Darrowlands. Aislinn remembered holding onto her mother's skirts as she dealt with their vassals and yeomen, in awe of how easily she handled others, meeting their questions and requests and demands with the patience, charity, or firmness they required.

From a young age, Aislinn realized that she wasn't like her mother and indeed, didn't think like most others at all. The social graces and nuances effortlessly practiced by her mother and other nobles often eluded her, especially when she was younger, and she rarely understood or played along with games or politics. She didn't see the point in not just saying what she meant and couldn't comprehend why so many spoke in half-truths or even lies. Sometimes it felt as though she tried to work the delicate weave of social interactions with a hammer. Her mind much preferred to turn over how things worked, the mechanics and intricacies of parts that made a whole function.

Her mother and father had always been patient with her. Lord Merrick indulged her learning and ideas. Lady Róisín had taught her etiquette and diction, manners and negotiation. When one method didn't work, her mother tried another tack until she was sure Aislinn knew how to read someone or a situation—even if she didn't understand them.

*"You don't always have to understand them or agree,"* her mother told her, *"what's important is learning enough to act appropriately in accordance."*

With her mother, Aislinn hadn't felt so different, or at least that what differences she did have weren't to be hidden or ashamed of. *"Your mind is different, it's true. But that's what makes it so beautiful."*

Her mother's words imprinted upon Aislinn's heart, a small thing to hold onto in the dark days after her passing.

Aislinn hadn't remembered much about her mother's confinement and delivery of Jerrod, she'd been too young herself. Just that there had been long stretches of days when she wasn't allowed to see her mother, and when she was, she found a diminished woman, her skin wan and her eyes dull. It'd taken a long while for the mother she knew to rekindle inside.

All the physicians had warned Lady Róisín that she mustn't risk becoming pregnant again. And so, with two children already, the Darrows had been content.

Until Róisín fell pregnant once more. It'd surprised everyone—Aislinn's parents hadn't been trying for another, and Róisín was already in the later years for women to bear. All but Róisín had met the news with dread; they remembered the physicians' dire warnings. A determined woman, though, Róisín soothed their worries. She delegated her duties. She followed all the physicians' instructions. Her pregnancy was normal, eventless.

Until it wasn't. Two months too soon, she had her labor pains. They lost the baby first, and in that first tumultuous night, Aislinn sat huddled outside her mother's chamber with the ugly thought that she was glad it was the baby and not her mother, at least. That of the two, she wanted her mother more.

But by the following night, Róisín hadn't improved. And by the next, she'd worsened.

By the third night, there was no strength in her.

Her father had taken her by the hand and Jerrod with the other and led them to see their mother one last time.

Jerrod had cried and refused to look.

Aislinn bent to kiss her mother's clammy cheek, hearing for herself how reedy her breath had gone. Róisín's eyes flickered behind her lids, but otherwise she lay motionless, a corpse with a little breath left inside it.

For a long time after, Aislinn hated everyone. She hated the baby for trying to grow inside Róisín. She resented her father for getting Róisín with child in the first place. She despised Jerrod for his incessant wailing. And she hated Róisín for not intervening in the early days when she could have.

Their family had shattered that night, and they buried their heart with Róisín.

It'd taken a long while to find happiness again. At first, Aislinn was ashamed of any small joy she experienced, thinking how Róisín would never feel anything again. As she grew from a youth to a woman, though, she began to understand that her mother would never want her to dwell in grief. And so Aislinn persevered, and she tried to help her father and Jerrod do the same.

Her father found a channel for his grief in the form of attacking the insidious slave trade that had grown in the chaotic years of the Eirean wars of succession. Although the fighting had ceased with the betrothal of the half-Pyrrossi, half-Eirean Prince Marius to the Eirean Crown Princess Ygraine thirty years before, the slavers had only grown bolder.

His crusade meant Merrick Darrow was often away from Dundúran and the Darrowlands. Aislinn contented herself that at least he was doing something good with his grief.

The same couldn't be said for Jerrod.

She could admit, in hindsight, that Jerrod's fate might have been avoided. Her love for him had never been a deep well—he was the type of boy who teased to make himself feel superior, and she was often the target of such teasing. This only worsened when their mother perished and their father sought solace far from home. He became a braggart, a drunkard, a womanizer. He strained Aislinn's patience, yet she'd always held hope that someday, he would come around. He was young—soon he'd learn the way of the world and accept his place as a Darrow and heir.

Instead, Jerrod went and did something unforgivable.

Her own brother arranged for Aislinn's dearest friend Sorcha Brádaigh to be kidnapped by slavers and sold to brutal orcs. All because Sorcha refused his childish attentions and lecherous overtures. Honestly, at the time, Aislinn had thought Sorcha fairly polite in her rejection, her careful refusal soft compared to Aislinn's sharp reprimand for Jerrod afterwards.

It still left her breathless to think her own brother could do that to someone, condemn them to a fate worse than death. Aislinn never presumed to understand most, but she'd thought, after living her life beside her brother, she understood Jerrod. She thought she knew his weaknesses and the bounds of his spitefulness. To be so utterly wrong . . . and that he spat in the face of everything their father worked for . . .

It seemed their father's efforts had only educated Jerrod in how to find slavers and orchestrate a kidnapping deep within the Darrowlands—somewhere that was supposed to be *safe,* far away from the rough, ugly reality of the slave trade.

Luckily, Sorcha had met a valiant half-orc named Orek who freed her and brought her safely home. Sorcha's return revealed Jerrod's treachery, and their father allowed Sorcha to decide Jerrod's punishment, as was only fair. She chose banishment to the Ward, an ancient fortress converted into a house of healing overseen by warden monks. She also asked that Aislinn be made heiress, Jerrod's inheritance stripped away.

And so it was. Aislinn was to be the next Liege Darrow.

She would oversee the Darrowlands and rule where her father had one day. She would atone for her brother's sins.

Which was how, on a pleasant late-summer afternoon, Aislinn found herself hiding away in her mother's overgrown rose garden, turning a letter from the Ward between her fingers nervously.

Jerrod hadn't taken to the Ward. Neither she nor their father thought he would, but after weeks and then months, they'd both hoped he would come to accept that this was his lot now. That if he was ever to atone and earn forgiveness, he first had to confront the ugliness inside him.

Unfortunately, Aislinn came to find that Jerrod's spiteful stubbornness ran deeper than she'd ever thought.

For months, he wrote her. Begging, pleading, threatening. He wanted out of the Ward. He didn't like the wardens or the quiet life of self-sacrifice. He was bored. He was unhappy. If she was truly his sister, she would appeal to their father. If she truly loved him, she would help bring him home. He wouldn't even demand his birthright as heir back. He would let her remain heiress and do whatever she wanted with the Darrowlands—if only she'd help him.

*Help me, Aislinn. Please. I've never asked for anything from you but this. Please.*

Perhaps she might be moved—if he didn't also write to their father.

Merrick Darrow was too disgusted with his son to even consider reading the letters, so Aislinn did. In them, Jerrod was all humbleness and atonement. He spoke of how sorry he was, how the wardens had taught him to care for others and therefore himself. He thanked their father for sending him here, that he hoped someday to return a changed man.

It saddened her to know that her letters were a closer representation of Jerrod's true feelings and self.

Pulling in a deep breath of sweet-smelling air, Aislinn broke the seal.

Unfolding the parchment, her fears thickened to find the missive wasn't in Jerrod's frantic scrawl. Her eyes devoured the message, her stomach sinking to the ground with every word.

*My good Liege Darrow,*

*It pains me to write to you with such news. This morning, upon checking his quarters, it was found that your son Jerrod is missing. The grounds were searched thoroughly and the few wardens and patients he spoke with were interviewed. We understand from what little was said by him that he has run away. He took his belongings and several provisions from our stores. It is unknown where he has gone.*

*Please accept our deepest apologies. He was not taking to life within the Ward, and it is not wholly unexpected that he would think to run away.*

*I have sent inquiries to the surrounding villages and*

*several wardens I know of serving outside the Ward. We
here will send along any information on his whereabouts
we can find.*

*Once more, you have our utmost apologies.*


*Colm, Head Warden to Her Majesty Queen Ygraine II
Monaghan*


Aislinn read the letter twice, just to be sure.

By the third time, her eyes began to blur with tears. Panic clutched her throat, and she put a palm to her cheek to feel how it burned.

Since she was young, Aislinn had had trouble not only reading the emotions of others, but hers as well. They bubbled inside her, sometimes so potent she could taste them on the back of her tongue. As she grew, she was better able to deal with them, to understand when they were getting to be too much and she needed to either seclude herself or redirect her attention.

It was when the emotions were left without an escape, a kettle left to boil too long, that she erupted. She couldn't control or stop it, everything pouring out of her in a forceful purge that left her empty, shaking, and terrified.

She feared her fits so much that she had put great effort into learning to control them. At first her parents and then Aislinn had rigorously controlled her environment, introducing change slowly—trusted staff were kept for years, familiar meals were served, and surprises were limited. In doing so, and working to learn about what could bring about a fit, she'd gone years without feeling so much as a stirring of those thrashing emotions that threatened to overwhelm and overpower.

But the Warden's letter, his news—

Aislinn drew another breath, the air wobbling in her sticky throat.

Her tongue stuck to the roof of her mouth, and suddenly the verdant air was too thick. She gasped and slid to her knees, the tears coming fast and hot as frustration and grief bubbled over.

*How dare he?*

*How could he do this?*

The tears coming easier than her breathing, Aislinn grabbed great fistfuls of the overgrown grass and began to rip. Soil splattered onto her skirts and into her loose hair, but she went back for another fistful.

Her feckless brother was out there somewhere, doing fates knew what!

What would he do?

*What will I tell father?*

Aislinn bit down on a sob until her cheek bled. Fates, she'd have to tell her father.

Every spear of grass within reach was plucked or shorn from its place until Aislinn was left panting and shaking.

She sat back on her haunches and wiped her damp cheek with the back of her dirty hand.

*Get hold of yourself,* she told herself sharply. *This accomplishes nothing.*

In increments, she was able to pull back all that wanted to spill and unspool. She liked to imagine it like a fisherman pulling back their nets. Everything back on the boat, where it should be.

As the moments passed, Aislinn was able to compose herself. When she stood up to brush the dirt from her kirtle, her knees barely wobbled.

She waited until the heat had left her face and hoped her eyes wouldn't be too puffy and red. Brenna would know the signs, and the last thing she wanted was Brenna's overbearing concern.

She looked around the garden instead, hollowed out from her tears. And as she looked, a new project laid itself out before her mind's eye.

*I should fix mother's garden.*

# 3

There was plenty to marvel at as Hakon followed behind his friend Orek into the great hall of Dundúran Castle. Whereas many of the homes and halls of Kaldebrak were carved into the mountain itself, the humans of the Darrowlands had made a mountain out of stone blocks, wrought iron, and carved wood.

Hakon took it in with wide eyes as he followed a step behind Orek. The hall was a towering space, peaked arches converging on heavy beams carved with animals and branches. Dozens of banners hung from the rafters, dominated by the standard of the Darrows, a crossed arrow and sword over a field of deep blue.

The warm stones of the hall almost glowed in the late-summer light, streaming inside the hall through rows of paned glass windows. It seemed to light their path, straight to a shallow dais of three short steps. A wide wooden chair, not quite a throne, had been placed at the center, and an older human man sat upon it, leaning forward to speak with another human standing before him.

The hall was hardly full, only five others inside, which offered Hakon a sliver of relief. Their steps echoed on the stone floor as they approached, and Orek slowed their pace the closer they came.

Glancing over his shoulder, Orek said, "Don't be nervous."

*Impossible.*

It'd been one thing to make the long journey north, questioning his right mind with every soggy step as the spring rains soaked him and his gear through. It'd been one thing to arrive in the Darrowlands and struggle through his limited Eirean to finally find a friendly harbor, with Orek and his human mate's large family. He and many otherly folk had begun congregating on or near the Brádaigh estate, seeking the help of the halfling who'd started all this.

That long journey, those days of indecision and nights of regret, all somehow felt shorter than the walk from the massive doors to the dais at the other end of the hall.

Hakon had told his aunt Siggy, had told *himself* this was what he wanted—to work his craft and make a life for himself and a future mate. That had all become far more than an idea in the space of two days, and his head was still trying to catch up.

Sitting around the large communal fire of the makeshift village of otherly folk, talking with his fellows about where they'd come from and where they hoped to go, Hakon had divulged his craft as a blacksmith and his hopes of finding a village that needed his skills. Hearing this, Orek and his mate Sorcha had informed him that, not a village, but Dundúran Castle itself needed smiths.

They would bring him to Liege Darrow himself.

At first Hakon didn't think he'd heard them correctly. It was bound to happen, with all the languages and noise of their patchwork settlement. He'd had Orek repeat himself just to be sure.

*"Yes, up at the castle,"* Orek confirmed, looking to his mate.

*"On her last visit, Aislinn said the previous under blacksmith left for Gleanná, so they've been making do with just Fearghas."* Sorcha, a comely, buxom human woman who was all warmth and smiles, said this as if Hakon knew any of these names, but it didn't matter that he didn't. What was important was a chance at a position—at the castle of all places.

And Hakon wanted it.

It'd been a vague sort of longing for months now, a partial idea of where he might stoke his forge fire. He'd assumed, being only half-human, a village smithy would be what awaited him. As he'd stumbled through the Eirean countryside, finally finding his way to Orek and Sorcha, he'd begun to worry over his plans. Nothing was available or no one wanted him to stay.

Upon arriving at the Brádaigh estate, he'd found most of the other folk were hoping for land to cultivate. A pack of bachelor manticores hoped for prime forest land for hunting—and pretty meadows to woo prospective mates in. A lone fae warrior and his unicorn steed were looking for an estate of their own, needing a home and land to absorb his magic. A dragon and his halfling sister looked to possibly ranch or build a school or both. A small flock of four harpy sisters had come to avoid a larger conflict within their previous flock and hoped to find homes and mates. And the handful of other half-orc had all expressed a desire to farm.

Amongst all this talk, Hakon's hopes had begun to wither.

He knew nothing of farming, and he'd certainly seen plenty of the wilderness on his long journey here. Doubts began to slither around his heart, and for several days he'd sat with a cold, slimy sort of desperation sucking at his guts.

*What have I done? Did I forsake* gadaron's *forge fires for nothing?*

But then Orek and Sorcha delivered the heartening news.

As Hakon followed Orek through the city of Dundúran, through the towering castle gates, and through the expansive castle courtyard, that hope had flickered anew.

With every step, Hakon grew surer that this was where he wanted to be. Born and raised within a mountain city, he was far more content within the great stone walls of a castle. Every stone felt familiar, every sconce and door hinge fascinated him.

A castle, *this* castle, was full of opportunities.

So there was little chance that Hakon wouldn't have nerves gathered in his gut as they approached the human lord. Not when he wanted this so badly, he could taste the yearning on the back of his tongue.

Hakon stood beside Orek as they waited for their turn to speak with Liege Lord Darrow, willing his ears to keep from turning that ruddy red they often did with emotion.

He was grateful Orek had kept to his left side, nearer his good ear, when his friend leaned over to say, "Darrow is a good man and a friend. He'll welcome your skills, I'm sure."

Hakon nodded but couldn't offer a response. He clenched his small tusks to his gums, the nerves and all his hopes clutching his insides in tight fists.

If Liege Darrow turned him away . . . Hakon didn't know what he'd do.

After another moment, the man speaking with Liege Darrow bowed and turned to walk away. He gasped when he saw two green halflings towering above him, jumping nearly a foot before skittering away.

It certainly wasn't the worst reaction a human had had to Hakon's presence.

Orek stepped forward and Hakon followed, bowing his head when Orek did in deference.

"I received Sorcha's message just this morning. I'm intrigued," said Liege Darrow, smiling at them from under his voluminous but neatly kept beard.

Darrow was still large and strong despite his years, with a mane and beard that had once been golden blond but were now fading to white. The rich velvet and silk of his doublet and robes couldn't hide a warrior's body, although it was his eyes, a leonine hazel and bracketed by fanning lines that drew Hakon forward. They looked down upon him and Orek with polite shrewdness, and Hakon kept his shoulders squared, knowing he was already being assessed. Probably had been since they entered the room.

"Orek, it's good to see you. What have you brought me?" The lord's voice was loud without booming, and confident—it rang clearly in Hakon's ears as he stood stiffly, awaiting judgment.

"Lord Merrick, we were told by Aislinn not long ago that the castle was in need of a new blacksmith." Orek's large green hand landed on Hakon's shoulder. "I've brought you a blacksmith. This is Hakon Green-Fist, newly arrived from Kaldebrak."

Hakon bowed his head. "My Lord Darrow, it is an honor to be here."

Darrow's brows arched. "You speak Eirean already."

"Mostly. I still have much to learn."

"You came here by yourself?"

"Yes, my lord. To work."

"They don't need blacksmiths in Kaldebrak?"

"There are already too many smiths in Kaldebrak." It was why the mountain had been mostly hollowed out long ago, the Green-Fist clan almost too industrious. Orclings learned to cast weapons before ever training to use them.

Darrow grinned in good humor. "I can hardly imagine. It seems like we're always in need of a smith." Leaning forward, he rested his elbows on his knees and took another long look at Hakon.

For his part, Hakon held very still, reminding himself that he was clean from his journey, wearing his best clothes. The shoulders of his jerkin had been tooled with steel, his arm bands molded to fit only his forearms, and his belt crafted from an eight-stranded braid of silver. His shoulders were broad, his arms thick from the work he'd done over a lifetime. He was a male in his prime, ready to prove himself.

*Give me the chance,* he urged. *Let me show what I can do.*

"You have experience at the forge?"

"My clan raises younglings to work the fires. I have worked iron since I was small."

"You can do all the everyday forging? Nails, horseshoes, the like?"

"Yes, my lord. Easily."

"But will you want to do them? I'm afraid not every project will be exciting. We go through more horseshoes than swords."

"If it needs doing, I will do it, my lord." And, because Orek had said Darrow was a friend and he'd shown good humor, Hakon dared to add, "And to be truthful, I prefer making axes to swords."

That earned him a smile through the beard. Sitting back in his seat, Darrow chuckled, "A fine axe will get you far in this world." He nodded once and looked to Orek. "You'll vouch for him?"

"Of course, my lord."

"Very well." Rising from his seat, Darrow descended the three shallow steps and held out his hand to Hakon. "Welcome to Dundúran Castle, Hakon Green-Fist."

Chest clenching with amazement, Hakon took the lord's hand and shook it in the way of humans. The lord's grip was firm, and Hakon returned it, pride having him stand a little taller.

Everything he'd hoped, everything he'd wanted was happening. He could hardly breathe, fearing it would disappear quicker than a spooked deer on a hunt.

"I won't fail you, my lord."

Darrow gave him a pat on the shoulder. "Wait until you meet our head blacksmith Fearghas before you make too many promises," he laughed.

When he turned to shake hands with Orek, the other halfling said, "There are more wishing for an audience with you, whenever you have the time, my lord."

"Word certainly has spread," said Darrow. "I'm glad for it. But next time you come, it's Aislinn you'll want. I'm putting her in charge of this—she'll oversee the suits and decide what can be done." And, leaning in, he said conspiratorially, "I'm sure between her and Sorcha, they'll have it all figured out in an afternoon."

"No doubt," Orek agreed, his look growing fond at the mention of his mate.

Talk turned to Sorcha and how the latest batch of horses she trained was coming along, but Hakon only half-listened. His attention drew to the mighty arches and wide span of the great hall. A marvel of engineering and workmanship.

This mountain of stones was where his start would begin, and he relished the thought of leaving his mark on such a magnificent place.

He'd been given his chance. Now, he was determined to make a life for himself here, by the strength of his arm and depth of his skill. The life he'd dreamed had just begun.

# 4

Aislinn hurried down the corridor, annoyed that she was late to the summer council meeting but also dreading having to attend in the first place. Since all the vassals and yeomen had arrived, Aislinn hadn't known a moment's peace.

Her skirts swished along the stone floor as Brenna bustled behind. The chatelain muttered unhappily about how late Aislinn was and how this would look as she attempted to stick needless pearl pins into Aislinn's plain plait.

Stopping before the arched doorway of the council chamber, bracketed by a guard on either side, Aislinn bit her cheek and reminded herself to be understanding. Brenna took the moment to secure a silk ribbon around her waist, as if that would hide the plainness of today's kirtle.

"Leave it, Brenna," she said with tried patience. "What I wear is of little consequence to them."

Brenna frowned back, her face falling into familiar grooves of disapproval. "What the future Liege Darrow wears is of *great* consequence. Especially now."

Now that Aislinn was heiress, she meant.

"When you're finished here, we still have tomorrow's banquet to go over and the afternoon entertainments. Earl Starley and Lady Lisbet have each requested different accommodations for the night."

"Just have them switch rooms," Aislinn muttered under her breath. Brenna sniffed, unamused.

Stepping forward, she left Brenna behind as a guard opened the chamber door for her and slipped into a meeting already well underway.

The melee of vassals talking over one another didn't abate, but it did lull as she stared down thirty of the Darrowlands' vassals and yeomen. Her mother had prepared her for such moments, even if the sudden attention and fact that she was late itched at her like rough wool, and she remembered her mother's lessons well. She held her head high and glided through the chamber, taking the seat to her father's right.

*"Never rush. Enter the room like it's yours."*

So she didn't rush, and didn't apologize either, merely placed her notebook on the table and opened it to a fresh page to begin a new sketch of her latest design.

She did, however, catch her father throwing her an amused if exasperated look—one Aislinn was far too familiar with. Bowing her head demurely, she threw him a wink back.

The meeting resumed around them, Margrave Cravan continuing with his complaints over this year's dues from the upcoming harvest. It was a time-honored tradition to have these seasonal meetings with the vassals and yeomen to hear their complaints over too many taxes, it seemed. Aislinn couldn't remember a time when her father wasn't complaining himself over dinner about the dues owed to the crown and the earful he'd get from his landholders because of it.

Yet, as he'd always stressed to Aislinn, and Jerrod when he was still in Dundúran, it was the liege lord's place to hear their complaints. The liege lords of Eirea ruled over their demesne for the benefit of everyone—the nobles, the craftsmen and tradesmen, the farmers. *"It's a system of many parts,"* he liked to say, *"and each part needs to work with the others to be most effective."*

Jerrod always rolled his eyes, but Aislinn found comfort in the familiar metaphor. It was something her logical mind could comprehend, and she never tired of her father's quip. She enjoyed the reminder that their family was a part of a whole, their role within it to keep the system running smoothly.

An unpleasantly familiar swoop of her stomach accompanied the thought of one day being Liege Darrow. Over the past decades, the Eirean nobility began to follow a more Pyrrossi style of inheritance, from father to eldest son, thanks to the half-Pyrrossi King Marius and his Pyrrossi cousins that now dominated the court in the capital of Gleanná. With an, albeit younger, brother, Aislinn had spent her life assuming the mantle would never fall upon her shoulders, even if she performed many of the duties anyway in Jerrod's absence.

The only new responsibility she truly enjoyed was the task her father had just recently given her: integrating all the otherly folk who were coming to settle in the Darrowlands. There was once a time, more than fifty years ago, when nonhumans were commonplace through the human kingdoms of Caledon, Eirea, and Pyrros. However, most fled during the wars of succession, when the Eirean royal family ripped itself apart and drowned many in their undertow in an effort to eradicate the other. After decades of fighting, the rift was only mended by the union of distant cousins, the half-Pyrrossi Prince Marius and the full-Eirean Princess Ygraine, now the King and Queen of Eirea. However, despite thirty years of relative peace since their betrothal, otherly folk had yet to return to Eirea in any significant number.

That was until her friend Sorcha returned from her ordeal mated to a half-orc from the southern wilds. Orek was a darling and made her friend wildly happy. His presence and union with Sorcha had opened the possibility of welcoming back more otherly folk, something her father was keen to foster. *"Having strong bonds with the others can only strengthen the demesne,"* he believed.

Already, she had ideas about where the otherly folk might like to settle, a few choice places near various towns and villages outside

Dundúran. Her father thought it wise for them to establish themselves nearby but not directly on top of existing villages; they couldn't force their people to accept newcomers immediately. Yet, if the rumors from the taverns were anything to go by, the manticores in particular were already quite popular.

The numbers of otherly folk trickling into the Darrowlands was beginning to flow, and Aislinn was excited by the prospects. She'd need to go out to the Brádaigh estate soon to have Orek introduce her to any new arrivals.

Her other duties were far less . . . stimulating. Or far too stimulating—namely, greeting guests and organizing banquets. There was always this lordling or that magistrate dropping by, expecting to be entertained and chatted with. It was an exchange of sorts, one in which Aislinn always felt a step behind. She also didn't quite understand the ease with which some dropped in uninvited on others' homes and expected everything to pause for them. Ghastly.

"Forgive me, my lord, but it may make us all feel more assured in your stance if your heiress would do us the courtesy of paying attention rather than *doodling*."

Aislinn's quill paused, as did all conversation. She looked up to find everyone staring at her with mixed expressions. It'd taken practice, but she was fairly good at determining expressions now, and it helped that most of those currently directed at her were similar—general exasperation and annoyance.

*I haven't even said anything yet,* she grumbled to herself.

The man who'd spoken, Baron Morraugh, sat imperiously across the table from her, his beard twitching. The stares and sudden quiet had her wanting to shrink into her seat, but Aislinn kept her spine stiff and met each stare. *"Never look away first,"* her mother had instructed, *"you don't need to be belligerent or rude, but don't waver."*

Aislinn counted her breaths, heeding her mother's advice. Beside her, her father leaned forward to place his folded hands on the polished tabletop.

"If you want my assurances, Baron Morraugh, be assured that my daughter is paying attention and has heard every word."

Morraugh sniffed behind his impressive beard, twitching the overlong whiskers beneath his nose. Aislinn looked away before she became fixated on the uneven cut of the hair at his lip.

Her father gestured for her to speak.

"I'm not doodling," Aislinn explained, "I'm sketching plans for the new bridge we intend to build upriver of the existing one to relieve load and expand the industrial section of Dundúran. Keeping my hand at work helps me listen."

She looked to her father, who nodded for her to keep going. "As to your complaints, it's unfortunate that dues are rising, but it isn't my father's doing. The crown has imposed higher concessions from all liege lords, and this in turn is passed on to all landholders. My father's rate is the lowest in the region. We ourselves are making concessions in Dundúran to ensure that rates are not so painful for you and your people. Should we ask for anything lower, we wouldn't fulfill the crown's demands, which may cause my father to fall out of favor. King Marius has been looking to appoint his relations to demesnes further from Gleanná. Should he see the opportunity, there is every possibility that the king would replace my father with a Pyrrossi cousin who would charge you the maximum or more. So no, Baron Morraugh, we don't enjoy the higher rates, but we all must make do until the crown decides on another course of action."

Aislinn sucked in a breath, a little winded, and attempted to keep her cheeks from reddening. Fates, she was trying to be better about that. Be more succinct.

Her father nodded. "There you have it."

After a heavy pause, the meeting continued when Morraugh decided not to push the matter. The vassals' tenor lowered now that the obvious had been stated.

Aislinn took up her quill again, but the ideas wouldn't come quite so quickly with the embarrassment prickling her chest. She resisted the urge to truly doodle.

When the meeting adjourned, she rose with her father to bow and thank the council for convening. Hands were shaken, pleasantries were exchanged, and the vassals left in what Aislinn considered decent spirits, considering the tone of the meeting when she'd arrived.

*"They need to speak and be heard,"* her father had explained when she'd questioned him on this, after attending her first council meeting. *"Sometimes that's all they need. Think of it as a lid being taken off a boiling kettle; some of the steam is released and the water is allowed to boil peaceably."*

Her father had a way with metaphors that Aislinn found invaluable.

Merrick settled back in his seat once the last vassal had left, so Aislinn rejoined him at the table.

"Well, let's see what you were doodling," he said.

Aislinn threw him a mock scowl before sliding her notebook over the table to him. "These are my initial ideas for the bridge."

Her father looked between the pages of her models and measurements and notes, and Aislinn held her breath. She enjoyed immersing herself in her projects. The castle was littered with them, failures and successes both. She'd engineered a more effective irrigation system for the castle gardens, worked with the blacksmiths and draftsmen to create a more efficient mechanism for the drawbridge, drawn up plans to reroute the chimneys to help keep smoke out of the kitchen, and much, much more.

This bridge, though. It would be her biggest endeavor yet and would affect many of the people of Dundúran. She wanted it to be for the better. She wanted to help wherever she could. She might not be a beautiful, graceful noblewoman like her mother or Queen Ygraine, but she could and would use her talents and skills to better the Darrowlands however she could.

"Wide enough for three carts abreast?"

"Into town, out of town, and passing. Several guild-masters and merchants have complained about how it slows everyone getting across, not having that additional width."

"Already spoken to the guild-masters, have you?" His hazel eyes, so like Aislinn's own, flicked to her over the notebook, crinkling at the corners.

The knot in Aislinn's stomach released.

"Yes, I wanted to get their input before committing to a design."

Merrick took another look through the plans before handing them back to her. "Well, you know what I'm going to say, kit. Brilliant as always."

Aislinn bit her cheek trying not to smile too widely. Making her father proud still felt as good as it did when she was a girl showing him her first clumsy wooden models of the catapult she wanted to make for getting rid of kitchen scraps.

"Thank you. I'm sensing a *however,* though."

Merrick sighed, rubbing at his eyes. "You know full well that we'll be accepting designs from several architects. The king is sending his own from Gleanná eventually."

"If we have a plan, one based on the needs of the people who will use it, why wait for outside opinions?"

"Because it'd be rude otherwise. The king wants to seem magnanimous, so we must let him."

"But . . ." Aislinn let out an annoyed huff. It was so *silly* to delay plans just for the king's feelings. Although, she wasn't naïve enough to dismiss that if anyone's feelings were important, it was a king's.

"I know, kit. If you had your way, we'd have broken ground last week, no doubt."

"And be well underway, yes."

Merrick shrugged his wide shoulders in a tired heave. "I'm afraid you'll have to humor me on this. We'll get our bridge built—just not as quickly as you'd prefer."

They spent a while longer discussing ideas and who should be brought into early discussions when it was finally time to begin building, and Aislinn hid her disappointment well, she thought. In truth, this bridge project promised a challenge, one she was anxious to take on. At least in this sort of duty, she was assured in her abilities to complete it well. Without any awkwardness or long-winded speeches.

She left her father outside the council chamber with the promise to continue their discussion over dinner tonight.

Skirts swishing around her ankles, Aislinn headed for the kitchens. The stress from attending the meeting and disappointment over not moving forward with her design had emotion welling inside her, uncomfortable, ugly feelings that she knew needed to be dealt with.

Her outburst in the rose garden had taken her aback and left her shaken. She couldn't allow herself such a fit again, certainly not with so many of the vassals in residence still. She was keenly aware that they all thought her an oddity—bookish, unmarried, informal, and lacking the social graces of her beautiful mother. It was one of her many duties now to instill confidence in them for her eventual position as Liege Darrow, and crumbling into a puddle of frustrated tears certainly wouldn't do that.

One of the ways she controlled her emotions was helping in the kitchen. Cooking and baking made sense. Food, meals, were a sum of parts. Add this and that together, heat for a certain amount of time, and out comes food. She enjoyed the routine of chopping, the methodology of cooking.

Hugh, the surly head cook, hadn't exactly enjoyed her presence in his kitchen at first, but he'd eventually been won over when Aislinn proved an unobtrusive help. That, and she'd never been the demanding type of noblewoman requesting braised swan an hour before dinner.

Walking with her notebook, Aislinn distracted her spinning thoughts with the golden views through the arched windows of the castle corridor. Late afternoon sunlight spilled through the diamond-patterned mullions, making the stone of the floor appear a quilt of gold. She loved this castle, especially at this time of day, the sky a saturated azure, the late-summer afternoon pleasant and vibrant.

She took the back stairs down to the kitchens, feeling a little better for the pools of sunlight. As she descended, the serenity was broken, however, by loud barking. Actual dog barking, too, not just Hugh being particularly cranky.

Of course, then came Hugh's bark.

"Get that beast out of here! His sort isn't welcome!"

Aislinn hurried down the last steps and around the corner to a commotion.

Hugh loomed in the arched doorway to the kitchen, standing guard over the threshold with his big fists planted on his hips and a thunderous frown etched on his brow. Before him, a huge gray dog sat on its haunches, barking up at him.

None of that was what surprised Aislinn. Several staff kept dogs, as did her family, though they hadn't in years.

No, it was the enormous green hand on the dog's collar, attached to the greenest, most muscular arm she'd ever seen. She tracked the bulging bicep up to massive shoulders, clad in a well-worked leather jerkin with tooled silver at the collar and shoulder.

Kneeling beside the biggest dog she'd ever seen was the biggest man she'd ever seen. Even on his knees, his head was nearly level with Hugh's chest, and Hugh wasn't a small man.

At first glance, Aislinn's mind immediately went to Orek. But no, this wasn't Orek. He had longer hair, hazel eyes, freckles. This man . . .

He saw her then, head turning to behold her. Eyes of the warmest brown met hers. He was indeed a halfling, his green skin evidence of that, but he had the noble features of the handsome knights painted in her favorite books, all high cheeks and sharp jaw and jutting chin. Where Orek's face was as beautiful as it was brutal, this halfling's face was all beauty, every line finely wrought. Even his green lips were pleasingly formed, parted just the smallest amount to reveal the tops of two short tusks on his lower jaw.

"Milady," Hugh huffed.

The cook's rough voice brought Aislinn round. Clearing her throat, she approached.

"What seems to be the matter?"

Hugh scowled down at the panting dog, the beast's long pink tongue lolling from its mouth.

"This beast thought he could come in and steal the evening roast."

"I apologize," the kneeling halfling said. The deep timber of his voice rolled over Aislinn like warm syrup, and her fist tightened on her notebook. "We're still learning. He meant no harm."

Hugh eyed the dog again. "That thing is tall enough to take whatever he wants right off the block!"

The halfling's pointed ears darkened to a ruddy brown. "He's just hungry is all."

Stepping forward, Aislinn asked, "Has the roast been spared?"

After a bit of grumbling, Hugh admitted, "Yes. Just barely."

"Then no harm done." Turning to the halfling, she gestured for him to stand. Her stomach did a funny flip, emotions churning there. Not bad emotions, though. No, under his warm gaze, she . . .

She stuck out her hand. "Aislinn Darrow."

The halfling's nostrils contracted in a sharp breath. He took her hand in his much, much larger green one so carefully, their fingers hardly touched. Still holding onto the dog, he said, "My lady, it is an honor," and bowed over her hand.

Blushing, Aislinn nearly forgot to pull her hand back when he straightened. She usually didn't enjoy touching strangers, but something about the halfling's broad fingers and warm calluses was . . . utterly enjoyable.

"And who's this?" She nodded at the giant dog, currently panting hot, wet breath onto her notebook.

"Wülf, my lady." He spoke with the same rugged accent Orek did, holding onto syllables in a way a human mouth couldn't. "I am Hakon Green-Fist. Your father has brought me on as a blacksmith."

"Ah, yes! I remember now. I hope you're settling in Dundúran."

"Yes, I—"

With an exasperated noise, Hugh threw up his hands and turned on his heel to disappear back into the kitchen. "Keep that mutt out of my kitchen!"

Hakon's ears went ruddy again. "I apologize, my lady, he—"

"Don't trouble yourself, Hakon, please. That's just Hugh."

His ears deepened in color at her use of his name. "He couldn't resist when he smelled the good cooking."

Smiling, Aislinn replied, "He isn't alone. Quite a few people stray into Hugh's kitchen around dinnertime. I promise, he doesn't mean anything by it. You and Wülf are welcome here."

"Not in the kitchen!" came bellowing from inside.

Aislinn winced, but a small smile formed around Hakon's tusks. She marveled to see it, as well as the dimple it made in his right cheek. Fates, that little divot softened his whole face.

Bowing again, Hakon hustled his dog away from the door. "It was a pleasure to meet you, my lady. I hope I can be of service to you and your father."

"Of course," she said by rote, her stomach still in strange knots.

She watched as the halfling led his dog away, his short, dark hair glossy in the late afternoon sunshine. It wasn't until he disappeared around the corner that Aislinn realized emotions bubbled in her middle still, but they weren't . . . bad. No indeed, the flutter of excitement in her chest was most pleasant.

Smiling to herself, Aislinn ducked into the kitchens, her mood lightened.

*Excellent. We needed a new blacksmith.*

<h1 style="text-align:center">5</h1>

The fires of Hakon's forge often burned late into the night, partly because he enjoyed working in the evenings, when the air was cooler and the dark afforded a better chance to accurately gauge the color of the heated iron, and partly because there was just that much work to do.

Hakon hadn't made nails nor chain link nor horseshoes in years, and never so many. Only a handful of days at his new position and he felt he could make a hundred hobnails in an hour in his sleep. It was always good to practice the basics, he told himself. Not every job could be a beautiful breastplate or wicked axe. Plow heads and hatchets and serving knives all served important functions, too.

At night, at work, when it was just him and his hammer and Wülf, Hakon could clear his head of everything else. He practiced his human words with every hammer stroke, forming his lips around the new words and phrases to memorize what they felt like, which would help him with what they looked like on others.

When he could hear what was said, he found the Eirean tongue easy enough to follow, although he was still baffled by some of their idioms and verbs. The problem was when people mumbled or pointed their faces away from him. Human lips were harder to read, moving much quicker without the hindrance of tusks.

He was undeterred.

A few days within Dundúran Castle and Hakon knew it was where he was meant to be. The work was steady and soon he hoped to be trusted with more challenging work. The smithy itself was an impressive thing, a huge circle of connected forges set in a stone circle, divided into cells by stone and brick. The ring of a room faced the west bailey, aired by a wall of wide windows. It had everything a smithy could want, with several work areas to choose from. Hakon already had a mind, since it was just him and the old head blacksmith Fearghas, that they could divide the space into specialties, so that specific tools and molds didn't have to be fetched or traded out every time.

He was waiting for Fearghas to warm to him before bringing this up, however. Although, he wasn't sure Fearghas warmed up to anyone. The tetchy older human man was big and burly, his head shaved to reveal a shiny scalp, but a wild beard grew to touch his chest. Hakon hadn't determined the color of his eyes yet, so often they were squinting or scowling.

Fearghas had deigned to give him a succinct tour of the smithy on his first day, but after that it was only barks to assign Hakon the busywork. For his part, Fearghas seemed solely focused on making intricate, decorative goblets set with braided metal and precious stones. These he took to his favorite tavern most nights to drink and sing shanties.

Hakon had to hope that his steady work of nails and horseshoes would eventually earn him some modicum of trust with the older man. He knew a skilled blacksmith when he saw one, and Fearghas was skilled—if abrasive. And set in his ways. Hakon would give the man a few more days before he brought up his suggestions.

Fearghas aside, there was much to recommend his new circumstances.

A small but well-kept room had been given to him just off the smithy so he could keep the fires stoked. Staff were welcome to use the heated baths below the castle, as well as take their meals in the dining hall with the liege lord and his family if no banquet was being held.

The best part, though, was all the pretty human women who inhabited the castle. The castle staff was a small army of people, half of whom were female, and many of them young and hearty lasses. His head had turned to behold more than one as he walked to find himself and Wülf food or on his way to the baths.

For the first time in his life, a woman flirted with him.

His ears burned hotter than his forge fire thinking of it.

He'd harbored dark doubts deep inside him during his journey north that he wouldn't, in the end, find human women attractive or suitable—or worse, none would find him appealing. He'd lived his life in Kaldebrak being passed over and ignored as a potential mate, but more than one human woman had already run her gaze over him appreciatively.

*It will work,* he thought to himself. *This all will work. I'll make you proud yet,* gadaron.

Now it was just a matter of talking to one of them. He was growing more confident in his Eirean every day, and he thought soon he'd be able to hold a conversation with a woman without fumbling his words.

He wasn't opposed to sampling the fruits, as it were, thinking of how one of the kitchen maids had given him a particularly lusty look as she ladled his supper into a bowl. His aim, though, was always to find his mate.

With so many women here, not just within the castle but the city of Dundúran itself, there had to be a woman who might fancy him and whom he could love in return. This was all for her, after all, his journey and new life.

So while he might sample, he had to keep his head. A mate was his aim, and he doubted she'd appreciate him looking for her in every maid's bed along the way.

His blood ran hot with the prospects—of which there were many.

He hadn't been this lusty since his randy days as an untried youth and the first nights he'd spent with Feeli. The possibilities almost overwhelmed him.

He had to think with his head, though, and not with his cock and make a good choice. And a wise one. For all that he yearned for a mate now, he'd spent much of his youth resenting it and its powerful hold over bonded mates.

The mate-bond took his mother from him, so strong was its pull to despair when his father perished. His grandfather couldn't bear to be without his grandmother and quickly died of a broken heart. So it often was for bonded mates, which was why many kin were cautious in bonding with a mate. They were much more carefree about bedmates, but he knew of plenty of kin who eschewed liaisons that lasted too long for fear of the bond beginning to take root.

The mate-bond was sacred to orcs for good reason, and Hakon learned to appreciate it in his maturity and long for the bond his grandparents shared, the one Siggy and her mates had.

He wanted that something fierce. To be everything to someone. To be loved and wanted and needed so fiercely . . .

Knowing that he was on the precipice, so close to finding it, eased a bit of the aching in his cock to be around so many pretty women—as well as the heartache of missing home more than he cared to admit.

As Hakon hammered, wanting to finish a few more nails and horseshoes before banking the fire for the night, the thought of pretty women and mates eventually lured his thoughts back to yesterday. To *her.*

He'd already heard plenty of talk about the Darrow heiress in his short time there. Hakon was pleased to find that talk of her, and of Liege Darrow, was almost always positive; they seemed truly beloved by the staff of their castle.

None of that had prepared him for seeing *her,* though.

He feared he'd been struck dumb in her presence.

Hakon thrust another iron bar into the fire, ears going ruddy at the memory.

Fates, he didn't know women came so fine.

It wasn't that the other women of the castle were mostly common folk while she was noble born. There were others just as or more beautiful than she; there were those who also had glittering eyes and more still with blonde hair that fell in soft waves down their backs. Plenty had freckles dotting their noses and pink, plush lips that curled just so into a warm smile. Orek's mate Sorcha was taller and more buxom, while many other women he'd seen were smaller than the heiress.

She was all of these things and so much more. What that was, though, he didn't know for sure, and thought perhaps knowing might lead him into danger.

Something moved in his peripheral vision. At first thinking it was just Wülf shifting on his preferred thatch mat, he ignored it.

There it was again, though. Clearly a human hand waving at him.

Hakon turned his head to look—and nearly dropped molten iron on his foot.

Lady Aislinn stood in the smithy entryway grinning at him, holding a book in one small hand and waving her other to get his attention.

Ears burning, Hakon hastened to safely put down his tools. Her mouth moved as she took another step into the room.

He lifted a hand, startling her, and quickly pulled the beeswax from his ears.

"Forgive me, my lady," he said, bowing his head.

"No need." She looked down in surprise when Wülf appeared before her and nudged her with his long muzzle.

Whistling between his teeth, Hakon warned, "Wülf, behave."

Lady Aislinn held her hand out for the dog to sniff, and in amazement, Hakon watched his unfriendly, aloof hound thrust his head into her hand for attention. He rarely let Hakon or his grandmother pet him, let alone strangers, but was happy to make a fool of himself for the pretty heiress.

*That makes two of us.*

"What did you have in your ears?" she asked.

Hakon's mouth opened and closed, his heart still racing to have Lady Aislinn there as if his thoughts had summoned her. Her glossy waves were brushed back from her face, offering him a clear view of her lovely face and sparkling golden eyes. A simple blue gown adorned her, the neckline dipping to reveal the top swells of her ample breasts and the skirt falling in a draping cascade around her round hips.

He caught a rumbling noise in his throat. *Fates, how lovely she is.*

Then—his heart stuttered when he realized she stood there, expecting his answer, but he didn't know the Eirean word for *beeswax.*

Clearing his throat to stall, he finally said, "*Tek'tek.*"

Her head of golden hair tipped to the side in curiosity. To his astonishment, she drew closer to him, holding out her hand. "May I?"

Whole face burning in a ruddy blush, Hakon swiped his thumb over the ball of wax to clean it best he could before he placed it in her soft palm. Fates, she had fine fingers—long-boned, soft, the nails perfect little crescents.

Angling her hand into the firelight, she smiled when she realized, "Beeswax."

A relieved breath rushed out of his tight lungs. "Yes, my lady."

"You use them to protect your ears?"

"My hearing, yes. Forging can get very loud." He mimicked the motion of hammering metal on an anvil.

Handing the wax back, her smile widened. "That is a smart practice, master blacksmith."

"An old practice," he told her. "My grandfather used it and so do I."

"Your grandfather was wise. Perhaps you'll be able to convince Fearghas to follow your example. Maybe then he'll keep what hearing he has left." She smiled good-naturedly, as if she was fond of the surly older blacksmith, and Hakon hesitantly returned the gesture.

It was true, even with protection, smiths tended to go deaf from all the loud noises of the forge. A cold, sickly dread always crept up Hakon's neck to think of losing any more of his hearing.

His grandmother too had had difficulty hearing in one of her ears. Hakon supposed, like his eyes, it was something that proved he was one of them.

"Do you usually work so late into the night, Master Green-Fist, or is Fearghas setting you that much to do?"

Fates, his ears would never return to normal at the rate they heated.

Clearing his throat, Hakon's answer was diplomatic. "A bit of both, my lady. Although—" he winced to think it "—if I'm disturbing you with the noise . . ."

"No, no! Don't think of it. I only wondered—the night is quieter and cooler and it seems—what I meant . . ." He thought it must be a trick of the light, but her cheeks flushed with color. Taking a moment to collect herself, Lady Aislinn said, "All I meant to say was that I like working at night, too." She nodded toward the open windows of the smithy, at one of the upper-level windows of the castle. "I was working myself and saw the fires still burning from my window."

Those blunt teeth caught the plush curve of her lower lip between them, catching Hakon's attention just as surely. Something fluttered in the pit of his stomach, and he watched dazedly as she took another few steps into the smithy to stand before him.

Wülf followed her stride for stride, pushing his head into her hand again.

"I was hoping . . . well, you may not have the time for it, of course. I'll understand if there's too much to do. But, if you'd be willing, I have a special project I'd like your help on."

Pleasure, sharp and aching, lodged between his ribs.

"Anything, my lady."

A smile, brighter than the sun and just as warm, broke across her face. She tempered it quickly, but Hakon already saw it seared across his mind's eye, like a green burst across his eyelids after staring at the sun.

The sight stunned him long enough that she was already opening the book she'd brought with her and showing him a page before he got his wits about him.

It took him a moment to realize—she was showing him a notebook, full of drawings and notes. The page she held up to him was a sketch of what looked like a wicked pair of gardening shears, the blades curved like a scythe.

"I was hoping you might make me these," she said, pulling the book back to rest on her shoulder so she could point out different aspects of the drawing. She told him in great detail what she'd imagined, from the spring coil to the angle of the shear blades to how she couldn't decide if wood or leather would be better for the handle.

Hakon stood on, a little dumbfounded, a lot impressed.

Her plan was sound—and better, it was certainly something he could create for the pretty heiress.

He realized a little too late that she'd stopped talking. Pulling his gaze up from those fine fingers as they traced the page, it landed on her mouth. Her plush, pink, unmoving mouth.

Lifting his eyes finally to hers, he found her looking away again, another blush staining her cheeks and a consternated frown marring her brow. He immediately disliked it, wishing he could take his thumb and soothe it away.

"Forgive me, I . . . I get excited talking about my projects."

"You are passionate," he argued. "Nothing wrong with that."

That earned him a little smile, which Hakon took greedily. Fates, what he wouldn't give to earn more of those.

"The castle has shears, of course, but Morwen told me to stay out of her good gardening tools—I've borrowed a few too many, you see—I always mean to return them, but something inevitably happens and—" she cleared her throat "—and we must respect the head gardener." Another shy, almost self-deprecating smile. "I thought to design something specifically for rose bushes. They'll need to be long and strong."

Thinking of Lady Aislinn, with her warm smile and fine hands, wrestling with thorny, overgrown rosebushes gave him pause. "Is there not . . . someone to do that?" he asked, choosing his words carefully.

Her smile turned sad, making Hakon's heart hammer faster than a striker on an anvil.

"Yes, there are plenty of skilled gardeners in Dundúran, but this is . . ." Her gaze fell away, those elegant fingers fiddling with the corner of the leather-bound notebook. "It's my mother's rose garden, you see. No one has touched it since her passing."

Something heavy vibrated between Hakon's ribs. Her sadness was apparent, and he hated it.

*A female such as this should never know sadness.*

"It's probably not worth doing," Lady Aislinn muttered, almost to herself. "I'm sure it's more trouble than it's worth. I just thought . . ."

Pulling in a long breath, Hakon could feel the ache in his own heart reaching out to hers.

"I know what it is to miss a mother, my lady. If it will bring you some comfort, then it's worth doing. I will help you any way I can."

Those luminous, leonine eyes of hers looked up at him with understanding, and something fundamental shifted inside Hakon.

"Truly?" she whispered.

"Anything, my lady. Whatever you need, I will do it."

To his relief, the sadness in her ebbed, replaced with an effervescence he wished he could grab with both hands and hold close to his chest.

"I appreciate it, truly. The last under blacksmith had no time for my projects."

"My time is yours." His mouth was running away from him, but he couldn't help it. If it kept her smiling, he might promise just about anything.

The smithy door opened with a clattering *bang,* making even Wülf jump, and in stumbled Fearghas. The man got a few steps inside before he saw Lady Aislinn and Hakon staring at him.

"Oh, milady, apologies—"

"No need, Fearghas. I'm sorry for disturbing you and your new blacksmith. We were just discussing a project." She threw Hakon another dazzling smile over her shoulder. "I'll return tomorrow with more detailed plans for you?"

"Of course, my lady. I will find you several choices for the handle grips as well."

That smile widened, and she clutched her notebook to her chest, holding it tight and making Hakon intensely jealous of a ream of paper.

"Gentlemen," she said with a nod, "I'll bid you goodnight, then."

"Goodnight, my lady."

"G'night, milady."

Fearghas shut the door softly behind her and wasted no time turning a scowl onto Hakon.

"What are you about, bothering the heiress?"

Hakon frowned. "She came to me with a request."

"So the horseshoes aren't done?" His scowl traveled over Hakon's shoulder to spy the unfinished, unmolded iron bars.

"Is a request from Lady Aislinn not more important?"

Blustering under that big beard, Fearghas wobbled further into the smithy. "Got a lot of projects, that one. Always needing something." That scowl returned, and Fearghas pointed it and a warning, meaty finger at Hakon. "You keep those puppy looks to yourself and leave the lady be. She's well loved here, and no one will stand for her being toyed with."

A growl worked up Hakon's throat, and all at once, he realized it for what it was—his once docile beast rumbling to life.

Hakon's heart stuttered again, even as his beast grew louder inside him.

"I mean only to help her," he told Fearghas through gritted teeth.

He would *never* toy with a woman like Lady Aislinn. A woman such as her was meant only for good things, for devotion and passion and love. To have a mate such as Lady Aislinn—

The old blacksmith *hmphed.* "See that you do. Best to figure out your place now and stick to it."

Hakon's fists clenched, emotion seething hotter than the molten rivers that flowed deep below Kaldebrak. He knew the old blacksmith was drunk and always surly, but to warn him away? To imply that he might hurt her in any way?

*Impossible.*

His beast, an inner instinct that drove all orc-kin to fight and fuck and find a mate, rumbled possessively. Some kin had beasts that drove them to berserker strength in battle; others had one that leant them a well of empathy and understanding of others that made them excellent healers. His had never been so strong before, not even when he'd spent years pining over Feeli.

He'd thought perhaps, as a halfling, his beast was only half, too. Half as strong or potent.

The instinct roaring in his chest felt nothing by halves. It was all snarling aggressiveness at another male warning him away from *his*—

The breath squeezed from Hakon's lungs.

No. No, the beast couldn't be right.

He just liked her and her quick mind and her smile, was all.

It . . . it couldn't be more.

Rationality meant nothing to the growling thing inside him, though. A few minutes spent basking in the warmth of Lady Aislinn Darrow and the infernal instinct was ready to make declarations that were impossible.

*Impossible,* he told it.

*Nothing's impossible,* it growled back.

# 6

Aislinn thanked her maid, Fia, as the redheaded beauty set down both Aislinn's plain fare and a hearty portion of Hugh's nightly feast for Merrick.

"Will that be all, milady?" asked Fia with a cheeky wink, making her brown eyes and many freckles dance.

Lithe, tall, and confident, the redhead was all easy smiles and jokes, exuding a warmth that put even the most anxious noblewoman at ease. They took to each other well, and Aislinn counted Fia as her closest confidante.

It was Fia who helped Aislinn choose what to wear when more than a simple kirtle was required. It was Fia who'd taught her to flirt and what to ask of a man to please her. It was Fia who made sure she ate when Aislinn would otherwise have completely forgotten in favor of drafting a new project.

Aislinn lived in constant terror that some handsome knight would finally turn Fia's head and sweep her away. Thankfully, Fia seemed unaffected by either men or women—although she certainly enjoyed being the one others fawned over. *I'm just waiting for something . . . special,* Fia had explained one evening as she brushed out Aislinn's hair. *Pretty promises are just that.*

Aislinn knew that day would come eventually, so in the interim, she kept Fia well compensated and thanked her every chance she got. With her friend Sorcha often busy with work and siblings and now a handsome halfling, it often felt like Fia was Aislinn's only friend.

"For now," Aislinn replied, making a show of unfolding her napkin into her lap. "Unless of course I'm displeased with the food."

"Hard to get mashed peas wrong," laughed Fia, and with a toss of her red ringlets, she strode from the high table to join the other staff. More than one head went up in anticipation of her coming.

Settling into her seat, Aislinn took up her spoon as her father tucked into his dinner with relish, a seasoned fillet with a swirl of cream sauce over it and accompanying roasted vegetables. It was hardly an elaborate meal for a lord's table, but then, her father had never been fussy. That was much more Aislinn's territory.

She didn't mean to make Hugh's life difficult—she just couldn't bear certain textures. Fish being one of them. But she was more than content with her hearty bowl of pea soup, a plate of the roasted vegetables, and a generous cut of the crusty loaf she'd helped knead that very morning.

Merrick made a few more appreciative noises before asking, "Which did you do for this?"

"Not much," admitted Aislinn, "just the bread. I couldn't stay long helping, there were another three guild-masters who requested an audience, and we're still trying to recover our stores of soap cakes after the council meeting."

In truth, it was a bit of a blessing that they hadn't enough soap to continue washing the *volumes* of bedding used to accommodate Dundúran's many guests last week. So many staff were needed for laundry that other tasks had fallen to the wayside. The gardens were going unkept, the corridors unswept. Hugh and Brenna were united for once in their chagrin.

Not a situation Aislinn wanted on her hands. *"Leave the bedding that hasn't been washed until we can get more soap. Our things must come first if we have enough for an errant guest."* Brenna hadn't liked that answer, her lips pinching, but Aislinn would much rather she, her father, and the staff had clean underthings than all the extra bedding usually kept in the vast linen cupboards was clean and ready for a possible guest.

*If it means we can't accommodate more guests, all the better.*

She didn't tell Brenna that, of course.

All of it only proved her point that having too many guests was a formula for upheaval. Unclean bedding and a lack of soap had upended the balance of Dundúran Castle, and Aislinn wouldn't rest easy until that balance was restored. She'd already lost two nights' sleep over it.

The thought of ever having to receive a royal visit, when a member of the royal family stayed with their courtiers indefinitely, sent a shudder of horror down Aislinn's spine.

"Ah yes," Merrick said. "I've heard rumblings of this soap cake crisis. Brenna is none too happy."

"When is Brenna ever happy?" Aislinn muttered. She didn't mean to be uncharitable, but little sleep rendered her cranky and short-tempered.

"Point taken." Merrick pulled apart a bit of bread, nodding appreciatively as he chewed. "Another excellent effort, kit."

"If only every problem was solved with a little kneading."

"Eh, it often is. Just in the more metaphoric sense."

Aislinn grumbled, making her father laugh. His jolliness lifted her spirits a little, and she decided to put her crankiness away for a while, her tasks and duties, too, and simply enjoy a meal with her father.

It was one reason why her father always insisted on taking evening meals together. It was a time to slow down, talk. He invited any staff who wished to eat in the dining hall to join them, five long tables laid out for the staff with cutlery and deep wells of stew, mounds of bread, and plates of whatever feast Hugh pulled from his ovens.

Watching the cheery talk of their people improved Aislinn's mood a little more. For all that she worried, her people were content. They rose to the challenge of the council meeting every season, and they'd all earned this respite.

"Well," Merrick said when he neared the end of his meal, "we may be lacking soap cakes, but we're rich in horseshoes. The new blacksmith is proving very industrious."

Aislinn's cheeks bloomed with heat, and she hid her face behind her goblet. The sip of mead wetted her throat but didn't cool her blush.

"Hakon is very talented. And driven," she said, hoping her father couldn't hear how her heart *pitter-pattered* at the mention of their handsome new blacksmith.

She wouldn't soon forget the sight he'd made that night in his forge, lit by firelight as his strong arms brought the hammer down on the iron. She'd lingered in the doorway, mesmerized by the methodical rhythm of his work, and although she didn't enjoy loud noises, somehow it wasn't so bad, the sparks that flew from the iron exciting, and the sure way he handled it enthralling.

"He is indeed," Merrick agreed. "Though I fear Fearghas is setting him too many tasks."

"Hopefully not. I've asked him to make me something already."

Her father made a noise of interest as he sipped his mead.

"A pair of shears. Morwen said I wasn't allowed another pair of hers, and I'll need something strong to get those brambles under control. The blooms are almost finished, so they'll need to be trimmed down for their winter dormancy."

"For your mother's garden?"

Aislinn realized too late that she'd not mentioned wanting to tame the garden to her father yet. She knew he'd have no objections, but any mention of Róisín always brought a somber pall to Merrick's face.

Just as it did now.

"Yes," she answered softly. "I . . . it's a peaceful place to sit. It reminds me of her."

Not looking up from his goblet, he traced the rim with his thumbnail. "Good. It will be nice to see it restored to its former glory. But wouldn't you rather Morwen and her staff took care of it?"

"No, I . . . I want to do it."

Finally, her father met her gaze. A look passed between them, short in length but significant in depth. Merrick reached out to squeeze her hand. "All right, kit," he said. "Let's see what you can do."

Aislinn's smile was bittersweet. She always loved her father's *"Let's see what you can do."* Where other fathers may have forbidden or reprimanded, Merrick Darrow only ever encouraged and advised. Even when Aislinn, and especially Jerrod, deserved reprimand.

*Speaking of which . . .*

Her father's good humor still hadn't returned, and Aislinn didn't see a reason to ruin it again.

*Best do it now.*

With a heavy heart, she pulled the Warden's letter from her pocket.

"We received this not long ago." Handing it to Merrick, she explained, "Jerrod's run away. Nobody can find him."

Her father's frown deepened as his eyes skated across the page. Stark lines carved across his face, making him look much more his age. Aislinn hated the reminder that he was growing older—she hated the hairs that had gone gray, the wrinkles that fanned around his eyes.

She hated Jerrod for putting such a look on their father's face.

After a grave stretch of silence, Merrick cast the letter down on the table in disgust. Sitting back in his seat, the look he finally turned on Aislinn was stoic, but she knew her father well enough to see the hurt pooling beneath the surface.

"As the Warden says, it's not wholly unexpected. It was perhaps too much to presume he'd accept his punishment with any grace."

The words weren't half as harsh as Jerrod deserved, but Aislinn couldn't help wincing. Whatever she felt, or didn't, for Jerrod, he was her brother, and if nothing else, she pitied him.

Yet Aislinn held her tongue, for what was there to say? Perhaps she might've mustered something in his defense were she able to forgive him for what he'd done, but she hadn't and couldn't.

Sorcha was like a sister to her, the sibling of her heart. A friend who *knew* Aislinn and accepted her for all she was. A friend such as that was invaluable—and came before even blood. Aislinn knew what it was to be misunderstood, to question why someone paid her any attention; neither was true with Sorcha.

His gaze faraway, Merrick brought his goblet to his lips and swallowed the last of his mead in a single gulp. Sitting straight in his seat, his look hardened, and Aislinn prepared herself for something she wouldn't like hearing.

"If he wants to make his own life, I suppose I can't fault him that. But we should find him, at least. Your brother has a penchant for trouble."

"Shouldn't he be returned to the Ward?" Six months hardly seemed a true punishment.

"Yes, but who will keep him there? Shall I send knights to guard over him and watch as he tends to the sick?"

*If that's what it takes. If that will finally make him learn.*

"No," Merrick answered his own question, "there's no point to it. Let him try on his own."

He sighed, his face gone haggard, and Aislinn bit her cheek to keep silent. The decision sat like lead in her stomach, uncomfortable and heavy. Were they to just never see him again? Never speak his name or know what became of him?

Her father took in her silence and raised his hands. "I know, kit. I just . . . what he did is . . ." Merrick shook his head. "I suppose it will be worthwhile to keep an eye out for him. If he's gone south, we'll surely hear word of him."

"South?" Aislinn repeated, frustration prickling at her neck to think she'd missed something.

She didn't miss her father's wince.

"Yes, that." Leveling her with a look, he said, "Ciaran and I have decided to make another expedition south. It's obvious we haven't accomplished nearly as much as we'd hoped against the slavers, and the ones who took Sorcha are still at large."

The words rang in her ears with an echo of disbelief.

"But you and Sir Ciaran have retired from that. I thought Connor and Niall Brádaigh were to take up the mission."

"They certainly are, but there's much their father and I must show them. People they must meet. And . . ." here he sighed again, "Ciaran and I . . . our work isn't complete. I can't rest knowing that, kit. To have slavers *here,* so close—I won't have it. Those who took Sorcha must be punished and made an example of. Else what will all our work have come to? Nothing."

Aislinn shook her head vehemently. "That's not true. You've already done so much good—it's time for others to take up the work."

"Soon," he said, as if that would reassure her. "And we don't intend to leave until after Sorcha's wedding. Wouldn't miss that, of course."

"You can't just leave again."

She hated how petulant she sounded even to her own ears. And how small.

Merrick's brows drew low in concern. He offered his hand in comfort, but Aislinn sat back in her seat, out of his reach.

"We must see this through, kit. I'm sorry."

"I'm not ready to be Liege Darrow."

"We both know your brother rarely carried out his duties—you've been in charge of Dundúran since you were small."

*I shouldn't have had to be. I shouldn't have to be now.* The words squeezed her throat until she could hardly breathe.

"It's not the same."

"It's just this once more. It has to be done."

"*Father—*"

Merrick shook his head once. "I'm decided, kit. This needs doing. You'll get on fine, you always do."

To her horror, hot tears pricked her eyes. When she stood to leave, he gaped up at her.

"Kit—?"

Upset unsettled her stomach, what food she'd eaten churning around inside her in a tempest. Her skin felt too tight, her throat, her chest, her very heart squeezing past discomfort.

*Fates, not again!*

Rounding her chair, she hastened from the high table and made for the side door, left ajar by one of the serving maids.

*Why must he leave?* Always her father had to find peace outside Dundúran, outside the Darrowlands. He made something good out of his grief, but why did it have to be *out there,* so far away?

*Don't go,* the girl inside her always begged. *Don't leave me by myself.*

Aislinn could hardly see through the watery blur of her gathering tears as she hurried through the castle corridors, but then, she didn't truly need to see. She knew every stone of this castle, every nook and corridor and hidey-hole.

Her whole life was in this castle, all her hurts and secrets and projects.

She'd left the Darrowlands only twice in her whole life. If Liege Darrow was needed at court in Gleanná, someone had to stay behind and steward, and that was never Jerrod.

*Aislinn will see to it. Aislinn will take care of it. Aislinn will understand.*

And she did. No matter the cost, no matter how she laid awake at night counting the things she had to do and dreading most of them.

She couldn't disappoint her parents. They'd given her so much, been so good and patient with her—she could oversee the home they built and loved. She could help her brother until he learned for himself. She could she could *she could*—

Aislinn sobbed. At first, she'd thought to flee to her study, but the stones of the castle seemed to warp, closing in around her. Aislinn picked up her skirts and pace, hurrying down down down into the west bailey below.

The night air was cool on her skin, damp from her flight and contained tears. Her breaths came in great heaves, each a battle to keep her dinner in her stomach.

Hand clasped over her racing heart, Aislinn slowed to an aimless walk. She shut her eyes tight, against her tears, against her reality.

Already she barely kept her head above the surface with all her tasks and duties. There was the new bridge to plan, too, and soap cakes to source, and two kitchen staff were leaving soon and would need replacements, and more otherly folk had sent petitions asking for an audience, and she still had to meet with the bricklayer and stonemason guild-masters to start negotiations for the supplies for the bridge, and Brenna would always have something for her, and she needed to draw up plans for the rose garden and and and—

"Are you well, my lady?"

Aislinn gasped, skirts snapping as she jerked toward the deep rumble.

She'd come to a stop in the center of the bailey and blinked owlishly at the voice coming from the smithy. Hakon the handsome blacksmith sat on a stool just outside the well-lit smithy, his elbows on his knees as he bent over something in his hands.

*Fates, he has lovely, strong hands.*

Turning away so he couldn't see her face, Aislinn quickly wiped away the escaped tears.

Mortification crept up her neck, but the surprise of seeing him there seemed to have shocked her roiling emotions, allowing her to bury them back into the pit she kept inside her just for them.

It was a long while before she turned to face him again, long enough that she knew it was rude, but there was nothing for it. She wouldn't allow him or anyone else to see her tears.

"Forgive me," he said, "I didn't mean to startle you."

She shook her head. "I should've paid more attention." The last thing she needed was to turn an ankle. That wouldn't spare her from her duties.

Out from the smithy trotted the mighty Wülf, tongue lolling. He headed straight for her, pushing his snout into her hand.

Aislinn petted him enthusiastically, welcoming the distraction.

"He's very fond of you," said the blacksmith. "He doesn't usually take to others. Or even me, really."

"Truly? But he's such a friendly hound." A deep scritch behind his ear with her nails had his back leg thumping on the cobblestones.

Hakon chuckled. "Only with you. I'm not sure he sees me as more than the one who fetches the meals."

"I'm sure that's not true." She bent to peer into the dog's eyes, finding them a soulful brown. "You're a noble beast, I'm sure."

"Careful, my lady. You'll spoil him."

A smile strayed onto her lips, surprising her. All the ugliness she felt was still there, still bubbling inside her, but out in the fresh air, petting a dog, talking with the handsome blacksmith, it didn't feel quite so . . . *unbearable.*

Shoring up her courage, she nodded at his hands. "What are you working on?"

"Ah." Straightening, he held up the little bauble.

Captivated, Aislinn crossed the bailey, her curiosity piqued. He held the object out to her with his fingertips, and Aislinn took it as gently as she would spun glass.

"Careful," he warned, "I need to smooth it."

Holding it up to the light, she marveled, "It's a rose."

"Yes, my lady." His gaze drifted dreamily, and his voice pitched even lower when he said, "Your project had me thinking of the mountain roses that grow on the southern slopes of Kaldebrak. In summer, the mountain is covered in their blooms."

Enchanted, another wider smile pulled at her lips. "That sounds so lovely." Handing the rose back to him, she said, "My mother's garden has the only roses here, I'm afraid. But there are lovely tulips and daffodils in spring. And for a few weeks, the wisteria blooms. It's beautiful."

"I look forward to it, my lady." He smiled up at her, his own soulful brown eyes catching the firelight from the forge.

Aislinn's stomach swooped—not with weighty worries but airy lightness.

"You whittle as well," she said to distract herself. "What can't you do, master blacksmith?"

"Plenty, my lady," he chuckled. "But I find it is good to practice different crafts." He held up the small knife he used to carve away flakes of wood. "In truth, it helps me think."

"Does it?" she asked, charmed.

"I've been thinking over your garden shears, planning it in my mind. This keeps my hands busy and my mind clear."

"I do the same, with my designs. Drawing helps my mind focus."

His smile returned, somehow even warmer than before. That dimple appeared, casting a captivating shadow across his cheek.

In the firelight, he might have otherwise struck an imposing figure, even sitting down. Those wide shoulders cast a wide shadow, and the darkness emphasized the slightly inhuman shape of his mouth. Yet, it also offered a velveteen softness to his skin, and the firelight caught in the dark swoop of his short hair and along the ridges of his knuckles.

The soft darkness suited him. And so did that dimple.

"If you come tomorrow, I'll have a . . ." He frowned, pausing as if to think of the word. "An example to show you."

Her heart leapt in pleasure. "A prototype? Already? Wonderful! I can come tomorrow afternoon?"

"Whenever suits, my lady. I hope you will approve of them."

She assured him she would. After a few more questions on what he liked to whittle—animals, mostly—and what Wülf liked to do—sleep, mostly—Aislinn bid him goodnight, her spirits lighter as she climbed the stairs back into the castle.

She could already hear the scolding from Brenna, that she hadn't the time to spend lollygagging in the smithy over a project, but Aislinn would make time. As she quietly walked the corridors of her castle, she found herself eager to discover what else the handsome blacksmith could create with those big hands.

# 7

The new blacksmith didn't disappoint.

Aislinn settled herself comfortably in the chair he'd obviously set out for her in a tidy corner by the window, with a cushion and everything. She grinned to herself, setting her notebook in her lap as she watched the giant half-orc bustle about his space.

She wasn't entirely sure, but she thought he might be . . . nervous?

Aislinn didn't know him well, of course, and always struggled to discern the feelings of new people, but the thought that this big man might be a bit flustered with her there in his forge tickled her with amusement.

A cloud of dust and soot puffed a foot in the air when Wülf flopped down beside her to watch the spectacle.

As she waited, Aislinn figured yes, he must be nervous. He knew she was coming, of course. She said she would the previous night, and she'd executed one of her better sneaks through the castle to avoid Brenna. He'd found a chair and cushion for her comfort. Yet he hastened about the smithy gathering everything, his ears that ruddy brownish color at the charmingly pointed tips.

In the bright daylight, she noticed a detail she hadn't before—several small gold rings hung from his ears. One pierced the left lobe with three more studding the shell almost up to the point of his ear. His right only had one. By the shine of them, they were true gold, and she found herself a little entranced by the glimmer.

It was from the sound of him clearing his throat that she finally realized he stood before her. His ears had deepened in color, and he tilted his head to angle the left one toward her.

"My lady?"

"Oh, forgive me, I was just admiring your earrings." She touched her own with a fingertip. "They're lovely. Do they mean something?"

"For orcs, it is a symbol of . . ." He gestured with his hand. "A new one is earned with every . . ."

"Achievement?" she offered.

"Yes. Achievement." He cleared his throat. "There is another word I have to learn."

"You've already done remarkably well learning the Eirean tongue. Did you speak it before coming to Dundúran?"

"No. I learned on the journey from Kaldebrak."

"Well, I don't speak orcish, but I'm glad to help you any way I can with Eirean."

His eyes crinkled at the corners. "You are kind, my lady." Reaching for something on a worktable, he presented her with an unfinished set of gardening shears. "Before that, let me see how you like the prototype."

Aislinn gasped in delight as he lowered it into her greedy hands. *This is only a prototype?* It looked perfect!

"Oh, Hakon, this is marvelous!"

She held the shears up to the light, appreciating the wicked curve of the blades. Although metal, the shears weren't too heavy, and she turned them this way and that to inspect and admire.

His dimple teased along his cheek as he explained the spring he'd made, as well as the catch for safety. He then presented her with options for the handles—smoothed pine and soft leather and tightly wrapped canvas.

"Knowing now how talented you are, I have to choose the pine," she said.

"Of course, my lady. I'll have it ready for you very soon."

"I appreciate it, Hakon, truly. This is so much better—and faster than I ever expected. I hope it didn't interfere with your other work."

"There will always be horseshoes to make," he replied in good humor.

She handed back the shears for the final touches, although reluctantly. Something about holding them, feeling how fine a creation they were, made her greedy.

"I hope you will enjoy using the shears as much as I did making them," he said as he pulled out several pieces of wood for her to choose from. "If you need anything else made, I will help any way I can."

More beautiful words had never been said—at least not to Aislinn.

"I wouldn't want to impose . . ."

"What else is a blacksmith for?" His smile turned cheeky, that dimple elongating. "All those designs in your notebook are very . . ."

It was Aislinn's turn to flush. "Messy?"

"Impressive," he decided. "You have so many ideas."

Aislinn shrugged, not knowing what else to do when faced with such praise. "It's just how my mind works, I suppose. If I didn't draw them and get them out, they'd crowd around in my head and leave me no space."

When her explanation was met with silence, she dared look up—to find him staring at her in . . . she didn't know what, but it had her heart fluttering like bird wings.

"I hadn't considered that." A slow smile spread across his handsome face. "I like it. The drawing frees your mind for more ideas."

"A blessing and a curse," she agreed. "It means there's always a new idea to distract me from the last one."

"A mind always at work."

"Yes." That was exactly right. He put into words how she felt in a way no one had before. With it came a sharp pinprick of truth, though; her mind truly was always whirring, which could be exhausting.

Not right now, though. As she sat speaking with Hakon Green-Fist, she found herself on the edge of her seat, greedy for what he might say next in that brogue accent of his.

After choosing a solid piece of pine, Hakon said, "Let me get a few measurements of your hands, if you wouldn't mind staying another moment?"

Mind? He'd have to throw her out.

"Of course," she said, adjusting her skirts to hide her happiness.

Pulling over a stool, he sat before her with a ball of string. Although the stool sat him a little below her in her chair, his head still rose above hers. The impact of his size was even more acute like this as he leaned forward, attention on unspooling a length of string. He took up most of her vision, and so close, she could smell the heat of the fire on him, the crisp scent of wood and iron just beneath, along with a heavier, deeper tone of male. His scent reminded her of a bonfire, like crackling orange sparks and fragrant wood in conflagration.

When he offered his large green hand, she didn't hesitate to give her own. She bit her lip at the feeling of his skin against hers as he held and moved her hand so, so gently. He touched her with his fingertips, as if she was delicate, precious. The string whispered across her skin as he took the length and width of her hands, a soft, teasing whisper followed by the warm scrape of his calluses.

She watched, mesmerized by the slow, almost sensual movements of his hands. How the tendons flexed under his skin, how the blunted fingertips held the string, how his palms almost burned her with their warmth as they held her hand.

It was a long while before Aislinn realized that the string no longer touched her, that it was only his two hands holding hers. Breath stuttering, she looked up between her lashes to find him looking at her much the same way under the shadow of his heavy brow.

A frisson of . . . something passed between them. She could only describe it as *sparkling* and *exciting*.

Aislinn held her breath, waiting.

For what, she didn't know.

For once, her mind was blessedly quiet as she took in every detail of the handsome blacksmith. The fleck of gold in his right eye. The small scar that bisected his left brow. The few freckles dotting the bridge of his nose. The perfect arch of his upper lip, hiding the tips of those small tusks.

Her lips parted—to say what she didn't know—and she watched his gaze drop to her mouth.

*Fates, what am I doing?*

Pulling her hand back, Aislinn dropped her gaze to her notebook.

"Thank you, my lady," he said, sitting straight on his stool.

"Of course."

Silence stretched between them as he stood, then Aislinn heard him rummaging about on the worktable.

She thought perhaps she should leave, but reluctance kept her in her seat. A blush still warmed her cheeks, and she still didn't know what she'd been thinking, mooning over him like that, but none of that meant she wanted to leave.

*It's too soon to return to schedules and soap cakes.*

Hakon came to her rescue once more.

His big hand appeared in her vision again, and she looked up to see him holding two small bars of beeswax.

"I can adjust the handles now, if you'd like. But it gets quite loud."

She took the wax curiously. "Should I warm it up?"

"Yes, between your palms."

Aislinn watched as he deftly worked the beeswax between fingers and palm before sticking it into his ear. Amused, she mimicked his procedure, her nose wrinkling at the unfamiliar feel of something clogging her ear.

"It's strange!" she said, probably too loudly, and shuddered.

He nodded with a smile, though she wasn't sure he actually heard what she said.

When the wax was in place, Hakon began his work.

Aislinn sat back in her chair and watched in awe.

Using tongs, Hakon buried the handled end of the shears into the forge to heat the metal.

"How long must they heat for?" she asked loudly.

He remained facing the forge, as if he hadn't heard her. Aislinn repeated her question and was met again with silence.

*The wax must work.*

Although, when he pulled the shears from the fire, the hilts of the handles glowing orange, and began to strike them into shape, the clang of metal on metal still pierced her ears. The wax dulled it enough to be bearable, but she still winced with each strike.

Still, it was a joy to watch the work. She always found these things fascinating. How did each step, each part, come together to make a whole? She'd spent many afternoons following behind the craftspeople of Dundúran, learning how they performed their art.

Witnessing the creation of a new thing brought a thrill, and watching Hakon was no different. In fact, it was better.

His hammer was an extension of his arm, muscles flexing and releasing in a perfect rhythm as his other hand turned and positioned the shears. It was a synchronized marvel, and Aislinn enjoyed every moment of it.

If she lingered over his bulging arms and the sheen of sweat gathering at the hollow of his throat, well, she was a mere mortal. She'd challenge anyone not to be arrested by the sight of his thick neck and the tendons that flexed there as he worked.

It ended all too soon. With the handles reformed, he held them up with the tongs and made a few gestures with his other hand. Unsure what they meant, she could only nod.

The shears then went into a barrel of water, steam sizzling through the open windows out into the bailey.

He let them soak for a set time—Aislinn observed him murmuring under his breath—then pulled them out to set on the worktable. When he pulled the wax from his ears, she did, too.

The world seemed overloud without them, her ears ringing with all the little sounds she'd missed.

"How do you know how long to heat them?" she asked. "Forgive me for asking again, I'm just curious."

His ears flushed a deep, ruddy brown again.

"I'm sorry, my lady, I didn't hear . . ." He cleared his throat. "You heat the metal to the right color."

"Color?" *How fascinating!*

Seeing her interest, Hakon was good enough to explain how smiths looked for the metal to heat to a certain color to tell when it'd grown hot enough. Sometimes they wanted just a glowing orange, others a yellow so bright it was nearly white. She listened raptly to his explanations as he worked the wooden grips onto the handles.

"And what is it you meant when you . . ." She repeated the hand gestures he'd made.

"Oh," he chuckled, "the hand-talk. My grandmother and I would use it when my grandfather was hammering."

"The gestures mean certain things?"

"Yes, they mean words. It is helpful when it's difficult to hear over the forge."

"Indeed. I'd love to learn, if you'd teach me."

His brows ticked up in surprise. "Of course, my lady. Perhaps then you can explain to me your many Eirean idioms."

Too soon, he was finished, and from the light pouring into the smithy, Aislinn knew the afternoon waned. There was still so much yet to do, and she was honestly surprised, and pleased, that no one had found her to disturb her afternoon.

Hiding away with the blacksmith was a treat—one she'd never consider with the surly Fearghas.

Thanking him again for humoring her and explaining his craft, Aislinn stood. "I can come back for the shears in a few days, then?" she asked, already counting the hours until she could come again.

"Tomorrow, if you'd like. I can begin on anything else you'd like."

Aislinn glowed with pleasure, grateful for the chance to duck her head when Wülf pressed into her side.

*Fates, you'd think I'd never seen a handsome face before,* she chided herself as she gave the wolfhound a final, dusty pat.

*Not every handsome face can make you everything you've dreamed—and offered to do it, too.*

Well, there was that. What else was a woman to do with so many promises?

Although, Aislinn had never been swayed much by promises. She held herself to her own, but the promises of men rarely if ever kept her warm at night.

She was just enjoying his company, was all. She could admire brilliance when she saw it, and all the better for her that he was willing to share his talents and skills.

Still, she couldn't help asking, "Will we see you at dinner tonight? All are welcome to join us."

Aislinn watched that wide throat of his bob as he swallowed. Those brown eyes searched hers as she stood waiting, patting Wülf for something to do with her hands.

"Wülf doesn't like to eat alone, but I'll try to get away."

"Dogs are welcome—" She pointed a warning finger at Wülf, "Good, *well-behaved* dogs are welcome, too."

"Then we shall join you. Thank you, my lady."

"Good. Well, then, I've taken much of your time. Good day, Hakon."

"Good day, my lady. Oh—!"

Her heart did that funny flutter when she turned to look over her shoulder at his exclamation. He closed the distance between them again, pulling something small from his pocket.

"I finished this and thought . . ."

Curious, she held her hand out to receive the bauble. She smiled in delight to find, "The rose? You finished already?"

"I smoothed it for you and thought you . . . might like it."

She did indeed, running her thumb over the smooth, waxed surface. Always sensitive to textures, from her food to her fabrics, Aislinn's spirit hummed with satisfaction at the smooth undulations of the wood petals, warm from his pocket.

"I love it," she said, "thank you. Here barely two weeks and you're already spoiling me."

The words were out before she could think, and heat pricked her cheeks.

He had no mercy on her, that deep voice rumbling, "It pleases me to please you, my lady."

Aislinn couldn't quite meet his gaze, eyes fixing on that infernally masculine throat as she croaked, "Thank you, Hakon," and fled.

She slipped the whittled rose into her pocket, thumb running across the petals. The movement soothed her racing heart a little, though she didn't catch her breath until she'd made it to the safety of her study.

Shutting the door behind her, Aislinn had to laugh at herself.

*What am I doing?* Flirting with the handsome new blacksmith wouldn't accomplish anything.

But oh, fates, was it *fun*.

# 8

Hakon closed the smithy door behind him, cutting off Fearghas's grumbling. He'd told the master blacksmith he intended to visit the countryside days ago, but that didn't stop the old human from complaining that his work wouldn't get done.

Hakon was sure to be ahead of schedule so that Fearghas didn't truly have anything to fret about. Well, anyone *other than* Fearghas, at least.

Excitement lodged in his throat at the prospects of the day. He'd gotten word from Orek that another of their group of halflings had secured himself a farm. He and many others planned to visit and congratulate Varon, as well as take a look at the land surrounding his new farm. Whispers had it that the Darrows may be willing to part with more land, and Hakon wanted to get a look himself.

While he thoroughly enjoyed his position at the castle—and serving a certain brilliant heiress—he understood how important land was to humans. One day, he'd want land to offer a mate, to build her a fine home and anything she might desire. Founding his own forge also greatly appealed.

He'd stowed away a few of the uncut gems Siggy gave him deep in his pocket, just in case they'd help him today.

The day was clear and bright, a good day for walking.

With Wülf trotting at his side, Hakon strode through the inner bailey, ringed by the smithy and pottery on one side, a stone staircase up into the castle proper, and a southern castle wall, and out into the main courtyard of Dundúran Castle. The space was made to be a pleasure to walk through, and Hakon always did.

The symmetrically laid white limestone pavers and ornamental fountains spurting glittering droplets pleased his artisan sensibilities. Neatly trimmed trees and bushes lined three sides, interspersed with marble statues and columns, making a sort of airy colonnade of foliage, arches, and stonework. Flowerbeds added bursts of yellow, blue, and green and a subtle sweetness to the air.

Many meandered through the courtyard for leisure throughout the day; guards and castle staff and artisans alike. He'd watched the maids sit in the shade of a copse of poplar trees on the near side, taking their luncheon and gossiping. He'd seen the knights train on the far side, near the gatehouse, running exercises and sparring.

It was somehow both serene and always full of noise, the bustle of the castle slowing a little within the wide courtyard.

Within that unique cadence, Hakon didn't think he imagined the sound of Lady Aislinn's voice as he neared the stables.

The largest of the castle's outbuildings contained within the curtain wall, the stables housed over a hundred horses; warhorses for the knights, draft horses to pull heavy loads, and sleek white carriage horses.

His steps faltered, thinking he heard *her* voice.

*Fates, aren't I hearing it enough in my dreams?*

It was bad enough that he dreamed of Lady Aislinn Darrow. Bad enough that he greedily soaked in her presence whenever she came to visit him at his forge—and that he tempted her back with promises of bringing more of her ideas to life.

Now he was hearing her, too.

And following the sound of her voice into the stables, somewhere he'd no place being. He'd hardly even touched a horse, let alone ridden one.

"Really, captain, it's ridiculous. I don't *need* a guard."

Like a moth to a flame, he followed inexorably on. His mind told him to leave it alone; this was her castle, and if she needed him, she'd ask for him.

His beast would have none of it, urging him deeper.

The smell of horses and hay was heavy inside the stables, although he found it to be a brighter space than he'd expected. Dozens of humans and horses moved about, and somewhere a farrier hammered shoes onto a hoof.

Lady Aislinn was easy to find, standing not far from the entrance, her golden hair gathered up into braids and pinned to her head. His beast rumbled with desire at the curve of her long neck, wisps of hair falling along her nape.

*By the gods, stop it,* he told the beast and himself.

He'd no business here in the stables or with the lady of the castle if she wasn't at his forge. If he'd been back in Kaldebrak panting after one of Chieftain Kennum's three daughters, the chief wouldn't hesitate to lop off Hakon's head with a dull battleaxe.

A halfling had no place thinking of an orc chief's daughter, nor a human nobleman's daughter.

He had to stop thinking of her when she wasn't with him and longing for the moment she returned. He had to stop enjoying the sound of her voice when she spoke in that animated way of hers, hands fluttering and swooping as she explained this project or that idea. He had to stop admiring the sharp cut of her mind and bright sparkle of her eyes. And he most assuredly had to stop dreaming about how the nip of her waist curved out into wide hips that swayed mesmerizingly as she walked in those draping blue skirts and would perfectly fill his hands.

He meant to find a mate—something he couldn't do if he kept mooning over Lady Aislinn. It didn't warrant even entertaining the thought of claiming *her* as his mate, nor that she would ever accept such an affront.

Much as he begrudged the old head blacksmith, one thing Fearghas said at least was true. Hakon had to remember his place—and it wasn't with Lady Aislinn.

That rational part of him wasn't the one that snapped to attention, though, when Lady Aislinn made a noise of frustration at the man standing before her. It was the beast that growled inside him in warning as the man, Aodhan, captain of the guard, stood firm, frowning down at her.

He knew Aodhan to be a good, noble sort. Stoic and strict, his brown hair and beard were shorn close to his skin. A scar bisected the left side of his tanned face, perpetually pulling it down into something of a scowl. Still, from what Hakon had seen and heard of him, he was a fair captain, highly respected by the knights and castle staff.

But right then, with him frowning down at *her* like that, Hakon *hated* him.

"I insist, my lady. You cannot be without guards."

"I'm only going to Granach! An hour!"

"That's an hour any vagabond would have on us, my lady."

Lady Aislinn grumbled, arms crossing over her chest. "It's just unnecessary. I've gone to the Brádaigh estate hundreds of times—*without* a chaperone."

"Guards, not chaperones," said Captain Aodhan in a voice that spoke of having said so many times before. "And that was *before*."

Hakon couldn't see Lady Aislinn's face, but her displeasure permeated the air, and most everyone else in the stables had made themselves scarce as the heiress and captain locked horns.

The beast gnashed its teeth—*who was this male to deny her?* And, on his next breath, *How dare she ever be left unprotected?*

If anyone would protect her, it was *him*.

"I will go with Lady Aislinn."

Silence met his offer.

Lady Aislinn turned to behold him with surprise. Captain Aodhan just raised a brow.

Clearing his throat, Hakon dared another few steps inside. *Damn it all.*

"I'm headed to Granach myself. I can accompany Lady Aislinn."

Another beat of silence, Lady Aislinn blinking at him before—

"That suits me just fine. Hakon will go with me."

"My lady," Captain Aodhan sighed, "you still must have guards. No offense to Master Hakon, but you need *armed* protection."

Hakon had just enough sense, and control of his beast, to clench his tusks to his gums to stop himself from telling the captain he'd happily rip any threat to Lady Aislinn apart with his bare hands—or showing him the dagger and hatchet he always carried. It paid to be prepared.

"Who would dare attack with an orc beside me?"

"Criminals will always dare. The scum that attacked Sorcha Brádaigh is still at large. So you'll have a full complement."

"I don't need *six guards* to visit a friend. What will that say to the people? One and Hakon will be plenty."

"Four."

"Two, and I drive myself."

Captain Aodhan opened his mouth, but after a moment's thought, closed it with a *click*. Finally, he nodded. "Very well, my lady."

Lady Aislinn sighed in relief as the captain barked over his shoulder, "Tieran, Greenbriar, mount up. Bring the heiress's carriage."

Hakon stepped forward to follow Lady Aislinn further into the stables, still a bit dazed by the turn of events. Before he could get far, Captain Aodhan intercepted him. A big, leather-gloved hand landed on the center of his chest, and although the human captain was a head shorter than Hakon, he stared up at him with enough gravity to stop him in his tracks.

"I'm entrusting you with the safety of our heiress," Aodhan said in a low, threatening voice.

"I'll protect her with my life." The beast rumbled with displeasure that anyone would think otherwise.

"See that you do. I'll send someone to the armory to—"

"No need." Pulling back his jerkin, Hakon revealed the hidden dagger and hatchet.

Aodhan squinted at them before asking, "You any good with them?"

"I'm a halfling with all my limbs still."

The captain assessed him, his light-brown gaze uncompromising as he took Hakon's measure.

Hakon stared back, unwavering.

*Nowhere is safer for her than with me.*

Whatever Captain Aodhan saw, it apparently satisfied him.

"Don't fail me, halfling."

"I'd never fail her, captain." And, because he figured his measure was taken anyway, he added, "Tomorrow, come by the forge and I'll work that dent out of your cuirass."

Captain Aodhan's gaze fell to the miniscule dent on the side of his breastplate, hardly anything, denoted only by a small shadow.

With a chuckle, the captain stepped aside as two horses pulled alongside them. A set of those sleek white horses had been hitched to a small—Hakon didn't even know. It wasn't quite the chariots he knew were raced in the human kingdom of Pyrros to the south. It wasn't quite the cart or wagon used by the farmers and craftsmen, nor the stately carriage he'd seen Lord Merrick climb into.

Essentially a bench on two large wheels, it had a long, cushioned seat protected by a bucket of wood painted shiny black with a storage compartment mounted behind it. Lady Aislinn sat on one side, long leather reins in her hands.

"Shall we?" she said.

Hakon gulped. She wanted him to *ride* in that?

Captain Aodhan slapped him on the shoulder. "Bring our black-smith back in one piece, my lady."

They left Dundúran behind and were quickly subsumed into the countryside. The breeze invigorated Aislinn's senses, the bright sky and bird chirps lending a cheerful air to their journey.

Although, she'd enjoy it more if her companion wasn't gripping the chaise frame so firmly his knuckles had gone pale. Aislinn was a skilled driver; she hadn't crashed since she was a girl.

Still, it was proving a little challenging to compensate for the unbalanced weight distribution. They'd repacked her basket of gifts for the Brádaighs—rose petal sachets for Aoife, science books for Calum, poetry books for Blaire, butterscotch for Keeley, and a little of everything for Sorcha—directly behind her in a fruitless attempt to rebalance the chaise.

Finally, a few bricks had been added beneath her feet.

It mostly worked, but the chaise still listed slightly on Hakon's side. Aislinn leaned to her left to keep from completely sliding into his lap.

Although, if she was honest, she did delight in letting herself press up against him. There was little choice, really—he took up most of the bucket seat with those shoulders and arms of his. If it meant she had to sidle close to keep them balanced and feel all that warm muscle, well, that only brightened her already good day.

Outside the castle, into the fresh air of the countryside, on the way to see her best friend in the whole world. That spelled for a good day, even if she'd had to argue with Brenna, and then Captain Aodhan, to make it happen. She wouldn't be denied—especially since Sorcha and Orek were finally back from their latest trip south and their wedding was quickly approaching.

Sorcha assured Aislinn that things wouldn't change very much after the wedding; she and Orek would be moving into a new house near the Brádaigh family home, but that was it.

Aislinn had had enough other friends wed to know this wasn't true. Those noblewomen she'd counted as friends, although not as dear to her as Sorcha, had made stately visits around the Darrowlands and hosting banquets at Dundúran bearable. Now, all were married, many with child or onto their second or third.

Life had a way of changing, and Aislinn didn't begrudge them for it. Even if she often felt left behind.

Now that it was her dearest friend's turn, she meant to claim as much time as she could before the change—however big or small it truly turned out to be.

Getting out of the castle, away from her duties, was another boon. A pleasant breeze fluttered across the meadows and shallow valleys outside Dundúran, the green grasses swaying like the sea. Their path followed the curving valleys around thick groves of trees and mossy outcroppings. The first leaves had begun to turn, a few pinpricks of red and orange and yellow in an otherwise verdant tapestry of green.

Aislinn breathed it in, glad of the fine day and prospect of seeing her friend—and, honestly, for the company. She didn't dislike the two knights flanking them on either side, mounted on their warhorses and eyes scanning for threats between the beeches and blackberry bushes. She just didn't see the necessity, really.

Or . . . she did, she just wished it wasn't necessary.

It was a reminder that everything was *different* now.

Life had changed for Aislinn as well, but not in the more pleasant ways it had for Sorcha.

Although . . .

Aislinn peered at the halfling beside her.

"How are you holding up, master blacksmith?" She couldn't help teasing him a little, biting back a smile at how like a rabbit he looked, ready to jump and run.

"Do all noblewomen drive such . . . carts?"

"No, I designed this chaise myself. I wanted something small and light to get around. Although, once they saw them, quite a few other ladies desired their own. I believe there's talk of starting a long-distance race next summer."

"Like the Pyrrossi chariot racing," he said, his concerned gaze fixed on the path.

"Less cutthroat, I'd imagine. Think ladies in their finest racing their favorite carriage horses."

"You think noble ladies are less cutthroat than charioteers? Orcesses would race to win."

Aislinn laughed. "You know, you may have a point. I know several who'd race to win, too."

"What did you make this from? How did you conceive it?"

Aislinn glanced at him, trying to gauge his true interest. If she'd learned anything about the new blacksmith, it was that he was unfailingly polite to her. Oh, to be sure, he had a sense of humor and was good-natured and patient, but none of that meant he actually *wanted* to hear about her trial-and-error to make her beloved chaise.

She found him looking back at her, some of the creases of worry easing from beneath his eyes. If she had to guess, she'd say he seemed . . . genuinely interested in her answer.

"Well, I found the carriage cumbersome, honestly. And the suspension on it is horrid when the roads are rutted. I wanted something light, that I could use. When I accompanied my father to Gleanná five years ago, I saw the court racing Pyrrossi chariots and I thought—I want something like that. Father wouldn't hear of it at first, so we compromised on this more cart-like design. Then it was a matter of creating and affixing the axle . . ."

The trip to Granach took little time at all, dominated by her explanation of how she'd eventually come to the final design. She remembered to take moments to breathe and check to see how much his attention had waned—yet, each time, she found him more attentive than before. If anything, the more she talked, the more relaxed he became. His knuckles unclenched from his side of the seat, and he began to move with the chaise rather than holding so stiff.

He asked about the axle and the rigging, the suspension and the brakes. With her long answers, he seemed to finally look around him and began inspecting the chaise with more interest, seeing for himself what she'd done to design it.

Aislinn hardly noticed the journey had passed them by until they were pulling into the packed-earth courtyard of the Brádaigh estate outside of Granach. A pause in their conversation allowed her to finally hear the bustle of the estate; grooms led horses here, there, and everywhere, cadets roamed the practice fields, and staff worked to bring in the early harvest from the orchards and vast gardens.

Renowned for breeding, raising, and training warhorses, the Brádaigh estate was a complex of fine buildings, dominated by a stable that rivaled those at Dundúran. The main buildings were surrounded by paddocks, grazing meadows, and a small training arena. And that was just for the horses. Sir Ciaran Byrne, Sorcha's knightly father, had a small barrack full of squires and cadets, little knights-in-training. And of course, there were cottages for the staff and grooms, a vast apple orchard, gardens full of beds of sunflowers, squash, and more.

The family themselves lived in a typical country manor house, built of local stone and dark-stained wood. The gables had been carved to resemble horse heads, and the heavy front door had been tooled with a prancing horse on the face. Mats of thick ivy clung to the north and eastern walls. It was a handsome house, one Aislinn always adored visiting.

"Thank you for keeping me company," she said to Hakon in the few moments of peace they had left.

"Always, my lady," he replied, his gaze serious.

Aislinn looked away and ignored the *pitter-patter* of her foolish heart.

She grasped the side of the chaise as Hakon disembarked, biting her cheek to keep from giggling as the vehicle swayed with his heaviness. His ears had gone ruddy by the time both feet hit the ground.

When he offered to help her down, Aislinn placed her hand in his much larger one, jumping down.

Wülf, who'd trotted alongside the chaise whenever there wasn't something interesting to sniff, plopped down between them, his tongue lolling out of his mouth. Aislinn scratched behind his ear with her nails, and the beast leaned into it.

"Where are you off to?" she asked, suddenly curious as to why Hakon needed to visit the Brádaigh estate.

"I have business with Orek. Then we're off to congratulate a friend on his new farm."

Aislinn smiled in pleasure. "Yes, Varon. I hope he's settling in well. Please give him my best."

His face cracked with his own smile. "I will, my lady."

Fates, when he smiled down at her like that, her thoughts just melted right away. She could stand there looking back for—

"It's Aislinn!"

The peace was broken by squeals of delight, and then they and the chaise were swarmed by the younger Brádaigh siblings. Their antics incited Wülf, who barked and pranced around the chaise with them.

Giggling, Blaire, the penultimate sibling, patted him on the head and said with a grin, "I think he's big enough to draw the cart himself."

"Yes, but he's not disciplined enough," replied Hakon. "He chases after every squirrel he sees."

Keeley, the youngest, laughed and threw her arms around Wülf, who was taller than her sitting on his haunches.

"He's always been so patient with them."

Sorcha joined them, an affectionate smile making all those freckles on her face dance. Her green eyes sparkled, and Aislinn swore her friend was glowing. *Happiness looks good on her.*

She'd always worried about Sorcha overworking herself—acting as another parent to her many siblings while her father was away with Aislinn's, helping her mother run the family business, and overseeing the running of the estate itself. It was many burdens to bear for one person, and it was why she thought she and Sorcha got on so well. They understood each other.

Aislinn threw her arms around Sorcha, quickly enveloped in the taller woman's voluminous curls and strong arms. Sorcha rocked them back and forth, laughing.

"You didn't tell me you were bringing a blacksmith along."

"Happy happenstance," Aislinn quipped, finally leaning back to smile at Hakon over her shoulder.

"It's good to see you, Hakon," said Sorcha. "Are you going with Orek to Varon's new farm?"

"Yes. It will be good to see everyone."

Sorcha waggled her brows. "Everyone will want to know the gossip from the castle." She cast Aislinn a significant look. "Me included."

The children asked Hakon a few more questions, like how he was enjoying his position at the castle and what Wülf liked to do there, before Sorcha directed him to find Orek at the new house—the one she was strictly forbidden from peeking inside until it was done. She couldn't hide her jealousy as Hakon walked off with Wülf in search of Orek.

Aislinn pinched Sorcha's waist, making her giggle involuntarily.

"You'll get to see inside soon enough," Aislinn reminded her.

"*Not* soon enough," Sorcha insisted. "It's driving me insane. You try having a big, wonderful secret right next door."

Aislinn snorted with laughter as Sorcha led her into the house.

# 9

Hakon indeed found Orek within the nearly finished house he was building for Sorcha. He knocked on the open door and entered when he heard Orek call from deeper in the house to come in.

It was a beautiful home, all polished wood and warm hues. Very human in construction and design, but then again, Sorcha was human and Orek's clan lived in elaborate tents, so.

As he passed through the fine construction, all a testament to the fierce love of a halfling for his mate, Hakon couldn't help a twinge of jealousy. How long until it was his own home he walked through, built for the mate who held his heart in her palm?

All right, it was more than a twinge.

*Does Lady Aislinn truly enjoy living in a castle or would she prefer something cozier?*

The thought had him pausing in the kitchen entryway.

*Fuck.* He'd told himself to stop doing that.

A frustrated sound pulled him further into the kitchen. Orek stood at the freshly waxed countertops, three door handles laid out before him. A concerted frown pulled down his face, and if Hakon had to guess, he'd say his friend had been standing there debating handles and hinges for a while now.

"Which do you think?" Orek asked by way of greeting.

The brusque clip of orcish had Hakon huffing a laugh. He hadn't heard his native tongue since he'd last seen his friend, and the little reminder of home—even if Orek spoke with an odd sort of accent only found in the splinter camps of the Griegen foothills—was welcome.

He'd been fantasizing, living in his head too much lately, and an hour pressed to the subject of his fantasies hadn't helped matters. His pulse still strummed a little quicker from the extended contact, and he doubted his ears would return to a normal color until tomorrow.

Coming alongside his friend, Hakon peered down at the samples he'd made. His gift to Orek and Sorcha for the wedding was all the metal handles, hinges, and knobs they would need for their new home—but first Orek needed to decide which to have Hakon fashion.

"This one." He plucked one of the options from the counter. It was a simpler design but his favorite. "It's big enough for halfling hands and will be smooth on human ones."

Orek nodded gravely. "That's true. Sorcha has soft hands, even if she insists otherwise."

*Lady Aislinn's hands are softer.* She had exactly one callus, on the top of her right ring finger, from how she held her quill. Otherwise, she was all soft, smooth, supple skin, a small, warm weight in his hand.

Riding in that death trap beside her, his arm pressed into the contours of her side, he'd found her body just as soft and supple. She wasn't a small woman for a human, but Hakon was confident he could lift her with one arm, pull her up into his body, off her feet, off into the wilds where he'd hide her away and—

He hardly heard Orek holding the examples up to the cabinets and drawers one last time. Only when his friend finally admitted, "You're right," did he wake from his daydream.

"How many did you need?" Hakon forced himself to ask, to pull away from the woman who'd managed to make a harrowing ride not so stomach-churning with the mere sound of her voice.

They spent a few more minutes counting everything that would be needed and taking final measurements. Hakon assured his friend the metalwork would be finished with plenty of time to spare.

"I'll make a few extra, just to have."

Orek sighed with relief. "One day, you'll know the agony of choosing handles for your mate."

*By the old gods, let that day be soon.*

Hakon agreed, and then they left through the front door, prepared to make the short walk to Varon's new farm.

With a low whistle, Orek summoned his companion, a rotund raccoon he'd named Darrah. The animal chirped and scrambled up Orek's body to drape across his shoulders.

Hakon and Wülf exchanged a look.

He'd forbidden Wülf from chasing Darrah when they'd first arrived at the Brádaigh estate, but it warranted a reminder since they were castle folk now.

Pointing a finger at his mutt, he said, "Not food."

Wülf huffed in annoyance as they made their way into the forest.

The gifts were quickly distributed and then Aislinn, Sorcha, her mother Aoife, and aunt Sofie ensconced themselves around the expansive kitchen table with tea and pastries. Each of the younger siblings went off with their treats and the guards made themselves scarce as the women settled in for wedding talk.

"I didn't know there were so many flowers to choose from—or how many we'd actually need," proclaimed Sorcha.

If their hands weren't busy drinking or eating, the women prepared flowers. Only two hours and Aislinn had already braided dozens of stems and pressed hundreds of petals. The dining room had been commandeered for wedding day storage, full to the brim with baskets and crates.

Aoife fretted over where all the visiting family would sleep—she and Sofie came from an extensive extended clan.

"And of course you and your party," Aoife said to Aislinn. "We'll put your father in our room, but for you I was—"

"Please don't worry over us," Aislinn insisted. "We'll bring father's camp tent. It's quite spacious and can fit our retinue comfortably."

Aoife made a face. "I don't know if I can let the liege and heiress of the land sleep in a tent in the courtyard."

"Father has used it numerous times."

Aoife continued to mutter unhappily until finally Sorcha said, "Let them, mama. It's not like it's a one-bedroll tent. It's bigger than this room and the front solar combined. They'll be fine."

"I promise we will," Aislinn agreed.

If not happy, then at least mollified, Aoife poured Aislinn another hearty cup of tea and slipped more biscuits onto her plate.

They chatted the afternoon away like that, Aislinn soaking in the warm perfection of a visit with friends. The feminine laughter and banter, the soft teasing and praise, all fed something inside her that withered and nearly perished with her mother.

As the afternoon waned, though, Aislinn knew she still needed to tell them the main reason for her coming. She had much more important news than which guild-masters were feuding and which knights were wooing which maids. Yet, she didn't want the day to end, the Brádaigh kitchen so warm and welcoming. And . . . the news brought back a nauseating dread she'd carried ever since she discovered what Jerrod had done.

Still, when she finished the last of her braided stems, she made herself say, "There's something I must tell you."

Their gazes shuttered at her tone, preparing for something, and Aislinn detested being the one to do it.

Folding her hands on the kitchen table, she said to Sorcha's shoulder, "We received word from the Ward not long ago. Jerrod has run away."

A chorus of outraged gasps filled the kitchen.

"Where will he go?" asked Aoife.

"Has anyone had word of him?" asked Sofie.

Aislinn looked to Sorcha, her friend's face cast in a dark frown. She knew the expression wasn't directed at her, but she couldn't help her guilt and shame. Her own blood had done such a horrible thing to Sorcha, to the family who welcomed her as their own. Their families had always been so close, and to betray those bonds so completely . . .

The tea and cake churned in Aislinn's stomach.

"Father said he'll look for him when he and Sir Ciaran head south after the wedding."

The Brádaigh women all grumbled with displeasure. "Yes," said Aoife, "we've been told the new plan."

"Men who feel their business is unsettled can never rest," Sofie said, shaking her head. "They don't understand that their business can never truly be settled, only passed on."

"I was thinking of asking Connor to track him down. I know he's meant to go south with them, but if Niall is already going, I'd like to send at least someone to find out where Jerrod has gone."

Sorcha perked up at the mention of her eldest brother. "Niall knows Jerrod better, but I'd trust Connor more to find him."

Aislinn and Sorcha shared a nod. Niall, the second-eldest brother, and Jerrod had been friends once, before Niall got serious about his knightly training. Although Aislinn trusted Niall as a knight, she didn't know if she could trust that he would serve her over Jerrod.

And besides, when there was a choice, she'd always choose the older, calmer, wiser Connor. He was a kind man, a carpenter and artisan at heart, which was why many were surprised when he followed his father into knighthood. It may not have been his truest calling, but Connor was noble, loyal, and effective.

"All this would be after the wedding, of course," Aislinn hurried to add when she saw Aoife's worried expression.

"You'll have to tell that man of yours," Sofie said to Sorcha. "I doubt he'll take it well."

"No, he'll want to go after Jerrod at first light tomorrow." A sneaky smile spread across her face. "Although, I have my ways of convincing him. I'll tell him tonight."

Her mother and aunt chuckled and rolled their eyes.

Aislinn smiled at the joke, but she couldn't help the jealousy that nipped at her. She'd seen the way Sorcha was with Orek—and more importantly, how Orek treated her friend.

Aislinn had never seen a man more devoted to his woman, and she felt almost voyeuristic witnessing how connected they were. It was almost as if they could read each other's thoughts. The little looks passed between them, the small touches and gentle banter; they had a language all to themselves.

She was a little jealous of her friend's attention being lured away—but more so seeing what a true love story could be.

Aislinn knew it hadn't been easy for them, and there would always be challenges to a union between human and otherly folk. Yet, when she saw them together, Aislinn understood how meaningless those challenges were to them. The sacrifice, the battle was worth it.

Her friend deserved nothing less.

It'd been a long time since Aislinn had seen such love between people, or a couple so well suited to and supportive of each other. Certainly, there were always flirtations and affairs going on within the castle. Every now and then, staff married each other or a knight or someone from the city. Many of her noblewomen friends had married for love, and she'd seen how happy they looked at their own weddings.

None of it quite held the same luster and depth as the love she felt between Sorcha and Orek.

She supposed it could be nothing short of that sort of love that could tempt her, to make her want what she never truly had before.

Aislinn had vowed to never fall pregnant, to never be in a position to have her life stolen away like Róisín's had. That meant, most simply, that she never intended to marry. There were certainly ways of avoiding pregnancy that didn't involve abstaining, like silphium powder, and Aislinn practiced those too, but a nobleman with a high-born wife would want children, heirs. And with a Pyrrossi-dominated court, he would want sons.

Her plan had worked excellently so far. Her father never seemed anxious to marry her off. He and Róisín had married for love and companionship, as did many in the Darrowlands and elsewhere in Eirea. Yet, Aislinn wasn't naïve enough to think the world in which Merrick and Róisín married was the same one she now inhabited. In an Eirea devastated after the wars of succession, expectations were different for nobles, particularly noblewomen.

This change was being resisted by many of the country lords, as her father was. The rights of women had always been equal to those of men, and Eirean inheritance and nomenclature often followed matri-lineal lines. Sorcha herself was a Brádaigh, not a Byrne, and as the oldest daughter of an oldest daughter, would inherit the estate and business.

And yet, Aislinn's choice could never be as simple as love and com-panionship and who suited her best.

She'd known that since she was a girl. So she resolved never to choose.

Seeing Sorcha with such a well-suited match, with a man who looked at her like she was the sun in his sky, though, had Aislinn aching.

It wasn't that Aislinn had never been in love. Far from it. She'd fan-cied herself in love with her math tutor as a youth. He was a dashing prodigy from the capital, only a few years her senior, and she'd been dazzled by his brilliance. Her father had brought him to the Darrow-lands specially for her, as she'd surpassed her other tutors early in her learning.

Brenden's mind worked in such interesting, different ways—having someone who also thought differently, more analytically, had been almost addicting. Brenden had been the first person she let close since her mother's death, and they had fallen in love over theorems and diagrams.

Eventually, though, the dazzle of him began to tarnish. He believed all the things people said of him, that he was meant for greatness. Aislinn hadn't mourned his departure back to the capital.

Then there had been Sir Alaisdair, a noble second son and newly made knight. He'd come to train with Lord Merrick and Sir Ciaran and served under them for several years. Aislinn had allowed an affair to blossom between them, swept away by his good looks and easy confidence. He'd been easy to talk to, and Aislinn was flattered by his attentions.

Still, like Brenden, Alaisdair too had begun to push about marriage. To state what he would do differently if *he* was Liege Darrow.

Aislinn hadn't missed either of them by the time they left Dundúran. Her heart may have grieved for a time, but she'd known she could never truly love someone who loved not her but what she meant for their political future.

She would be no one's steppingstone.

Seeing Sorcha with Orek, their love outshone anything Aislinn had ever known. She understood that what they had was rare, as well as that such a love wasn't necessary to be content.

And yet . . .

"Speak and it shall be so," quipped Sofie. "There they are now."

Aislinn looked up, startled from her thoughts, out the kitchen window to see two huge green figures cutting across the courtyard.

Orek was striking in his leathers, and his height dominated any space he was in.

Hakon was a hair shorter but broader, those shoulders and arms bulging from his jerkin.

*Pitter-patter* went her heart.

"I wonder if they looked at land on their way back," Sorcha said absentmindedly, beginning to gather their cups and plates.

Aislinn's mind snapped around her words with a metallic *clank*. "Land?"

Sorcha nodded, her focus on stacking plates. "Before getting his position at the castle, Hakon had said he was interested in acquiring land as well. I don't know that he wanted to farm, but land all the same."

"It would be nice to have another blacksmith out this way," Aoife said. "Especially if we could catch him for ourselves. The horses always need shoes."

Sorcha threw a smile over her shoulder as she set the used dishes by the sink. "Careful, Aislinn. Sounds like my mother intends to steal away your new blacksmith."

Aislinn forced a grin. "Well then, I'll have to make good use of him while I have him."

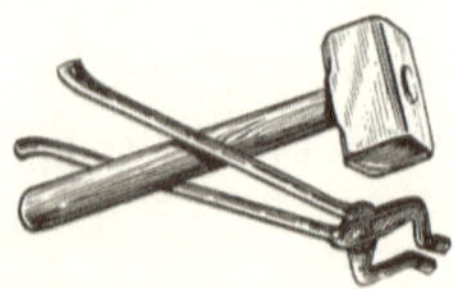

The pack of manticores led them in one last rowdy drinking song, their short whiskers twitching in merriment as beer and mead sloshed over tankard rims.

Over a dozen of them crowded outside Varon's tiny homestead, celebrating the new life about to be lived there. Green skin and golden fur and blue feathers all joined in a cacophony of textures, their toneless voices ringing in good fortune and fat harvests for the new farm.

As they all belted the last word, their loudness shaking the doorframe, the manticores led them in pouring their drinks on Varon's head in a show of celebration and good luck. The male took it well, grinning around his tusks as foam ran along his brows.

After slaps on the back and more well wishes, many headed to the cask to refill their tankards.

Before he could refill his own, Hakon looked down, feeling feathers rustling against his calf.

Maritza, the eldest of the harpy flock who now called the Darrowlands home, squeezed between him and Orek, smiling up at them in that unnerving way of harpies. They lacked beaks like birds, instead having rows of sharp teeth perfect for swooping down and taking a bite out of prey—or partners. Big round eyes, dominated by overlarge irises, dilated and focused on him.

He felt her tail of blue-black feathers swish against his calf again. She and her sisters were all of similar coloring; long inky black manes of hair; gray-blue skin on the face, chest, and legs; violet eyes that were always moving; and blue-black feathers. All harpies had wing-arms—not true arms but instead wings with a clawed, four-fingered hand at the middle joint—and legs with backward-facing knees that ended in birdlike feet with three talons each.

Maritza's sister Andreen scratched a few symbols around Varon's new house with those strangely elegant feet. The other two, Ysera and Nareeda, had already cornered Jör, another half-orc, their tails swishing behind them. When unfurled, their tails fanned around them at least five feet, and Hakon had learned in his time in camp that harpies flirted with their tails.

Looking between them, Martiza smiled, tossing her glossy black hair over her narrow shoulder. Martiza, though, flirted with everything she had.

"We miss you in camp, Hakon," she crooned. "And Orek's become a stranger, finishing that house."

Hakon could feel his ears burning, and Orek looked like he'd swallowed a rock.

Harpies were known to be lusty creatures, with a fierce love for hunting, flying, and fucking. They often mated for life, sometimes a flock of females taking just one male, but that male had to earn his place. In the meantime, harpies enjoyed testing potential partners.

Hakon knew that Orek being a mated male wasn't a qualm for

Maritza—he'd heard her invite Sorcha to join them more than once.

Their little camp on the outskirts of the Brádaigh estate was often a hotbed of intrigue and flirtation. He knew at least one of the manticore pack, probably Balar by the way he was glaring at Nareeda fawning over a flustered Jör, had taken the harpies up on their flirtations.

Hakon himself had been sorely tempted, but if he was honest, Maritza and her sisters terrified him. Something in their hungry gaze . . . he was male enough to admit he might not be enough male for them.

"They keep me busy at the castle," Hakon said, quick to put his empty tankard to his lips for something to do.

"There are many pretty human women there, I suppose." *Swish* went her tail.

"And men. Many knights."

Her brows arched in interest, feathers rustling. "Are there now."

Hakon had the sudden image of Maritza and her sisters descending on the courtyard of Dundúran Castle, catching Captain Aodhan unawares and unprepared. The knights of Dundúran wouldn't stand a chance.

"Perhaps you can visit the castle," said Hakon, happy for the diversion. "I'm sure Lady Aislinn wouldn't mind."

"You've spoken with Lady Aislinn?"

They looked up at the deep rumble, the festivities muting at the sound of Allarion's resonate voice.

The imposing fae warrior stood a few steps away, his face severe and attention trained on Hakon. It was unnerving, to say the least. Little was known about the fae and their kingdom in the western highlands. Tales told of great castles that overlooked the sea, sparkling cities that shone brighter than the sun, all ruled over by the powerful Fae Queen and her court. The fae were ancient; no one knew how long they lived nor how long they had inhabited the western coasts.

What little was known was that fae were deeply attuned and attached to their land. They imbued their own magic with that of the earth, intertwining themselves with the forests and mountains and lakes. Their kingdom was considered impenetrable, for how could any force break the combined magic of all fae.

So to see a lone fae warrior, detached, was startling enough. Although more human in appearance than harpies, they were no less striking. Their sclera were black rather than white, and their grayish-purple skin so pale the black blood in their veins was visible in patterns and whorls just below. Allarion's hair hung in a long sheet of silvery white, kept back from his face by the long points of his ears.

A cloak of purple velvet so dark it was nearly black shrouded him, in stark contrast to his pale skin. Those dark eyes, a rich amethyst color set in a whirl of black and framed in long white lashes, fixed on Hakon, and he made an effort to lock his knees. An ancient being looked at him now, older than the forest around them.

No one knew what drew Allarion here, nor how he'd come to be so far from the high court of his queen. The fae were known to be led by females, who were jealously guarded by the bigger, more aggressive males. There were stories that the females, while significantly smaller, had wings more beautiful and more delicate than stained glass.

An enigma, Allarion was nevertheless a pleasant enough male—so long as you got over your initial fright. He'd been nothing but polite, if aloof. Hakon had been a little surprised to see him at their celebration, but then, Allarion had been one of the first to arrive here seeking a new life in the Darrowlands.

Clearing his throat, Hakon answered, "Yes, I've spoken with Lady Aislinn. I came with her here, she's back at the Brádaigh estate."

Nodding once, Allarion said, "I will accompany you back. I wish to speak with her."

He said it in that mild way of his, without malice or aggression, but it didn't stop Hakon's beast from taking notice. He stood no chance against an ancient fae like Allarion; even so, he looked the male over, assessing the threat.

No harm was allowed to come to Lady Aislinn.

Allarion continued to stand there; his expression hadn't changed, but there was an expectance to the air now.

Maritza fluttered her wings and moved along to flirt with the dragon Theron and his half-sister Briseis instead while Orek and Hakon said their farewells and congratulations to Varon.

By the time they returned to Allarion, perhaps the most striking thing about the fae, as if the way he exuded magic wasn't enough, trotted from the forest to join them.

The hairs on the back of Hakon's neck rose, and he had to put a hand on Wülf's head to stop his growl.

Dark as the shadows he emerged from was Allarion's steed—the unicorn Bellarand.

Perhaps even rarer and more mythical than the fae were their terrifying steeds. Larger than the draft horses humans used to pull great loads, sparks seemed to burst from every great hoof-fall as the unicorn stepped forward. With a mane of midnight black and coat as dark as a starless night, the soft light of the meadow seemed to bend around him.

Fangs rested just behind his muzzle, and black sclera nearly obscured the dark red of his irises. The muscles of his great chest and flanks shivered under the velveteen coat. And his horn . . .

A long, wicked spiral, the horn thrust from the center of his forelock like an obsidian blade, the tip sharper and stronger than any spear or sword.

There were old stories, from when the orcs had first crossed the western seas, of the clans uniting to fight the fae and claim land for themselves. The idea of facing down a charge of unicorns, enchanted fae blades right behind them . . . it made Hakon's stomach curdle.

Nothing could stop, block, or break a unicorn horn.

When the unicorn tossed his head in expectation, all eyes stayed on that horn as it cut through the air.

Orek carefully extended his arm, Darrah all puffed up and holding perfectly still on his shoulders. "Shall we?"

Allarion nodded amenably, as if he and his steed didn't raise the hackles of every being there.

Hakon patted Wülf again, flattening those hackles. "Not food, either," he muttered to the mutt.

The walk back to the estate was quick and quiet. The only time Hakon's pace slowed was to take a look at a little nook of a meadow near the border of the estate. He'd spotted it many times before, but with the uncut gems in his pocket, he observed the lands around the Brádaighs' with fresh eyes.

He only had a moment to linger—something instinctual told him the unicorn didn't want him falling behind, where he couldn't be seen—but it was enough.

The meadow was a beautiful place, blanketed in clover and lined on one side by a tall outcropping. The tree canopy let in enough light for a thicket of blackberry bushes and splashes of blue cornflowers to grow. It was charming, and Hakon could just see his own home there, with a respectable forge on one side and a workshop on the other.

His homestead would be larger than Varon's, something much more akin to Orek's house for Sorcha. Hakon's mate deserved nothing less.

He hurried to catch up with the others, his mind made up and his spirit content. It was a good plot of land; one he'd happily share with a mate.

Work, along with everything else, seemed to stop on the estate as they passed into the courtyard. The many horses being trained or reared nickered at Bellarand in awe, their ears swiveling forward and their long heads bobbing, as if acknowledging a king among beasts.

They'd almost made the house when the front door opened and out walked Lady Aislinn and Sorcha, followed by the knights from Dundúran and the three younger Brádaigh children. All gaped at the fae walking alongside his horned steed.

Even though she smiled in greeting, Sorcha held her arm out to prevent her youngest siblings from drawing any closer to the unicorn.

"Allarion, we haven't seen you here in some time."

The fae's attention settled on Sorcha, and Hakon could feel Orek stiffen beside him.

"I have been searching the western forests for the right place. I believe I have found it." That eerie gaze moved from Sorcha to Lady Aislinn. "I have written several times petitioning for an audience."

A frown erased the shock from Lady Aislinn's face. "I'm sorry, I . . . Varon's farm was the only petition I've seen."

"I have sent you numerous requests."

"No other land grant petitions have passed my desk."

The fae shifted infinitesimally, and though his expression didn't change, the air around him cooled.

"I am not a liar, Lady Aislinn."

Her frown deepened, bewilderment plain on her face. "I never said you were, only that I haven't received your petition."

"Then someone on your staff is keeping things from you."

Lady Aislinn's mouth fell open in affront. The air crackled, and Bellarand's great head bobbed, the point of that wicked horn pointed Lady Aislinn's way.

His beast howled, and Hakon stepped forward, angling himself between the fae and Lady Aislinn.

"I'm sure it's just a misunderstanding," he insisted. "There's no need to accuse Lady Aislinn or her people of wrongdoing."

Allarion's frigid gaze turned on Hakon, but he felt no fear. Perhaps a smarter male would, but he'd stand between far worse than Allarion and Lady Aislinn.

After a fraught moment, the fae finally nodded.

"I apologize. I am short-tempered in my haste. Being untethered as I am, my soul calls to choose a home. I have found a place that would suit Bellarand and I."

Lady Aislinn nodded slowly and extended her right arm. "Shall we talk in private?"

"My lady . . ." one of the knights argued.

"You can't protect me from a fae, even standing right next to me. So what will a few yards truly mean?" She said it so matter-of-factly, and the knight's clear distress mirrored Hakon's own.

His heart lodged in his throat as Allarion stepped forward.

"I would never harm a woman, especially not an innocent," the fae hissed at the knights.

And as if in defiance, he came alongside Lady Aislinn and offered his arm. She blinked at it once before slipping her hand in the crook of his elbow, just her fingertips touching the fine black leather of his coat.

Hakon watched with all the intensity of a predator as Allarion led her a short distance away, his head bent toward her as they spoke softly.

Jealousy writhed under his skin—that the fae would touch her so easily, would presume to claim her attention.

Their words were hushed, and Hakon didn't know if he'd be able to understand even with all his hearing—but he hated that his right ear couldn't pick up the soft tone of her voice. They bent their heads together with their faces pointed away from the others. He hated the small intimacy, of seeing her standing so close to another male, one who was powerful and worldly and clearly of noble blood.

*Everything I'm not and never will be.*

The thought gnawed at him like Wülf on a bone, tearing him to pieces.

"Look away," Orek muttered to him in orcish. "Others are starting to stare at you."

The warning had his beast growling. He couldn't look away, he couldn't risk it. *What if she needs me?*

He heard Orek let out a long sigh.

"Are you sure?"

The question surprised him enough to finally draw his gaze away. "What?"

"Are you sure she's your mate?"

Hakon's blood ran cold.

"She's not my mate," he forced through his lips.

Orek huffed, obviously unmoved. "That's why you're standing here glaring like you want to attack *a fae*. And growling louder than your dog."

Hakon realized only then that his chest shook with the heavy vibrations of a growl. He bit down on the sound, muffling it, but his beast wouldn't totally relent. His throat ached with the strain of keeping it inside.

"I didn't know if I had a beast myself, being halfling," Orek told him. "It was dormant for the most part. Until the night I walked into a supply tent and found Sorcha."

The words cast their spell, trying to lure Hakon's attention away from Lady Aislinn and the fae. He heard the warning, and worse the truth, ringing in Orek's admission.

He knew what danger was about to come.

"It knew I couldn't leave her there. It knew I couldn't let her travel home alone. It knew she was the one I wanted. Didn't matter how I tried to stop it, the beast knew. Sounds like your beast knows, too."

"She's not my mate," Hakon repeated, for himself as much as for Orek. The words grated against his throat.

"Not yet. But know, my friend, that once it's begun, it cannot be stopped."

"I know." That's why he had to forget his foolish infatuation. There were many lovely women in Dundúran—any would be a better choice, a safer choice than the heiress of the Darrowlands, a woman he would never, could never have.

He wanted a good life, a simple life, one filled with family. He didn't want intrigue or complication.

*Yet I want her.*

Except he'd never be accepted as her mate. It may have been fine for Sorcha, the daughter of a knight and yeoman, but the chieftain's daughter? Never.

He was stupid for even entertaining the thought.

"I know what hell it is, for the mate-bond to go unrequited. Whatever you choose, decide now. You must be sure."

Hakon could feel the tendons of his neck pressing against the skin as he clenched his jaw closed, keeping back the roaring frustration.

*Fucking fates, it wasn't supposed to be like this!*

Everything inside him, all his hopes and dreams and aspirations, roiled beneath the onslaught of a beast that was already sure. He felt himself ripping in two, between two desires, two fates, and worried that he stood on a precipice too high and dangerous to leap from.

For what could truly await him if he leapt? Nothing ended with *her* as his mate, safe and comfortable in the homestead he'd built for her.

That dream would never be.

*So she can't be your mate.*

The truth sliced him down past the marrow, into his very spirit. His heart cracked under the strain.

Hakon watched in a daze as Lady Aislinn and Allarion came to some sort of agreement. The fae escorted her back to their party, and with a final bow to Sorcha, he leapt onto the back of Bellarand in one graceful arc of his cloak.

"My lady," he intoned, and then the unicorn turned toward the forest.

No one spoke until the two had long since disappeared between the trees.

Sorcha blew out a breath. "Well, that was something."

"What did he want?" Hakon asked, unable to help the desperate bark of his tone.

He could feel everyone staring at him, but he didn't care. He needed the answer like his next breath, the unknowing crawling over him like biting ants.

"He wants to claim the abandoned estate on the north side of the forest," Lady Aislinn said, her expression unreadable.

"Scarborough?" said Sorcha.

"Yes. He's sending his petition in again for me. The previous ones must have gotten lost—or father didn't remember to send them over. I'll have to look into it."

Her answers were solace enough to herd the beast back behind the cage of his ribs. With effort, his temper cooled, and the rumbling in his chest went quiet.

When he glanced at Orek, his friend only looked on gravely.

Nothing else needed to be said.

"We should return before it gets dark, my lady," said one of the knights.

Lady Aislinn agreed, and so farewells were said and promises of a future visit made. Hakon shook Orek's hand in the human way and accepted a small peck on the cheek from Sorcha. The Brádaigh children all patted Wülf a final time and extracted promises from Lady Aislinn for more gifts on her next visit.

Hakon held out his hand to help her climb into the chaise. She took it without hesitation, slipping her palm along his. A frisson of awareness crackled from his arm down his spine, and he couldn't help a deep breath, taking in her sweet scent.

*Fates, I'm a stupid male.*

He climbed up after her, the children tittering at seeing the chaise sway under his weight. When they were settled, they waved farewell as the knights mounted their horses.

With a gentle *crack* of the reins, Lady Aislinn had them back on the road, on their way home to Dundúran.

The day had long since waned, and it would be dark before they reached the outskirts of the city. Still, Hakon wouldn't take this for granted—a little time with her would soothe him, he knew it.

He opened his mouth to ask her a question, to get her started on one of her topics, when she turned to him first, her eyes glittering with interest, and said, "Tell me everything you know about the fae—and unicorns."

# IO

Even if he could never have her as his mate, Hakon resolved that he could at least be a friend to Lady Aislinn. Surely that would be all right. It sated the beast, who was restless and unhappy until she was near, and gave his more reasonable head time to select someone he could truly build a life with.

His beast may have grumbled at the thought, but Hakon knew living in a fantasy would get him nowhere. The life he planned to build and have was simple, stable. What his grandparents had.

So, he could chat with the heiress, admire her brilliance, and build her new contraptions to please and delight her. If he so happened to save the image of her smiles, the golden hue of her curls lit by the afternoon sun, or the angle of her brows as she puzzled over a problem, well, so be it.

He was sure once his head was turned by someone else, he wouldn't remember those things so vividly. He just had to give himself the opportunity to have his head turned.

Hakon took Lady Aislinn's suggestion of eating with the other staff in the dining hall. Wülf took to it quicker than him, learning that by sitting on his haunches looking stately, more than a few hands were likely to slip him scraps. Hakon forced himself to go, and eventually, he grew accustomed to the pleasant chatter that flowed around him.

He was slowly getting better at reading human lips, and he practiced during the meals, making sure to track who was speaking and listen carefully to what was said.

There were more than a few maids, cooks, and gardeners who eyed him across the table. He did his best to pay them some attention, to learn names and faces and who did what.

He found one cook, Tilly, quite humorous, and she always had the table in stitches with her stories. Brigitt, Claire, and Fia were all beautiful—although Fia was his favorite, mostly because she often spoke of Lady Aislinn. Hakon swallowed every tidbit more greedily than his meal and was always hungry for more.

Yet as the weeks passed, he was no closer to finding someone he might want to ask for a turn about the courtyard or to take into the city for a meal. There were many more people in the city itself he'd yet to meet, but his time was consumed with castle work—and Lady Aislinn's projects.

He'd long since finished her sharp little shears, and afterwards quickly made himself a pair of his own.

"You truly don't have to," Lady Aislinn insisted as they stood together in her mother's rose garden one afternoon. She'd been throwing him concerned looks for at least ten minutes.

"I want to," he assured her. He grinned down at her, hoping to relieve her worry, but then she smiled back, dazzling despite being shaded by her floppy straw hat. Another treasure for his hoard of her, more precious than the gems that sat hidden under the floorboards of his room.

Clearing his throat, he added, "It's good to get out of the forge. See the sun."

"That's certainly true," she laughed. "We can't have you going pale." Then her brows arched nearly to her hairline. "Does orc skin darken in the sun? Can the sun burn you?"

Her eyes caught that glint of curiosity, and suddenly her hand was on his bare skin, her fingertips running down the curve of his upper arm.

Hakon's heart kicked violently in his chest—and his cock with interest in his trou.

Lady Aislinn's hand was painfully soft, her fingertips branding his skin.

With a little gasp, she pulled her hand back.

Her gaze fell away, and she hid her blush behind the brim of her wide hat. "I-I'm so sorry. I merely . . ."

Hakon cleared his throat again, luring her attention. Peeling back the collar of his jerkin, he showed her the line of lighter green skin below his throat.

"We do darken under the sun," he said, bemused but inordinately pleased when she blinked and blinked at his exposed skin, not pulling her gaze away. "Orc hide is too thick to burn. Or too stubborn. Halfling skin . . ." He rocked his open hand in an undecided gesture. "It's a bit more sensitive."

She stared at his throat for another long moment before nodding decidedly, her mouth set in that determined way of hers. "You should have a hat, then."

He laughed at the thought of him wearing something like her floppy hat, but when he next came to help her, he found she was serious, awaiting him with his own wide-brimmed straw hat.

Lady Aislinn held it out to him expectantly, and he knew, mate or not, he'd never disappoint her.

He sat the hat on his head, his ears immediately cooler under the shade.

She made a humming sound of pleasure, reaching up to tighten the strings under his chin.

Those fingertips brushed him again, and his ears were suddenly not so cool anymore.

She seemed pleased with her work, so Hakon was pleased, too. Under the shade of the hat, he could easily watch her more than was strictly necessary as she taught him the proper pruning of garden roses.

He took to the work faster than he did eating in the dining hall, especially when he saw how the thorns cut and scratched at Lady Aislinn's soft hands. Even with gloves, the roses fought them, determined to keep their brambles and wild shapes. He insisted on battling the more difficult plants, where the shears had to get in deep. They had their retribution, scratching his arms and face, but better his than hers.

With his help, the garden slowly but surely began to reveal itself. Lady Aislinn was overjoyed with the progress they made, and Hakon happily listened to her talk of the roses and what colors they would be next spring.

As they worked, they also spoke of Aislinn's ideas for future projects—namely, the bridge she meant to build on the southern side of town.

"I'm determined to start soon," she told him on another sunny afternoon.

Autumn had begun, though it'd been strangely mild so far. Still, a chill rode on the breeze, prompting Lady Aislinn to want to finish preparing the garden for its winter dormancy before the first large storm.

Hakon followed behind her with a barrow full of mulch, listening in amazement as she described her plans for the bridge, from the angle of the arch to the width of the footpath to the composition of the mortar.

"I suppose if I'm to be left in charge of Dundúran, I'll have my way with the bridge at least. I'd like to begin soon so that at least the preliminary work might be finished before the snows, but soon that won't be possible."

It wasn't the first time she'd mentioned the approaching time when she would rule over not just Dundúran but the whole of the Darrowlands. Hakon had had to piece together the story from Orek's account of Jerrod Darrow, castle gossip, and what Lady Aislinn said.

That Liege Darrow intended to leave soon, and not to look for his wayward son, sat unwell with Hakon. Resentment on behalf of Lady Aislinn grew faster and more numerous than the weeds that wanted to claim the rose garden, and he often didn't know what to do with the feelings, other than throw himself into helping her any way he could.

So when she turned to him near the end of their work that day and asked, "Would you . . . accompany me to speak with the guild-masters when it's time? I'd appreciate your opinion," there was no other answer for him to give than, "Of course, my lady."

And not just because it meant more time at her side. He genuinely wished to help. If the brilliant heiress wanted to build a bridge, then Hakon would make it so.

*There will be time later to get to know more of the women and find a mate.*

Yes, he was sure when winter settled on the land and everyone kept indoors, he'd have the time. For now, he could offer his to Lady Aislinn.

For a few weeks, as the autumn air began to carry a crispness that heralded harvesttime, Aislinn found uninterrupted refuge in the castle smithy and her mother's garden. For a blissful fortnight, Aislinn's little hideaways went undiscovered, her afternoons her own for the first time in what felt like a long while.

She was grateful to Hakon for letting her monopolize so much of his time. Fearghas was certainly already tired of her in the smithy, grumping about not liking being watched as he worked, but she and Hakon just threw each other furtive grins as he got on with his work.

Whatever she brought to Hakon, no matter how outlandish, he agreed to at least try to bring her vision to life. He was spoiling her with his agreeableness, and it was quickly becoming addicting. She was actually running out of the bits she'd wanted to have made as prototypes or experiments and was spending the late hours of her evenings sketching any idea that came to her—if only for the excuse to steal to the smithy again.

She had a little treasure trove of items he'd made her, from scissors to quill nibs to coal tongs to new hinges for her study door, so they'd never give her away when she slipped out. Her favorite, though, was still the little wooden rose.

Aislinn kept it in her pocket always, a little token that made her smile. She'd taken to running her thumb over the smooth petal faces while Brenna read her daily list of tasks, the silky glide a soothing, repetitive motion to focus on rather than her anxiousness.

When the duties seemed to pile around her and her emotions bubbled over the brim inside, she breathed easier knowing she could escape to her little refuge to see her friend. Sometimes she brought work or reading with her, but most often, she was content to settle in for a chat. At first, she'd simply enjoyed the dark peace of the smithy, but as the weeks passed, Aislinn had begun to realize . . . it was Hakon she went to see.

She enjoyed his easy smile and how he never seemed to bore of her. Aislinn knew how others reacted to her monologues—she easily overexcited herself and got carried away. Yet, she never felt rushed by him or that he'd rather she be quiet. If anything, he prompted many of her long ramblings, encouraging her to talk through an idea or explain a decision at length.

His help in reclaiming the rose garden was invaluable—she'd thought to do it herself, but when the idea struck to ask for his help, she hadn't hesitated. It'd just sort of spilled out, and she never would've held him to it. But every time she asked, he arrived, earnest and eager under that wide-brimmed hat she'd found for him.

She could easily spend a whole afternoon sitting in what was now her chair in the smithy, watching him work. The methodical processes of heating and shaping the metal appealed to her, and he was patient in explaining each step. Aislinn loved learning how things were made and worked, and Hakon offered up his knowledge on a platter for her hungry mind.

And, if she was honest, that wasn't the only hungry part of her.

There was something almost poetic about him at work. The way he wielded the hammer and tongs . . . the concentration on his face as he worked the metal . . . how his hands flexed and his muscles bunched as he hammered the iron . . .

It wasn't just the heat of the forge that flushed her cheeks.

Multiple times a day, she ran her fingers over the wooden rose as she thought of that moment he peeled back his collar to reveal the line of lighter green skin at his throat.

Aislinn had never truly considered what she found most attractive in men. Her two paramours had been vastly different in size and shape—Brenden had a willowy elegance, his limbs long and finely formed; Alaisdair had been all hard edges and brutal strength. Hakon was both and neither, everything and more.

That day, she watched his shoulders bunch and release as he buried an iron bar beneath the glowing coals. Aislinn crossed her legs, the apex tingling with desire. Fates, but he was a fine man. Big and brutal, yes, but there was something so elegant and refined about his face. And the way those warm brown eyes looked up at her through his long, sooty lashes as he bent to stoke the forge fire . . .

Sucking in a breath, Aislinn raised her hand and made the gesture for *done?*

Hakon nodded, replying with *for now.*

Aislinn quite enjoyed the hand-talk he used. In their afternoons together, he'd taught her basic words, and she was always excited for more. She liked how straightforward it was—the gesture meant one thing. To be sure, he could make whole sentences with his hands and form complex thoughts and questions, but it wasn't up to interpretation the same way spoken words were. Her mind enjoyed the directness of it.

She also liked feeling included, as if they had their own secret language.

Pulling the beeswax from her ears, Aislinn took a moment to readjust to all the sounds. The forge fire crackled, and she could hear the whirr of the pottery wheels nearby.

As Hakon removed the beeswax, he made the gesture for *water?*

Aislinn shook her head and tried very hard to pretend not to watch as he picked his waterskin up from the worktable and took a long draught.

That wide throat of his worked and bobbed with every swallow, a single drop escaping to glisten on the curve of his chin. Her mouth ran dry, lips tingling with the desire to catch that droplet on her tongue.

Fates, she'd never found a man's throat so fascinating before.

It took her a moment to realize it now moved as he spoke.

"Come again?" she breathed, blinking quickly to refocus on him.

"I said I heard another for you to explain to me."

Aislinn smiled, leaning forward in her seat. It was another of the things she greatly enjoyed about her time with him—their little game of language.

She thought he'd fairly mastered the Eirean language, but he remained unsure, almost shy over his skill. Sayings and idioms were particularly baffling, and he'd taken to bringing her ones he found mystifying.

"Let's hear it."

"Putting the cart before the horse." He planted a big hand on the worktable, leaning his weight on it as he drank again from his waterskin. "Why would anyone think to put the cart before the horse?"

Aislinn snorted with laughter. "They wouldn't! It's supposed to be nonsensical."

"Then why must humans remind others not to do it?"

"It means not to get ahead of yourself. To do things in the proper order."

"But then . . ."

They debated the merits of the saying for another ten minutes, Hakon's arguments growing more outlandish—she suspected just to make her laugh.

Her soul was lighter for the laughter, her heart a bit fuller at having a companion. She hadn't realized how sorely she missed having a friend, someone to talk to. Fia was often her closest confidante, but Fia had a position to fulfill and her own life; her family ran a bakery in town, and she often visited to help them when Aislinn didn't need her for the day.

To have someone's attention, to gorge herself on companionship, wasn't something Aislinn took for granted.

Especially once her refuge was finally found out.

Feeling the afternoon waning, Aislinn pulled herself up out of her seat. She was beginning to say her goodbyes when a little yelp fluttered in from the bailey outside.

Fia grasped the sill and leaned inside the open window, exclaiming, "*There* you are!"

Blushing, Aislinn straightened her skirts. "Here I am."

Fia blew out an exasperated breath. "Brenna has everyone looking for you."

"Let's not tell Brenna where you found me," Aislinn said with a wince.

But the maid just waved her hands, dismissing Aislinn's worries. "Never mind that. You're needed in the great hall. Baron Bayard is here."

The name of their nearest neighbor had Aislinn's heart sinking—and just like that, the glow of the day faded.

It seemed she could hide all she wanted—her duties would find her no matter what.

# II

Aislinn bobbed her head in acknowledgement of Baron Bayard's fine courtly bow upon her entrance to the great hall.

"Ah, Aislinn, there you are," said her father in relief. Neither of them overly enjoyed entertaining Padraic Bayard when their neighbor decided to grace Dundúran.

Bayard strode forward to meet her, holding out his hand. Aislinn bit her cheek, offering as little of her hand as she could. She'd never cared for this custom, especially when it meant being touched and kissed by strangers—or worse, Padraic Bayard. Using the fingertips she offered, he pulled her closer and bowed his head to kiss the back of her hand.

"Lady Aislinn, you are a beautiful sight this day and every day," he pronounced.

"And your compliments are numerous, as always, Baron Bayard."

He smiled warmly, making her stomach clench. That was the problem with Bayard—she could never quite tell how much of him was true and what was prevarication or tact.

Similar in age to herself, Bayard had inherited the estate of Endelín and its vast vineyards at a young age. He had a boyish charm to him—although, this was perhaps fading as the both of them neared thirty.

Still, he was a handsome man, with chestnut curls and sparkling blue eyes that he used to great effect.

He and Jerrod had been friends—of a sort. Mostly, they enjoyed outdoing the other. They lived to see who could goad the other into the more preposterous prank or throwing the most lavish banquet. If Bayard purchased a new gelding, then Jerrod had to have one, too—if Jerrod seduced a beautiful widow, then Bayard had to woo an even more beautiful heiress.

Unfortunately for Aislinn, she was the latest in his string of attempted courtships. She'd made her feelings about him, about marriage itself, clear multiple times, and yet he wouldn't be dissuaded or discouraged.

She'd hoped, with Jerrod's fall, perhaps Bayard would relent. Part of her suspected his interest was motivated by a desire to somehow get the better of Jerrod by bedding his sister. That she could believe it of him, and her brother, filled her with disgust for both.

Now that she was heiress, Bayard had only grown more ardent.

Like Brenden, and Alisdair too, Padraic Bayard was an ambitious man. The hand of Lady Aislinn Darrow carried weight, offered prestige, and promised position.

Not that it changed her opinion of him, but Aislinn couldn't say for certain that Bayard's professions were all conceit. Sometimes he seemed . . . genuine. In those times, she thought perhaps there was a person beneath the smart clothes and suave manners she might come to like—or if not like then tolerate.

The charm was on full display today, though, as he threw smiles her way and at her father.

"Has something happened, to bring you back so soon after the council meeting?" Aislinn asked. She doubted it, but it warranted asking since Bayard would be the type to bring up the plight of his commonfolk last.

"The harvests have begun, and I opened the cellars just yesterday." He waved forward his manservant, bearing a green glass bottle of wine, the cork sealed with black wax. "This was a particularly good year, and I thought we might celebrate."

Aislinn exchanged looks with her father.

Merrick extended his hand, and the manservant dutifully presented the wine. Her father made the necessary sounds of pleasure, holding it up to the light to see how none passed through the deep red.

"Nine years?"

"Ten," Bayard said, pride oozing from him. "I thought it would be a fine addition to your table and wanted to present it myself."

"Then you must join us for dinner," said Merrick, handing back the bottle and giving Bayard exactly what he'd come for.

Aislinn held in her sigh. "I will have Brenna arrange accommodations. Your usual room will do, I trust?" Although he was their nearest neighbor, Bayard never came for a short visit.

"If you would be so kind," he said. "That room has the loveliest view."

Bobbing her head again, Aislinn made her retreat, despite her father's obvious *don't you dare leave me with him* expression. Brenna already knew Bayard was here, as she'd sent Fia to look for her, and therefore also likely had his accommodations well underway.

Still, Aislinn took the excuse, escaping for the time being.

When she rejoined her father for dinner in the dining hall that evening, she was prepared for recompense. Perhaps Merrick crying off early or inviting someone else to round out their numbers at the high table.

Instead, she found her father alone. A third place had been set for Bayard, but the baron had yet to arrive. A bottle of wine sat unopened on the table.

Slipping into her seat, Aislinn was relieved at least that their meal hadn't been moved into the smaller, more intimate dining room that adjoined her father's study. She preferred, as her father did, to take meals in the dining hall, surrounded by their people.

When she dared look up at him, she found her father's gaze far-away and contemplative. The laugh lines around his eyes and mouth sat downturned, again reminding her of his age.

He didn't seem morose, which was something.

Aislinn gave him time as she poured herself a goblet of her preferred mead.

She was just bringing it to her mouth when her father asked, "Are you still determined not to marry, kit?"

Just stopping the mead from sliding into her lungs, Aislinn coughed into her napkin and replaced her goblet. She gaped at her father.

"Why do you ask?"

Sighing heavily, Merrick leaned forward, folding his hands on the table.

"Things are . . . different now. You are heiress. You'll be expected to marry."

"You didn't."

Merrick looked up at her chilly words, only to frown in affront. "No, no, kit, I wouldn't do that. You know what I think of him—and I know what you think of him. I only meant that as heiress, you'll be expected to take a spouse."

"Must I?" she whispered.

His face went almost haggard when he looked at her to answer. "Yes. The king is looking for ways to consolidate his power in the country. That's why he's sending an architect for a mere country bridge project. When he hears the heiress isn't married, not even betrothed . . ."

Silence and Aislinn's dread filled the void left by his implication.

She'd never considered . . . hadn't even thought . . .

She'd met King Marius exactly once, had exchanged the required pleasantries for a total of twenty-three words spoken between them. She found him to be a regal man, handsome in the way some older men were, with gray around his temples. He hadn't paid her much mind, more interested in Jerrod at the time.

That this man she'd met once would presume to dictate a marriage—*her* marriage . . .

Her vision narrowed, her breathing growing labored.

The possibility that she'd be traded like meat, forced into a union with one of the king's cousins, hand over her people, her home, her body to a stranger—

A warm hand enveloped hers and squeezed.

"Breathe, kit. Damnit, I'm sorry, I didn't mean to worry you."

Aislinn clutched her father's hand and breathed through it. After a few moments and deep breaths, her stomach stopped revolting.

When she could finally look up at her father, his expression was contrite. Acidic shame burned the back of her throat to think he might see her as unable to handle the difficult realities of their situations. She valued that he spoke so freely with her, that he trusted her enough to tell her the truth.

With another squeeze of her hand, Merrick said quietly, "As heiress, it'd be wise for you to marry, yes. Before the king pushes a choice on you. That's why I bring it up now—to give you time. I'm sure you can find someone you like. Someone who will be a good husband, a good partner."

Aislinn nodded shakily, giving her father the reassurance he needed that she was all right.

Except she wasn't.

She hardly heard the dining hall around her, hardly noticed when Bayard finally joined them, richly adorned in a velvet doublet. She dutifully sipped the wine he'd brought, hardly tasting it.

She managed to keep minimal conversation, just enough not to seem rude, but her mind was far afield.

*A husband. A partner.*

Her soul didn't cry out against the idea as it might have when she was younger, but her reluctance was still firm.

*Where to even begin?*

Her gaze, affixed to the table during the meal and chatter, rose to look out upon the dining hall. Without issue, she found the big green form of the new blacksmith, sitting with his peers, Wülf lounging at his side.

*Pitter-patter* went her heart inside the fist of despair clutching it tight.

*Just because Sorcha got a storybook love affair with a halfling doesn't mean you'll get one too,* she told herself.

And yet . . .

And yet.

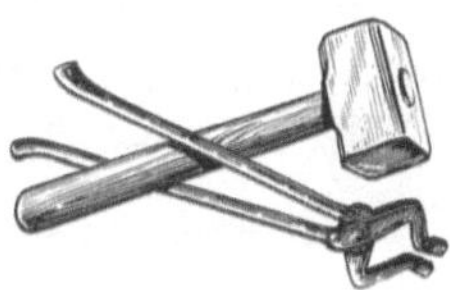

Hakon and the rest of the staff looked up from their meals when the visiting lord entered the hall, dripping in finery and smiling beatifically ear to ear. Baron Bayard was exactly what Hakon imagined of a nobleman—refined, clad in his riches, and easy with his smiles and compliments.

Hakon hated him on sight.

"Do I enjoy having to make up that monstrosity of a bed in the room he prefers? No," said Claire, one of the chambermaids, as she refilled her goblet with more of the expensive wine Bayard had brought. "But at least this time he came bearing gifts."

"And even better that milord and milady don't care for wine," added Owen, a potter sitting on Hakon's left. He held out his cup for Clarie to fill.

"He comes often?" Hakon asked.

His beast snarled and snapped at the sight of the nobleman sitting at the high table, but Hakon thought he kept his tone even, not letting on to the searing curiosity that'd consumed him since Fia came to fetch Lady Aislinn.

Fia herself snickered into her napkin. "Too often." She rolled her pretty brown eyes, smiling wide at him. Fia had a pretty mouth, with lush lips that spread wide. Hakon liked her mouth—it was easy to read.

"He's been after the lady for years now," said Brigitt, another maid. She leaned forward conspiratorially, her bright eyes dancing with mirth. "She's denied him already, but he can't seem to give up the game."

"Can't truly blame him," said Liam, another potter on the other side of Owen. "Prize has only gotten bigger."

The three maids booed and hissed at his remark.

"Milady isn't a prize broodmare," grumbled Claire.

"She can do far better than him," agreed Fia. "*Especially* now."

Brigitt nodded imperiously. "She can have *any* man she wants." And as she raised her cup to her lips, she winked at Hakon over the rim.

His ears heated, and his instinct was to drop his gaze—but he couldn't afford to, not when the conversation darted faster than hummingbirds between flowers.

The maids and the potters began to debate better marital options, Fia arguing that none but a prince of the realm would do for Lady Aislinn. Hakon listened on, his chest tightening with every name they suggested and a growl building. Finally, it slipped past his lips.

He patted Wülf's head, pretending it was him who made the sound when those nearest him looked up.

Hakon swallowed his growls and grumbles, shoving them deep down where he was trying to contain his ever-growing interest in the Darrow heiress.

*She isn't for you,* he reminded himself. Not for the first time that day.

Still, he couldn't help it when the conversation lulled and, without a mouth to watch, his gaze strayed to the high table.

Hakon's heart kicked against his ribs when he found Lady Aislinn looking out across the hall—at him. She was as far away as she could be within the hall, all the way at the high table with her father and Baron Bayard, and yet, Hakon clearly saw the unhappy strain in her gaze.

She blinked, a blush overcoming her cheeks when she realized he looked back at her. Her gaze shifted away, back to the baron, who leaned nearly halfway across the table toward her, obviously trying to snare her attention.

The beast's roar inside him was so loud, Hakon couldn't hear anything else.

His eyes fixed on the baron, jealous rage incinerating his good sense. He could feel the growl rumbling in his chest, a bestial language older than words that meant but one thing—

*Mate. Mine.*

"Hakon?" A hand covered his.

His attention snapped like ice on a lake, disturbing his quiet, frigid focus.

He stared at the small female hand on his fist, willing away his no doubt murderous glare at the baron. By the time he looked upon Brigitt, he hoped at least he didn't resemble the beast he felt raging just beneath the surface.

The maids and potters were all looking at him expectantly—Fia stared, something too close to understanding glinting in her eyes, but it was Brigitt who'd touched him and said his name. She smiled at him, though the expression had gone tight.

"Forgive me," he hurried to say. "What did you ask?"

Brigitt smiled wider, leaning forward until her breasts pressed together atop the table.

"I just asked if orcish courtship is anything like that."

Ears burning, Hakon cleared his throat to buy time. Her hand was still on his, her smile and breasts right there.

*A female's flirting with me.* He'd grown a little more used to it over his weeks in the castle, although most of the women, and a few men, had soon looked elsewhere when he fell into work, leaving little time to flirt back or show anyone else any attention.

Her fingertips ran in circles over his hand, and her eyes had gone sultry. What he'd at first found thrilling, Hakon now didn't know what to do with.

Words didn't immediately come to him, and it was an awkwardly long time before he finally forced himself into an explanation of orcish customs. He told himself to look only at Brigitt, to turn his hand over so her palm would fall into his.

*Explore this. Let your head be turned.*

He told them of how an interested orc in Kaldebrak would often start with gifts, showing off their skill to catch the eye of their desired partner. Orcish courtship emphasized performative acts of interest; declarations were all well and good, but orcesses in particular were won over with consistent action to prove a potential mate's devotion, commitment, and passion.

These acts were meant to foster a mate-bond, to help the potential partners decide if they would carry through with the final act of intertwining their lives, their hearts, their very souls. He left this part out, though—the mate-bond was a closely kept secret amongst orcs. It was their greatest strength, yet also their greatest vulnerability. Mated orcs were highly prized as warriors, for the need to protect a mate could quickly trigger a berserker rage, the likes of which were immortalized in the sagas.

He also didn't tell them the old way of orcish courtship—when males would take their desired partner over their shoulder and disappear into the wilderness, sequestering away until a strong mate-bond formed. Partners were supposed to be willing, but the tradition fell out of favor when a few too many weren't. In Kaldebrak, such a thing would be considered barbaric now, and Hakon figured the humans would see it that way, too.

What he did say seemed to please Brigitt, as her smile only grew. "And what sorts of gifts would *you* give someone?" she asked.

*Tooled silver quills. A gold torque the very same hue as her hair.*

*A whittled rose.*

Fia coughed into her napkin.

*Fuck.*

His gaze skittered to Fia, and they exchanged a look full of under-standing.

*Fuck!*

He hardly heard when Brigitt finally straightened, a satisfied smile on her lips despite Hakon having no answer for her.

"It sounds awfully romantic," she breathed.

"So if I show up tonight with a pot fresh out the kiln, you'll be my forever-love?" said Owen.

"We all know your pots are for Tilly," Brigitt sniped back, throwing Hakon a wink.

He managed a wan smile before retreating back into silence.

The conversation resumed around him, and he was relieved to fall back into watching mouths and listening as he pretended to eat.

Hakon didn't taste the food. He couldn't meet Fia's searching gaze. He focused solely on not seeking out Lady Aislinn across the hall.

He couldn't look upon her now. Not when another glimpse would surely have him marching across the hall, throwing her over his shoul-der, and making off with her.

*By the old gods, what a fucking mess.*

# 12

Aislinn heard Brenna bustling into her room but didn't accept that it was time to rise until the heavy drapes around her four-post bed were tossed back. Light spilled across the dark cavern of her bed, and Aislinn grumbled, squeezing her eyes shut.

"No wriggling, please, you'll send your breakfast flying."

She carefully sat up against the headboard as Brenna laid the breakfast tray on her lap.

Aislinn had asked Brenna to do this the night before, needing an early start to the day, but that went unappreciated in the bright light of morning. As she nibbled a bite of toast, cut into four perfect pieces, Brenna pulled her infamous list from her pocket.

The chatelain patted Aislinn's knee at the face she pulled. "I know, dear. But such is the life of an heiress."

Aislinn muffled most of her grumbling behind her toast.

Brenna was unimpressed, but her eyes crinkled in that way they did sometimes, on those rare occasions she showed affection. As Aislinn dutifully ate and listened, Brenna listed off the day's tasks and various things she herself needed the heiress's opinion or direction on.

"There's the matter of the wine Baron Bayard sent—would you like the kitchen stocked with it?"

Fates, the wine. Bayard had come with so many bottles, most of the staff had sore heads and irritable attitudes for days. And once he'd finally returned home after two agonizing days of *visiting*, he sent even more.

*My finest vintages for the finest heiress in the kingdom,* his note read.

"Let Hugh have what he wants for the kitchens and add the rest to the wine cellar."

"Very good," said Brenna, leaving a note for herself with the portable quill Aislinn had designed for her. Such things were commonplace in bigger cities like Gleanná or Kilgaran, but Aislinn had made her own prototypes.

"He'll expect a response," Brenna commented, flicking her a look over her list.

"Add it to my correspondence list," Aislinn sighed. Fates, there was never an end to those who needed a note or letter from her. Simple thanks or congratulations were most common, but then there were legal inquiries, suits, and requests from throughout the Darrowlands, her own personal correspondence with friends and extended family, as well as purchases, writs, and grants for Dundúran itself.

The Darrowlands thrived, which she was grateful for, but it meant a veritable mountain of paperwork. When she was young, her parents had often kept ministers to help run the demesne. After her mother's death, though, as the ministers left, retired, or passed away, her father didn't replace them. Instead, he decided to take on the duties himself; as a way to distract himself, Aislinn suspected.

It was admirable for a liege lord to take such an interest in and command of their demesne, and her father had instituted several popular reforms. However, those duties easily began to build up when Merrick was distracted by other things—such as his campaigns in the south. More of these duties now fell to Aislinn as her father prepared for his next excursion with Sir Ciaran. She enjoyed some of it, tolerated most of it, and loathed a handful of things. Her favorite was still helping the otherly folk who—

"Oh!" Aislinn sat up straighter, apple slice halfway to her mouth. "Do we have any petitions from the otherly camp for land grants? Specifically from an Allarion?"

"Not that I've seen," said Brenna. Her tone was the same, but curious red splotches appeared high on her cheeks.

"Strange. He spoke with me when I went to see Sorcha. He said he'd already sent two petitions and I said to send another."

"Perhaps he changed his mind."

"Hm. Can you leave me a note to write Sorcha? I'll have her make inquiries in the camp."

"Of course."

Brenna resumed her recitation of the list, though Aislinn couldn't help noticing her demeanor had chilled. Aislinn's breakfast sat uneasily in her stomach, thinking she'd perhaps displeased Brenna somehow. Although she always seemed to be doing it, she never liked disappointing the chatelain. Brenna was a last tangible link to her mother.

Her manner may have been stern, but Brenna cared deeply for Aislinn and the Darrow family. She was always quick to defend Jerrod, always sure to see that Aislinn's needs were met. Liege and Lady Darrow had kept many staff on for a long time not just because they were good people who did good work, but because change was difficult for Aislinn. Brenna too now ensured that life ran as smoothly as possible.

Although Aislinn complained, she'd be absolutely lost without the steadfast chatelain. Brenna was her breakwater, keeping back the deluge.

When she'd finished with the list, Brenna replaced it in her deep pocket and took the empty tray. Before leaving, she arched one of her severe brows, telling Aislinn, "And no sneaking away to the smithy today. There's too much to do."

Aislinn's cheeks heated under that admonishing stare. She felt twelve years old again, being scolded for doing something naughty.

Aislinn nodded, which seemed to satisfy Brenna. "Good," said the chatelain. "I'll send Fia in to help you dress."

Heart suddenly heavy, Aislinn crawled out of her large bed, even as she wanted to roll back into the soft, comforting darkness. The day stretched out before her, long and arduous, without the promise of her refuge to look forward to.

Part of her mourned that her hideaway was no longer secret.

A larger part already missed getting to see her blacksmith.

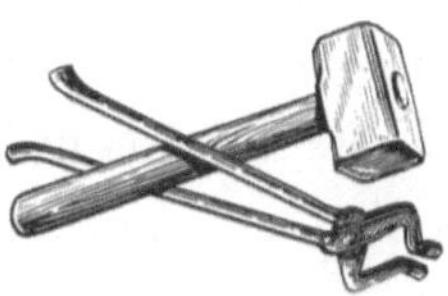

"This doesn't go here."

Hakon scraped his tusks against his upper teeth, checking the temper heating faster than the forge in his blood.

"It does now," he told the head blacksmith with as much patience as he had left. Which was admittedly not much.

"And who said you could move things about?" Fearghas glared from over the spare anvil Hakon had had the audacity to move.

In the midst of their squabble, Hakon almost regretted resituating the smithy. Making stations for different tasks made the most sense with it only being the two of them, and he'd made faster progress through his work in the two days it took Fearghas to notice the change.

He couldn't completely regret it. He needed something to *do*.

She hadn't come. Today, yesterday, or the day before.

Lady Aislinn hadn't gone three days without coming to see him since she brought him their first project. But now, he'd only caught glimpses of her in the dining hall or walking through the courtyard.

The beast inside wanted to hunt her down and never leave her side again. How could he protect her if she wasn't with him? How would he know how she fared and what she thought if she didn't come to him?

*Why wait,* his beast demanded. *Go to her!*

He couldn't do that, though. He had enough sense, common and self-preserving, that if he were to go to her, that would be the end.

She'd send him away—or her father would. Then he'd truly not see her, and neither he nor his beast could live with that.

So Hakon grew restless and agitated, trying to deny reason and reality. The smithy was rearranged in one afternoon as a result. Now his temper was flaring far too easily.

Fearghas stomped around the smithy, scoffing and grumbling over the different stations and where the tools had ended up.

"It makes sense, with only the two of us," argued Hakon, not for the first time.

"It's nonsense is what it is. This smithy has run just fine for years without you meddling!"

"It's not meddling, it's a better use of space."

Fearghas's beard twitched dangerously, and the red of his face deepened. "Put it all back."

"You haven't even tried—"

"Put. It. Back." And he took a hammer and slammed it on the anvil, the ring piercing.

"No."

Fearghas's glare darkened. "That's an order."

"If you hate it so much, you put it back. It works for me and the—"

"No, you work for *me,* halfling," Fearghas spat, pointing an accusatory finger. "You may have your fancy ways and orcish techniques, but this is *my* smithy, you understand? The heiress will tire of you— looks like she already has—and then where will you be?"

Hakon growled a warning, the harsh words hitting too close to his heart.

Eyes glittering with malice, recognizing he'd scored a point, Fearghas struck his hammer on the spare anvil again. "That one always tires of her projects. You aren't special, halfling. Now put everything back and get back to real work."

Hakon bared his tusks, frustration as much of a snarling beast in his chest as his actual beastly instinct. A snorting huff exploded from his nostrils, then he was pulling Wülf behind him as he strode from the smithy before he did something regrettable.

The courtyard was much cooler than the smithy, the difference punching through him. His bare arms prickled, but Hakon hardly felt it.

Stalking further away from the blasted smithy, Hakon took long, deep breaths, needing the burn of cool air in his lungs.

*Stubborn, hateful old bastard.*

Tugging a hand through his sweaty hair, Hakon slowed his pace.

The old blacksmith was set in his ways, and Hakon liked to think he wouldn't normally be so aggravated to have his ideas so thoroughly dismissed. He and Fearghas would never be friends, but he could acknowledge the human was skilled—when he actually put his mind to something.

None of that mattered with an unhappy, impatient beast snarling just below his heart, goading him to steal into the heiress's room to profess his undying devotion and then ravish her senseless.

*Gods, don't think of her naked!*

He did enough of that while in the baths late at night, alone with his daydreams. There were nights he rubbed himself raw with how long and viciously he tugged his cock to thoughts of the pretty heiress.

Three days without her and he was reduced to a slavering, irritable beast.

*Fuck.*

He scrubbed a hand over his face.

What was he to do now?

*Go to her. Claim her. Mate her.*

*I can't—*

"Hakon!"

He looked up at the sound of his name, hope lancing his heart.

A woman hurried toward him from the direction of the kitchens, and Hakon tried not to show his disappointment in it being Brigitt.

He attempted to match her bright smile as she came to stand before him, but he feared it was tepid at best.

"Good day," he managed.

"I've been looking for you," she said, her voice breathy.

She presented him with what, given the shape, was likely a large jar, wrapped neatly in cloth and tied with a tidy bow on top.

Hakon took it, mind racing. Had he asked her to bring him something and forgotten?

"It's blackberry jam," she said with that unrelenting smile. "I picked them myself, on my family's farm. Only the sweetest."

Hakon's throat ran dry, unsure what to say. He couldn't refuse the gift, nor tell her he, as well as most orcs, didn't have a taste for sweet things.

"Thank you," he said. "You didn't have to trouble yourself."

Impossibly, her smile widened, and she closed the distance between them.

"I wanted to give you a gift," she said, fluttering her lashes and rounding her big blue eyes.

His stomach dropped.

*Fates, she's—*

Brigitt took hold of his leather apron and pulled him down. Warm lips pressed to his, and her lashes swept against his cheek as she closed her eyes. Hakon stared at her brows in shock, unsure what to do, his back rigid as he held perfectly still.

Her lips moved, tempting his. He'd seen humans kissing, knew it to be a dance of lips and tongues. He himself had taken to imagining Lady Aislinn's plush lips. He stared at them enough to know every contour, every shade of pink, and dreamed of what they would feel like on his skin.

But this wasn't her. This wasn't what he'd dreamed.

It was wrong.

Brigitt leaned back, and Hakon retreated to his full height. She was smiling again, but it was small, unsure. A nauseating mix of embarrassment and pity swirled inside him, rendering him speechless. What did he say?

"Do orcs not kiss?" she asked, trying to laugh.

"No, not usually." He swallowed. "Brigitt, I don't . . ."

Her hands fell away from him almost as fast as her smile fell from her face, and she took a step back.

"Oh," she said.

Hakon hated how quickly tears filled her eyes. He'd done that. *This is all wrong.*

He'd come to Dundúran to find a mate. He had a beautiful, pleasant woman giving him gifts in the orcish way and kissing him. He should be grateful. He should be pleased.

But . . .

"I'm sorry."

Brigitt shook her head, hiding her tears behind a frown.

"But you . . . you made me think you felt the same!"

Cold washed over him. "I didn't mean to." What had he done? His shocked mind tried to recall, to think what might've been misunderstood, but he was too horrified to remember much.

"Then what's all this staring at my lips? A human does that when he wants to kiss!"

Shame turned his stomach. He always felt the vulnerability of his right ear—but that such a simple thing as reading lips could be misconstrued . . . to know it'd ended up hurting someone . . .

He *hated* that.

"Brigitt, I'm sorry. I . . . I'm still learning your language. Your customs. I didn't know." It was a sorry excuse, but it was all he had.

Her mouth scrunched to almost nothing, as if she could reclaim the kiss she'd bestowed. She marched up to him, and Hakon braced himself.

Brigitt poked him with a stiff finger as she declared, "You shouldn't lead a woman on like that!"

Hakon apologized again, and after a few pokes, Brigitt took back the gift and marched away.

He was left appalled in her wake.

*Fates, what have I done?*

He was constantly looking at lips to better understand people, particularly when the noise around him obscured voices.

He'd stared unabashedly at Lady Aislinn's lips.

*Does she think I want to kiss her?*

If she did, she'd done nothing about it. Perhaps he should've been relieved with the revelation, but it only stoked his temper and frustration.

If she knew of his feelings, she did nothing to encourage them.

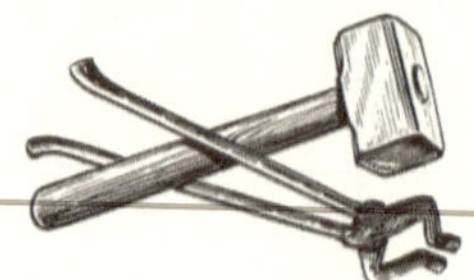

Aislinn shoved the hunk of buttered bread, all she had time for at the midday meal, into her mouth and chewed as she walked. Her morning tasks had taken her longer than expected, which meant she was late for the tailor, which meant she'd be late for everything after that, too.

It was aggravating to watch every task fall behind the previous one, like downed fence posts toppling one after the other, when just one thing went wrong.

Utilizing a shortcut to get back to her apartments, where she was meeting the tailor in her solar, Aislinn rounded the corner of the upper castle gallery to find a small group of maids gathered round. Their heads leaned out between the colonnade, peering down onto the courtyard below.

Aislinn stopped a few steps away, her curiosity invariably itching. She peeked down into the courtyard herself to see what the fuss was.

*Oh, my.*

Near one of the drains, Hakon had set up an old cask—and in it sat a soaked and unhappy Wülf, soap suds adorning his head. Into the cask Hakon poured great buckets of water, rinsing away the soap.

This seemed the final straw, and the big dog let out a baying cacophony of complaints. Wülf stood as much as he was able and shook his great gray body, sending water everywhere, but mostly onto Hakon.

The blacksmith yelped and stepped away dripping, his linen shirt soaked through and clinging to his wide shoulders. Even from up in the gallery, Aislinn could see the way the green flesh of his great chest undulated and bulged with strength.

*Ohh.*

Hugging her notebook to her chest, she couldn't pull her gaze away from the wet blacksmith as he attempted to finish bathing Wülf.

"No, no, no," he told the beast as Wülf tried to escape from the cask. "You're filthy. Either you get a bath or I throw you in with the rest of the pigs."

Wülf yipped and barked in protest as Hakon, apparently seeing the futility in trying to stay dry, leaned down and held the dog with one arm while he scrubbed with his other hand.

His soaked shirt clung to his wide back, and his dark hair had gone glossy with the dampness.

Aislinn watched on, mesmerized by the beauty of him. How his strong shoulders bunched and released, how he easily controlled the wriggling beast of a dog with the utmost gentleness.

Something warm and tingling took root deep in her belly, something she hadn't felt in a long, long time.

Her lips and breasts ached bittersweetly, and Aislinn touched a finger to her lower lip.

*Attraction. Desire.*

That's what this was.

For the halfling blacksmith.

Perhaps she should've been surprised at herself, but she wasn't, not truly. His fine form outlined by a soaked shirt was just the last in a string of qualities that drew her to him. The attraction had been growing for a while now, beautiful and unstoppable.

*Fates, I really do like him.*

She couldn't help it—not when Hakon was simply . . . everything she could want.

Aislinn could be reasonable. She knew there was something to seeing Sorcha so happy with her own halfling. But Hakon was his own person, and the companionship they shared, the way he helped her and encouraged her, the way he gave her his time, his attention, his patience . . .

What she knew of how Orek was with Sorcha may have given her ideas of what Hakon was like, but it was he himself who proved to her, every time she interacted with him, what a genuine man he was. Kind, patient, skilled. It was *him* she admired, not just the idea of a halfling lover.

She knew it wouldn't be proper; that when her father said to find a partner, he'd meant one of their own. Someone landed. Someone of good stock. Someone *human*. She acknowledged the wisdom and reason in all of it—but that didn't stop her gaze, and her heart, from wandering. For the first time in a long while, Aislinn was *excited;* she rose with the hope of spending time with her blacksmith. Days were better when he was in them, and that wasn't something she took for granted.

Her mood had quickly gone dour after not visiting him for days. Brenna reminded her every morning that her tasks were more important, yet Aislinn didn't think she was actually completing any more than on days she visited him. Her attention waned and she trudged through the work, slowed by her apathy.

Seeing him now, arguing with his unruly dog, was a balm to her sore spirit. She almost . . . wanted to go down and join them.

*What if I do?*

The dangerous thought expanded inside her, excitement clutching her throat. She was heiress, yes, but that meant this was *her* castle. She could do as she wished within it.

What she wished for was the blacksmith.

Aislinn laid her hand on her chest, feeling how her heart fluttered at her breast. Acknowledging her attraction somehow released the tension there, and it felt as if bubbles of joy burst in her blood.

She would have gone to him, had she not overheard what the maids said.

"It really is a shame," sighed Tilly.

"I was so sure," grumbled Brigitt.

The other maids made sounds of pity and comfort, patting her shoulders and squeezing her arms.

"So were we," agreed Claire.

"Looking at lips must just mean something else to orcs," said Fia.

"Hmph. Or he fancies someone else," Brigitt said.

Aislinn's mind suddenly filled with the sight of him in the dining hall, always surrounded by maids.

*Something must have happened.* Although unsure what, their words stuck in her mind, even hours later. The bubbling excitement inside her fizzled, leaving her confused and a bit more reasonable. She didn't hurry down into the courtyard, instead stole one last look at the blacksmith attempting to dry off his complaining wolfhound, then passed by the maids.

She met Fia's gaze for a moment, and she thought her maid might say something, but Aislinn was quickly deep within the castle.

The meeting with the tailor played out by rote, being fitted for a new gown and warm layers.

Aislinn stared at herself in the long mirror as the tailor measured and pinned fabric in place, chattering about new patterns from the capital that had just come in. She made the necessary noises of assent or appreciation, but her mind was far afield.

*Must mean something else to orcs . . .*

Hakon looked at her lips sometimes. Aislinn perhaps wouldn't have assumed it meant wanting to kiss, but then, she'd never been adept at flirting. She hadn't assumed any of his actions were flirting, yet . . .

Her palm itched to hold the wooden rose.

That didn't feel like nothing—but perhaps it meant something else to orcs. She knew little of orcish culture, just human stories that were unkind to them and their ways, and what little Orek had said.

Her stomach churned not knowing if she was again misreading someone, a person she'd thought she understood. She'd made that mistake with her own brother. Perhaps it was nothing more than a misunderstanding of cultures, but either option made unpleasant emotions begin to bubble inside her.

*I could ask.*

That idea just made her stomach clench with nerves.

Just ask him about orcish customs and whether any of it meant he might feel as she did? The prospect seemed . . . too daunting. She didn't think she could bear it if he said no, or worse, laughed at her.

She valued his friendship and companionship too much.

It would be safer to bury her feelings. To forget this attraction. Nothing could come of it, not truly. She was Aislinn Darrow, heiress of the Darrowlands. Even if Hakon was a prince among orcs and just failed to mention it, the idea of a noblewoman taking a halfling for a lover was scandalous, and taking one for a husband was inconceivable.

Her jealousy over what Sorcha had only grew.

Aislinn peered at herself in the mirror, the uncertainty plain on her face for even her to see.

Perhaps . . . it was for the best then that she continued not visiting him. Perhaps now she should finally do the wise thing and let go of her infatuation before her heart became anymore attached. She wasn't far enough down this path to be in true danger—there was still time to turn back.

That would be the smart thing, the responsible thing to do.

And yet . . .

She found no comfort in it. Her heart shuddered at the idea of being put away again.

Aislinn always found change frightening. Hakon was no different and yet like nothing before. He came with *promise,* the chance at something wonderful—if he reciprocated any of her feelings, of course.

Familiarity was safe. Wise. Comforting.

Aislinn knew what to expect in the familiar, knew how to read and understand it.

*And yet . . .*

The familiarity of her duties, of being alone, of not having *him,* wasn't the comfort it may once have been. It may even fill her with . . . despair.

She'd never liked keeping the gaze of others for long, but she'd taught herself to hold for a requisite amount of time. Now, she forced herself to look back at her own reflection.

The woman who stared back was torn, uncertain. Frightened of but longing for change.

Did she dare take the chance and risk heartbreak, humiliation? And, perhaps even more frightening, if she won her gamble, could she allow her heart to open itself again, when it had been hurt so many times before?

Aislinn didn't know. And she hated not knowing things.

# 13

Sweat and condensate ran in thick rivulets down Hakon's straining neck and back, his skin finding no relief as the warm water and steam of the baths swirled around him. The knuckles of both hands had gone pale, one with the effort of holding himself up against the far wall while the other fervently worked his cock as the water lapped at his bollocks.

A nightly bath had become his ritual, a way to wash off the day's soot and grime—and lust. He took to the baths late in the night, when no one else would be there to witness his weakness.

The ritual was simple—grabbing his angry cock and releasing what he could of his frustration. He cleansed himself of his daydreams, purged his fantasies, and in the hot water and steam of the baths, he renewed his resolve to finally put aside his desire for Lady Aislinn.

It didn't matter what he or his snarling, unhappy beast wanted, because *she* didn't want him.

It was that simple.

Hakon bared his tusks in agonized fury at the wall and pumped his fist harder.

She hadn't come to him in over a week. No projects, no requests. She wasn't even taking all her meals in the dining hall, so when he did see her there, he had to look his fill and make it last.

*She doesn't want you.*

That's what this had to mean. She found him enjoyable and useful enough, but she had more important things to see to. He was merely staff.

It's what he'd been trying to convince his beast of for weeks, but the dogged thing wouldn't listen.

And now look. No Lady Aislinn. A spurned potential partner—and Brigitt was likely to speak of him to the other maids, which meant his immediate prospects with anyone else within the castle were slim.

*Only want one person in the castle,* growled the beast.

Hakon violently wrenched the head of his cock, the pleasure-pain searing through him. That was all his beast ever said. Never anything useful, nothing that would help him build the life he wanted.

It was hard enough living as a halfling amongst humans and looking for a potential mate. It was difficult enough finding the woman of his every dream only to discover he could never have her.

He didn't need an unhelpful, stubborn beast making it more difficult.

And yet, that's exactly what he got.

Hakon shook his head from side to side as his orgasm ripped through him, a blazing moment of pleasure that never lasted long enough and never left him satisfied.

Oh, he could imagine her there with him, her skin glowing and rosy from the steam. He could see how her golden hair would pool around them on the surface as she smiled up at him. Those intelligent eyes would flutter at him as she took him in hand. That brilliant mouth would grin a precious little grin before bestowing teasing kisses up and down his length. She'd torment him for as long as she wished, testing his mettle, and he'd savor every moment of agony, waiting for that glorious moment when she'd slip his cockhead inside the hot well of her mouth.

The picture of her in his mind, those plush pink lips wrapped around the angry green of his cock, had Hakon shouting into the stones, ropes of spend hitting the water.

When it was all finished, he was left heaving. He leaned heavily into the wall for support, his legs weakened and shaking in the water.

The ritual was complete. A day's worth of frustration and unrequited desire purged.

But he feared he'd never be free of her. Every new day brought new hope, new dreams that would wilt and wither as the sun crossed the sky.

He was caught in his own trap, unsure how to escape. Everything he'd wanted, the sacrifices he'd made to come to Dundúran—they were all for nothing if he couldn't get his head on straight and give her up.

With a sigh, Hakon slumped backward into the water, floating aimlessly on his back.

The steamy air was heavy in his nose and lungs, but he couldn't seem to make himself leave.

Other than the smithy with Lady Aislinn in her designated chair, the baths were his favorite place within Dundúran Castle. Sourced from a natural spring beneath the castle and supplemented with a hypocaust, the baths were a sprawling network of heated pools. The natural spring had been hewn into rock formations with veins of glittering minerals, as well as columns that supported arching passageways. The floors were inlaid with small tiles and glass squares, set in intricate mosaics.

The baths were split down the center by a metal mesh screen, the openings just large enough to allow air but not to see into the other side. Should a woman be bathing on the opposite side, he'd be able to make out her silhouette, but no features.

He was always careful to wait and ensure no one was in either bath before taking himself in hand. Even if a woman could only see a silhouette, his was distinctive within Dundúran.

Hakon drifted for a long while, his body warm and spent.

The situation wasn't out of hand yet. If he could break his beast of its obsession with the heiress, perhaps then he could finally get serious about meeting a potential mate. One he could truly have and make a life with.

*Fates, it all sounds so simple.*

Nothing ever truly was.

Hakon grumbled and set himself upright. Pushing out of the water, he grabbed his bath sheet and made quick work of drying. He pushed his legs quickly into the loose linen braies he wore just to the baths and hung the sheet around his neck.

Determined to leave the morose thoughts behind, he climbed the stairs back up into the castle.

He'd made the convergence of the stairs leading down to the two sides of the baths when he heard quiet voices and steps coming down to meet him.

Hakon looked up in surprise.

Lady Aislinn and Fia looked back at him much the same, their faces cast partially in shadow by the lantern Fia held.

Both were obviously bound for the baths, linen chemises peeking out from brocade dressing gowns. Lady Aislinn's was a rich claret color that caught the light of the lantern where it curved around her body—her shoulders, her hips, her generous breasts. Her golden hair fell in soft, unbound waves down her shoulders and back, framing her lovely face.

She looked as undone as he'd ever seen her, and he knew the sight was branded onto his mind forever.

Ears burning, Hakon dropped his head. "My lady, forgive me, I…"

"No, no, don't mind us," she insisted. She cleared her throat as silence stretched.

Hakon dared pick up his head, unable to help how his gaze fell greedily upon her. Fates, she was all softness in the lantern glow.

Good thing Fia was there, for if she wasn't, Hakon didn't know if he'd have been able to stop himself from doing something foolish.

More foolish at least than murmuring, "It's good to see you, my lady."

He didn't imagine how her pulse visibly beat at her throat. A purr of desire gathered in his own, and although he knew he should look away, he couldn't.

"You, too," she said, her voice a low, breathy noise that drew him up, up the steps, until he was just one below hers.

Those brilliant golden eyes of hers searched his face, and he wondered if she could hear him crying out to her—*send Fia away, come back to me, come with me.*

If she did, she said nothing. Her lips parted, but no words came out. Hakon stared at those lips, his body rocking toward her as if she was a celestial body and he was pulled inexorably into her sphere.

"Goodnight, Master Hakon."

He looked at Fia in a daze, seeing her arched, expectant brows.

Hakon swallowed hard. *Fuck, what am I doing?*

He stepped as far back as he could, bowing his head once more.

"Goodnight, my lady, Fia," he said, and took the steps two at a time.

By the time he was safely sequestered in his room, his pulse pounded at his ears and his cock bobbed in his braies.

He'd never forget the sight she made—soft, glowing, perfect. And never to be his.

Aislinn lay awake for a long while, her body overwarm despite having long since dried off from the baths. The castle was quiet and still in the deepest hours of the night, all but the night watch having found their beds. Yet Aislinn couldn't rest, couldn't turn her mind from the sight of the blacksmith coming up from the baths.

Another wave of longing surged through her at the memory of him, glistening from his bath, every heavy muscle thrown into stark relief in the light and shadow of the lantern. She couldn't stop thinking of how his damp hair had been slicked back close to his head, nor how droplets of water gathered on the pointed tips of his ears. His cheeks had been rosy and his skin supple from the steam.

And his braies . . . clinging to his thick thighs from the dampness, they left little to the imagination over his shape. Aislinn's throat ran dry thinking of the outline she'd glimpsed of his cock, hanging against a thigh. She shouldn't have looked, but his head had been bowed and she was excruciatingly curious.

Had Fia not been there, Aislinn suspected she would've given in to temptation—thrown herself into the strong form of him, finally indulge and discover what his truest scent was, how his skin would feel against her cheek, how his arms would feel wrapped around her . . . what those big green hands would feel like as they pushed away her dressing gown and revealed her to the soft light . . .

Sucking in a breath, Aislinn pulled down the neckline of her nightgown to run her fingertips over one pert nipple. Bending a knee, she rucked up the hem to her waist and set her other hand to exploring between her legs.

She hadn't brought herself pleasure in quite a while. She'd certainly thought about it since meeting Hakon, but now, she couldn't go another moment without satisfaction.

Her fingers worked in a practiced rhythm, and Aislinn was quickly slick as her hips rolled beneath her hand. She pinched and worked her nipple and clitoris in unison, wringing her pleasure out with familiar movements and tricks she'd learned over her youth and womanhood.

She'd lain with two men before, but she herself was always the one to ensure her own pleasure. Her climax built, gathering tension low in her belly, until it all released in one bittersweet moment. Her thighs clamped around her hand as her hips rolled and rolled, chasing the pleasure.

His name was on her lips as she crested, pleasure pooling like syrup in her veins.

She lay for a long while in the center of her bed, the sheets tangled round her, staring at the canopy and thinking, *I wish I was with him. In the baths. In this bed. Anywhere. Everywhere.*

She'd tried to resign herself to distancing from him. She thought it would be for the best.

Her mood only worsened with every day she didn't see him.

The wooden rose she kept in her pocket was a constant comfort but also a reminder of him. That she hadn't spoken with him in days. Even if he was only ever to be her friend, she was grateful for it. There were few people in her life who she'd found it easier to talk to than Hakon.

*What am I to do?* She'd been asking herself that for days without finding an answer.

Somehow, tonight, it felt as though a line had been crossed or a rite performed. Something had happened, but she couldn't quite say what.

And as she lay there in her bed, her body still shaking with the aftermath of her orgasm yet aching for him, she wondered, *How can I stay away?*

In the end, Aislinn couldn't. She stole to the smithy again, her heart fuller for it when she saw his wide, welcoming smile. The way the dimple in his cheek appeared when he smiled like that . . . it set her insides to fluttering.

She couldn't go as often as she had before. Duties and work truly were piling up as her father shifted most of his focus to preparing for his venture south. Harvest was one of the busiest times of year as well, as all throughout the Darrowlands, crops were brought in for storage or processing. The silos, granaries, and mills were hives of activity, workers bringing in the harvests from the surrounding farms and tax collectors the dues from the nobles and yeomen.

Head full of accounts and numbers and tables, Aislinn hadn't been able to keep herself from visiting him. She needed the relief, the comfort of watching him work.

The smithy was safe and warm, a world unto itself. It made her *happy* to be there with him.

As the duties compounded, the letters from Bayard continued, Jerrod's whereabouts went unknown, and the vassals continued to complain about the raised dues, Aislinn savored those moments of happiness where she could find them.

She'd worried that when returning to him, she might find their friendship strained or awkward, but he only smiled at her and handed her fresh pieces of beeswax for when he hammered.

It was a relief that things settled into the way they'd been before. There was an easiness between them, one she longed for whenever she interacted with someone else and found it more difficult.

Day after day, she stole to the smithy and was happier for it.

Yet, it wasn't truly as it'd been before. There was something . . . different about their time together. Perhaps even about the two of them.

She caught him blushing more than once, and she didn't think it was from the forge fires. And when she noticed his gaze falling to her lips, her heart stuttered in her chest remembering what the maids had said.

It was on the tip of her tongue to ask, but for a while, she wasn't brave enough. She feared what his answer might be, and what might happen because of it. It was easy to settle back into their easiness, but she couldn't help feeling the change.

Finally, one night, she decided she had to know. No matter the outcome or how it changed what was between them. She spent her nights longing for him and her days missing him—she couldn't go on like that forever, her body always aching, her heart always pining.

When next they were alone in the smithy, once more discussing her plans for the bridge, she noted when his gaze fell to her mouth.

Drawing herself up in her chair, she smiled gently before asking, "Hakon, why do you look at my mouth so often?"

She'd surprised him.

He went perfectly still. She watched as his mind turned over her words, and his ears darkened with a ruddy blush.

Hakon turned away from her suddenly, giving her his profile as he worked a polishing cloth over the iron he held.

"I meant no offense," he said quietly.

"I know you didn't. I was merely curious. I just wondered if . . ."

The words, those said and more so those unsaid, hung between them for a terrible moment. Aislinn clutched her fingers into her skirts and made herself stay still, even as she wanted to fidget—or better yet, flee.

It was a while before he turned back to her, setting down his work. He wouldn't quite meet her gaze, but he did approach, stopping only a step away.

Heart in her throat, Aislinn kept quiet and still, feeling the weight of whatever it was he was about to say.

"I . . . I don't like to speak of it. But I'm mostly deaf in this ear." He touched a finger to his right ear, the one with but a single golden hoop. "I protect what hearing I do have because I fear losing any more."

"I didn't know," she murmured. He'd hidden it so well—she'd never have guessed he struggled with his hearing.

Hakon shook his head, gaze straying out the smithy windows. He seemed to find it easier to speak to the night outside, and so Aislinn listened patiently, not demanding his gaze or more than he was willing to give.

"My grandmother was, too. She taught me the hand-talk. With others, I can usually hear them, but reading lips helps. Especially if it's loud, like in the dining hall. I fear I may have given some the wrong idea by it."

Aislinn swallowed around the lump in her throat. "It's not your fault," she insisted. "You didn't know."

He nodded, though she wasn't sure he actually agreed with her. "Perhaps. It's made learning and speaking Eirean challenging."

"You've done wonderfully!" she was quick to praise him.

That earned her a faint smile. "Thank you, my lady. You . . . you've helped greatly. I enjoy listening to you talk."

Aislinn flushed from head to toe. That deep brown gaze of his returned to her, compelling her up out of her seat. Gently, she laid her hand on his arm.

"Thank you for telling me."

The corners of his lips, which had just begun to turn up again, fell, and his gaze grew evermore serious. Slowly, he took the hand she'd laid on his arm in his.

Keeping her gaze, he lifted her hand and bowed his head, pressing his warm lips to the back of her hand. *Pitter-patter* went her heart as her breath escaped her in a soft gasp. His eyes flicked to her mouth, and she couldn't help it, she drew her tongue along the bottom lip.

She felt the rasping breath he took against her skin, then a harder, more fervent kiss was pressed into her palm.

The forge fires crackled, Wülf snored, and the nightingales sang, but Aislinn hardly heard any of it over the rush of blood in her ears.

The way he looked at her now . . . the frisson of heat that arrowed between her thighs when he tasted her skin . . .

The smithy door clattered open, and Fearghas stomped inside.

She and Hakon gaped at the old blacksmith with surprise.

"Evening, milady," he said in his usual brusque way, but rather than shuffling off deeper into the smithy, he stopped to look at the scene before him.

His big bushy beard twitched.

"I'd better go," she murmured.

"Good evening, my lady," Hakon said just as quietly, allowing her hand to slip from his.

She tried to walk away, but under Fearghas's inscrutable gaze, it felt too much like fleeing. So she turned and told the both of them, "I like the new organization. It seems most efficient."

"Thank you, my lady." Hakon's smile was wide and, interestingly, a bit smug. She'd never seen quite that expression on him, a hint of wickedness, and she . . . rather liked it.

She couldn't help keeping his gaze for another moment as her heart tried to thunder right out of her chest.

She had her answer, even if she didn't know what it was.

Things were *changing*—and while that did frighten her, she couldn't help the well of excitement, too.

Giving him one last smile, she left the smithy, the hand he'd kissed curled against her breast, just above her racing heart.

# 14

Hakon wiped the sweat from his brow, heart lighter than it had been in days. His beast was . . . if not settled, then at least quiet as it lay in wait. A few afternoons in Lady Aislinn's company had soothed his gnawing discontent and renewed his enthusiasm for work.

Not even Fearghas's grumbling could deflate his spirits. There was nothing for the head blacksmith to truly complain about, not when Hakon was inspired enough to complete his work and much of Fearghas's with time to spare.

Without so much sourness in his demeanor, Hakon had a better time at being friendly. He made a point to take his breaks outside and chat with the potters. Captain Aodhan stopped by more than once for a fitting of the new breastplate Hakon had offered to make, and several of his knights followed suit.

Looking around as Hakon measured and made charcoal marks on the metal, Captain Aodhan had remarked, *"This is the cleanest I've ever seen the smithy."*

Fearghas *hmphed* from his anvil.

*"Oh, I figured it wasn't your doing, you old pack rat,"* the captain joked.

*"Nothing wrong with the way things were,"* Fearghas growled back.

*"No, there wasn't. And there's nothing wrong with this way, either."*

The head blacksmith sunk into a moody silence. Captain Aodhan tossed Hakon a knowing look and settled in for his fitting.

Hakon had even made inroads with Hugh, the surly head cook. Repairing knife handles and sharpening the blades were a constant need, and for a few spare bones for Wülf, Hakon was happy to do it.

Inspired by their brilliant heiress, Hakon made himself useful, helpful. He earned his place at the table and added to nightly conversation where he could.

He wasn't sure Brigitt had forgiven him yet, although the other maids soon warmed to him again. Hakon tried to look each over, to appreciate their qualities, but his eye was inextricably drawn to the high table.

More than once, he caught the heiress's gaze. She smiled at him prettily, which only made his beast that much more determined. He wouldn't let himself think or say anything aloud, but the beast had made up its mind.

Pulling the beeswax from his ears, Hakon adjusted to noise once more.

Or would have, had there been any.

Looking around, he saw that Fearghas had stopped his own hammering to stare flabbergasted out the window. The pottery next door had fallen silent as well.

Hakon turned to the windows to see a great shadow taking up the bailey.

Stomach clenching, he hurried outside, not quite sure he believed his eyes.

In the middle of the bailey stood Bellarand, his black coat absorbing what sunlight filtered in from the overcast sky. On his back sat Allarion, his form hidden by that purple-black cloak, his silvery-white hair falling down his back in a starlit cascade.

As Hakon walked into the daylight, Allarion's gaze fell upon him, making the hairs on his arms rise.

"Good day, Hakon."

"Hullo, Allarion. What brings you to Dundúran?"

The nostrils of the fae's thin nose flared, and with a sweep of his cloak, Allarion dismounted. Although he was a hair shorter than Hakon, his ancient presence made him infinitely bigger, his magic soaking into every nook and cranny of the bailey.

"I've come to petition for the Scarborough estate. It seems missives go missing here, so I've come myself and don't plan to leave without seeing a Darrow." His lips thinned. "Perhaps I'd have better luck with the father."

"He isn't here. Won't be back until tomorrow." From what he understood, Liege Darrow was visiting several of his vassals in preparation for his journey south after Orek and Sorcha's wedding in just a few days.

"I'm prepared to wait. I've given the girl enough time."

Anger prickled along Hakon's neck. "Lady Aislinn promised she'd see to your petition. I'm sure there's good reason why she hasn't."

Nothing in the fae's visage or stance changed, but the air temperature in the bailey dropped. Gooseflesh rose along Hakon's arms.

"There had better be." He nodded at the castle steps. "Take me to her."

"No."

The denial surprised Hakon just as much as Allarion. They stared at each other for a long moment, before Bellarand huffed and threw his mane impatiently.

"No?" Allarion repeated. There was no threat in his voice, but Hakon felt the danger skitter up his spine.

"No. Not until your temper has left you." It was entirely a guess that this was what Allarion's temper looked like, but it was different enough from the placid, if aloof, demeanor he knew from the fae that he was willing to risk it.

For he wouldn't risk Lady Aislinn. He'd not bring an angry fae to her door.

Those nostrils flared again. "Everyone assumes I mean her harm.

Why? I have said nothing of the sort."

"They assume by reputation."

Allarion frowned. "A fae hasn't slain a human in hundreds of years."

"They have long memories. But I won't take you because Lady Aislinn is . . . she's a friend and a good woman. She doesn't deserve your ire."

Allarion looked on for a long moment, and Hakon locked his knees to stay in place and bear the brunt of that intense gaze.

Whatever he saw, the fae eventually nodded once. The air returned to its mild autumn temperature, and Bellarand nickered.

"Very well. If you speak for her, I trust it is true."

Hakon worked to hide the surprise from his face but didn't think he succeeded.

"Please," said Allarion, "I wish to speak with the heiress and resolve the matter."

Slowly, Hakon nodded. "She'll be in her study this time of morning."

"Take me there?"

Hakon reluctantly agreed, untying his leather apron and throwing it across the sill of an open smithy window. He caught Fearghas's round eyes through the gloom.

"Best tell Captain Aodhan that the heiress has an otherly guest," he told the old human.

"I'm not sure the captain needs to know," Allarion said.

"But he'll want to. He's a good man. Fair. Just wants to ensure the safety of the heiress."

Allarion made a considering sound in his throat but otherwise stood still, waiting for Hakon to lead him into the castle.

With another nicker, Bellarand turned around to trot back out of the bailey.

"Yes, all right. Stay out of trouble," Allarion called after him.

The unicorn flicked his long tail.

"Dare I ask where he's going?" said Hakon.

"Back into the courtyard to inspire terror and awe. They are his favorite."

"I see." He didn't, but he was too unsettled to say anything else.

Hakon kept the fae in his peripheral vision as he led him up and into the castle. The beast wanted to lead him straight to the dungeons to lock up the potential threat, but Hakon swallowed the asinine desire. Allarion was right—he'd never been aggressive or threatening toward anyone, let alone Lady Aislinn.

Still, he didn't savor bringing the fae to her, if only because Allarion's business was likely to upset her. And mean more work. Which might threaten their afternoon together.

*The dungeon is starting to sound like a good option.*

It wasn't until the third floor, however, that Hakon remembered one vital detail. He didn't know which door was Lady Aislinn's study. He knew exactly which was her window and could make an educated guess—but he didn't want to barge into rooms.

Thankfully, the chatelain, Brenna, exited one of the rooms down the hall.

"Mistress Brenna!" he called.

The older woman looked on in shock—perhaps even horror—as they approached. Hakon tried not to take offense. Like Fearghas, she'd made it clear since he'd arrived that she didn't approve of him nor Lady Aislinn spending time with him in the smithy.

"What is this about?" she asked, eyes narrowing.

"Which is Lady Aislinn's study? Lord Allarion has important business."

To her credit, the chatelain didn't wither or quiver. She met the fae's chilly stare as she looked between him and Hakon.

"Lord Allarion doesn't have an appointment."

"I can wait," the fae said. "I'm a patient male. Just show me to the great hall where I might wait for the heiress."

A tendon in Brenna's cheek twitched. "That won't be necessary." She nodded to the door two down. "That's her study. But don't keep the lady long, she has important work to do." Gathering herself up to her full height, she leveled Hakon with a steely glare. "And she's far too busy to waste time with you today, blacksmith."

"Yes, mistress," he grumbled.

With a decisive nod, Brenna pushed between them on her way down the corridor.

They waited for her to disappear down the stairs before moving toward Lady Aislinn's door.

"That woman is unpleasant," said Allarion.

"She can be." Hakon decided that was as diplomatic as he could be. Brenna kept the castle running smoothly, but he'd never seen the woman smile. She didn't eat with the staff nor take part in any of the gatherings they held on rest days. She seemed to always be working and determined to keep Lady Aislinn that way, too.

Rapping a knuckle on the door, Hakon waited with impatience for the sweet, "Come in!" The sound of her voice soothed his temper, and he opened the door to her study with a smile on his face.

Inside was a trove of books.

The room was oblong, with some of the limestone blocks of the castle showing through the worn plaster walls. Wooden shelves had been mounted on the walls, books spilling over onto the floor in great piles that reached almost to Hakon's shoulder. Two arched windows on the south wall let light stream inside.

Magnifiers, rulers, scales, weights, compasses, pens, and sharpening knives sat atop books and folios. It was a chaotic cavern of scholarly delights that smelled of parchment, ink, and Lady Aislinn.

Hakon loved it immediately.

Sitting at a battered desk on the far side, Lady Aislinn herself looked up in surprise at their entrance. She was enchanting as always, her hair gathered in a braid that followed the slope of her head, and her limbs clad in a lovely green gown. Ink stained her fingertips, and she had a charcoal smudge on her cheek.

"Oh. Oh! Hakon—Allarion!" A blush overcame the tanned skin of her cheeks, and she looked with increasing worry between them.

"Good day, my lady. Allarion and Bellarand have come to see you today with business."

She glanced at the still open door with trepidation. "The unicorn isn't right outside, is he?"

"Rest assured, he's perfectly content in the courtyard being admired from afar." Something of a fond grin curved on the fae's lips. It was more disconcerting than his temper chilling the bailey.

"All right." She cleared her throat. "What can I do for you today, Lord Allarion?"

"I've come to settle the matter of the Scarborough estate."

Lady Aislinn's brows arched in comprehension. "Oh yes! I've been waiting for your petition. I asked Brenna, the chatelain, about it not long ago and she said she hadn't seen it." She winced with embarrassment. "I apologize, I looked everywhere for the petitions you sent but couldn't find them. I'm sorry you've had to come all the way here."

Laying a hand over his heart—or where in the chest most others' hearts were—Allarion assured her, "It's no trouble, my lady. I just wish to resolve the matter."

"Of course."

Turning to her left, Lady Aislinn rifled through several volumes and parchment rolls, pulling out a large, leather-bound folio. She flipped to a large map of the Darrowlands, the land covered with names written in fine scrawling script that had long since faded to brown. Tracing the map with a finger, Lady Aislinn followed the curve of the Shanago River north, to a place that's name had been scratched out.

"You're sure you wish to let the Scarborough estate? It's sat fallow for decades."

"No, I don't wish to let it. I wish to purchase it."

Lady Aislinn stared at the fae for a long moment. "Purchase it? But it has no farms, no village."

"Precisely why it will suit me."

"You would be beholden to attend council meetings, as a land-holder."

"A good excuse to socialize."

Lady Aislinn bit her lip, still looking uncertain.

"You seem to have no need of it," Allarion reasoned. "If it has sat abandoned for so long, then no one has cared about it in a long while. I will restore the estate and land. I will pledge loyalty to the Darrow name, and none shall be a timelier taxpayer."

That got a grin from the heiress. "You make a strong case. I only worry that the land is far away from the community you have on the Brádaigh estate. It's far from anyone, really."

"You're only making it more alluring to me, my lady."

Lady Aislinn thought a moment before smiling and stretching out her hand. "All right, then. The estate is yours. I look forward to seeing you at the next council meeting."

"As do I."

Allarion took her hand, and they shook in the human way.

Hakon swallowed the growl building in his chest that another un-mated male might touch that which wasn't his.

Although sure he hadn't made a sound, the fae's unnatural gaze slid to him, one brow ticking up in an interested arch.

"Would you prefer we decide today on a payment schedule or wait until my father returns? The deed will need his seal of writ before it's final."

"No need," said Allarion. From beneath his fathomless cloak, he pulled a clinking velvet sack and laid it on the open map. "I believe this will do?"

Lady Aislinn blinked at the coin purse. "Quite so," she murmured, as surprised as Hakon at the sight of such a bulging purse.

Shaking herself, Lady Aislinn pulled a fresh piece of parchment from a stack and began writing up the terms of the sale and deed. When everything was decided and final, she signed it and then passed it to Allarion for his signature.

Rather than taking the quill she offered, Allarion ran the tip of a finger over the parchment. A spark and sudden smell of ash filled the room. Allarion's burnt signature appeared alongside Lady Aislinn's.

"My father will need to sign it as well and add his seal," said the heiress, staring in wonderment at the fae's signature.

"That will be soon?"

Blinking, Lady Aislinn looked up to nod. "Yes, he returns tomorrow for the wedding. I will personally ensure he signs it and give it to you at the wedding, if that is agreeable?"

"Indeed." Pleased, the fae swept into a low bow, his long hair nearly touching the floorboards. "Thank you for seeing me, my lady."

"Of course! I apologize again that it's taken this long to sort out."

Straightening from his bow, Allarion's face went hard again. Gone was the pleasant charm as he negotiated with Lady Aislinn.

"I don't mean to presume, my lady, but you might consider looking into the matter of how correspondence makes its way to you."

Her lips parted in surprise, but then the fae was bowing and saying his farewells.

"I will see you both at the wedding."

And with a swish of his cloak, he departed, leaving behind whispers of magic.

Hakon and Lady Aislinn stared after him for a long moment before blinking at each other.

"I can't believe there was a fae warrior in my study," she whispered.

"At least he didn't bring the unicorn with him."

Her lips scrunched and then Lady Aislinn let out a peal of laughter. Hakon joined in, lighting up at seeing her amusement.

She settled back in her chair, the smile still on her lips. "A visit from a fae and the largest land sale in a decade—all before luncheon."

"All the other heiresses will be envious."

Lady Aislinn snorted. "Hardly."

Hakon's gaze stole to the map, still open on her desk. Reaching into his pocket, he approached her, his throat going tight.

"While the map is out . . . I wondered if I might claim my own land sale."

Lady Aislinn looked up at him, her bright golden eyes wide with surprise. "We don't have any more unclaimed estates, I'm afraid."

"No need for something so grand. I was thinking of something like Varon's farm."

"I didn't realize you had farming aspirations," she teased.

"By the old gods, no. I'm not suited for it. But land of my own—that I aspire to."

He held her gaze as the merriment of before morphed into curiosity. Lady Aislinn cleared away the parchment from atop the map and traced a finger from Dundúran toward the Brádaigh estate.

"There are several parcels available. Did you know which one?" she asked.

Hakon leaned over the desk, putting their heads close, and followed the path of her finger. His bumped hers over the Brádaigh estate.

"Here," he said, "with the meadow. Do you know it?"

He watched as her expression went soft with fondness. "Yes. Sorcha and I used to pick flowers there in the spring. It's a lovely place."

She liked the plot. She had fond memories of it. It was near her friend.

His beast howled in triumph.

*Take her there. Mate her there. Build her a fine home.*

"What will you do with it?" she asked, voice gone low and soft.

"Build a home. A forge." His gaze dropped to her lips. "Have a family."

"Is that why you came to the Darrowlands, ultimately? For a family?"

The question felt far more serious than her voice implied.

He held that gaze of hers, enthralled, and knew he had to choose his answer wisely. He didn't know why, only that he did.

"I came to find a purpose," he finally answered.

*And it's you.*

She pulled a long draw of air into her lungs, and Hakon couldn't help his eyes flicking down to see how it made her breasts push against the neckline of her gown. He pulled his gaze up only to find her watching him, her eyes gone heavy-lidded.

Hakon swallowed on a dry throat.

The motion pulled her gaze to his throat, and then up to his mouth, where it lingered.

*Kiss her. Do it. She wants you to!*

Hakon swayed toward her, hardly hearing how the papers rustled beneath his hand. Her pupils blew wide, and her lips parted. He could feel the heat of her on his lips, needed only the smallest encouragement to close the breath's distance between them.

"Shall I draw up another deed for my father to sign?"

She turned her head away, and Hakon retreated. Only a little.

*She feels it.*

His heart pounded harder than a hammer against an anvil in the confines of his chest.

*She feels it, too.*

"Yes," he said, too dumbstruck to say more.

From his pocket he pulled three uncut gems. It wasn't enough for the parcel, but it was enough to surprise her.

"I can bring more for the full price," he said.

"Are those . . .?" She tentatively reached to touch one with a fingertip.

"Sapphires."

Her mouth opened and closed as she brought one closer to inspect. She turned it round, catching the light in the dark blue depths.

"Oh, Hakon, these are beautiful. Where . . .?"

"Not half as beautiful as you, my lady." She blinked up at him, and for a moment he didn't think she'd heard his bumbling declaration. Then pink suffused her cheeks and her lips twitched with a smile.

Heart in his throat, Hakon rounded the desk and reached for the hand holding the gem.

"Even when it is cut and polished, it won't shine half as brightly as you do."

Her blush deepened, and she seemed to squirm in her seat.

"You're flattering me."

"I'm only speaking the truth."

He brought the hand he held to his lips and kissed each knuckle.

"Hakon . . ." Perhaps his name was a warning, perhaps a plea. All he knew was its breathy tone and how it lured him closer.

"I would make you the finest crown, the brightest torque inset with these. No one would be able to look away from how you shine."

She stared up at him, her lips parted. "I don't shine," she murmured.

"Oh, you do. So brightly, it burns hotter than my forge fires."

His heart ached to see the way her eyes went wide and vulnerable at his words. She wasn't ready to hear his praise—which meant she wasn't ready to hear how deeply he adored her.

Reluctantly, he let her hand go and resumed his place on the other side of the desk. He kept his expression open and friendly as they worked out the details of the deed. He didn't tell her how her hair caught the daylight, shining like spun gold. He didn't say how he admired the slope of her shoulder or careful flex of her fingers as she signed the deed. He didn't even admit how thoroughly he wished to kiss her as he bent to add his own name.

He didn't know Eirean writing so instead signed his name in orcish. *Hakon Green-Fist.*

He more than liked the way it looked alongside *Lady Aislinn Darrow*—he relished it.

"Thank you, my lady."

She smiled shyly up at him, having regained her composure. "I look forward to seeing the life you build there, Hakon."

# 15

The ensuing days were so hectic, Aislinn barely had time to sleep, let alone solve the mystery of the missing missives.

When her father returned the day after Allarion's visit, she had just enough time to slip his and Hakon's deeds beneath her father's hand before more business intruded.

Merrick's brows rose. "The Scarborough estate?"

"He seemed determined. And the sale will cover all the extra dues for the year." The additional funds required by the crown were one reason her father had been willing to sell land to the otherlies wishing to settle in the Darrowlands, but neither of them had dreamed anyone would want something as large as the Scarborough estate—and be willing to pay.

Her father quickly read the deed before dipping a quill in ink and adding his name to the deed. "Well, a fae for a vassal. This ought to be interesting."

"And this."

He quickly read Hakon's deed. "Do we want to grant our best blacksmith a reason to leave us?" He looked up and winked at Aislinn.

She attempted to smile back but couldn't, too worried her father *knew*.

*Is it plain on my face how I feel?* She often had trouble hiding her emotions—and she had so many for the halfling blacksmith.

The matter of his land sale gave her no shortage of turmoil. He had the means to pay, and her father had promised the otherly folk they could settle in the Darrowlands. And yet . . .

Aislinn didn't relish the idea of Hakon leaving Dundúran. She didn't enjoy the idea of him building a house for himself and a new wife. She especially didn't like the idea of his taking a bride.

*Fates, I'm jealous of an imaginary woman.*

The feeling was an overwhelming one, as were all the realizations that came with it.

She was jealous of an imaginary woman because she herself wanted to be the one he chose. She wanted to be his woman. She wanted to be with her blacksmith in any way she could.

Because she . . .

"There." Her father held up the second deed and blew on his signature to dry the ink and wax. "We'll just have to make sure he doesn't want to leave the castle."

*Never. I never want him to leave.*

The thought clutched her by the throat, panic roiling her chest so violently that she hardly paid attention to the formal procedures for granting her authority over Dundúran and the Darrowlands. Accords were signed, regent grants sealed. All of it gave Aislinn, as heiress, authority over her father's demesne and all the people who lived within—from the highest baron to the lowest vagabond.

Perhaps on another day, Aislinn might have lingered over the importance of such an act. She'd been left in charge of Dundúran plenty of times before, but always it was Jerrod who'd been vested with a regent's authority. With the papers signed and sealed by her father, Aislinn could issue edicts, sentence criminals, and purchase anything she wanted.

*Finally, we can start on the bridge.*

There was one advantage to having this new burden, at least.

Still, even with the papers safely locked in her room, the responsibility they bestowed followed her through the castle and her daily duties. Already, she could feel their weight hanging about her shoulders, and her father's looming departure stalked her like a shadow.

Attending to her usual tasks, as well as packing for their overnight stay at the Brádaigh estate, was why it took her over a day to finally find and ask Brenna if she could explain why it'd been necessary for Allarion to come in person.

"Brenna!"

The chatelain stopped and waited for Aislinn to catch her up.

"My lady." She pulled the list from her pocket. "Did you forget your appointment with—?"

"No, I'm going now. But I wanted to speak with you. You know Lord Allarion, the fae, came the day before last?"

Brenna's lips pinched in displeasure. "Yes. Did those two bother you? I told them not to keep you long."

"I'm glad they came. Lord Allarion has been very patient trying to get this solved. Father signed his and Hakon's deeds this morning."

"The halfling is buying land, too?"

Aislinn frowned at her tone. "Yes. And they both paid in full." She looked the chatelain over, noting her stiff stance and how she wouldn't quite meet Aislinn's gaze. "Allarion sent a third petition after our discussion at the Brádaighs'. It never got to me."

"The maids must have forgotten," Brenna sniffed.

"The maids and pages know to bring everything to you, no matter what. They're all too terrified of you to not." A sinking feeling overcame her, the truth right there but too much to bear. "Why didn't you give me his petitions?"

Brenna frowned back, and for a long moment, Aislinn thought she'd keep her silence.

Then, blowing out an annoyed breath, Brenna said, "I kept them because you didn't need them. They don't concern you."

Aislinn blinked, baffled. "I'm in charge of settling the otherlies within the Darrowlands. It's my business above all."

"But it shouldn't be." Brenna raised her hands. "I know it's your task, and I know you mean to do it, but they shouldn't be given land. We don't even know who these creatures are! If Sorcha Brádaigh wants to bring one into her family and marry it, fine, but we shouldn't be encouraging them."

A cold, sickening dread held Aislinn like a fist.

"That isn't your decision to make, Brenna. Your position is to bring me correspondence. *All* correspondence."

"My position is to take care of you and this family. It's all I've done since the day I came here with your dear mother. Allowing otherly folk here, letting them become *landholders,* will weaken your family's position—in the Darrowlands and at court."

"They come seeking a new life, and they've done nothing but enrich their communities. We're giving them a fair chance, just as we would anyone."

"Life isn't fair, Aislinn. If it was, your brother would have minded himself better and kept his position. If it was fair, you'd be off in the capital, at the great academies learning and inventing—not stuck here at a position you're unsuited for. If it was fair, your mother wouldn't—"

Aislinn staggered back a step, Brenna's words hitting her like a physical blow.

How had she never realized Brenna thought this way?

*Unsuited.*

Aislinn didn't always take to her duties, no, but she tried her very best. Certainly, the duties were often overwhelming, and she longed for more time of her own, but that didn't mean she disliked the work. Aislinn enjoyed the challenge and puzzle of it, but above all finding ways to better the lives of her people. Always.

Brenna took a moment to compose herself. "I didn't feel you needed the added burden," she said. "You're already struggling. This shouldn't be a priority."

Tears slipped down Aislinn's face before she realized she wept, and she shook her head in denial before she knew she did so. Hands on her face to catch the sudden tears, she said, "It isn't your place to decide that."

"When your dear mother passed, I promised her I'd—"

"You aren't my mother!" Aislinn cried, shocked at herself for it—but more so for what came out next. "And neither am I."

Brenna's face fell, but Aislinn was done. Fleeing the corridor, she hurried to the nearest staircase. Clapping a hand over her mouth to keep in her sobs, she raced down the spiraling stairs, slowed only by a chambermaid who called after her in alarm.

Emotions tumbling like the sea in a storm, Aislinn fought against them, a ship caught in the tempest. Panic and bile rose in her throat, and she knew it was too late. Her fit was coming, and she wanted to be *nowhere* near Brenna when it happened.

Her vision blurred by tears, Aislinn managed to stumble her way to the rose garden. It took multiple tries to get the key in the lock and open the door.

Once inside, she didn't know if she closed the door behind her. She staggered to the lawn, cut short weeks ago by Hakon as they finished reclaiming the garden from the brambles.

*He thinks I shine.*

Slumping to the grass, Aislinn buried her face in her hands and succumbed to the sobs. She didn't feel shiny or brilliant or capable. In fact, she felt about as tall as the grass beneath her.

She sank her fingers into the lawn, soil wedging beneath her nails, and pulled.

Brenna thought she hated being heiress.

Brenna didn't think she was right or good for it.

Brenna thought . . . Brenna thought . . .

Aislinn thought she could trust her.

*I was wrong. Again.*

Wrong about yet another person she'd known her whole life. Someone she considered family.

Wrong. So, so wrong.

She couldn't trust Brenna. Or Jerrod. Or herself, for she'd trusted both of them once and now—

*Stupid.* She was so stupid!

Aislinn slapped her chest and shoulders, the emotions needing *out.* The tears came fast and hot, scalding her face on their way down to soak the soil below. Mud streaked across her face as she tried to wipe them away with her dirty hands.

She didn't know anyone, not truly. She never expected anyone to lie to her, especially not those closest, and yet that's all they did. Lie and leave and disappoint.

Turning her face up to the sky, her eyes stinging with dirt and tears, Aislinn cried and cried and cried.

The tears didn't abate, and her chest ached with the sobs—so much so she thought she imagined the big, warm hands coming around to hold her own. That her imagination tried to manifest the comfort she always longed for but never received.

"Shh, shh," a deep voice rumbled in her ear, "it's all right, *vinya.* It's all right."

Aislinn could hardly see through the tears and could hardly believe it when she was lifted from the lawn and carried into the shade of the trees at the back of the garden. So, so gently, she was placed back on the ground, but those warm hands didn't leave her.

"Oh, gods," she croaked, the green of Hakon's skin just discernible through the tears that wouldn't stop.

"I'm here, *vinya,* you're all right."

She shook her head viciously, pawing at her face. "I'm sorry," she gasped. She didn't want him seeing her like this—so unkempt, so undone. So . . . vulnerable. "I'm sorry, I'm sorry, I'm—"

"There's nothing to be sorry for."

Those big hands grasped hers, pulling them away from her face. With another tug, she was brought into the warmth of a great chest, the heart beating steadily beneath soft skin.

Despite herself, her dirty hands clung to the soft leather of his jerkin, afraid he'd suddenly rescind his comfort. She held on for all she was worth, held on through the sobs as they wracked her chest and the tears as they scalded her skin.

She'd have a monster of a headache tomorrow and be sore for days. She'd need a cold compress all night to ensure she wasn't red and puffy for the wedding. This had to run its course now; there was nothing else for it.

None of that mattered. Not then, under the autumn sky in her mother's dormant rose garden.

What mattered was the steady beat of his heart under her ear. The way his hand ran in soothing strokes up and down her back, up and down, up and down. How he drew her heavy hair from around her face, allowing the breeze to cool her nape. When his big hand cupped the back of her head and held her there when she otherwise might break apart.

Words tumbled out of her mouth; she wasn't sure if they made any sense or explanation, but that didn't matter. He made noises of agreement and assurance as she told him of what Brenna did, of what Brenna expected, of everything Brenna had done for her and her family. She told him about Jerrod and his apathy and anger, how she often wondered if she'd been a better sister if he'd have chosen a different fate. And she told him how she'd so rarely left the Darrowlands, and even Dundúran, that she loved her place as Lady Aislinn and wanted to take on the role of heiress, but that the castle often felt like a burden, a prison of its own.

Like she was nothing without it.

"No, *vinya*," he whispered into her hair. "You are *everything*."

She wanted to protest, but she hadn't the wherewithal. In fact, the tears were slowing, the sobs lessening—and the exhaustion coming swift on their heels.

Within another few moments, she'd stopped shaking and her senses began to return. A breeze blew across the garden, rustling the branches of the trees. The smell of earth and iron and male finally registered in her nose, and she blinked at the thick green column of Hakon's throat.

*Oh, fates.*

Embarrassment surged through her, but on that cool autumn day, her body was too tired, her heart too battered to do anything about it. Instead, she kept her place—atop her blacksmith, she realized.

He'd propped his shoulders against a tree, his long legs spread out before him and Aislinn set between them. Laid upon his chest, his arms cradled her as if she was precious, and there was nowhere in Eirea she'd rather be.

Too exhausted to check herself, she turned her nose into the hollow of his throat and nuzzled there, claiming a long draw of his scent. The word that came to her slow mind was *decadent*. This felt decadent, laying here with him through an autumn afternoon and indulging in his intoxicatingly masculine scent of leather, iron, and soap.

His legs shifted beneath her and his arms tightened around her, bringing her impossibly closer to him.

In a moment she'd be embarrassed. In a moment she'd apologize for crying all over him.

Until then, she enjoyed the moment she had now.

*I want more of this.* Wanted it more than she'd wanted anything before.

Aislinn lived her life content with how it was. Change was frightening, the unknown dangerous. She'd made up her mind about husbands and children and romance long ago—yet as someone who enjoyed science and invention, she well knew that plans changed. Challenges and opportunities always arose, and the successful innovator was one who adapted to them.

Hakon, and everything he could mean for her, was frightening, to be sure.

And yet . . . he could be so much more.

Barely louder than the breeze, he asked, "Are you all right?"

*I am now.*

Aislinn's sigh was long. The answer wasn't so simple.

Pulling herself up, she rested her weight on a hand and tried to smile back at him as she wiped away the remaining tears with the back of her other hand. He let her go but didn't release her entirely.

From his pocket he pulled a kerchief, and so, so gently, he wiped away her tears. Aislinn wanted to curl and hide away in embarrassment, but even though she couldn't meet his gaze as he touched her so, so tenderly, she made herself stay still and accept his comfort.

"I'm sorry for that," she said quietly. "I don't . . ." *Know what came over me.*

Except she knew exactly what.

"Does this . . . happen?"

"Sometimes." She swallowed past her dry throat, summoning the words. He'd been so honest with her about his hearing, she owed him no less. "It was worse when I was younger. Things just . . . emotions become too much and just need out. Unfortunately, that's how they decide to come out."

"Nothing helps?"

"Plenty helps." With her free hand, she pulled the wooden rose he'd carved her from her pocket. Running her thumb over one of the smooth petals even now brought her a little peace and pleasure.

His face went almost pained as he watched her hold the rose. "You like it?"

"Very much. I carry it everywhere. The smoothness helps ground me. Lots of little things help to keep me calm and divert the more unpleasant emotions. It's about not getting overwhelmed by them. There are just times when I can't stop them."

"I'm sorry you've dealt with this alone."

Her lips parted in surprise, and her heart ached. She hadn't always borne it alone. Her parents always helped her manage. When her mother passed, Brenna had . . .

Brenna's methods had been heavy-handed. Literally. She could feel the slaps on her cheeks still. But the shock of it, and the threat of another slap, was often enough to pull Aislinn out of an impending fit.

As she grew older, she hadn't needed Brenna's intervention. What fits she did have she tried to hide—mostly from her father. He relied on her, and she never wanted to disappoint him or for him to think less of her.

She . . . felt similarly about Hakon. She didn't want to seem lesser to him because of this.

"I manage," was all she could think to say.

He nodded slowly, his expression contemplative. She didn't know if he realized, but he ran a finger over his right ear.

"Thank you for caring for me." She couldn't quite hold his gaze as she said it, her blush too sudden and warm. "It's nice to not be alone."

"I'll always care for you, *vinya*."

*What if . . . what if he . . .*

Everything about him spoke of his earnestness, if shyness. His shoulders were stiff, his hands clenching nervously, but he held her gaze, never wavering.

She wanted to ask—she wanted to be right about someone.

*What if he feels it, too?*

Change was certainly frightening, but at least, for once, this time, the change would be one of her own choosing.

*And he'll be worth it. I know he will.*

Shoring up her courage, Aislinn leaned forward into his space. He watched her come, eyes tracking her and not closing even when her lips brushed against his.

Her breath left her in a happy sigh, and she moved a little closer, deepening the kiss. Her lips teased over his, which held still—not rejecting but not welcoming, either.

Pulling back a breath, she whispered, "Is this all right?"

From one moment to the next, something overcame him. That shock burned away by something heavier, more intense. He suddenly looked as if he wanted to lay her down in the grass and gobble her up.

Heat pooled between her thighs at the thought.

His big hand cupped her face, and his fingers dug into her hair, keeping her in place. She savored the little tug at her scalp, rocking forward. Their lips brushed again, and she felt his words when he said, "Yes, *vinya, yes.* Just show me how."

*Orcs don't kiss.*

The thought flitted across her mind but was gone again the moment his mouth took hers.

Enthusiastic and fervent, his lips followed hers, learning how to move and suck and nibble. She lost herself to the soft press of their mouths, a scintillating dance. She gasped when she ran her tongue along his bottom lip and he opened for her, allowing her to trace the wicked points of his small tusks. She loved that they only appeared when he talked or smiled, yet she saw them often.

He was a quick study—she knew he would be. He was brilliant whenever he turned his attention to something, and to be what he focused on took her breath away.

His mouth moved in caressing strokes and presses and nips over hers, and his hands, oh, his hands. They ran up and down her back and carded through her hair. They pulled her into that wide chest, which thrummed with something like a purr deep beneath his ribs.

Aislinn nearly purred herself and arched like a cat at the way his calluses rasped against her scalp and skin. A little moan of pleasure escaped her lips, and he swallowed the sound, an answering rumble emanating from his throat.

She spread her fingers over his chest, feeling that rumble and how his heart hammered there. His skin was so warm, she wanted to curl up and lay in the sun all afternoon beside him.

"Aislinn," he whispered, and her whole body clenched with desire. Not *my lady* or *heiress,* her name. Just her name. She loved the sound of it on his lips.

Happiness expanded inside her until she felt like she could float away, out into the sunshine and high above all her worries. Those big hands kept her grounded and tethered to him, though, exactly where she wanted to be.

She didn't know how long they laid in the shade of the tree, indulging in kisses and slow caresses. Aislinn claimed it all greedily, soaking up the comfort and pleasure.

*He feels it, too!*

It wasn't until the dinner bell sounded that she realized the sunlight had long since waned and the air had grown chilly. The sound of the bell pulled her back into herself, and she couldn't help her blush.

Hakon's head fell back against the tree, his gaze heavy-lidded as he watched her. Aislinn's heart fluttered in her chest to be the recipient of such a look, her lips aching for more of his kisses. Yet she . . .

"You must go," he said.

"Yes." She didn't move from her spot between his legs, though, reluctant to leave the little dream they lived in that moment.

What if she left and it disappeared? She didn't think she could bear it.

"Hakon, I . . ." What did she say? How could she make him understand?

He lifted a lock of her hair and pushed it behind her ear.

"Find me when you can, *vinya*." He leaned in and claimed another kiss. "I'll be waiting."

She flushed, a smile drawing across her lips. "Nothing will keep me away," she promised. Swooping in for her own final kiss, she pushed herself to standing.

Allowing herself a moment to admire the view of him, sprawled against the tree, Aislinn blew him a kiss and then made herself retreat from the garden.

Her heart was full to bursting from everything that happened within the rosebushes, it burned away the lingering exhaustion from her fit. She nearly ran through the castle, so giddy and excited and—everything. She was *everything*.

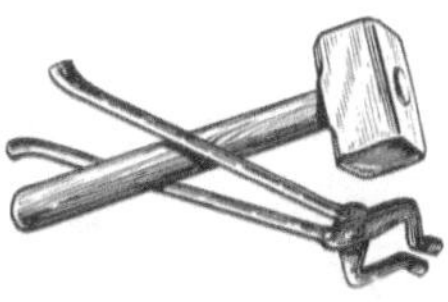

Hakon drew in a long breath and settled back against the tree, still stunned. All the promises he'd made himself, all the time he'd spent resisting his desires and . . . *her.*

In a matter of moments, everything had changed.

He couldn't help himself—like running down a steep slope, he careened into his obsession with her, heedless of the danger and unable to stop. All for a very simple reason—she was everything to him.

*Mate,* roared his beast.

He wanted her for his mate, needed it with a sharpness that blurred everything else.

The mate-bond was already forming—had been since the first time she walked into his forge. Every day brought him closer to her, every day proved she was the one for him. Her brilliance, her kindness, her spirit of iron, all of it drew him inexorably to her.

Her kiss lingered on his lips as night fell around the garden, and Hakon was loath to move for fear of losing it. He held hope, so much hope, inside him, and he was determined that it wasn't to be the last of her kisses he claimed.

He needed a plan.

His old one meant nothing now. Things had changed.

*She feels it, too.*

That's all he needed to know.

What mattered now were just two things—firstly, that she was his mate. The one his beast and his soul cried out for. He'd long since known she was everything he could ever want in a woman. It wasn't fair to himself or to anyone else to try finding it in another when all he wanted was her.

He also wouldn't let the little fact that he was a halfling blacksmith stop him from claiming her.

For the second thing that mattered was this: the life of heiress and eventually Liege Darrow could bring her only misery.

Seeing her like that, crumpled in the grass and beating at her breast as she wailed, nearly broke him. *Nothing* should be allowed to make her feel so low, so broken. Hakon wouldn't stand for it any longer.

He would fill her life with only goodness and pleasure. He would make her happy, give her a life that would make her smile. She deserved nothing less.

He'd build her whatever life she wanted on that land—free of duties and tears.

What had to be done, then?

He had to convince her. Woo her. Pursue her as he'd forbidden himself from before.

Hakon would show her what a mate he could be. He'd claim her in every way he could, support her and please her and encourage any affection she already had for him. He'd spend his days proving himself to her, that the life they could build would be so much better than her life as Liege Darrow.

And then, with a little luck, she would choose him over being heiress.

Just as his mother had chosen his father. Just as his grandfather had followed his grandmother. Hakon's mate would choose him.

He'd accept nothing less.

# 16

The wedding was as beautiful as she'd hoped and sweet enough to cause a toothache. Aislinn arrived early in the day on her chaise to help with Sorcha's preparations, her father following with their small retinue a few hours later.

Sorcha was all nervous chatter, her fingers finding different ways to fidget as Aislinn braided her hair with flowers and her sisters twirled in their dresses and her mother shoved biscuits and tea down her throat.

"It won't do to faint from hunger," Aoife reminded her daughter sagely.

Men were barred from the house, although more than one of Sorcha's brothers attempted to sneak inside to see her. Aislinn intercepted each one and sent them away.

"Not a chance," she told Niall, wagging a finger under his nose, "we know you're doing reconnaissance."

"Have you seen the size of the groom? You try telling him no!"

"Try harder," Aislinn laughed as she shut the door in Niall's face.

In truth, it pleased her to know Orek was so anxious to behold his bride. It had her thinking of her own halfling.

Perhaps some of her joy and giddiness wasn't just for her friend's wedding.

She hadn't found a moment to speak to Hakon since the garden, duties and preparations consuming all her time and sending her to bed downright exhausted. Still, the chance, the promise of something more, of something *coming,* had her aflame with excitement and expectation.

Tonight was the night. Something would happen, she was sure of it.

Weddings were times of promise, of change, of celebration. Aislinn was determined to claim a little bit of it for herself.

For now, though, her focus was her dearest friend.

Sorcha was the most beautiful bride, and when the afternoon waned and she emerged from the house, she was the picture of a woodland goddess come to bless them. Prettier than a storybook princess, she seemed to glide across the grass to her groom, and all held their breath, in awe of her.

Aislinn's cheeks hurt from smiling so wide, and her eyes leaked happy tears as the couple exchanged vows and made their promises to each other, her father tying a red ribbon around their joined hands to seal it. The ceremony drew tears from nearly everyone, even some of the harpies and manticores.

When Orek bowed his head to take Sorcha in a passionate kiss, declaring them husband and wife, a loud cheer rang out from the large crowd gathered, then a laugh as the kiss went on a little longer than necessary.

Over Orek's broad shoulder, Aislinn spied Hakon, cheering and clapping with the other halflings. His grin went lopsided when their eyes met, and Aislinn flushed from her head to her toes.

*Find me when you can,* vinya, he'd said. And oh, she meant to.

Tonight.


Although a chilly evening soon crept across the Brádaigh estate, the crackling bonfires kept the celebration lit and warm well into the night. Aoife and Sofie presented the feast that'd taken days to prepare, and over one-hundred guests ate and drank their fill.

As mead and wine flowed, a group of musicians struck up, and revelers crowded around the central fire to dance.

With a belly full of mead and Aoife's fine cooking, Aislinn wove through the dancers until she found Sorcha and pulled her into the dancing.

Her friend glowed with happiness, and as they skipped and twirled barefoot around the fire to the music, they giggled like the little girls they'd once been. Tonight, they were both just as full of hopes and dreams as they'd been as girls, tomorrow brimming with promise. Nothing seemed forbidden or out of reach in the firelight, and the beat of the music and dancing filled Aislinn with an effervescent hope of things to come.

Aislinn laughed until her sides hurt, her mind wonderfully quiet.

The flowers in Sorcha's hair shed petals as they danced and filled the air with a sweet fragrance. The joy for her friend, the happiness Sorcha exuded, was unstoppable, uncontrollable. It was as if everyone there felt it too, the singing loud and joyous, hope and goodwill for the new couple overflowing faster than the wine.

When the song ended, Sorcha threw her arms around Aislinn and hugged her tight. She returned the embrace, pressing a kiss to her friend's cheek.

While she was still monstrously jealous of her friend's new life, seeing how Sorcha had made her own way gave Aislinn a little more courage. They weren't the same, and neither were their situations, but tonight, nothing felt impossible.

"You deserve every happiness," Aislinn whispered to her friend.

Sorcha squeezed her tight before releasing her. "So do you. You'll tell me if there's anything I can do to make it happen?"

"Of course." She pinched Sorcha's arm and turned her around back into the celebration. "But not tonight. Tonight is your night!"

Sorcha threw her arms up, more petals falling from her wild curls, and then she was pulled away into another dance by her sisters.

Aislinn watched on as she caught her breath. It was a good excuse to . . .

*There he is.*

Weaving through the throng of people, Aislinn smiled and nodded where she needed but didn't let herself be snared into conversation. Instead, she walked with purpose around the bonfire to where Hakon stood, watching the dancing.

Heart pounding, Aislinn came to stand alongside him. "Beautiful, isn't it?"

"Indeed. They are well suited." Hakon grinned fondly. "To be honest, I'm glad the ceremony at least is over. Orek was nervous all morning."

"He'd no reason to be. Although, I take it as a good sign."

"A groom should be nervous?"

"At least a little, I think."

"That his bride won't appear?"

"That he might faint when he sees that his bride is more beautiful than he ever dreamed."

Hakon rumbled in thought. "That's certainly a possibility." The lopsided grin he gave her had her stomach flipping with anxious delight.

Clearing her throat, Aislinn pulled in a breath and all her courage.

The music, the dancing, the mead—it all helped. Mead was her preferred drink; she enjoyed the taste and she'd experimented over the years to know exactly what specific amounts did to her. At two goblets, she wasn't drunk, merely brave—and a little tingly. The perfect state to open her mouth and ask—

"Do you dance?"

Hakon's heavy brows rose, and he glanced at the revelers dancing merrily around the bonfire.

"I don't know your human dances," he admitted, his grin falling.

Aislinn smiled through her sudden anxiety. "It's all right! We can stand and talk."

Hakon grimaced, looking around for a moment before raising a finger. "Stay right here," he told her, before disappearing into the crowd.

She blinked after him, not sure how to interpret that. Not dancing with him and now not in his company, either. Not how she'd envisioned this.

Her brows sank into a confused frown, and the pleasant tingling in her lips and fingers began to fade.

*Fates, now what do I do?*

Certainly not chase after him through the crowd. Too conspicuous. Dancing together might be too, but it was a night of revelry and possibilities. There was a good chance some might not even remember after a night of celebration and drinking. The perfect opportunity to feel her halfling move and have him all to herself.

"My lady."

Aislinn startled, looking up into the fathomless gaze of Allarion.

"Forgive me," he was quick to say as Aislinn rubbed at where her heart pounded.

She dismissed his concerns with a wave, and then stood in shock at the sight of the mysterious fae. Gone was his long cloak. He was still covered from neck to toe in a fine black doublet that fit tightly to his muscular chest and dark trou tucked at the knee into black leather boots—but all his limbs were visible, and his long fall of hair had been tied back. Those pointed ears jutted back from his head, the many hoops and studs glittering in the firelight.

He almost looked . . . casual without the cloak.

A small smile touched his lips, sending Aislinn reeling in shock.

"It is a fine night. They give me much hope."

Aislinn watched Allarion look out into the crowd, his gaze finding Orek and Sorcha across the courtyard, speaking to each other in low tones with warm, loving smiles on their faces.

"It's wonderful," Aislinn agreed. "Oh!"

Snapping her fingers, she dug through her pocket to produce the folded but signed and official deed.

"I believe this is yours," she said, presenting him with the papers. "As is Scarborough estate."

Eyes crinkling at the edges, Allarion gently took the deed, running his fingers over the parchment. "I thank you, Lady Aislinn. You cannot understand how much this means to a fae like me."

There was a wealth of questions Aislinn wanted to ask him then—but the fae and his inscrutable smile were saved by the heavy beat of a drum.

Aislinn turned back to the bonfire to behold dancers clearing the way for all the orcs to converge in a great circle around the fire. About a half-dozen halflings, including Hakon and Orek, joined the ten or so orcs from Orek's old clan who'd come for the wedding. They stood tall and silent around the crackling fire as the drumbeat grew louder and faster, and the crowd held its breath, waiting.

One of the older orcs let out a long shout, and then the others joined in, declaring something in orcish. The drum picked up pace, and as one, the orcs began to move. They whooped and yelled, their tusks flashing and the golden loops that decorated their green ears sparkling in the light.

Muscles bulged as their great bodies danced, their feet stomping the ground to create a rhythm that harmonized with the drumbeat. They clapped and hummed, dropping down before bouncing up, legs kicking. They jumped through the air, far more graceful than their size implied, spinning and pounding the ground again with feet and fists.

They circled the fire as a unit, undulating like an encroaching wave about to crash against the shore. Aislinn's pulse beat hard at her throat and between her legs, the powerful sight of their big bodies lurching and spinning inciting a deep, hot lust. She put a hand to her cheek to feel how it burned.

She couldn't tear her gaze away from Hakon, how he moved his body through the maneuvers. It was something like a dance and the exercises she saw the knights doing, everything demanding strength and discipline and poise. It was somehow both brutal and elegant, and her lips parted to watch how his arms bulged and his chest expanded with every heaving breath as he moved with his fellow orcs.

"It's one of their mating dances," said Allarion.

"O-oh?" she stuttered, having entirely forgotten the fae was there.

"Often done during celebrations, I believe. To impress potential partners."

"It's certainly impressive." She hoped she didn't sound as breathless with lust to Allarion as she did to her own ears.

She wasn't the only one watching on with awe and longing, the crowd nearly silent as they beheld the show of strength. From somewhere near the house, someone began to clap along with the drumbeat, and then everyone was, whooping and cheering with every impressive move.

Their dance gained momentum, the drumbeat like a heart, pounding and pumping as the bonfire cast shadows across the orcs' powerful forms. More than once, Aislinn found herself holding her breath, hungry to see what happened next as well as desperate for it to end and Hakon to return to her.

When it finally did end, with a roar of triumph from the orcs and matching applause from the crowd, Aislinn's body burned.

The orcs were soon subsumed back into the crowd, many hurrying to speak with and admire them. Aislinn watched as Hakon wove his way back toward her, not stopping for anyone.

"I will leave you," Allarion said, perhaps a note of amusement in his voice. "Good evening, my lady."

She thought she bid him goodnight, but all she really knew was that her lips were parted when Hakon finally did come to stand before her.

His big chest rose and fell, a few trickles of sweat along his temples catching the firelight. Those deep brown eyes seemed to burn brighter than the bonfire—a match to Aislinn's own desire.

She couldn't bring herself to say anything, longing holding her throat tight.

Hakon said nothing, either. Just moved to stand alongside her again.

The celebration resumed around them, full of familiar noises and sights. She could have resumed their friendship in that moment, too. Let things slip back to the way they were.

It may have been the safer, wiser thing to do, but it wasn't what she wanted.

And so . . .

She slid her hand into his, pulse fluttering at her throat to feel how large his palm was against hers. With a little tug on his hand, she said softly, "Come with me?"

He turned his face to hers, his expression full of hunger.

"Anywhere."

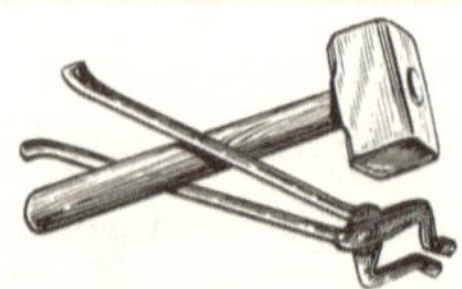

Hakon's body burned even as they passed from the light of the bonfire into the cool, murky shadows of the estate's outer buildings. Other figures moved in purple blurs out in the darkness, but Hakon paid them no heed.

He let Aislinn lead him into the darkness, enthralled by the hypnotic sway of her hips. He'd seen her in finery before, but there was something about this dress—a deep, flushing pink that nearly matched her cheeks when she blushed—that had his blood running hot ever since he spied her in the early afternoon.

Fates, he'd been so envious of Orek all day. The male fretted over nothing, there was no question that his bride would emerge at the appointed time. Still, his anxiousness to see his mate and officially begin their new life in the eyes of the humans was endearing.

Hakon's own anxiousness was sharper. Ever since that afternoon in the garden, he'd been filled with nothing but agonizing hopes that sank their fangs into him and wouldn't let go.

His beast was insufferable; even now, as he held her hand and followed her into the soft darkness, the infernal thing wouldn't be silent. Anticipation held his heart in a tight fist, and he could barely breathe beyond it.

The darkness wasn't too thick, and his orcish eyes had no problem seeing that she led them to the far side of the stables. She found her way without error, and under a tree, after a moment of waiting to hear if anyone was nearby, she turned to face him.

Hakon wondered if she could hear his heart beating thunderously, for to his ears it was louder than the drums had been.

Her small hand came to rest on his chest as she stepped forward into the curve of his body, and he leaned down to meet her. Her scent filled his nose, a sweet mix of roses and honey and . . . mead.

He looked at her eyes, but of course the pupils were blown wide in the dark.

A little tug on his tunic brought his attention back to her.

"Kiss me," she whispered, breath honey-sweet from mead.

"Because you're jealous of your friend getting married?" He didn't care, not truly, not after the garden, but he still needed to know. He was playing this game to win.

"Because I want you to kiss me."

A rumbling purr rattled to life in his chest, and he dipped his head even lower. She got on her toes to meet him, and although the angle put a crick in his neck, it was one of the best moments of Hakon's life.

Their lips met in shy reunion, tentative and soft. He tasted the mead on her lips, yes, but also *her*.

His beast needed nothing else.

Straightening to his full height, out of her reach, his gaze devoured her.

She pouted up at him, misunderstanding why he pulled away.

Then, she gasped in delight when he bent to pick her up and carry her.

"Fine," she sighed into his neck, pressing a kiss there that made him shudder with need, "I'm a little jealous of her getting wedded. But more so that she's getting bedded."

Hakon's groan was long and with feeling. He hustled her to the far side of the stable, where great bales of hay were stacked neatly. He lifted her onto one pile before climbing up on the one below it. Sitting like that, tucked away in the hay, they were nearly the same height.

Her smile was wide and full of joy, drawing him back into her glow. Her hands sought his face, cupping his jaw to pull him nearer. He rested his arms on the hay around her, the fine fabric of her gown teasing his skin.

"Are you not a little jealous that they get to make love all night?" she whispered against his lips.

"Intensely," he said. "But if it was me, with my beautiful mate, it wouldn't be a night of making love."

"No?" She carded her fingers through his hair, her soft gaze watching her work. "What then?"

"Nothing but rutting."

He filled his hand with her waist, feeling her warmth and how her breathing stuttered at his words. Those plush lips parted, and he couldn't resist any longer. He swooped in and claimed them, savoring her taste.

Gone was the shyness of before. He devoured her, claiming and tasting and gorging himself. She gasped against his lips, her nails scraping against his scalp.

His cock kicked in his trou, overeager for her, but—*Not yet. Not yet.*

He had wooing to do first.

Pulling her closer across her bale, Hakon drowned in her taste and feel and scent. She was everything he'd wanted for so long, he hardly believed he held her, warm and enthusiastic, in his arms. She squirmed and pressed against him, her hands exploring the length of his neck and width of his shoulders.

He lived for the little noises she made deep in her throat, wanted to swallow them down with her taste and hold onto them forever. He chased every one, needing another, greedy for all she could give him.

The night around them was cool and purple-tinged, almost like a dream. It was a dream to him, and he prayed to the old gods he'd never wake.

Her blunt teeth caught his lower lip and tugged, inciting a growl of lust. He answered by running his hand up her waist to her breast, daring to tease his fingers across the neckline of her gown and then down, finding the needy point of her nipple through the fabric.

She gasped against his mouth, a decadent moan escaping her lips. He kissed her chin, her jaw, down her neck. Aislinn exposed her throat to him, and he lavished her with his tongue for the show of trust. He kissed and sucked at her pulse, feeling how it throbbed under his lips, before straying lower.

Her fingers clutched at his shoulders as his lips skimmed across the petal-soft tops of her breasts. He knew they'd be a perfect handful and watched as his green thumb teased at the embroidered, plunging neck of her gown. It was delicious and wicked to see the contrast of their skin, how the night rendered him nearly as dark as the forest while her peachy skin almost glowed in the moonlight.

*Fates, she's so beautiful it hurts.*

Her hand came to rest over his, pressing it to her breast. She moved again in that needy way of hers, and he felt her groan of desire against his head, where she pressed kisses to his temple.

Unable to resist, Hakon sank his face into those plush breasts, taking a long draw of her scent. It was heavier here, thicker, and she tasted of warm woman and salt from the dancing. He rained kisses and nips to the tops of her breasts, plumping them for his attention with their joined hands.

"Hakon," she gasped, raking her nails down his neck.

His purr grew almost violent, shaking his chest and hers. He held the whole world in his hand, and he wouldn't be foolish enough to let it go. She was everything to him, the axis around which his world spun, his guiding star.

He hadn't been able to explain to Siggy why he wanted to leave Kaldebrak for the human lands. He hadn't truly known himself.

*It was for her. I came for her.*

That was so perfectly clear to him now, even in his thick haze of lust.

He teased a finger into her gown to draw it down, and his greedy mouth was ready when her nipple popped free of the bodice. Aislinn clutched him to her as he filled his mouth with her, lashing her with his tongue and pulling on her tender flesh in deep, long pulls.

"Aislinn, *vinya*," he murmured against her skin. *Rose,* he called her. His rose, vibrant and sweet.

"Hakon," she whispered back, her hand straying down from his chest to his belt.

"Oh!" Another voice punched through the quiet night, and someone giggled drunkenly below them. "This is taken."

Two sets of footsteps staggered away, and while Hakon logically knew the most anyone could see from below was their legs, not who they were attached to, his hunger cooled and hardened like iron to know they'd gotten so close without him noticing.

No one was allowed near his mate while he pleasured her. Her pleasure, her noises, were for him alone.

He could hear her heartbeat quickening at her breast, and her touch was less lustful and more frantic as she tried to pull him back into their lovemaking.

She moaned in unhappiness when he pulled away and righted her bodice.

"Hakon." She moved quicker than his addled mind was ready for, capturing a kiss and resting her hands over his, trying to pull him back to her. "Make love to me. *Rut me.*"

It was his turn to moan, and he hung his head. It would be so easy to give in, and as she pressed her body to his and kisses into his skin, he wanted to. Oh, gods, how he wanted to.

But he still smelled the mead on her breath. And the tang of horse from the stable.

*Not like this,* he told himself—and more importantly his beast. *Not like this. She deserves much better.*

If he was to show her all that he could be for her, he could and would do better when he made love to her for the first time.

"I will, Aislinn. Fates, I want to." He let his mouth fall to hers, taking one last taste of her. "But only when your head is clear and you're sure it's what you want."

A frown gathered at her brow. "Hakon . . ."

"You must be sure, *vinya,* for there will be no going back. Once I have you, you'll be mine, do you understand?" He skimmed his lips across her brow, the whisper of a kiss, a promise of much more. "You'll ruin me for any other, and I intend to do the same for you. So you must be sure."

She blinked at him in astonishment, and he took the chance to retreat. Sliding to the ground, he helped her down. Aislinn looked up at him in bewildered silence, allowing him to take her hand and lead her back to the celebration.

His beast thrashed inside him. *Fool!* it roared. *Don't let her get away! Take her, claim her! She wants you to!*

Fates, yes. The thought kept him incandescent. She wanted him— but when she came to him, it had to be with a clear head. He'd accept nothing less of her than everything, and while he risked never having his chance again by denying her now, he couldn't risk that she would regret tonight and turn away later.

*Smart, we have to be smart,* he told the beast—and his angry cock.

The confusion was plain on her face when he turned to her on the fringes of the firelight. Lifting her hand, he placed a kiss just above her knuckles.

"I'll be waiting, *vinya*," he whispered before making himself turn away.

If he stayed a moment longer, he'd forget himself and his plans and take her right back to that hay pile.

Hakon gritted his tusks against his gums and put on speed, hurrying around the center of the estate and keeping to the low light on the outskirts of the dwindling celebration. Music still played and people still danced and ate and sang, but others had moved to smaller groups or disappeared entirely—including the bride and groom.

His pace was unforgiving as he strode across the estate. He recognized someone calling his name, Varon and a group of fellow half-orcs gathered round a smaller fire and drinking, but he ignored it. The blood in his veins burned too hot to stop.

Soon, he left behind the celebration and the light, finding his way by the moon. He didn't stop until rocks and water scraped and sloshed beneath his boots.

Baring his tusks at the night, Hakon pulled off his boots and flung them back onto dry land. His nicest jerkin and tunic went next, then his best trou. Naked, he walked into the lake near the manor house, the chilly water sending gooseflesh up his legs.

He hardly felt it past the burning ache in his blood.

Hakon wrapped a fist around the angry cock bobbing between his legs and pumped. He hissed with hunger and desperation.

Was he a fool for stopping? Had he missed his only chance?

Only time would tell.

Hakon had been patient already. He could be again now.

But fates, he didn't want patience. He wanted Aislinn. He wanted his mate.

His hand slid up and down his throbbing shaft, collecting slick that leaked from the tip. Spend dribbled into the lake, and the water lapped at his legs as he worked himself mercilessly. The memories of her softness under his lips and hands were a stark counterpoint to his roughness, and he wished with everything inside him that it was her he thrust into, not his own hand.

*Soon,* he promised himself.

More than a promise—a vow.

*Soon, soon, soon.*

His hips thrust to the rhythm of that promise, and with one last brutal pump, Hakon released into the lake, his lips pulled back in a snarl.

He heaved as the desire poured from him, and before he'd even finished, he threw himself into the lake headfirst. The cold water rushed past him, shocking his body and bringing a measure of relief.

Without it, he was liable to storm back through camp and, in front of everyone, throw Aislinn over his shoulder to find somewhere quiet and sequestered in the old way.

*Soon.*

Aislinn wandered the outskirts of the celebration for a while, mind turning over all that'd happened. Or *not* happened, as it were.

The noises of the revelry didn't register as she pondered what Hakon said—and rued that the mead she'd drunk sabotaged her chance at laying with her blacksmith that night.

*Be sure,* he'd said.

*I am sure!* What about letting him expose and lick her breast made him think she wasn't?

Honestly, men were impossible.

"Milady?"

Aislinn looked up, startled at the sound of Fia's voice. Her maid stood only a few feet away, looking concerned.

"Men are impossible," she blurted.

Fia's concern faded into an amused grin. "That they are, milady.

Sometimes wholly insufferable. But there are a few good ones yet."

"Even those are impossible sometimes."

"Certainly." Fia looked her over, no doubt noting how her dress was slightly askew. Aislinn could only hope no hay was sticking from her hair.

"Are you all right, milady?"

"Yes," she sighed. "Just tired. I think I'm turning in."

"Your bed is ready for you. Shall I—?"

Aislinn waved her back toward the revelry. "No, no. I can manage. Enjoy your night." *Someone deserves to.*

Fia made a few noises of protest, but Aislinn ultimately entered the dark, quiet tent alone. Her father hadn't retired yet and none of their attendants had returned. No matter, Aislinn had practice in getting herself out of gowns.

With her stays loosened just enough, she was able to slip out of her gown, then collapsed into her cot in just her chemise.

Rolling onto her back, Aislinn stared at the tent ceiling, grumpy and forlorn and trying not to despair.

Her fingers made idle circles around her right breast, and she swore it was warmer than the other, the memory of his mouth still burned into her skin.

She shifted in the blankets, overwarm, with unfulfilled desire scratching under her skin. She was in no mood to bring herself pleasure in a camp tent when her father could walk in at any time, though.

No, she was in the mood to have a certain halfling blacksmith satisfy her lust.

*Fates, what if he decided he doesn't want me after all?*

Was that why he'd stopped and brought her back?

*Be sure.*

She *was* sure. Sure she wanted him.

But as the night deepened and she turned the words over in her mind, she began to think that perhaps he meant more than just sex.

Aislinn knew whatever was between them was about more than

just physical desire. She counted Hakon as her friend, and in truth, that was most important to her. That she wanted to feel his hands and tongue touch her *everywhere* was just an added boon.

She didn't know where this could lead. Likely only to heartache.

Aislinn wasn't like Sorcha. Her life wasn't her own, inextricably tied to the Darrowlands. Her life wasn't hers to give.

But her heart, her body, those she could give. She so wished to give both to him.

*If only he'd take them, hay or not,* she grumbled to herself.

Fates, what did she do now? How did she make him understand?

She feared it meant being brave once again. The night truly had brought change and promise, but Aislinn feared what the morning would bring. Could she still be brave in the light of day, at home in Dundúran, and take what she wanted?

Aislinn didn't know.

Whatever she did, though, it'd be without the help of mead.

# 17

*I'm a fool.*

That was the only thing Hakon could think beyond the mire of despair that weighed him down in the ensuing days. He hardly saw Aislinn as she and the castle staff prepared and bid farewell to Lord Merrick when he left with Sir Ciaran. Hakon himself was up late into the night to ensure all the parties' horses were properly shoed and every metal piece of all the supplies was shining and strong.

He'd held hope that with her father gone, Aislinn might find time to slip away, but in the glimpses he stole of her, she was always busy, her nose buried in papers or listening to three people at once. He wished he could walk up to her and smooth away the line of consternation between her brows, but without her encouragement, he didn't know where he stood.

Hakon hammered his frustrations into horseshoes and breastplates and anything else that needed a beating. Mercifully, Fearghas seemed to recognize another of his dark moods and left him alone rather than picking at the wound. It was a mercy Hakon didn't appreciate, instead frothing for a fight—anything to distract him from the hours that staggered by without her.

*I've ruined it. She thinks I've rejected her and won't return.*

The doubts clawed at him, their tenor louder than the hammer even as he struck the molten iron with all his might.

Just when he'd committed to his plans, to her, he went and ruined everything. What could he do? How could he woo her back?

Hakon spent any of his free time trying to shape gifts from iron and wood, working his fingers to beyond pain, but could finish nothing. None of the gifts were good enough nor expressed his devotion. How could he make iron tell her that she was the most perfect creature to walk the earth and he was lucky to even stand in her presence?

Hurling away a useless chunk of wood that'd begun to take the shape of Wülf, Hakon hissed at himself in disgust. The real Wülf trotted over to the discarded wood and began gnawing on it, oblivious or apathetic to Hakon's unhappiness.

Slumping into a seat, Hakon raked his hands through his hair, no doubt spreading soot and grime all over himself. He didn't care. She hadn't come today and it was already early evening; she never came too late, not since the first time.

Another day without her, without knowing.

Fates, how did anyone do this? Being lovesick made it sound almost romantic, poetic. This sinking dread and apathy in all else was nothing of the sort.

He'd no desire to go to the dining hall for dinner—nor even to find some scraps in the kitchen. He wasn't hungry, he could barely sleep. His mind merely kept showing him memories of her, soft and willing on that bale, and how he'd denied her.

Was ever a male so stupid?

He tried reassuring himself that she was busy with her duties. With Lord Merrick gone, full authority over the entire demesne now rested with Aislinn, and it wasn't a responsibility she took lightly. He loved that she was devoted to her land and people—and hated it, too.

*She would be a wonderful Liege Darrow, but she could be happier as my mate. I'll make sure of it.*

That was, if he ever saw her again.

Fates, what if she didn't remember what they'd done, what he'd said. His sore fingers went cold with horror at the thought. He didn't think she'd been too badly affected by the mead—just on the right side of drunk. But then, she was so much smaller than him. Could it be that she didn't remember his profession and promise of more if she came to him?

Hakon opened and closed his hands nervously, not knowing what to do with the realization.

He had to try again. There was nothing else for it and no turning back now.

Nothing was promised in this world, not a mate, not happiness. Hakon knew this well, knew the dangers of the mate-bond and how it consumed all around it. The bond didn't care what it left in its wake as it sought fulfillment.

He couldn't be a mindless beast, lost to his love and desire for her. He had to be smart.

For once, he wanted the mate-bond to do right by him.

Standing so suddenly he startled Wülf, Hakon hurried to collect his bathing sheet and loose linen braies. First, he needed a bath. He wouldn't woo his lady love dirty from the forge.

Second . . . well, he hoped he'd have that figured out by the time he returned from the baths. At least, a better plan than scaling the wall outside her balcony.

Aislinn lay awake late into the night, restless yet again. She hadn't slept well since the wedding, and her exhaustion was beginning to get the better of her. Emotions tumbled like leaves in a gale through her, one quicker than the last, giving her no time to make sense of any of them other than *frustration*.

Grumbling, she rearranged her pillows, wishing her mind would just go quiet long enough to fall asleep. Instead, it ran rampant through everything she needed to do the following day and everything she hadn't accomplished today and whether Connor Brádaigh would have any luck locating Jerrod and if she could ever forgive Brenna and and and—

Whether she had the courage to return to the smithy.

She wanted to. Oh, she wanted to.

Falling into her duties and preparing for her father's departure had been an easy distraction. However, now that he was gone with half their company of knights for the south, work was the only distraction.

And it wasn't the kind she enjoyed.

Aislinn struggled with the realization that she didn't want to distract herself. She didn't want duties. She wanted her blacksmith—and to know if he meant everything he'd said to her at the wedding.

*Fates, I hope he did.*

She'd never hoped for something more.

Aislinn would never go on the adventures Sorcha did with her mate nor get to go to academy like Maeve Brádaigh. She'd never experienced the freedoms even Jerrod did.

She couldn't leave Dundúran, her father, for so long. She couldn't be selfish. At least not in that.

*I want to be selfish about him, though.*

And yet . . .

*What if it's wonderful but then all goes wrong?*

That was a distinct possibility. What future could they really have together, a blacksmith and a noblewoman? Sorcha had the support of her family and neighbors, and even King Marius had granted permission for otherlies to live in the Darrowlands and, feasibly, marry humans. But what would happen if such a marriage came with the promise of an otherly lord consort?

She hardly dared to think it, but could the Darrowlands and Eirea herself accept a half-orc for an heiress's husband? Brenna couldn't be alone in her opinions and prejudices. It was all well and good when the otherlies were in their own camp, making friendly with rural villagers—but what happened when there was a dispute? Sorcha and Orek's wedding was a fine example of harmony, but it was bound to be tested eventually.

Aislinn didn't know any of the answers to these questions—and she hated not knowing.

But did not knowing truly mean it wasn't worth the chance?

*No.*

That simple answer rang in her mind, clear as a tolling bell.

Her breath caught in her throat, and she sat up in her bed.

Not knowing did her no good, only robbed her of the little sleep she managed. If nothing else, even if heartbreak was what it brought her, at least it came with a clearer mind—it would be worth getting rid of some of these emotions crawling just beneath her skin. Better to find out one way or another now and be done with it.

And . . . the chance to be with Hakon, for however long, to whatever end, was worth the risk. Come what may.

Heart racing, Aislinn threw back the coverlet and grabbed up her dressing gown. Her hands shook with excitement and terror as she shoved them through the sleeves and tied the waist.

He would be awake still, she was sure of it. What he would say, would think, she was less sure. But she had to find out.

She'd never get to sleep now—she needed to *know*.

It felt as though she didn't breathe at all as she stole through the castle. With her fingertips on the cool stone of the achingly familiar walls, she made her way down from her chambers, her slippers silent on the flagstones. The castle was quiet in its slumber, only a few of the night's watch on their rounds to break up the darkness.

A handful of torches lit her way, but she hardly needed them. The sky was clear and the moon nearly full, just enough for her.

It wasn't Aislinn's first time creeping through the castle at night. She'd suffered with bouts of insomnia before, as well as with ideas that wouldn't leave her and demanded she return to her study to draft.

However, she'd never stolen from her bed to meet a lover—or potential lover—before. Not even in the height of her ardor with Brenden, when every tender moment they shared was stolen, had she done such a thing. It hadn't even occurred to her.

The illicitness of the act was delicious, and Aislinn's heart beat hard under her breast with the thrill. Just a few more steps, and then she would *know*.

Her hair and the skirts of her dressing gown flowed behind her in her haste. In just a few moments, she was in the bailey and opening the smithy door. In another breath, she was inside, the soft glow of the forge fires filling the space.

And revealing—

Hakon wasn't there.

Neither was Fearghas, which was a relief, but . . .

*Where is he?*

A cold dread sucked at her stomach, and Aislinn pressed her fist against her sternum.

Terror, cold and sharp, lanced her middle and made her lips tremble. What did she do now?

The high whine of a boiling kettle filled her ears, and tears gathered at her lashes. Fates, what did she do now? Even her panic didn't know what to do.

What if—*what if he's*—

"Aislinn?"

# 18

The sound of her name popped her burgeoning panic. Aislinn turned to behold Hakon in the smithy doorway, blinking at her with obvious surprise. His chest was bare, his bath sheet hanging around his neck, and a pair of damp linen braies draped loosely from his hips.

*Fresh from the baths.*

Aislinn's lips parted, her body overwhelmed by a sudden punch of lust so potent, all thought left her.

Wülf knocked the door wider and trotted inside, unaware or uncaring why his master had stopped in the doorway. He loped up to Aislinn and sat, whuffing for a pat.

"Aislinn?" Hakon said again, voice pitched low.

Not *my lady* or *heiress*. She took some hope from that.

"Did you mean what you said?" she blurted, heart thundering against her ribs.

His throat bobbed on a swallow. "About what?"

"About everything."

Aislinn watched in surprise as the uncertainty bled from him, and he somehow stood straighter, his shoulders thrown wide. Already warm, the smithy grew hot as she watched him fully enter then shut the door behind him, sealing them together.

"Yes."

A rumble vibrated through the warm air, and she realized with a gasp that it was him. Purring for her.

In three quick strides, he was across the small distance, his arms going around her to pull her close. Held tight to all that warm, damp chest, Aislinn really had no choice but to press her palms to it and sink her fingers into his flesh.

His hiss of pleasure made her clitoris throb.

"I'm sure," she told him. Not about where this would lead or how it would sustain itself—but him? Absolutely, yes.

That wide chest expanded with breath, as if he'd been waiting to hear those words. "Thank all the gods for that."

Then his lips were on hers and everything was *right*.

Breathing her own sigh of relief, Aislinn sank into his kiss, his body, his warmth. Her fingers found their way into his hair, and she raked her nails across his wet scalp.

That purr hummed against her lips, and when she gasped in delight, his tongue was there, chasing down hers. He sealed their mouths together in a hot rasp, a moan sounding from deep in his throat as he banded his arms around her back and lifted her off her feet.

Toes dangling, Aislinn kissed her blacksmith for all she was worth.

*Fates, what an answer.* It wasn't quite what she'd been expecting, but whatever other doubts or concerns she had, they were drowned in the uncompromising tide of her hunger for him. It didn't matter what tomorrow brought—so long as the promises of that night were fulfilled, Aislinn would be satisfied.

So, so satisfied.

"Fates, you feel too good," he murmured against her lips.

"You promise you won't stop this time?"

Another rumble, and to her horror, Aislinn was set back on her feet. She clutched at the bath sheet still around his neck, refusing to let him get far.

"Only if you tell me to," he said, a fascinating little grin teasing at his lips. He pressed that grin into her mouth in a kiss before telling her, "Stay right here."

Aislinn stayed, more so out of bafflement than because she was told to. She watched as Hakon closed up the smithy for the night, shuttering the windows, banking the fires, and closing the metal forge doors, leaving only a small vent at the top of each open for ventilation.

Finally, he returned to take her hand and lead her deeper into the smithy, up a set of three steps, to a door at the rear she'd never been through. Together they entered a dark chamber, cooler than the smithy but not cold.

Not letting go of her hand, Hakon used his other to light and turn up a lantern hung on a peg near the door. Soft illumination fell across his bedchamber.

It was a small but cozy room, with a narrow window looking out into the bailey. No hearth, but this part of the castle was kept warm from the smithy with purposefully designed ducts and chimneys. A wide bed took up most of the space, with a finely carved trunk at its foot. A small table with washbasin and bathing sheets sat in one corner, a well-worn chair with whittling tools in the other.

It was humble. Practical. Best of all, it smelled of him, a rich scent of male and iron and soap.

Muttering in orcish, Hakon backed Wülf up when he would have followed them in, shutting the door with him still in the smithy and Aislinn and Hakon in the bedchamber. Alone.

A distinctly canine huff and groan echoed from the other side of the door, followed by the sound of a big hairy body trudging back down the steps.

Aislinn grinned in amusement, but she couldn't hold it for long. Drawn further into his room, her pulse fluttered in her throat with anticipation.

The bed was neatly made and laden with blankets, pillows, and furs. For all that he worked with fire and hammer, it seemed he enjoyed soft things, too. She dared to reach out and run a hand over one of the furs at the foot of the bed. Had he brought it all the way from Kaldebrak?

He came up behind her, warmth radiating from his bare chest and raising the hairs at the back of her neck. A big hand slid around her waist to pull her into the rigid line of his body.

Tipping up her chin with a knuckle, he captured her gaze with his serious expression.

"This goes however you want it to, *vinya*. I'm yours, tonight and all nights hereafter. But if you come to my bed, it's as Aislinn. Just Aislinn. And I am just Hakon."

Fingers trembling ever so slightly, she reached up to cup his face. When he leaned into her touch and turned his face to kiss her palm, she couldn't help but smile.

"That's all I want," she assured him.

Just her, just him. Nothing could be better.

His own smile spread across his face, revealing that dimple in his cheek, and desire curled low in her belly to see it. He was entirely too handsome looking at her like that, the longer hair at the crown of his head falling to his brow, those sooty lashes drawn low over his hungry eyes.

"For now," he said. When she frowned in confusion, he lowered his mouth to hers but didn't quite kiss her. Instead, he ensured she not only heard but felt and tasted his next words, too. "Soon, you will understand you can ask more, much more of me. Anything at all, *vinya*, and you shall have it."

His promise sank inside her with a terrifying joy. She didn't think she truly understood or grasped his promise, not yet, but to have it at all fed the vulnerable, doubting parts of her. Under his piercing gaze, none of her was able to hide; he saw all and didn't look away.

"I want you," she murmured against his lips. When he would have kissed her, though, she gave him a gentle push backward. "And I want to see you."

Hakon straightened, looking down at her with such desire she thought she might combust. Nodding once, he positioned himself in the center of the room, his bare feet spread, and hands held loosely at his sides.

Swallowing her fears, Aislinn followed him, pulling the bath sheet from his neck and hanging it on a spare peg to dry. Bare and still slightly damp from the baths, his skin almost glowed in the soft lantern light. Two flat nipples were a darker green than the rest of his skin, and shadows danced along the heavy slabs of muscle that formed his chest.

A smattering of hair trailed down the center of him, following the valley between his pectorals and bisecting his abdomen. It disappeared under the waistband of his loose braies, which hung low on his hips and left little to the imagination.

Catching her bottom lip between her teeth, Aislinn touched her fingertips to that glorious chest. She watched in delight as gooseflesh followed in her wake as she traced over his thick waist, and his pulse visibly drummed at his throat. He hadn't the lean, defined abdomen she'd seen in some men like Sir Alaisdair. Hakon was instead wide and heavily built, slabs of muscle on his sides from wielding hammers and iron.

He held perfectly still for her, save for his eyes, which tracked her as she skated her fingers across every bit of flesh she could reach.

It never ceased to amaze her what a joy he was to touch. Softer than she expected, and smoother, it was almost like touching the finest leather, and yet better. The way his flesh shivered or jumped under her fingers was more than flattering, and by the time she'd circled around to his back, her blush was deep and her grin of pleasure wide.

It was Aislinn's turn to shiver with gooseflesh at the sight of his broad, strong back. He was nothing but muscle, two winging shoulder blades making great swooping shadows. She followed the line of his spine, in a valley between the thick clusters of muscles spread across his ribs and hips.

Her fingers strayed into the dimples winking at her from just above his buttocks, and she couldn't help slipping one below the waistband of his braies. It took little effort to slide the damp linen over the rounded swells of his backside, and within one breathless moment, the braies pooled at his ankles on the floor and he was absolutely, gloriously naked.

Pulse beating a cacophony in her ear, Aislinn slid her fingers over the firmness of one buttock before trailing them over his flank and hip and finally rounded his other side to—

*Oh, bless his parents and every ancestor.*

His large cock stood proud against his lower belly. The thick shaft sprung from a thatch of hair, with heavy bollocks tucked between his thighs. Green, with a large vein snaking up the underside, his cock looked like a handful even for him, the cockhead flared and almost angry looking, already leaking pearlescent spend. He was familiarly shaped but certainly unfamiliarly sized.

A dash of trepidation only sweetened her curiosity and hunger as she let her fingers trail down, down, down—

She gasped to feel the heat of him on her hand, but it was drowned out by his hiss.

One big hand grasped hers, stopping her exploration.

Aislinn couldn't help pouting up at him, more than a little frustrated in all the best ways. She'd seen her prize, and she wanted it now.

Hakon adored the sassy little pout she lobbed at him when he stopped her questing hand. In truth, he didn't want to stop her, but it was imperative that he do this correctly. Already dribbling spend, he wouldn't survive her hands if she grasped him right now.

"Can't I touch you?"

"Fates, yes," he groaned, "but if you touch me there now, I'll flip you on your front and rut you through the bed."

A choked sound escaped her. "What's wrong with that?"

Hakon sucked in a breath. Fates, she'd kill him with those big, luminous, hungry eyes.

He had to do this right—savor. There was every chance this would be his only chance; he trusted her when she said she was sure this was what she wanted, at least for the night, but only time would tell if he could woo her back again. His last rational thread of thought knew he had to make memories to last him.

Still, he couldn't help promising, "Next time, love."

That pout lingered another moment before her brows arched and she stepped forward into him. Fates, if he adored her pout, he fucking *loved* her flirtatious smile. Running her hands up and down his chest and shoulders, she captured his desperate cock between them.

The fine fabric of her dressing gown rasped in a silky glide against the underside, and Hakon couldn't help another hiss of ardent agony. Filling his hands with that dressing gown, he kneaded it, feeling how her warm flesh gave beneath his fingers.

A low, pleasured hum deep in her throat nearly sent him wild.

Sucking in another breath for strength, Hakon set her back from him a step, earning him another pout. It was his turn to smile smugly at her as his fingers made quick work of the knot at her waist holding the dressing gown closed.

The red fabric slid off her shoulders in a cascade, and he hung it from a bed post. The lantern light rendered the white of her nightgown nearly transparent. His mouth ran dry to see the shadowy contours of her, the thick thighs and rounded hips and feminine swell of her lower belly. Her heavy breasts pushed against the neckline, her nipples puckering against the fabric, begging for his attentions.

Bending down onto a knee, Hakon caught the hem in his hand and began to pull it up over her legs. He watched her face, even as he desperately wanted to behold every precious inch of skin he revealed, to ensure she didn't want him to stop.

She was only about a head taller than him like that, and he had no trouble drawing the nightgown up to her hip. Biting her lip, she looked at him with nothing but desire and excitement. All he could ever want.

Heart nearly beating out of his chest, Hakon lifted the nightgown up her middle. Aislinn raised her arms, and then her nightgown was free and cast onto the trunk.

She stood bare before him, incandescent and far more beautiful than he'd ever dreamed. Wasn't that what she'd said at the wedding—a groom should be worried about fainting from the beauty of his bride?

He did feel lightheaded as he leaned back on his other leg so he could look his fill.

With her soft golden waves falling down her back, he had an unobstructed view of her perfection. Her strong arms were lithe and golden from the sun, and her collarbones two graceful wings just below her throat. A few freckles dotted her chest, and her perfect breasts sat teasing him with their large pink nipples. Her waist nipped in before flaring in wide hips. A neat patch of hair hid her mons just below the slight curve of her belly. Her thighs were perfect handfuls, her calves shapely, and her ankles strangely precious.

It was some moments before he realized he gawped at her as she stood there, and he knew from how she tried not to sway or fidget that it was an effort to stay still and let him look.

"Oh, *vinya*," he rumbled, filling his hands with her hips and drawing her to him, "you are perfection."

Her smile was shy, not the same pout or sass from before, but he would take it. Soon, they'd know each other in every way. It was his purpose in life, his duty and his pleasure, to learn her and everything she liked. Always.

Hakon pressed leisurely kisses to her belly, catching hints of her pleasure scent. It was there, thank the gods, but he needed her to drown him in it. His thumbs played across her hipbones as he kissed up her body, to her sternum, then nipped the warm undersides of her breasts.

With a moan, he buried his face between her breasts, breathing heavily of her scent. Perfect, she smelled so perfect. She smelled like home. Like his.

*Mate.*

Nothing would ever smell or feel or taste better than her. Nothing.

Her little gasp puffed against his forehead when he banded his arms around her and stood, taking her up with him. In a moment, he had the blankets and furs flung back and Aislinn laid out in the middle.

She wiggled a little, running her hands over the blankets and sheets, and Hakon rumbled with pleasure at the sight. This was where she belonged, in his bed, beside him.

Hakon swung himself over her, keeping his weight on his hands and knees. His cock kicked against his belly to behold her under him, how she smiled in welcome and carded her fingers through the hair on his chest.

The sight did give him pause, though. She was so much smaller than him. He'd always known this, but somehow, with her laying there beneath him, he acutely understood how he could crush her in carelessness.

*Never. Never hurt her, only please.*

That was his intent, but this first time, slow. He had to go slow.

No matter what the beast, or the vixen, said.

"Have you lain with anyone before?" he asked. So long as it wasn't anyone he saw daily, he thought he could temper his jealousy.

"Yes, but it's been a long while. And always with a human man." Her hands smoothed over his chest and shoulders as a considering look stole across her face. "Have you?"

"Yes."

"Always with human men for you, too?" she teased.

He snorted a laugh. "An orcess, I'm afraid."

"Hmm." That considering expression returned. "Quite a bit bigger than me, I suppose?"

"Yes."

Lowering himself to her, Hakon couldn't help a groan when her legs parted to cradle him between them. He fell into her body, their forms fitting together so perfectly he needed a moment to catch his breath. The soft give of her body nearly drove him mad, and his bollocks drew up tight in need.

Hakon rained kisses onto her face and neck before asking, "Tell me what pleases you, *vinya*."

She made a considering noise, those wicked hands teasing up and down his flanks. "This rutting business sounds intriguing."

He huffed a laugh into the crook of her neck. "Are you ready for rutting?"

Hakon slipped a hand between them, fingers seeking the warm cunt hidden between her thighs. He felt her sharp inhale when he delved down, ignoring her clitoris to instead tease a fingertip against her opening. While she wept for him there, it wasn't nearly enough.

"Not quite yet," he told her, "I've more work to do."

He silenced her protests with a kiss, taking her lips and tongue for his own. Fates, she tasted so good. Distracted by his teasing tongue, Aislinn consented to play his game, nipping his lower lip and tracing his tusks with her tongue in revenge.

One of her thumbs found and circled his nipple at the same moment her lips caught his tongue and sucked.

Hakon rocked forward, cock thrusting against her thigh.

"Fates," he groaned.

He pushed himself back up onto his elbows, granting him a little distance from that wicked mouth of hers. His cock throbbed at her smug expression, and he wanted to see it again.

But first . . .

Hakon set himself the enviable task of making love to her, one kiss at a time. He started with her brow, following it down to the curve of her cheek and bridge of her nose. He tasted her lips but didn't linger, no matter how she tempted him by curling her tongue around his, and followed the elegant line of her neck down to her throat.

He tasted the hollow there at the base, licking between her collarbones before pressing kisses into her shoulders and upper arms. No part of her was spared—he sat up to kiss her forearm, the inside of her elbow, her wrist, her palm. Every fingertip got a kiss, every knuckle. When one hand had been given its due, he placed it on his shoulder and went to the next, feeling almost drunk on how she watched him with heavy-lidded eyes.

Next, he kissed her sternum, where he could feel her heart beating beneath his lips. Each breast received thorough attention, kisses and nips to the underside and long laves with the flat of his tongue against her pert nipples.

Aislinn moaned and rolled her hips, trying to find a little relief, but he wouldn't give it, not yet.

He could have spent all night there, teasing and playing with her breasts, but when she squirmed again, Hakon made himself move lower. He kissed each rib he could feel beneath her downy skin, then swirled his tongue in her belly button. She shuddered with a laugh, then moaned when he pressed a nipping kiss just above her mons.

Next was a growl of disapproval when he ignored her cunt and instead spoiled her hips and thighs with attention. His tongue teased the hollows of her hipbones and the caps of her knees. He kissed down the line of her shin as he held her small ankle so, so gently. The tops of her feet got a kiss, and so did every toe.

When all of her had been thoroughly kissed, Hakon sat back on his heels and smiled up at her. She returned it as he began to crawl over her, but it quickly disappeared with an outraged huff when he reached beneath her and flipped her by the hip onto her front.

Flicking her hair over her shoulder so she could scowl back at him, she said, "What happened to this going however I wanted?"

"I said nothing about how quickly," he replied, kissing her bare shoulder. "Trust me, *vinya*. Can you be good and patient for me?"

Reaching around to hold her throat in his hand to support her head, he felt her half-hearted grumble. "I suppose I've waited this long. What's a little longer?"

Hakon chuckled, but she received a gentle swat to her flank for that sass.

"Not much longer," he told her as her face fell into the pillows with a moan.

Releasing her, he returned to his ministrations. He learned the angles of her shoulder blades and curve of her spine with his lips and tongue. He charted each of the freckles along her back, charmed at the speckles of color along her perfect, supple skin.

When he reached her backside, he couldn't help himself. He buried his face against one buttock and filled his hand with the other. His fingers sank into the plush give of her, and with a groan of his own, he pressed many, many kisses along every curve.

It was a long while before he pulled himself down, to kiss her thighs and calves. The arches of her feet each got a kiss, as did her ankles and backs of her knees.

Hakon lifted up again, already so full. Fates, what he wouldn't give to spend the rest of his days in this bed, gorging on her. He'd kissed almost every bit of her there was and wanted to again, forever, always.

His stubborn mate had other ideas, though.

"And now?" she asked him over her shoulder, her brows arched in that way that made him throb.

He smiled wickedly at her. "Now we see if you're ready."

She opened her mouth to ask, but instead a gasp of delight filled the chamber when he palmed her thighs and drew them apart. He coaxed her knees up, and he rumbled with hunger when it opened her to his questing fingers.

Her scent punched through him, no longer a hint but all-consuming. His chest rattled with a pleased growl, and he couldn't help burying his face between her legs for a taste. Aislinn cried out and bucked as he ran his tongue from clitoris to cunt.

"*That,*" she groaned, "that pleases me."

He licked his lips when he sat back, grinning to see how she'd begun to tremble.

"I think you're almost ready, *vinya,*" he said as he came up behind her.

"*Almost?*" she croaked indignantly.

Hakon rumbled in assent, savoring her moan when he rested his cock between the generous globes of her backside. He watched the shudder run up her spine, and she rocked back into his hips.

The sight of his green flesh against hers nearly snapped the last thread of his control. The leisurely kisses had done their work on him too, lulling him into a haze of softer pleasure—but the taste of her, feeling her cradle his cock so perfectly . . .

*There's not a male alive luckier than I am.*

Hakon planted one hand on the bed near her head, and his heart beat faster when she immediately reached out to grasp his wrist. Rocking his cock against her in small, controlled movements, his other hand claimed what he'd been waiting so desperately for.

The pads of his fingers slid through her slick, immediately soaked with her desire. He teased her clitoris for a moment, rewarding her patience, and devoured the sight of her rocking back into his hand, seeking her pleasure, her eyes shut and her lips parted in concentration.

Before she could work herself to release, he slid his finger back to her opening and pushed inside. The first finger met no resistance, her muscles pulling him greedily deeper. The second finger took several slow thrusts, moving with her hips as she chased him down. The third was tight, and he pushed against a ring of muscle before finally feeling her resistance give way.

Aislinn's whole body shuddered and shook, and her head thrashed back and forth on the pillows when he touched a textured patch of slick skin inside her. "Hakon," she groaned, "Hakon, Hakon . . ."

"Just like that, *vinya.* Come for me just like that."

Her knuckles went white clutching the sheets, and with a little cry, she came apart under him. She clenched at his fingers, milking them and drawing them even deeper as her hips rolled against him. The wet slaps of their flesh filled the room, and Hakon nearly lost himself to the scent of her release, thick and syrupy.

Seed leaked from his cockhead, beads running over her backside and pooling at the small of her back. Their scents mingled, inciting every primal part of him that he'd tried so hard to put away.

He waited as long as he could, but her noises and the feel of her coming on his fingers shredded the last of his control and his sanity. Before she'd entirely recovered from her release, he rolled her onto her back.

Looming over her, he used a hand to guide his cock through the hot, throbbing lips of her cunt. Coating himself in her slick. Branding her desire into his skin. Imprinting her scent in his mind.

*Fates, yes.* He wanted everything.

She watched him with those sultry eyes and her lower lip caught by her teeth as he worked. He held that gaze, drowning in the golden glitter of her eyes, as he soaked himself.

Her cunt throbbed against his cockhead, and that was it. Hakon couldn't take any more.

Notching the head at her entrance, he pushed an inch inside before falling over her. She welcomed him with open arms, her thighs cradling his hips and ankles locking at the small of his back. As if he'd try to get away. Never, he never wanted to part from her. She was stuck with him now, forever.

He was hers.

"*Vinya,*" he grated against her cheek as he sank deeper.

He pushed inexorably on, not quick and brutal like he wanted, but unstoppable nonetheless. Aislinn threw her head back, and he kissed the long line of her throat, feeling her moan vibrate under his lips.

Even with all the preparation, she was still so tight it stole the breath from his lungs. He burned to move faster, to buck and thrust and fight his way home, but he made himself press on slow and measured.

The tendons in her neck stood out in stark relief as she panted heavily beneath him. Her fingers were claws, sunk into the meat of his shoulders.

When he'd sheathed half his shaft inside, he made himself stop and ask, "All right?"

She nodded once jerkily, but he didn't resume. The sight of tears glittering at the corners of her eyes almost sent him into a panic.

"Aislinn—"

"It hurts but good," she murmured.

"Good?"

"So *good*." She took a handful of his hair and yanked. "Don't you dare stop."

That was all he needed. Hakon angled her hips up with a hand on the small of her back. She gasped when he much more easily slid in another inch, and Hakon held her still as he worked himself in steady thrusts until, finally, *thank all the gods old and new,* he slid inside to the hilt.

Body shaking, Hakon could hardly believe he was buried deep inside his mate.

An orcish curse fell from his lips at the sight of her around him. It was almost obscene, her pink flesh spread so wide, the dark green root of his cock disappearing inside her.

*Exactly where I belong.*

Falling to his elbows, Hakon was no longer thought or word. He was only motion, hips thrusting inside his warm, soft, perfect mate. She met every thrust, hips rolling in tandem. Their slick dripped between them, coating his thighs and making the most obscene, delicious sounds.

They shared breath as their bodies rocked together. She followed him up and he chased her down, a perfect rhythm that stole the thought from his mind and the breath from his lungs. A sheen of sweat rendered her luminous in the low light, and he lapped at where it pooled in the hollow of her throat.

His pace grew faster, the bed creaking beneath them as he hunted the release that'd haunted him since he'd first met her. His hand was nothing compared to her, would never be good enough again. No one would. He was ruined for anyone, anything else.

"Perfect," he rumbled, "you're perfect."

"Hakon!"

He consumed her plea, sealing their mouths together just as he sealed his cock inside her on a downstroke. Lifting her a little higher, he angled her just so, ensuring his cock caught against her clitoris with every thrust. She clenched tight as a vice around him, her heels digging into his back as her rocking hips stuttered and grew frantic.

Aislinn's head thrashed on the pillows, and he felt the powerful ripple of her release. Hakon buried his face in her neck and let go, pouring himself inside his mate. The wet slaps of their furious lovemaking were nearly lost to his blood rushing through him and the hard beat of her heart at his ear.

He immolated in her arms, heated and reformed again.

She made room for him inside her, and as he collapsed into her arms, they molded together. Like links of mail, he heard the mate-bond *snick* into place, his center realigning around her.

She would be his, one way or another, but now, at this very moment, he was hers. For always.

"*Th'rat rus tenyar,*" he rumbled in orcish as he thrust one last time. *You have my heart.*

He didn't know if she heard it over her release; he barely remembered saying it as the throes of climax consumed him. It didn't make it any less true, though. And when, many moments later, their bodies had cooled a little and their heartbeats began to slow, Hakon's resolve hardened.

*I will have her for always.* He kissed that promise into her skin.

# 19

Aislinn woke in an unfamiliar bed, under unfamiliar blankets, surrounded by an unfamiliar but deliciously warm scent. An equally delicious set of lips pressed warm kisses to her cheek and the corner of her mouth.

"Good morning, *vinya.*"

Reluctantly, Aislinn peeled back an eyelid to behold the devastatingly handsome face of her blacksmith. He looked soft and warm in the morning, his hair mussed from his pillow—and her clutching hands.

A blush overtook her, and Aislinn curled up under the blankets in shock and delight. Fates, she'd gotten her answer. A decadent soreness accompanied her memories of the previous night, of his ferociousness and devotion. The slap of their bodies echoed in her ears, an answering throb low in her belly a telltale sign that she wanted more. Much more.

"Good morning," she replied, smiling up at him.

It was only then that she realized she was actually alone in the bed. He knelt beside it, dressed already for the day.

She tried to ignore the shard of disappointment that lodged in her chest. She couldn't quite decide what was her favorite part of the previous night—having that monstrous cock buried inside her or falling asleep with her cheek squished to his hard chest. She'd actually . . . looked forward to waking up with him. Seeing what he looked like in sleep. Maybe even kissing him awake.

"You're up," she said, trying to keep her tone light. She sat up in the bed, holding the blankets to her chest.

"The day starts early for blacksmiths." He leaned back to reach for something on the trunk then set a tray of food in her lap. "And I wanted to fetch your breakfast."

Aislinn stared in surprise. "You brought me breakfast?"

"Of course." Leaning in, he kissed her brow before standing to his full towering height. "You have to keep your strength up."

"For what?"

He smiled wickedly, and Aislinn realized he was flirting.

Bending at the waist, he placed his lips just beside her ear to whisper, "For rutting."

Her heart kicked in her chest with excitement, and her cunt gave another throb of desire. "O-oh?"

His grin was insufferably male and had her whole body blushing. "Indeed. I mean to keep you captive today. You aren't to leave this room."

She blinked in confusion. "But . . . what am I to do all day?"

"You'll eat your fill. You'll take your rest. And you'll think about what the night will bring."

Aislinn thought steam rose from her cheeks, her blush was so hot at his words. She squirmed in the bed, rattling the utensils on the tray.

"I-I have much to do. I can come back—"

"No." Holding her chin with a finger and thumb, his gaze was sure, hungry, and set her alight. "You're my captive, remember? And I say you take the day off."

She swiped her tongue across her bottom lip as she considered, and his eyes tracked the movement. That deep, rumbling purr rattled to life in his chest, and Aislinn nearly choked to feel how quickly she ran slick at the sound.

The guilt of wasting an entire day sat heavily on her shoulders, but was there anything else to say but, "All right."

"Good." His smile was her reward, as was the long kiss he bestowed, his tongue teasing and playing with hers.

She'd raised a hand to clutch his tunic, nearly forgetting the tray of food, when he pulled back. She wasn't proud of the mewl of disappointment she made, but she stood by it.

"I know, *vinya*. The day will be even longer for me, thinking of you here, warm and naked in my bed."

"Well, at least we're in it together."

His smile was wide and happy and took Aislinn's breath away. It stayed with her even as he left her to eat and start his day.

The memory of that smile alleviated some of her shame at taking such an indulgence. She ate her breakfast at a leisurely pace and ate it all, her appetite large after the previous night.

She could still hardly believe it, and when she finished her food, set the tray aside to lay in the depression Hakon had left in the bed. Everything smelled of him—and of their lovemaking.

He'd been so gentle as he cleaned them both before rejoining her in bed, but the blankets tangled around her still held the scent of their exploits. She wouldn't normally, but there was something thrilling about laying about late into the morning in the blankets that smelled of them. It was a visceral, primeval sort of pleasure, and Aislinn decided she enjoyed it immensely.

She managed to doze for about an hour, but before long, she inevitably grew bored. Never good at sitting still, her mind turned over everything she should be doing. Fates, Brenna was probably hunting for her. Aislinn thought she was likely safe ensconced in Hakon's bedchamber; Brenna might think to look in the smithy but wouldn't check his room.

Still, the illicitness of not only laying the day away but doing so naked in the blacksmith's bed held its own pleasure. Although she was bored, she nevertheless delighted in the slowness of the day—and promise of the night.

Curiosity was a sharp complement to her desire to finally see what this rutting was all about. She thought she'd heard Sorcha mention something similar, that orcs often sequestered themselves away with their partner and didn't emerge for days.

She squeezed her thighs in anticipation. Aislinn couldn't fathom *days* of lovemaking, let alone staying in bed that long. She hadn't spent so long in repose since the last time she was ill.

As the morning waned, Aislinn pushed out of bed, not sure she could lay down any longer. She wanted to honor her promise, but there was nothing to do. It was a bit of a conundrum—she could dress in her nightclothes again, but there was no chance of sneaking back to her own bedchamber without being caught. Late morning and early afternoon was the busiest time of day within the castle, and even waiting for the midday meal, she risked being seen.

The staff had seen her in odder attire, to be sure, but nightclothes would garner questions. Inquiries she wasn't sure how to answer.

She wasn't ashamed of Hakon, nor of what they did—or would do. Now that she'd had her curiosity sated, Aislinn was determined to have more of him. He wasn't just a curiosity or craving; she wanted to spend her time with him, her nights with him. Fates, she didn't sit around bored for just anyone!

None of that answered what to do about this new thing between them. Their friendship had been one thing. She was friendly with all the staff to varying degrees—mostly determined by the other person. She could confide in Fia, joke with Morwen and Hugh, but wouldn't dream of that with Captain Aodhan, who insisted on a level of decorum in their exchanges.

Aislinn and Hakon were far beyond *friendly* now.

Her past liaisons had been kept secret, too. The fear of being found out with Brenden had had its own kind of thrill, and she and Sir Alaisdair had eventually been found out. Both had felt good in their own ways, but eventually it was the romance itself that withered.

*Do I just like the secrecy?* she had to wonder. Aislinn couldn't deny that three made a pattern, nor that she found the secret nature of the relationships stimulating.

Yet, she didn't like reducing Hakon to that. If she wanted a secret romance with staff, she had many to choose from, all of whom she'd known before Hakon.

Logically, then, Hakon was special.

Yes, she liked that much better.

He *was* special—in his own right and to her. She liked how his mind worked, and his hands, too.

The memory of how his fingers ran circles over her clitoris had her holding her heated cheeks in her hands.

*Fates, focus!*

She'd burn away to coals at this rate.

She liked how talented he was and how devoted, too. It took both to be successful, and Hakon rose to every challenge. He was kind, good-natured, and had a sense of humor. She could list so many excellent qualities—but he was more than them and their sum. He was Hakon, and right then, he was hers.

Aislinn could think herself in circles over the question of what their futures held. Her stomach clenched with nerves over it in a way it hadn't with Brenden or Alaisdair. Somehow, even in the throes of early, passionate love, she'd never considered that she had a long future with either of them. When the end of their romance came, she hadn't been surprised nor overly hurt.

It was different with Hakon. She couldn't say she envisioned anything specific, nor that she suddenly longed for marriage and children. This new, beautiful thing with Hakon didn't change who she was fundamentally.

But she was willing to give it room to grow. She wanted to be with him, in whatever way she could.

And perhaps that was best done in secret. She didn't need furtive glances and malicious comments poisoning what they had before it even had time to develop.

Hands on her hips, Aislinn nodded to herself, decided. She would—

"I *knew it!*"

Jumping in surprise, Aislinn threw her hands over her breasts and whipped toward the narrow window. Two hands clung to the outer side of the sill, and Fia's copper hair glinted in the daylight. Just her arching brows and wide eyes were visible over the stone of the sill.

Heart sinking, Aislinn didn't know what to do with herself as her maid dropped back down into the bailey and out of sight.

Fumbling, she grabbed her nightgown and tugged it over her head. She'd just gotten her arms through the sleeves of the dressing gown when Fia came marching through the door with all the confidence of a conquering general.

Closing the door quickly behind her, Fia took a long look at Aislinn.

Aislinn held perfectly still, as if Fia wouldn't see her if she didn't move.

After a terribly long moment, a smile broke across Fia's face. Insufferable and smug, she waggled her brows before handing Aislinn a bundle of things.

She took them numbly, waiting for Fia to say something.

"Brenna has the maids searching the castle top to bottom for you," said Fia, "but I had a feeling I'd find you here."

Aislinn cleared her throat, although she didn't know what to say.

Nodding at the bundle in Aislinn's arms, Fia said, "I brought one of your work kirtles, a book, and your notebook. I figured you'd be bored by now."

Deflating with relief, Aislinn finally looked at the items in her arms. Just as Fia said, one of her worn kirtles sat atop the book she'd been reading on the bridges and other maritime structures of the seaside city of Adrigoll, as well as her notebook with a portable pen stuck in the spine.

"Thank you, Fia."

Throwing her a wink, the maid said, "I know you aren't one for laying about."

Aislinn nodded absently, teeth chewing at her lower lip. "Fia . . ."

"I won't tell anyone," her maid assured her. "Besides, you deserve this. The laying about and the handsome blacksmith."

Aislinn looked up in surprise. "I do?"

"Of course." Fia patted her arm. "He makes you happy."

*So happy.* Hearing that put into words, the acknowledgement of it, touched something deep inside Aislinn. She was happy. Despite the added responsibilities and worries.

The happiness he gave her outweighed the despair that always lurked on the fringes of her spirit.

"Look at you, eyes twinkling." Smiling, Fia pulled a small bottle from her kirtle pocket. "One last thing."

Her blush only worsened to see the bottle of silphium powder.

"I thought you'd want to be safe. Unless you wanted a little green heir."

Aislinn stuck her tongue out, and Fia matched it. Soon, they devolved into making faces at each other, which was what Hakon walked into when he entered with luncheon.

Fia snorted with laughter seeing his crestfallen face as he looked sheepishly between them.

"Your secret is safe with me," she said, patting Hakon's arm as she practically skipped out the door. "I'll tell Brenna I saw you leave for town. That ought to keep her occupied." Fia pulled the door behind her, but before it closed, she leveled Hakon with a serious look. "And blacksmith? You make her happy or I'll chop you up and feed you to the pigs. There won't be anything left to find of you."

The door shut behind her in a deafening silence.

Hakon turned back to Aislinn slowly, face slack with shock.

Aislinn could only shrug. "Unfortunately, she's not exaggerating."

Hakon grinned ruefully, setting her tray of luncheon on the bed.

"Oh, I agree with her. A male who doesn't please his woman should be fed to the beasts."

With her book and a little work, Aislinn spent the afternoon in a pleasant frenzy of ideas. She drafted more of the bridge, and for the first time, she didn't worry about not being prepared for her meeting with the guild-masters in a few days.

She was actually *excited* for it.

At least her temporary authority had a few benefits. She looked forward to breaking ground and at least getting scaffolding up before winter, to show the people of Dundúran that the Darrows were committed to improvements and the higher dues hadn't been for nothing.

The afternoon passed by quicker than she thought possible. Left alone with her book, she let her mind wander and play, and the drafts flowed freely across the pages of her notebook. By the time night fell, her heart was full, her spirit satisfied. It hadn't been a waste of a day as she'd feared, and taking the time to sit still and do something she enjoyed nourished her in a way that she unfortunately often took for granted.

Still, by the time night followed Hakon in with their dinner, she was more than ready to set aside her book.

They shared the tray of food Hakon brought from the kitchen. Prepared to eat whatever he didn't want, Aislinn was surprised to find everything was one of her preferred foods.

"Don't you prefer more meat?" she asked.

"Yes, but I'm not feeding myself."

He wouldn't hear her protests, nor of leaving again to find himself more. He only ate what she didn't, finishing off the tureen of pea soup and hunk of bread and platter of spiced carrots and beets.

She listened happily as he told her of his day, turning away maids looking for her as he and Fearghas prepared a large order from Captain Aodhan for new spearpoints. Brenna would no doubt have her suspicions but smoothing them over could wait for tomorrow.

As their meal settled, Hakon took up a comb and brushed her hair. Aislinn sat still, too amazed to contribute much to the conversation. Only Fia and sometimes Brenna brushed out her hair in the evenings. Having a man do it, having Hakon do it, was . . . divine.

Her lids slipped closed as she soaked up the care and comfort, the comb rasping pleasantly on her scalp. She fell into something of a trance listening to his deep baritone, surrounded by his warmth and scent.

She'd relaxed, almost gone boneless when she heard the comb being set down. His lips tickled at her ear, and flames licked through her body when he whispered, "Are you ready?"

Without opening her eyes, Aislinn leaned back into him, her head falling onto his shoulder. She reached an arm back to bury her fingers in his hair.

Aislinn hummed in pleasure. "And what does my captor intend to do with me?"

"Anything he wants." Hot kisses fell along the curve from her neck to shoulder. "It's not every day he has a beautiful lady caught in his arms."

His hands came to clasp her upper arms, and he began to slide the sleeves from her shoulders.

"First, I want you naked."

The kirtle fell away from her chest, exposing her breasts to his waiting, greedy hands. He filled his palms with them, plumping the soft flesh to tease the callused pads of his thumbs over her nipples.

Aislinn arched against him, her grip tightening in his hair.

"And second?" she asked breathlessly.

"Second—" Without warning, he whirled her around to face him and took handfuls of her kirtle, pulling it down until it pooled at her feet. "I want to fuck you all night long."

Aislinn choked on her gasp, reeling with delight as she was picked up by the waist and set back on the bed. She bounced amongst the blankets, biting back her giggling.

He quickly took her breath away, pulling his tunic over his head and unlacing his trou. He threw his clothing aside without dropping her gaze, his eyes intense as he watched her watch him take his cock in hand and pump once, twice.

She shuddered with lust, her legs falling open in welcome. "Do you intend to finally make good on your many, many promises?"

"Very good," he rumbled.

Aislinn nearly quivered to see the animalistic way he stalked toward her. The power of him, the strength suspended above her, sent a wicked thrill through her that had her cunt clenching with desire. Fates, she needed him badly. More than she needed him the night before.

She suspected she'd need him even more tomorrow.

He loomed above her, and for a moment, he kept her in delicious suspense, that hot gaze devouring her from head to toe. Finally, his hands came up to grip her knees. He pushed her even wider, opening her to him, and she shivered at the cool air whispering against her weeping cunt.

With deliberate movements, he got on his knees and lowered his mouth to exactly where she needed him. Aislinn watched on, holding her breath, not sure if she could bear to feel his hot mouth and teasing tongue there or if she could survive another moment without it.

Keeping her gaze captive with his, he spread her with his fingers and lapped at her with the flat of his tongue. Nearly arching off the bed, Aislinn saw stars, body quaking as his mouth began to move. His lips nipped and teased, his tongue coming after to soothe.

He lavished everywhere but her clitoris with attention, tasting and suckling until she whined and throbbed. Raking her fingers through his hair, she tried to pull him closer, to where she *needed* him, but he only smiled against her slick flesh and pressed lazy kisses to her inner thighs.

Aislinn didn't know how long he kept her there, on the edge of the bed and knife's blade of oblivion. His tongue speared inside her, making her cry out, filling the room with her sobs and pleas for release. He took no mercy on her, swirling that wicked tongue and running a finger teasingly along the edge of her mons.

"Hakon—!"

Gripping her thighs, his mouth finally fell on her clitoris. He wrapped his tongue around it and nearly felled her with a single pull.

Aislinn's hips rolled, but she found no relief. Her cunt clenched around nothing, and she growled at him with desperation.

He bared his small tusks at her in return. "I need you at least half as desperate for me as I am for you."

She opened her mouth to retort, but then she was on her front, her legs being spread wide and her knees pushed up under her.

"Yesyesyes," she sang when his cockhead teased her entrance.

His great chest seared her back when he fell over her. Caged by his bulging arms, Aislinn did everything she could to push her hips back to meet his.

"Once I start, I won't stop." The words fell hotly against her ear.

"*Good,*" she growled, setting her teeth in the meat of his forearm.

With a rumbling growl, he breached her. Aislinn's mouth fell open around a moan of agonizing pleasure. Her arms gave out, dropping her front to the bed, and Hakon's cock slid home in one thrust.

Stretched wide, full to the brim, pinned beneath him, Aislinn could only lay there. Her ears rang, her mind struggled to form a thought other than—*more, move, please!*

Her hips twitched and then pushed back as much as she could. It was less than an inch perhaps, but it was more than enough.

A growl buzzed in her ear, and then one of his hands was holding both of hers in front of her, stretching her torso, while the other delved beneath them to find her clitoris. That merciless finger ran circles around the sensitive flesh with every thrust, drowning her in sensation.

She didn't know where to focus or what to think. Reduced to only movement, she could do nothing but receive his brutal lovemaking.

His cock pistoned inside her, his hips crashing against her in a maelstrom. Slick dripped onto the bed between them and soaked his hand, his fingers sliding through her folds in a frenetic rhythm. He reached inside her with every stroke, emptying her of all that came before. She cried out when he retreated, only to cry out in ecstasy with his return.

She didn't know how many times she climaxed or if she ever stopped. She lost time, she lost all sense. Her body was a single exposed nerve, surrounded by Hakon. He bore down on her, unrelenting, unforgiving.

He bit the blankets beside her as he filled her with spend, the hot ropes burning her from the inside out. Aislinn shuddered, and his arms closed around her tight. His hips lost their rhythm, and as he snarled with release, she thought she finally understood what it meant to be rutted.

She had no idea, though.

For it was only a moment later that he reared up and rolled her onto her back. His cock glistened with their fluids and dripped with spend, and although it'd gone a bit soft, he wasted no time spreading her legs and burying himself to the hilt.

Aislinn gasped, flesh oversensitive and overwhelmed. When he lowered himself to her, she grabbed him in her arms, their mouths seeking and desperate. Their tongues mimicked the rhythm of their hips, slick and smacking.

It wasn't long before Aislinn found release again, her pleasure bordering on pain as her muscles clenched greedily around his cock. Her body never wanted to give him up, never wanted to let go. She wrapped arms and legs around him, refusing to part.

She'd hardly caught her breath before he rolled both of them this time, putting her above him. Still buried inside her, he guided her hips with those big hands to find a rhythm. Aislinn could hardly hold herself up, but she splayed her hands across that glorious chest and moved, chasing down another searing climax.

He had a little mercy on her near midnight, ensuring she ate and drank. But when she expected to be taken into his arms and fall asleep again listening to his heartbeat, she was instead pulled down the bed and her legs thrown over his shoulder. Her mouth opened wide around a silent scream, her throat already sore from her cries and moans.

His cock sank inside, and he told her in a rumbling growl to play with her breasts. She did mindlessly, her limbs boneless, her breasts overstimulated. He watched her avariciously, thrusting harder whenever she kneaded or played with herself.

The sight of him watching her somehow drew another climax out of her. She didn't think it possible, nor the next one or the next. He wrung pleasure out of her she didn't think herself capable of. The night sank into the wee hours and still he was hungry for her.

It wasn't until the gray light of predawn filtered through the small window that he relented. Aislinn fell exhausted into the blankets and let him arrange her how he wanted, spread over him like another blanket.

A tender kiss was pressed into her forehead before she fell into the deepest sleep of her life.

*My mate. My beautiful, perfect mate,* echoed in her dreams.

# 20

Hakon offered his hand to Aislinn, helping her use the blocks the stonemasons had brought as steps. She gave him a grin of gratitude, but the true gift was, with her back turned to the gathered crowd of guilders, the flash of trepidation across her face.

She trusted him with her fears, and Hakon would do the utmost to vanquish every one.

He clasped her hand and nodded, stepping back when she turned to face the guilders.

*My brave mate.*

Standing three blocks up, she was high enough for all to see. The two dozen or so guilders watched on in silence, anxious to see what their heiress would say.

As they lay in bed together the night before, Aislinn had confessed her worries over this meeting to him, how she wished to gain their support and respect. He assured her they would listen; she had worked with all of them before, and her plans for the bridge were not only sound but magnificent.

She'd blushed when he used that word, making him think for a moment that he'd gotten it wrong. He was coming to realize, though, that his pretty mate was unused to praise.

It was perhaps surprising for a noblewoman; Hakon would've thought all manner of people had showered her with compliments and flattery, so much so that she would expect it. Aislinn was just the opposite, and Hakon had to wonder if it was because of a lack, or because she mistrusted it.

Whatever the reason, he was determined now to praise her whenever he could, enough that she would finally start to believe it.

"Good morning," she began. "As you can see, construction on the south bridge is scheduled to begin in spring. Today, I wanted to demonstrate the dimensions I had in mind and offer the chance for input."

Hakon's chest swelled with pride to see how the guilders gave her their attention, how she commanded them not with orders or fear but competence. She had nothing to fear; these craftspeople hadn't woken early to come hear her speak for lack of respect.

She outlined her plan in a speech she'd practiced with him over several afternoons as he manned his forge. Hakon watched as some nodded, others scribbling notes onto notebooks.

Using gestures and the demonstrative blocks, she described her ideas for the bridge. Although it was early, she, Hakon, and several staff had arrived to hammer stakes into the ground on either side of the river and tie ropes between them, showing the planned dimensions of the construction. Stonemasons had arrived next with sample blocks of local limestone, showcasing the planned graceful façade.

It didn't take her long to have the crowd riveted, and Hakon watched, just as enchanted, as she used words to help them imagine the elegant triple arches of the bridge, the wide lanes, and how the bridge would benefit everyone of Dundúran.

When Aislinn finished and asked for questions or concerns, several stepped forward—not to challenge her but instead ask over supplies to be sourced and labor projections. Already they agreed to her plan, whether or not she realized it, and were quick to inquire how they could help make her ideas real.

*They love her.*

How could they not? Gentle, kind, and brilliant, all of them could see what a leader she made. She greeted them with patience and good humor, offered a detailed, thoughtful plan, and ensured everyone would benefit not only from the bridge itself but the work of constructing it.

It would make asking her to step down as heiress all the harder.

The more time Hakon spent beside her, the more he doubted he could. And yet . . .

*I love her more.*

The love of her people was certainly something to admire, but he could love her better. He could give her everything else. He'd give her himself, be her mate in every way, her husband if she wanted it. Without the title of lady, she could have everything.

When it was time to show her drafts, Aislinn stepped down from the blocks. Hakon offered his hand again, and she took it with a grateful smile. She looked a little pale from having to stand up and speak before so many, and he hated to see the strain around her eyes.

*It will be for the best.* She could still help her people, could still draft and imagine and work—just without the worries and pressures of being heiress. He would give her a home, a family, a life so full, she'd never miss her castle or position.

He'd do anything to make it happen, anything for her.

*My mate.*

On nights when Aislinn couldn't slip away to his bedchamber, she at least managed to meet her blacksmith in the baths. She'd taken to joining his nighttime ritual, showing him the secret way to open the grate that separated the sides of the baths.

She needed to rise early again the next morning for another day of receiving each of the guild-masters individually to discuss orders and labor costs, but she could at least steal an hour with Hakon.

Floating along the surface, her head propped on his shoulder and her fingers playing through the steam rising from the mineral water, Aislinn let the stresses and worries of the day seep away. They'd long since finished washing each other, taking opportunities to run their hands greedily up and down their slippery skin.

Limbs lax and head delightfully muzzy from the orgasm that still sent little sparks of pleasure through her body, Aislinn didn't know if she'd ever been so relaxed. Certainly never so much after a day of public speaking and negotiating with guilders.

Hakon's big hands were pure magic as they massaged away what felt like years of strain, that charming purr rumbling in her ear. Her eyes slipped closed as they floated, so warm and content, it defied belief.

In the fortnight since first laying with him, she'd come to not only crave her blacksmith's touch but need him in a way she hadn't anyone else before. She went to him with her worries and problems. Some afternoons they spoke of nothing but forging or gardening or old orcish legends. Not everything was about sex—not every meeting led to a liaison; although, those were often the most exciting. She enjoyed spending time with him, whatever they did.

There were even times when . . . when he pulled her back from the brink of a fit. Overwhelmed with her duties, exacerbated by the fractured state of her relationship with Brenna, frustration and anxiety had nearly gotten the better of her twice now. Each time, she made it to Hakon, and somehow, he made it all right.

His calmness, his caring, his patience, it all helped soothe the worst edges of her panic. Enough that she could get hold of herself.

As if her body didn't crave him enough, she sought him out whenever she could. For comfort, for pleasure, for reassurance. He was quickly becoming her favorite person, and Aislinn wasn't sure if she was more pleased or terrified of this.

Such thoughts were far from her mind tonight, though. After a long day of meetings with guild-masters, negotiating and writing contracts, a bath with her blacksmith was a luxury she couldn't help indulging in.

"Have I told you today how beautiful you are, *vinya?*" His lips whispered across her cheek, scrawling the words on her damp skin.

Aislinn blushed. "You haven't."

"An unforgivable oversight. You are more beautiful than the moon in the night sky. More beautiful than the purple mountains at dawn. More beautiful than every pearl in the sea and all the jewels in the ground."

Her grin was wide listening to his praise. His Eirean vocabulary had certainly improved leaps and bounds.

"Every single one?"

"Every. Single. One." He punctuated each word with a kiss along her shoulder, and his questing fingers made looping patterns down her back.

She hummed in pleasure, reaching back to trace the inhuman point of his ear. "Why do you call me *vinya?*"

"Because it's what you are to me. My rose."

Her eyes opened, staring up at the stone ceiling of baths. The stalactites had been smoothed, minerals glittering along the conical slopes.

"I'm like a rose?"

"*Vinya,* yes."

It took her a long moment to push out her next words, and she nearly let herself be distracted by the slow, warm kisses he lavished down her neck.

"So I'm delicate and fussy?" She tried to make it a joke, but she heard how her voice caught on the words. She couldn't help thinking of her mother's roses, so easily out of control without careful pruning, their stems riddled with hidden thorns for protection.

Without stopping his ministrations, he purred his answer in her ear.

"*Vinya* aren't your garden roses. They are the mountain roses that bloom along the slopes of Kaldebrak. They defy the mountain, clinging to the rocks." His hands slid up her body to cradle her breasts, his fingertips sinking into the plush flesh. "They are hearty, determined. They weather every storm, only to bloom brighter after the rain. That is why you are *vinya*—you are all this and so much more."

Aislinn's lips parted in surprise, her heart *thump-thumping* heavily in her chest.

Flipping over to face him, she found him gazing at her with such softness, such affection.

She didn't have the words to . . . did he understand how beautiful . . . could he really think . . .?

Throwing her arms around his neck and her legs around his thick waist, Aislinn molded their bodies together. Her mouth sought his, and she held his strong jaw in her hand, keeping his head still to receive her fervent kisses.

Fates, no one had ever said such things about her.

His purr deepened into a lusty growl as her hand traced down his body to take hold of his cock. She guided him into her body, and with a smooth stroke, he slid deep inside her.

Sealing their mouths together again, Aislinn kissed him greedily, swirling her tongue along his short tusks and nipping his lower lip. She kissed him with a frantic sort of need, a counterpoint to the unhurried rhythm of their hips.

The water lapped gently at them, hardly disturbed as she held his face in her hands and he held her hips in his, guiding their lovemaking. When climax finally came, it was no less devastating for its gentleness. Aislinn clutched him to her in every way she could, holding on as she came apart in every way imaginable.

Cracked open, he put her back together with his kisses and his care.

"*Vinya, vinya,*" he chanted to her, as if she were a goddess of old to be prayed to.

With his cock pulsing inside her and her love for him growing in her heart, she felt divine then. A woman who could do anything, one who had everything she could ever want.

*Him. I just want him.*

Hakon was quickly learning that his mate liked games. The thrill of a challenge was always sure to get her blood running hot and her cunt dripping slick.

He was the luckiest of males.

Aislinn waved to him through one of the open smithy windows, just out of sight of Fearghas, working on the opposite side. Her smile was all mischief as she used hand-talk to tell him to meet her in the rose garden at luncheon.

There and gone again, she slipped away through the bailey, leaving Hakon hot under the collar and the morning to crawl by. His skin itched all over, and it was more work to keep his cock under control than to shape and hammer spearpoints. He nearly smashed his thumb and nailed his hand before he stopped and took a breath to refocus himself.

It wouldn't do to show up with bloodied, bruised hands. He needed them for much more pleasurable work.

Hakon waited for Fearghas to leave for luncheon with impatience. Once he was gone, Hakon pulled out a bone to keep Wülf occupied and banked his forge fire.

He mopped at his brow as he strode for the rose garden, hoping he wasn't too dirty or sweaty. Although, his mate seemed to delight in it, never turning him away even with grime smudged across his face and sweat sluicing down his chest.

The wooden gate had been left unlocked, and after taking a furtive glance around, Hakon slipped inside, closing and locking it behind him.

The garden was bright and fragrant, despite the burlap covering the tall bushes for winter dormancy. The air held a chill, the promise of winter to come, but Hakon felt nothing but a deep, consuming need for his mate.

He looked upon her with something akin to awe as she sat waiting for him on the marble bench, the breeze picking up locks of her golden hair. Her lovely face turned when she heard him coming, and she smiled up at him in welcome.

Hakon fell to his knees before her, overcome.

If he thought his beast would go silent when he finally gave in, he was . . . partly right. Without the conflict between them, the beast was far quieter; although, Hakon was always aware of it, a sharpness between his ribs. The purr in his throat was all the beast and all for her.

"How are you today, my darling?" she asked, her smile brighter than the summer sun.

Hakon took both her hands and kissed each palm. "Far better here with you."

Leaning forward, she drew him closer so their faces were near. "What if I told you I had ideas of seducing you right here in the rose garden?"

"I'd tell you it wouldn't be difficult."

Her laughter filled him with warmth, a brightness that reached all the cracked, battered parts of him. She wrapped her arms around his neck and bore him to the ground, a cascade of flaxen waves and green skirts and gold, sparkling eyes. Her mouth found his in the flurry, and Hakon settled onto his back, more than content to let his *vinya* do whatever she wished with him.

Especially when what she wanted was to take him for a noonday ride.

Clambering down his legs, Aislinn straddled his knees as she worked his belt and trou loose. When that playful gaze flicked up to him, Hakon smirked and folded his hands under his head.

He wasn't so calm when she reached into his trou and pulled out his hardening cock. Her soft hands pumped him with deliberate strokes, and Hakon's mouth fell open when that golden head dipped and those rosy lips stretched around his cockhead.

A moan fell from his own lips, and it took effort not to buck and shove his cock into her throat.

"Shh," she hummed around him, "someone might hear."

Gritting his tusks against his gums, Hakon rumbled with frustrated hunger. So this was her true game. Test his control, his patience as she played with him.

She could play as long as she wished; he wouldn't break, not when holding tight to his building climax meant more swipes of her wicked tongue and pulls of that talented mouth.

Unable to fit more than half of him in her mouth, she worked his lower shaft with her hands, wringing beads of spend from him, and skated her fingers across his sensitive bollocks. Hakon nearly choked on his roar, clenching his jaw so tight he heard a *pop*.

He couldn't help shifting beneath her, but he stayed like that, prone and receiving her attentions for as long as she wanted.

It felt like a long while before she had mercy on him, swirling her tongue one last time around the cockhead and across the slit before crawling up his body. His greedy hands were there to meet her, helping her gather her skirts so she could grip him to guide into her weeping cunt.

"Fates," he hissed as her soft flesh kissed his cock, "you burn hotter than my forge."

Her thighs trembling, spread wide across his waist and hips, she lowered herself onto him. With little circles of her hips, she worked him deeper until, with a mischievous bite of her lower lip, she let herself fall the rest of the way. She bared her teeth to hold back her moan as she impaled herself on his throbbing cock.

His hands dug beneath her skirts, needed to feel her skin. He grabbed hold of her plush thighs, matching the steady rhythm her hips set.

It took effort to hold back, to not just flip her over and rut her into the soil, but Hakon kept hold of himself as he held her, watching in awe as she rocked above him.

"That's it, *vinya*," he praised, "take everything you need."

She rewarded him with that mewling noise she made as her peak mounted.

Hakon slid a hand up her thigh to run his thumb over the pearl of her clitoris, swollen and glistening. It stood in relief against her spread cunt, and a dark, satisfied growl rumbled in his chest at the sight.

"Look at you stretched around me. What a sight you make, *vinya*."

He teased his thumb across the hood, making her shudder and lose her rhythm.

"Do you know how it feels to have you like this?" she asked him breathlessly. "To have such a big, strong man beneath me?"

"Like the goddess you are."

She smiled wide. "Exactly."

Seeing her flushed with hunger and confidence was what finished him. Head thrown back across the grass, Hakon bit down on his growl and rasped his callus against her clitoris mercilessly. He needed to bring her with him with a desperation that bordered on pain.

With a gasp, her cunt clenched him tight as a vice. Hakon thrust his hips up to meet her, needing as deep inside as he could be, needing to be a part of her now, later, always. He spilled inside her, her slick and his spend dripping down his cock.

Her nails dug into the leather of his jerkin as her body quaked with release. Hakon held her through the throes of climax, devouring the sight she made, shining in the midday sun. She was more glorious than he could express, and the way she looked down at him as her cunt pulsed with aftershocks broke him apart.

A soft moan escaped her lips as she melted onto his chest. She pressed her ear to his chest, where she had to hear his heart thundering, all her doing, all for her.

His cock began to soften, but still she didn't move nor try to pull away. Hakon held his mate there in the garden, warmed by the sun and her affection.

"One day soon," he told her, "I'll have you do that to me on my land."

She lifted her head to prop her chin on his chest, grinning dreamily. "Oh?"

"We should visit it," he said, trying to keep his voice light. He wanted her in all ways, but most especially to hear her screams of pleasure echoing through the trees. He wanted to fill her with his seed, see it spill out of her with her slick to soak the soil. It would be their land, their home.

"That would be nice," she said.

"In spring, I'll lay you down in the flowers there and take you under the full moon."

Her cheeks darkened with a blush, and she buried her face against his chest. "Is that a promise?"

Hakon ran his hands up her legs to fill his palms with her backside. He squeezed and kneaded, earning him a gasp of interest.

"Most definitely," he answered her. "You know I keep my promises."

She squirmed on his chest as his cock began to harden again inside her.

Hakon grinned, heart almost painfully full. He would promise her everything if she was ready to hear it. He intended to give her everything, too. Their life together was nothing but promise, full of possibilities, and he awaited it with impatience.

For now, though, he would be content to claim his mate amongst the rosebushes.

# 21

Aislinn hurried down the castle steps into the courtyard, not caring that the cold air nipped at her face. Sorcha stood up in the footwell of the cart as it clattered to a stop, waving back and calling her name. A loud chorus followed, her three youngest siblings in the back of the cart leaning over the side and waving and shouting happily to see her.

Aislinn bounced on the balls of her feet as a patient Orek brought the horse to a stop. He jumped down lithely, rounding the back of the cart to help a squirming Sorcha down. Her feet had barely touched the cobblestones before she was flying into Aislinn's waiting arms.

They rocked together, giggling, as Orek picked each of the younger Brádaighs out of the cart, swinging them before depositing them safely on the ground. Even Calum, sixteen and prone to bouts of surliness, whooped as his big halfling brother swung him through the air.

Soon Blaire and Keeley were clinging onto Aislinn too, and she was thoroughly caught by Brádaighs. They all laughed as Calum rolled his eyes and Orek looked on with fond amusement, his eyes crinkling at the corners.

"And how are my favorite horse folk?" asked Aislinn.

The younger siblings groaned before launching into a loud description of everything that had happened on the estate since the wedding. They all talked over one another as Sorcha shook with bitten back laughter.

Aislinn managed to catch that several grooms were caught up in a love affair with one of the gardeners, and there was talk of a Choosing being called for, a Choosing being an ancient Eirean custom that saw potential suitors press their suit for the hand of their intended, who had to decide within moments whether to accept any of the suits made. Several of the manticore males were after their other sister Maeve even as she prepared to return to academy in Gleanná, Sorcha and Orek were all moved into their new home but it was *so unfair* that they didn't let siblings stay the night—oh and Aunt Sofie was feuding with a neighbor in Granach over his pig breaking into her herb garden again.

"The same man she was arguing with over the pumpkins last year?" Aislinn asked.

"The very same," answered Sorcha, eyes twinkling. "I think it's their way of flirting."

Aislinn wanted to know everything, but even more, she wanted to tell Sorcha *everything*. Thrilling as it was to sneak around the castle to find secret places to romance her blacksmith, it was its own agony that only Fia knew.

She could feel what she had with Hakon growing stronger, its roots buried deep inside her, around her very heart. She scarcely let herself think what it truly meant, or could mean, and wanted the perspective of her dear friend—and someone who herself had a halfling lover.

Aislinn was also intensely curious over what Sorcha knew about orcish culture and courting.

When the younger Brádaighs finished their litany of news, Aislinn clapped her hands and said, "As promised, Hugh has your sweet buns and—" A round of cheers went up from the excitable children "—and the books you requested have been pulled and are waiting for you in the library."

"Thank you, Lady Aislinn!" they called as they tore off in the direction of the bailey. Thankfully, the castle staff had been warned in advance of the coming Brádaigh invasion, and the children were favorite guests, even to Brenna.

"I'll make sure they get where they're meant to go," said Orek. "The smithy is that direction, yes?"

Aislinn tried but failed to contain her blush. "Yes, it's just there. With all the forges."

Orek nodded, either unaware or gracious enough to ignore her blathering. "And Hakon is in?"

She cleared her throat and tried to shrug. "I haven't seen him this morning, but I would assume so. It's where he often is."

Orek and Sorcha exchanged looks, and Aislinn watched as a whole conversation passed between them within an arch of a brow and tilt of lips. In the span of a few seconds, they'd communicated a wealth of feeling between them, before Orek leaned down to receive a kiss from Sorcha.

"Enjoy your bath," he murmured against her lips.

"I will. It'd be better with you, though."

Aislinn coughed. "I'll have to do."

Orek and Sorcha chuckled before he waved farewell and headed off after the children.

Sorcha lost no time linking her arm with Aislinn's. They wended through the castle on their way to the baths. Aislinn always enjoyed her friend's visits and the opportunity to steal away for a slow afternoon in the baths, catching up and sharing their news. She was grateful this at least hadn't changed after the wedding.

"Horses are a herd, wolves are a pack. I wonder what a group of siblings is called," laughed Aislinn.

"A hassle," Sorcha replied with a mock grumble. "But don't change the subject. What was all *that* about?"

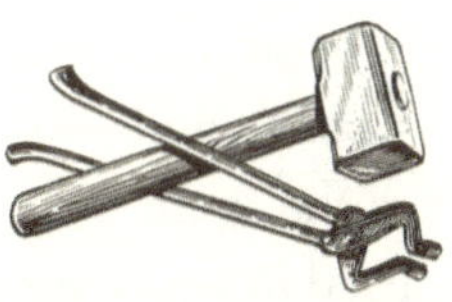

Hakon and Orek laughed as Wülf pranced around the bailey, letting Blaire and Keeley chase him. The faint *clink* of metal behind him told him that Calum was examining the castaway tools from the smithy that he was welcome to take.

"Does Sorcha visit Dundúran often?" Hakon asked in orcish. The language would make Fearghas squint even harder than he was from inside the smithy at them, but it felt good to feel his mother tongue in his mouth. He also didn't need the old blacksmith to hear or understand everything he said. As obstinate as he could be, Fearghas was an irredeemable gossip.

"Before being taken, yes. She's been looking forward to it, and the children could use the distraction. They'll be bored when winter sets in and they're kept to the house."

"Keeping to that new house of yours this winter, are you?"

Orek grinned. "Don't plan to come out for days whenever possible."

Hakon chuckled. "I envy you, my friend."

Orek turned his head to peer at Hakon. "How long?"

"Almost two fortnights." And they'd been the best days of his life without question. He couldn't spend nearly as much time with her as he wished, but when he was with her, the world was right. The mate-bond sung inside him, a harmony that made the sunshine a bit brighter, the wine a bit sweeter. Aislinn made his life better.

She was his life.

He lived for her hand-talk directions and finding her in hidden nooks, thrilled when he finally caught up to her and kissed her senseless in a disused part of the castle. She wasn't the only one finding clever ways to steal time together, though.

With the requests from Captain Aodhan and coming bridge construction, Aislinn had brought on two more blacksmiths, a woman named Caitlín and an orcess named Edda—business and romantic partners both, who'd come from the south for a new life, just as so many others had. Hakon was shocked to see an orcess here, mate-bonded to a human female no less, but welcomed the help.

Two human lads from the city were also taken on as apprentices. Hakon gave up his room at the back of the smithy to them and claimed another on the north side of the castle. Few rooms were inhabited here, as it was draftier and further from the kitchen. That served his purposes nicely, and almost every night, Aislinn stole into his room unseen.

Orek was quiet for a long while. He stood watching the children play, his expression mild, but Hakon could feel his mind working.

Hakon checked his temper as he waited for his friend to say something. This was the first test he needed to pass—if he didn't have support amongst friends, he'd have none at all.

"You're sure?"

"Yes. The bond is already in place."

That got Orek's attention. "Hakon . . ."

"She's my mate," he rumbled. "What else can I do?"

Silence fell between them for another long moment, Hakon's guts clenching with rage. Why could Orek have a human mate and not him? It was unfortunate that Aislinn's noble blood stood in their way, but he wouldn't find a finer mate. She was everything to him, perfect, and he meant to—

"I understand. Truly, I do," Orek sighed. "Even after I accepted my beast's demands that Sorcha was mine, the burden of an unrequited mate-bond weighed heavily. I wasn't sure how I could ever fit into her life here. Some days, I'm still not sure."

Hakon's brows rose in surprise. "But she's your wife now."

"Thank fates for that. But I'm still learning my place here. All Sorcha and I can do is take things as they come and build our life. My mate deserves nothing less, and I will do it, whatever it takes, for her."

Orek's look was grave when he turned it on Hakon. "Can you be what your mate needs?"

"Always." Hakon would give her whatever she needed or wanted, whether it was a new tool or the moon itself.

"Can you fit your life to hers?" Orek pressed. "I don't envy your plight—a human woman is one thing, a human noblewoman is much more."

Hakon ground his back teeth, his answer grating against his throat. He didn't know how to tell his friend that Aislinn's life as a noblewoman wasn't what was best, that although she was gifted and devoted, she would surely be happier with a simpler life full of only what she wanted to do.

He would give her that. He'd promised to make and build her whatever she wanted, and that included a new, better life.

Yet, the words didn't come easily. His confidence wavered when it was time to say them aloud. He couldn't help thinking of just how gifted and just how devoted she was. It'd be no small thing for her to give up the life of Liege Darrow.

It was the only path he saw forward, though. He wouldn't be welcomed as her mate and husband within the human nobility. Fates, there were times he didn't think himself worthy of having her for a mate, even in secret.

Hakon couldn't give her up—but he also didn't know how long this half-life they had could last. A love confined to the shadows could never truly grow.

Orek gave his shoulder a supportive slap. "She's a fine woman. I don't know what is to come, but if there is a way, she'll think of it."

Hakon nodded, trying to be content.

He had his mate in his bed most nights. He shared her laughter and her worries. Soon, he would win her heart. Then, he would brave asking her to choose him over all else, just as he loved her above all others.

Fates, he loved her. Of course he did, she was his mate.

That love had to be enough.

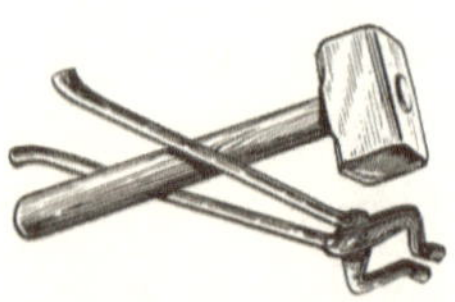

Sorcha squealed in delight before Aislinn slapped a hand over her mouth. Her friend wriggled in the warm water, her smile evident even under Aislinn's hand.

"You wench!" Sorcha giggled when Aislinn finally removed her hand. "How long?"

"Almost two fortnights now. But even before . . ."

Sorcha slipped under the water and came back up with a smug grin on her face. Aislinn splashed her for the grievous offense.

Folding her arms on the stone ledge of the bath, Sorcha propped her chin on her forearm and waggled her brows expectantly. "*And?*"

Aislinn groaned, covering her flushing cheeks with her hands. "He's wonderful. In every way."

"You know how highly I think of halflings, so I'm biased," Sorcha said. She poked Aislinn's bare knee. "I'm happy for you! You deserve this!"

"People keep saying that . . ." she muttered.

"Who else knows?"

"Only Fia, but she said just the same thing to me when she found out."

"Well, it must be true, then. You work yourself ragged here. I'm glad someone's looking out for you." And she included a saucy wink so Aislinn would know exactly what kind of *looking out for* Sorcha meant.

With a little more prompting, Aislinn admitted how it had all come about; from their first meeting to her finally shoring up her courage to go to him. She told her friend of the wonderful things Hakon had made her, of how he'd helped her with the rose garden and accompanied her on meetings with the guilders.

"He's my friend and . . . so much more." The admission felt good to say aloud.

Sorcha hummed dreamily in agreement. "You're well-suited." With a laugh she added, "That clever bastard. Leave it to a blacksmith to find the way to your heart is with projects."

Aislinn's smile was uncontrollably wide. Who would've thought they'd suit each other so well—it all felt fated or meant to be, in a way that she didn't quite believe in but couldn't wholly dismiss.

"Has the mate-bond begun yet?"

"Mate-bond?" she repeated.

The joviality fell from Sorcha's face, and she turned to look at Aislinn seriously. "Has he not said anything about the orcish mate-bond?"

Aislinn shook her head, her stomach sinking.

A small frown marred Sorcha's brow as she said, "He better have a good reason."

"I'm sure he does." Though Aislinn couldn't think of one. Despite the warm water of the baths, her fingers began to go cold. "Why don't you explain it to me."

Sorcha did, describing how orcs had an internal instinct, a beast they called it, that pushed them to fight and fuck. Some had stronger inner beasts than others, particularly in battle, with stronger beasts pushing an orc into a berserker rage. Many orcish sagas told of the destruction a berserker could mete upon an enemy, especially a mated berserker.

Not all orcs formed mate-bonds, and to Sorcha's knowledge it wasn't preordained like other folk believed. When a compatible partner had been found, and the desire was there, a mate-bond formed between lovers. This bond was everlasting, tying mates together for the rest of their days. Such a bond, and the consequences of it, meant that some feared it.

"Once it's set, it's there for life. Always they will feel a pull toward their mate. An orc with a mate-bond will do anything for their partner."

"And you share one with Orek?"

A smile cracked across Sorcha's serious face at the mention of her own mate. "Yes. He said it began to form not long after we met, but he fought it, thinking we wouldn't remain together. He said it usually takes a while to complete, with sustained contact and sex." She arched her brows deliberately.

"Hakon hasn't said . . ."

Sorcha reached out to take her hand. "He might not think you're ready to hear it. Orek didn't tell me at first. He didn't want me to feel tied to him if that's not what I wanted." Her friend searched her face, and Aislinn wanted to squirm away. She knew what Sorcha would ask even before she did. "Do you want to be his mate?"

*Yes.* "I don't know."

To be a mate, to share a mate-bond, it all seemed so . . . final. Such a bond sounded as though it carried far more weight than a human marriage—tied together through blood and instinct rather than just paper and vows. Someone would have to be sure the one they bonded with was truly the right one.

The idea of having to find such a right one, to not only determine it was them but also that they could be trusted with her heart and her future, had panic clawing up Aislinn's throat.

*What if you get it wrong?*

"Hakon purchased land," she made herself say to distract from her panic. "That meadow north of your estate? With the outcropping?"

Sorcha nodded slowly. "I know it."

"He bought it outright. He's talked before of building a big house and forge there. And . . . he hasn't said as much, but I believe he came to the Darrowlands to start a family. That would require a mate, wouldn't it?"

"Not always, but . . ." Sorcha chewed her lip, considering. "I'm a little surprised, honestly. He didn't seem like he wanted to farm—and there's so much for him here at the castle."

"His life is here." *I'm here.* "But, he's asked me to come see the land sometime soon."

"One conundrum after another," Sorcha muttered. "He gives you gifts but hasn't said anything about the mate-bond. He buys land away from Dundúran but wants your approval."

Conundrum was right. Aislinn didn't know what to think now, a seed of worry already planted in her mind. When she made herself consider the mate-bond again, she found she wasn't so terrified of it. Perhaps there was comfort in the finality of it. To know who your mate, your person was. If someone was thoughtful and deliberate in their choice, if they met and chose the right person, then the mate-bond would no doubt be a boon.

For herself, it would be a comfort to know that she'd be able to trust that the bond was there, tying them together, rather than a desire for her title. She didn't have that fear with Hakon per se, but she hadn't forgotten the bitterness of discovering that she was her title first, Aislinn second to her previous lovers.

A noblewoman always had to consider her title when it came to marriage—whether she married because of that title or needed to safeguard it against avaricious suitors.

"Perhaps it's for the best," she made herself say. "Father's beginning to insist I find someone to marry before the king does."

"You, marry?" Sorcha guffawed. "You've been avoiding it so long."

A twinge of frustration pinched Aislinn's chest; it wasn't that she was altogether opposed to marriage. She'd just never found someone she wanted to marry. Not marrying also meant no one expected her to produce heirs and put her life in danger doing it. No man or potential family had been worth the risk before.

Until . . .

Sorcha squeezed her hand again. "I'm so sorry, Aislinn. This is so much to bear, especially on top of everything else. I wish I had answers for you. I wish . . ." Her expression fell. "I wish I'd known what a burden it would be when I asked you to be named heiress."

Aislinn hurried to reassure her friend, even though an ugly, hurting part of her was glad of the acknowledgement. Some days, she resented that this had been bestowed upon her. Some days, she rued the mantle placed on her shoulders.

This part of her wasn't the whole, though, and in the end, she was grateful for the chance to serve her people. In so many ways, she'd acted as heiress even before Jerrod's exile. At least now, there was an acknowledgement of her status and the work she did, and she was honest enough with herself to recognize that that satisfied her pride.

With more power over the Darrowlands, Aislinn intended to improve where she could. She'd make the most of this and leave her mark on her demesne. She just needed a moment to collect herself and catch her breath. Sort out her plans. Figure out what to do with Brenna, what to do about Jerrod when Connor Brádaigh found him, and what she meant to do with Hakon.

But the panic simmered inside her, making Aislinn wish she could solve all problems with a good soak with her dearest friend.

Nothing was ever so simple, though.

*Enjoy it while it lasts,* she told herself. She'd never been good at it, but there was never a better time to start.

# 22

That night, Aislinn laughed along to Sorcha's ridiculous story of what Darrah the raccoon had been up to over the last few weeks—mainly, disappearing into the stables and eating most of the apples, making him many equine enemies.

The dining hall buzzed with warmth and chatter, the tables full of good food and lively people. Hugh made a rare appearance in the hall to graciously accept a round of applause for a wonderful meal, as did Captain Aodhan to sit with some of his seconds and play drinking games.

Aislinn hadn't accomplished much that day, but her spirit was lighter for it. Spending time with Sorcha—while creating more questions than answers about Hakon and orcish courting—was always good for her own morale. The little party planned to stay the night, and Aislinn already looked forward to breakfast with them and stealing a few more hours with her dearest friend.

Sorcha, Orek, and the three youngest Brádaighs were a welcome addition to the high table, the conversation bouncing between all the siblings. It was a marked difference from her staid, lonely dinners since her father had departed. Usually, she brought a book or work to read while she ate.

This was much better.

Although . . .

Her gaze strayed over Sorcha's shoulder, following a familiar path to the rear of the hall. As if he could sense her gaze, Hakon's attention shifted from the potter beside him up to her. Aislinn offered a small smile, wishing he could join them at the high table.

It was while she looked across the hall at Hakon that she noticed a figure walking quickly toward the high table. Aislinn's attention pivoted, and she watched with growing curiosity as one of the maids, Siobhan, hustled toward them, her face blotchy with color and her expression grave. Aislinn might have been worried were it Fia, but Siobhan was known to be of an excitable, meek disposition.

Siobhan dipped into a curtsey when she made the high table. "Forgive me, milady," she whispered breathlessly. "A courier just came, he said it was urgent." She held out a neatly folded missive, sealed with yellow wax.

Aislinn's sense of dread lessened when she saw it was neither the royal seal nor her father's. Orek reached for the missive and handed it to her.

"Thank you, Siobhan. Please, enjoy your dinner."

Curtseying, Siobhan wrung her hands, her gaze stuck worriedly on the missive for a moment before she finally turned away.

Aislinn met Sorcha's curious gaze before using a nail to pop the seal. Yellow was a common color, available in any tavern or waystation, but much less so was the prancing horse standard pressed into the wax.

That dread prickled once again up her neck, and opening the missive and looking at the signature confirmed her suspicion.

"It's from Connor," she told the table.

The siblings all went quiet.

"What does he say?" Orek asked gravely.

Aislinn ran her eyes over his brief message thrice, just to make sure she understood.

*My Lady Aislinn,*

*It is with a heavy heart that I write this to you from the seaside town of Malton.*

*I have followed your brother's trail from the Ward to several towns along the Shanago. He has traveled north, toward the Strait and may attempt to cross into Caledon. He has been using his name to attempt to marshal a mercenary force. Several sellswords in Culdan confirmed that he is offering a fortune to anyone willing to help him reclaim his title.*

*He has gained a following of about thirty but seeks more in the Strait. There is word of a large mercenary force there planning to winter just on the Caledon side of the border.*

*I will send further word when I have it.*

*Yours, loyally,*
*Connor Brádaigh*

An icy ball lodged deep in her stomach as Aislinn handed over the note to Sorcha. As Orek and the children anxiously watched Sorcha read, Aislinn caught Fia's eye and waved her over.

She weaved her way across the hall, smiling and winking at several as she passed, but her smile disappeared when she saw Aislinn's expression.

"Milady?"

"There's a courier from the north who's just delivered a missive. Have him set up for the night and outfitted to leave again at dawn. And secure another courier to ride south and find my father."

Fia went pale, her freckles stark against her white cheeks. "Right away, milady." And she picked up her skirts and darted from the dining hall.

When Aislinn turned back to her dinner party, Calum was quietly reading the girls their elder brother's missive while Orek and Sorcha looked to her with concern.

"Anyone would be mad to believe Jerrod's promises," Sorcha spat.

"People have done far worse for a few coins," said Aislinn.

"What do we do?" Orek asked, lines bracketing his mouth.

"We fight," Sorcha growled. "He has no right to—"

"Many will say he has every right." The words spilled from numb lips, Aislinn's calm exterior a mask to hide the icy rage gathering in her gut. *How dare he?*

"Fuck anyone who does." Keeley gasped at her sister's curse, but Sorcha didn't seem to notice, her frown thunderous and her gaze expectant.

Aislinn wished she could share her friend's fiery anger, but in that moment, all she felt was a cool indignation. If she was honest, this was exactly what they should have expected from Jerrod. Aislinn might've thought the mercenaries more likely to cut him down than listen to him, but then, her brother could be charming when he wanted.

The Darrowlands were a fine prize, blessed with rich farmlands and vineyards. Despite the increasing taxes levied by the crown, the demesne still thrived. As Liege Darrow, Jerrod could afford to pay his mercenary force a fortune and still be a rich lord thereafter.

*But he'll never be Liege Darrow.*

He'd lead the demesne and its people to ruin, and Aislinn wouldn't allow it. *She* was heiress.

The thought fed her indignation, which she clung to. If she let it, a gaping maw of fear would swallow her whole. Jerrod's scheme may come to nothing—mercenaries didn't like being paid in promises. There was still a chance, though, that a force could march on Dundúran. That violence and blood would be the only thing to stop it.

She feared that most. Violence curdled her stomach, and Aislinn never wished to ask others to lay down their lives for her position.

*Don't let it come to that.*

No, there were still things to be done. No force had been gathered.

She still had time.

To Sorcha she said, "We'll each write to our fathers and have the courier make all haste for the south. With them returned, Dundúran's full company will outnumber and outmatch any mercenary force."

Her father had left her with half of their company of knights, as well as the full castle garrison, and while capable, she didn't know if those left behind would be enough.

She'd always feared that her brother would only be stopped by violence and blood, but it hadn't come to that yet. *I still have time.*

Rising from the table, Aislinn looked out over the dining hall, stomach clenched with nerves. None seemed to notice the dramatic shift in tenor of the high table—except Hakon. He stood from his place, Wülf at his side, his gaze focused on her.

All she could do was shake her head.

Later, much later, when the letters were all written and sealed and the castle itself slumbered through the wee hours, Aislinn stole down to Hakon's bedchamber.

A faint line of light glowed beneath the door, confirmation that he was yet awake and awaiting her. Heart in her throat, Aislinn quietly opened the door and closed and locked it behind her.

Hakon sat in a chair near the hearth, whittling. He looked up immediately at the sound of her entrance, and quickly stood, casting away his knife and block.

"Aislinn—"

She walked straight into his open arms, burying herself against his chest. She banded her arms around his thick waist and held on tight, needing the comfort of his warm body. Those big arms came around her, holding her together when she otherwise might break apart.

"Lay with me?" she whispered.

Without a word, Hakon pulled her to his bed. He drew his leathers off and untied her dressing gown. Turning down the blankets and furs, he laid out on his back and held his arms open for her. She slipped in behind him, crawling over him until she could lay across him like a blanket.

He covered their legs with a fur before wrapping her up in his arms again. His chin rasped against the crown of her head as he tucked her tight to him. Aislinn nuzzled the divot between his pectorals, drawing in a long pull of his scent, and sighed with relief when a little of the terror fisting her heart loosened.

He rumbled that purr for her, not a frenetic vibration like during their lovemaking but instead a soothing cadence, one meant to lull and calm her. Aislinn's eyes grew heavy, and she sank into him and his comfort.

"Will you tell me what's happened?" he said softly.

Drawing a long breath, Aislinn did. She told him everything without exaggeration or embellishment. He listened in silence, the only sign of his growing anger the kneading press of his fingers along her back.

"I'll kill him myself if it comes to it, *vinya,* and any brigand he dares bring with him."

"I know," she whispered. That's exactly what she feared.

They lapsed into an unsteady silence. She could tell there were many questions and thoughts on his tongue, but he held them back. Perhaps he sensed just how tired she already was over this, how she only needed his comfort, not his battle plans. Perhaps he guessed that she had questions for him, too.

She didn't ask him what she'd come to ask, though.

Tonight, she didn't think she could bear his answer, whatever it was.

So, she lay with him through the night, sometimes sleeping, sometimes listening to the steady beat of his heart. She focused on that rhythm, forbidding herself from any more thoughts until the sun came up.

Like that, she was finally able to steal a few hours' rest.

# 23

Aislinn bit at a cuticle until Sorcha drew her hand away, before it could bleed. Her friend squeezed her hand sympathetically as they stood in the small posterior foyer to the great hall, where they could wait for everyone to gather before entering.

Orek had left earlier in the morning to take the children back to the Brádaigh estate, promising to return by the afternoon. Aislinn was grateful for her friend's continued presence; if she couldn't hold Hakon's hand and seek his comfort in the daylight, at least she could hold Sorcha's.

Leaning around the corner, Sorcha peeked out into the hall. "It looks like everyone's ready for you," she reported.

Drawing in a long breath to settle her nerves, Aislinn nodded and preceded Sorcha out into the hall. The eyes of all her staff found and followed her as she made the dais.

Aislinn had struggled over the decision but ultimately decided they deserved to know. It wasn't yet time to worry anyone outside the castle, for Connor's message didn't lead her to believe Jerrod's mercenary force was imminent. Still, there were things that now needed to be done, and she didn't want to keep secrets from the staff.

Well, any *more* secrets.

Her eyes skated across the gathered crowd; she saw green in the corner of her eye but didn't want to make it obvious. Still, when her gaze fell on Hakon, standing off to the side with the other blacksmiths, her heart went *pitter-patter*.

It was lonely atop the dais, in a place she was so accustomed to seeing her father, but the sight of Hakon gave her comfort.

Clasping her hands behind her back, Aislinn let her mother's training guide her. She'd never enjoyed public speaking, but this was her staff, the people she saw every day. She didn't relish standing before all of them at once, but they deserved to hear it from her.

"Good day, everyone. Thank you for taking the time. I wanted to inform all of you of recent developments." Whoever hadn't been giving her their full attention before now did, and the atmosphere of the great hall cooled to see the stiff, serious way she stood there. "As you all know, my brother Jerrod was stripped last autumn of his title and inheritance. He was sent to the Ward to serve his penance for crimes. In summer, he ran away from the Ward, and nothing was heard of him. Last night, I received intelligence that my brother has been using his name and promises of future favors to gather a mercenary force to retake Dundúran."

A nervous murmuration went through the staff, anxious eyes bouncing from her to their neighbors and back. She'd caught them by surprise, but then, she could hardly believe it herself.

Jerrod running away from the Ward hadn't surprised her. Neither had discovering he was looking to have others reclaim his life for him. Yet, going to mercenaries was a shock—that he'd endanger himself and throw his lot in with much rougher, more desperate people meant . . . Jerrod was just as desperate himself.

A desperate Jerrod was a dangerous one.

*Why couldn't he have just made a new life for himself somewhere?*

Away from Dundúran, away from the Ward—somewhere he wouldn't make more trouble for his family.

*That's not like Jerrod.*

No, it wasn't. And that was why Aislinn stood before her staff now. She wanted to be proactive and assuage any fears. As heiress, she would defend her people and her position. She would prove she was the one to lead them.

Even if everything about this terrified her.

"I tell you this now not to frighten you. Many of you have worked loyally for my father and me for years, and you all deserve to know. This is an ongoing situation, and I'm seeking more information before a decision is made. I have already sent for my father to return home."

The nervous energy of the staff swelled, and Aislinn gave them a moment. She understood what a shock this was; Dundúran hadn't come under attack since before Aislinn was born. Many staff couldn't remember a time when the city was threatened. Her own father had to go looking for danger in the borderlands with how safe and secure he'd made the Darrowlands.

Stepping forward, she said, "If you have any information that may be useful, please come forward. We don't suspect that Jerrod has much of a force, and nothing at all may come of this. Everything is to go on as it normally would. The autumn council meeting will still take place in three days, and we expect guests to begin arriving tomorrow."

Something of a sigh released from the staff, and Aislinn was proud to see her people rallying. The danger wasn't yet at their door, if it ever came, and ensuring normalcy would go a long way to allay fears.

"I will speak to Captain Aodhan today, and please come to him or me if you have any concerns. For now, keep this news within the castle walls. Before you go, I want to thank you all for your service to me and my family. Each of you fulfills an important part in Dundúran, and I'm grateful for all you do." And with a nod, she dismissed them back to their duties.

The staff rallied, and a few called out well-wishes to her. Aislinn descended the dais and met several of the more nervous staff, assuring them that everything was in hand and she would call them again to share any news.

As the crowd dissipated back into the castle, Captain Aodhan, Brenna, and Fia stepped forward, staying as she'd asked them to. Over Brenna's shoulder, Aislinn spied Hakon lingering, having only made a few cursory steps for the door.

She wished he could stand beside her, but for now, there was nothing for it. All she could do was offer a small smile before turning her attention to the group gathered around her.

"Captain, Brenna, I'd speak with both of you, please. Follow me."

Aislinn led their small party from the great hall toward her study. Her nerves gnawed at her and what she needed from each of them, but she made herself walk at a steady pace, her chin up and shoulders back.

It was only when they neared her study that she realized an issue. She couldn't fit all of them in her study, crowded with books and drafting tools. Aislinn's cheeks heated as she slowed to a stop.

Just imagining Captain Aodhan in there, amongst her piles of books and scattered papers, was laughable. Next to the stoic warrior with his shining breastplate and short-cropped hair, her study seemed almost . . . childish.

"We'll use my father's study," she decided, turning to lead them to the much larger room.

The space was a familiar one, and as she walked into it after Captain Aodhan opened the door for them, she took comfort from the scent of leather and wood oil. Her father's presence lingered in his study, in the wide, dark-stained desk and deep green cushions. His bookcases were orderly, his maps and tools organized.

She was so used to walking into this room; what grated against her with unfamiliarity was rounding the heavy desk and sitting in her father's chair.

Aislinn ran her palms over the rounded pommels on the chair arms, feeling the grooves her father had worn in them over his years as Liege Darrow.

*It's too soon,* her heart cried. She didn't want his place nor his title. Not yet.

None of that changed her situation, though.

So, Aislinn moved the chair closer to the desk and laid her hands on its cool surface.

"Was it wise to tell them?" asked Brenna as they gathered round the desk. "The news will undoubtedly find its way into the city. Tongues have a way of wagging."

Aislinn blinked, realizing that she could have lied, or at least kept silent about this to the staff. It hadn't occurred to her, honestly. They deserved to know.

"I don't wish to lie to them," said Aislinn.

"It wouldn't look well on Aislinn if they found out later, when Jerrod's at the gate," Sorcha argued.

"*Lady* Aislinn," Brenna corrected under her breath.

"I thought they should know. And . . . should there be any sympathy for Jerrod within the castle, best to know sooner."

"Indeed, my lady," agreed Captain Aodhan. "We will be vigilant. It's also why I must advise that at least two guards stay with you at all times."

Aislinn opened her mouth to argue, that she of course was safe within the castle itself, but had she not just admitted she waited to see if someone would betray her to Jerrod?

*I won't be able to see Hakon. Not without an audience.*

She trusted her knights to be discreet, but her situation had grown evermore fraught. Aislinn couldn't help remembering Brenna's warning about the Darrows seeming so cozy with otherly folk. She wanted to believe her swordsmen and staff wouldn't be so bigoted as to care either way, but it was naïve to think that the lady of the castle sneaking off to the blacksmith's bedchamber wouldn't at least cause gossip.

Aislinn swallowed that bitter truth with effort and a heavy heart.

"And no more disappearing for a whole day," added Brenna.

Lips thinning, Aislinn said, "I will agree to two guards. For now, have them keep back unless we know there is a possible threat. We must be cautious, not paranoid."

Captain Aodhan nodded stiffly. Aislinn knew he would have preferred to have her surrounded by six knights just to walk from her bedchamber to the dining hall, but Aislinn chafed against such an obvious show of defense. She wasn't scared of Jerrod, and she wouldn't allow him to dictate her daily life from over a hundred leagues away.

"I'm hoping none of this will be necessary in the end, but it may be worthwhile seeking new recruits to help round out the numbers."

"Yes, my lady. I will also increase patrols and send a few into the countryside, just to ensure we won't be taken by surprise."

Aislinn nodded. "I don't want the people to be frightened or feel a heavy hand, but we must be vigilant, as you say. I want to know if anyone is sympathetic to Jerrod. I'm hoping his plan will fall apart, but if he does manage to marshal any sort of force, we can't have a threat within, too."

"That won't happen, my lady, rest assured. The people are loyal to those who treat them well. I'm sorry if I overstep," Captain Aodhan pressed his fist over his heart, "but we all remember your brother. The Darrowlands rejoiced when you were named heiress—no one will want to see you replaced."

"Thank you, captain." Aislinn's heart stung with gratitude at the captain's words.

Bowing, Captain Aodhan said, "We will weather this, my lady."

"You're right. We will."

After a few more words, the captain departed to see to his duties, leaving Aislinn a little more confident in his wake.

Aislinn would take what time she had to find a solution—something other than violence and bloodshed. With a little luck, she'd find one before her father even returned home.

The alternative was to test the loyalty of not only her staff but her people. To call upon a force to defend Dundúran—something even her father had never had to do. She had the authority, and her father's seal of writ, but did she have the loyalty of all her people, from the farmers to the barons?

*I don't know.*

Aislinn thought she knew and could trust people before and had been proven wrong.

"Brenna."

The chatelain stepped forward, her expression even more closed off than usual. That unreadable face had upset Aislinn many a time. Left to fill in her own interpretation, she often imagined Brenna was disappointed in her, mad at her.

Now, it didn't matter so much. The sting was still there but buried under the cold indignation that Aislinn clung to.

"My lady?"

"I need to know everything that goes on in the castle. If there is sympathetic talk over Jerrod. If there's discontent with my father or me. Anything."

"Yes, my lady."

"That goes for you as well, Brenna."

That got a coolly arched brow. "Me?"

"I know Jerrod has long been a favorite of yours. I know you feel for him as if . . ." Aislinn pushed past her tightening throat. "I know he's dear. But what he's planning to do—it endangers us all. I hope I can count on you in this time."

Brenna's lips drew thin, and for a moment, Aislinn thought she was about to receive a classic, curt telling off. Brenna was a proud woman and held herself and her position to the highest standard. To have her loyalty questioned was no doubt insulting.

And yet, Brenna had let Jerrod get away with most everything. Always she had a reprimand or scolding for Aislinn, yet Jerrod could do no wrong. Perhaps if Jerrod had faced any consequences, from his parents or Brenna, things might have been different.

Perhaps, if their parents hadn't been so preoccupied with making sure Aislinn was given what she needed to not only survive but succeed with her different mind, they might have seen the angry, jealous boy their son was becoming. The first to notice was Brenna, and she spoiled him for it, giving him the affection his family couldn't. When he wanted something, he went to Brenna. When he didn't get something, he went to Brenna.

Brenna forgave him. Brenna loved him. Even when he wasn't lovable or kind.

She'd been more of a mother to him than Róisín or Aislinn had. Which was why Aislinn had to bury her guilt and ask now.

"He's just a silly boy," was what Brenna said. "I'm sure he'll give it up soon."

"That's my hope. But we both know how he can be when he truly wants something." Aislinn often lamented that he never translated that fervor into dedication to Dundúran and his duties. He could be single-minded and determined, but the darker side of this was when it still didn't get him his way. His disappointment was ugly and vicious, and Sorcha's ordeal was proof of it.

"Your brother has had a difficult life."

Sorcha audibly scoffed.

Aislinn bit her tongue to keep the retort inside. It was true, for all his privilege and position, Jerrod hadn't had an easy time of it. There were many reasons to show why he'd done what he did.

And yet—

"That's no excuse, though, for threatening his family and his home," said Brenna.

"Indeed." Aislinn sat back in her seat, trying to assess if Brenna spoke true. She thought so, but then again, she'd thought many things before.

The risk was too high to be wrong now.

"Very well. Keep me informed on whatever you learn."

"Of course." Dipping into a quick curtsey, Brenna departed.

The chatelain left an uneasy silence in her wake.

"I want you to keep an eye on her," Aislinn told Fia softly, whispering as if Brenna might hear through the very walls.

"Yes, milady."

"Is all this watching and reporting back necessary?" asked Sorcha.

"I hope not," Aislinn replied. "But there were a few who liked Jerrod."

"Not enough to threaten your position," insisted Fia. "Your people are loyal, milady. They've seen what you do for them, when your brother was heir and now. They understand who the better leader would be."

"He can't be very popular when people hear he's bringing mercenaries. Fates know what they could do to a city like this," added Sorcha.

The pit of dread gaping in her stomach opened a little wider at the thought. Fates, she couldn't allow whatever mercenary force Jerrod might rally anywhere near Dundúran and its people. Anyone desperate enough to take Jerrod up on merely promises would ravage the city and leave nothing behind.

"You look ill." Sorcha came around the desk and placed a comforting hand on her shoulder. "It's going to be all right. You'll see. The people of the Darrowlands are loyal to you."

She had to hope so.

The consequences of being wrong were too much to bear.

# 24

Not that it mattered to her anymore, but Aislinn had no doubt Brenna would be proud of her today. In preparation for the day's council meeting, Aislinn had woken early and sat patiently as Fia chose her an appropriately fine gown and wound her hair in braids and curls, fixed with pearl pins. A crescent cloth headdress encrusted with pearls and aquamarines kept her hair back from her face, and a long string of pearls accompanied the gold arrow and sword insignia of her house affixed at her throat.

Looking at herself in the mirror, the first thought Aislinn had was, *I look like my mother.*

This certainly wasn't a bad thing. Whenever she faced a situation like this, she wanted to emulate the elegant Lady Róisín as much as possible.

Still, her reflection plucked at her nerves—she didn't look like herself.

For now, that's just the way it had to be.

The pearls offered cool little points of sensation as she walked with Fia, Sorcha, and her two guards to the council chambers. Not unpleasant but almost distracting. Weighed down in finery, Aislinn told herself to think of it as armor, a shell to protect her vulnerable innards.

*Let them see and judge the shell.*

Sorcha offered a nod and Fia a small smile before they stepped up to the doors. Her guards opened them wide, and, holding her breath, Aislinn swept inside.

The gathered vassals and yeomen went silent upon her entrance, but rather than being met with annoyance, expectation hung heavy in the air. As heiress and the sole Darrow in residence, this meeting didn't start without her.

Faltering only a step, she made for the seat at the head of the long table. Fia came to stand to her side and just behind, holding onto documents she may need later. Sorcha found a place to stand with other yeomen, the seats around the council table reserved for the most senior nobles in attendance.

Aislinn stood at the head of that table and made herself meet the eyes of as many as she could. Padraic Bayard was there, of course, he never missed a chance to visit Dundúran. Earl Starley had come, no doubt in the hope of seeing Lady Lisbet. Baron Morraugh had unfortunately come, but then, it was said he looked for any excuse to escape his estate after his wife's passing. Several vassals and yeomen who hadn't been at the summer meeting were here now, bringing the total to at least fifty, well above the last meeting.

*Come to see the heiress squirm.*

Aislinn refused to let the thought further than that and the flush from overtaking her face.

*"Never let them have more than you're willing to give,"* her mother would say.

She was about to take her seat when the doors opened again.

One of her guards leaned into the room. "My lady, there's . . ."

Aislinn caught sight of a swishing black cloak. Pulse kicking, she said with more confidence than she felt, "Yes, let him in."

After another moment of hesitation, the guard opened the door wider, and in walked Allarion.

A gasp resounded through the room.

"My lady, what's the meaning of this?" demanded Lady Lisbet, her concern and bulging eyes speaking for those gathered.

"Lord Allarion, you are welcome here," Aislinn said instead.

Bowing, Allarion said, "Thank you, my lady. I'm honored to be here amongst my esteemed peers."

His footfalls, while quiet as a mountain cat's, were thunderous in the perfect silence of the council chamber. He quickly picked Sorcha from the crowd and made himself comfortable along the wall beside her. He took in the stunned council with a mild expression, although Aislinn thought he might have found the whole spectacle amusing.

Aislinn took her seat and folded her hands on the polished table. When no one else moved, she was forced to tell them, "Please, take your seats and let's begin."

Those with chairs slumped and slipped into their seats, gazes flicking between her and Allarion, as if they didn't dare turn their attention away for too long.

"Lord Allarion has taken possession of the Scarborough estate. As such, he is well within his rights to attend this meeting."

Several councilors gawped at her, reminding her of fish caught on a hook. She allowed them a few more moments with their surprise, but eventually her impatience won out.

*Let's get on with it and be done.*

"Now, as you—"

"He's *fae!*" insisted Padraic Bayard, standing up to emphasize his point.

"Yes, my lord. I know."

"He can't . . . he shouldn't . . ." Bayard threw what Aislinn considered to be an imminently stupid frown at the fae in question.

"As you all know, we have King Marius's blessing to integrate interested otherly folk into our demesne. Allarion has the deed, signed by myself and my father."

"But, my lady," tried Baron Burgoyne, one of their vassals to the south, "to allow an otherly such rights . . ."

"No one has claimed or wanted Scarborough for decades. Allarion is doing us a favor by occupying and restoring the land. And what's more, the sale has helped Dundúran cover this year's dues. Once my brother is dealt with, I will be giving you the difference between this and last year's dues."

That earned a round of interested mumbles. It was true what her father said sometimes, *"Money speaks, even if it has no mouth."*

"Now," she continued, "I won't hear more argument about it. The otherly folk in the Darrowlands have worked hard to integrate into our communities. From all accounts, they are good neighbors. My father has always upheld the Darrowlands as a demesne of freedom and dignity for all. *All* includes humans and otherly folk."

"But a fae . . ." croaked Earl Starley. "They are loyal only to their queen."

"If I may?" Stepping forward, Allarion waited until Aislinn nodded in assent before explaining, "Not all are loyal to the queen. Dissent exists in her court. I wanted a life far from this intrigue and am grateful to have found a place as peaceful and good as Scarborough. I have pledged my fealty to Liege Darrow and the heiress, as have you all."

Allarion left a stunned silence in his wake as he retook his place beside Sorcha, whose own eyes had gone wide at his speech.

Clearing her throat, Aislinn said, "Thank you, Lord Allarion. Now, shall we begin?"

A few murmurs and disgruntled huffs met her question, but ultimately, the council settled in.

With Fia taking notes for her as she usually did, Aislinn led them through the meeting, finding the familiar rhythm of it once she got them on task. There were harvests to report and winter droving sites to negotiate and criminal cases to rule on. Alarmingly, the margraves reported an increase in thefts in their market towns.

"Do we not often see such increases with winter coming?" Aislinn asked.

"We do, my lady," said Margrave Holt, a pretty woman even younger than Aislinn who'd taken the mantle of responsibility from her mother at the tender age of ten. "But this is earlier than we'd usually expect. If it continues at this rate, many of my farmers will struggle this winter."

"Do you have any ideas for why there's such an increase?"

Margrave Holt blinked, as if she hadn't been expecting to give her opinion. Aislinn blinked back, waiting. Who else better to give an opinion than her?

"My sheriffs suspect there is disquiet in the borderlands. There are rumors from the orcish territories that one of their chiefs is trying to unite them under one banner to check the Pyrrossi incursions along their borders. This and your father's efforts may be pushing those who'd normally hide out in the borderlands further north."

*Interesting.* If this was true, it was all the more reason to call her father home and have him reassess his strategy.

"While you're here in Dundúran, I'll have you write a report of the problem and your suspected reasons for it. I will ensure this information gets to the capital. If Pyrros and the orcs mean to war with each other, Eirea must be prepared."

"Of course, my lady."

"Upon your return, please gather what information you can from your sheriffs and have those farmers affected compensated. We can also increase patrolling in the area if you think the show of force would help."

Margrave Holt grinned with relief. "It would, my lady. Thank you."

"Good. You may also keep anyone caught in the act through the winter, and we will try any cases in spring."

This drew approval from the other margraves, and the tenor of the meeting seemed to warm. They discussed the coming winter as well as any large construction anyone planned to undertake in spring.

Although she'd been dreading the meeting, Aislinn didn't look forward to the end she saw drawing closer. She kept her hands tightly knitted together to keep them from trembling, and listening to the landholders kept the worst of the nausea at bay.

Still, with the issues dwindling and the landholders beginning to look at the door in anticipation of the coming banquet, Aislinn knew she could avoid it no longer.

"There's one last thing we must discuss."

The vassals settled back in their seats, though she could tell she only held about half their attention.

"I have received credible information that my brother Jerrod is attempting to raise a mercenary force along the Caledon border. He aims to march that force and retake Dundúran."

The air in the room cooled, the gathered landholders looking on in shock.

"We don't know what, if anything, will come of this. Jerrod has his name only to barter with. I'm seeking more information and have already sent for my father to return. However, in the event it is needed, I hope I can count on all of you to send what forces you can to defend the Darrowlands."

"Of course we will, my lady," Margrave Holt was quick to say.

"A liege lord hasn't summoned a force in nearly forty years," said Baron Morraugh.

"And let us hope that remains true. I don't believe Jerrod will be able to rally much of a force to him, but I want to be prepared. I also want to be honest with you all. When there is more information, I will share it."

Her heart went reedy in her chest waiting for some sort of reaction.

The landholders looked amongst themselves, the more senior barons and earls no doubt calculating just how much they might be asked to contribute. Aislinn knew such a command would be unpopular—perhaps even more so than the raised dues.

The fact remained, though, that she was heiress of the Darrowlands, and everyone here owed fealty to her father. She could summon their forces to defend Dundúran.

How many would actually answer was the real question.

Aislinn's stomach twisted painfully.

Jerrod wasn't popular with the vassals, but she knew more than a few who may choose a strategy of attrition. Prevaricate until it was clear whose side would be victorious. Perhaps there were even those who disliked her enough to side with Jerrod.

Aislinn looked around the gathered landholders, that sinking dread inside her growing heavier.

She didn't know. She couldn't say with surety who they would support.

Of the fifty or so here, she felt confident about only ten of them.

Were it her father, there wouldn't be any questions, of course, but this wasn't a question of her father.

"Thank you for your time," Aislinn said. She stood, giving permission for the others to as well. "I don't mean to worry any of you with this, only to inform. Dundúran has met and crushed every threat to her. She will again."

"We're sure of it, my lady," said Earl Starley, surprising her.

"Thank you, my lord." Forcing a smile, she gestured for the doors. "Now, I think we've earned our feast."

The landholders burst with noise, murmurs and groans and cracking knuckles. They moved as an unhurried wave for the door, groups gathering and chatting as they exited the council chamber two or three at a time.

Aislinn took further questions from a few of her margraves, as well as several of her younger, inexperienced yeomen.

"It's only me, the wife, and the babe," said Samson Brightweather, a yeoman from the north. "I couldn't contribute much, but perhaps I could spare a horse?"

Warmed by the offer, Aislinn was quick to reassure him, "Please don't worry yourself. It's the nobles and other landholders who keep retainers who will send reinforcements if they're needed. You focus on preparing for winter."

"Thank you, milady," Samson sighed in relief.

When he and the lingering landholders finally left, Aislinn slumped into her seat, sighing herself. She could hardly move her stiff fingers and hid her trembling hands in her skirts.

"I may be of some help," said Allarion, stepping forward with Sorcha. "I am ready to defend my new home. But I must caution you, my magic is still . . . unsteady. For now, I fear it is only my sword I can offer."

"That's very generous. I hope I don't have to take you up on your offer, but . . ."

"I know nothing of your brother, but I do know that those who feel they have had something stolen from them find it difficult to let it go. Let us hope your brother is wiser."

Aislinn managed a weak smile in agreement, but she feared her own concern was plain on her face.

Jerrod wasn't that wise. That he'd run away at all and sought the help of mercenaries showed just how stupid he could be.

No, what Aislinn worried over was just how much his stupidity could cost them all.

"Let us hope," she said. Even if it was for naught.

What she did know was that this was the last time she let Jerrod's stupidity hurt her, their father, and the people of the Darrowlands. Brother or no, blood or no, Aislinn was done.

# 25

Hakon stood with Orek under the eaves of the smithy, watching the rain splatter on the cobblestones. The sweetness of the warm cider one of the lads had fetched them all from the kitchen warmed his mouth, a counterpoint to the damp cool of the rain, but Hakon barely felt the burn.

The rain came down in heavy sheets, obscuring the castle walls just across the bailey. The torrential sound of it filled Hakon's ears with a thick buzzing, and the gray damp matched his mood.

"Aislinn hardly comes to the dining hall. She's not eating," he told his friend in orcish. Although the new orcess blacksmith, Edda, could understand them, he thought the pounding rain would dull their words—if her enthusiastic hammering didn't already.

"The womenfolk are seeing to her," Orek assured him.

*Not as well as I could.* Hakon saw the strain around her eyes and mouth. The burdens she carried were beginning to crush her, and it drove him mad having to stand to the side and watch it.

It was only a little comfort that she had Sorcha with her. She and Orek had taken up residence in the castle for the time being to help Aislinn with whatever she needed. For the most part, that seemed for Sorcha to be as a companion; Orek offered his help and brawn wherever it was needed but stuck mostly with Hakon in the smithy. She had Fia, too, the maid acting more as a seneschal and messenger. Aislinn was always guarded by at least two knights, even if they weren't obvious or close beside her.

*So many people to perform my duties. I should comfort her. I should protect her. I . . .*

It was a mate's due and duty.

Yet, she wasn't his mate. Not truly. In his heart and mind, she of course was. But he'd never explained the bond to her. She'd never accepted his claim.

He'd gambled and lost.

With guards everywhere and the staff steeped with suspicion after the announcement of Jerrod's scheming, there weren't opportunities to see her. Being somewhere he shouldn't was noticed. Her guards would follow dutifully if she came to his chamber as she used to.

He wasn't afraid of wagging tongues, and he'd be a liar if he said being kept a secret didn't rankle. Hakon understood, though, that she was the one with everything to lose, and he'd never accept being a liability to her. If it was safer for her to keep away, he understood.

He didn't like it.

He didn't want it.

He understood why the separation had to be—but that didn't mean not having her near didn't drive him to insanity. All day and each night, the unfulfilled mate-bond clawed at his guts. If he allowed it, a keening whine escaped his chest, a pathetic sound the exact pitch of his longing for her.

Fearghas and Caitlín had insisted he take a break after shattering his second metal plate of the day. Caitlín was an orderly sort and didn't appreciate his mistakes. Her partner, Edda, likely suspected something as an orcess herself, and looked on sympathetically when he grumbled over his distracted work.

"They must have her rest. This is too much for one soul, they must make her—"

"You know as well as I do that there's no making Aislinn do anything she doesn't want," said Orek.

Hakon gritted his tusks. He did know that. He also knew that if it was for her benefit, Aislinn had to be made to rest and eat and calm herself.

A sucking, sick feeling took root in his gut thinking of her crying in the rose garden. Had she had another fit?

His chest ached with needing to hold and comfort her, to feel her skin against his and have her scent soaking his senses. He understood the distance but didn't know how long he could bear it.

"If only word would come, one way or another." This waiting was its own kind of madness. Since learning of Jerrod's plans almost a fortnight ago, nothing had been heard from either Connor Brádaigh or Lord Merrick.

The strain of so many unknowns was carved in the lines on Aislinn's face and echoed in the whispers of the castle. The merriment had largely disappeared from the staff, meals much more hushed and eyes downcast. Many took their cues from Aislinn herself, and although she carried out her duties with determination, they all saw the growing concern that hung about her. It was a miasma that followed her from one part of the castle to another, almost visible when she attempted to smile but it never reached her eyes.

"It'll take Liege Darrow time to get his party turned around."

Hakon grumbled. "Doesn't mean he can't send word ahead." He didn't need Orek's sense or agreeableness. His mood was darker than the rainy skies, and everything was wrong and nothing was right.

*None of this is right. I should be with my mate.*

His mood toward his friend wasn't improved by Orek getting to lay with his own human mate each night.

Jealousy was an ugly thing, but it was amongst good company inside Hakon.

Still, he appreciated Orek's steadfastness as he tried to let the rain dampen his temper and frustration. For now, there was nothing to do but wait.

When his mate needed him, Hakon would be ready.

The rain pattered against the windowpanes, an auditory distraction that Aislinn just couldn't ignore. Sighing, she sat back in her seat, abandoning the letter she'd been crafting for days. Rain usually offered a pleasant rhythm to work to, but Aislinn would take any distraction she could.

She scowled at the growing pile of correspondence that needed her attention. From reports to orders to letters, it seemed like everyone in the Darrowlands needed something from her.

Aislinn spent most of her days sequestered in her father's study, trying not to drown in paperwork. She ate and slept when she could, and even visited the bridge site to finalize plans with several of the guild-masters, but much of her life had condensed to that room.

She missed her study.

Her father's was large and comfortable and befit the work she did and meetings she conducted. Fia had helped move over her most pertinent papers and notebooks, but still, she missed her space; how it smelled of parchment, how the light streamed in around midafternoon and filled it with a golden glow.

She missed her father himself, too. It should've been him sitting in that chair, writing those letters. There was still no word from him, nor Connor, and each day that passed without news frayed the delicate strands of her sanity a little more. She worried it wouldn't be long before she was weak enough to snap.

So far, her fits had threatened but not manifested. There was always something to distract her. This needed doing, that accomplishing. Completing even a little task gave her some sense of control, and she was able to wrest herself back from the precipice of panic as she stroked the whittled rose with her free hand.

At least during the day.

At night, her mind had nothing to do but wander. Down the corridors of the castle, to his door.

She missed Hakon most of all.

She longed to write to him, to at least have one correspondence to look forward to, but he neither read nor wrote Eirean. With her guards, there was no question of going to him unseen. She knew her knights were discreet, but she didn't know if Hakon would want such exposure.

Their separation was a dark chasm that grew with every day, and Aislinn worried that the wider it grew, the less likely it was that they could bridge it.

Externally, there was no lasting proof of their affair. She'd been dutiful in taking the silphium Fia brought her and had already had her monthly courses. Other than the marks on her heart, nothing betrayed that she'd begun to fall in love with the halfling blacksmith.

She thought she could claim some of his affections—she'd no doubt that he cared for her, but what this distance did to such budding feelings, and what it meant as far as potentially being his mate, she couldn't say. Since learning of the orcish mate-bond, the idea had stuck like a splinter in her mind, breeding doubts and worries.

There was a soft part of her, in her heart of hearts, that wanted to be Hakon's mate. The one bonded to him. The sole recipient of his devotion.

If she only knew how he felt, whether it was a possibility at all . . .

*What would I do?* she asked herself, not for the first time.

She didn't know if there was any possibility that she might be or become his mate nor if he even wanted that. And, perhaps most importantly, she didn't know what she would do if she was. Could she give him that devotion and commitment in return?

If she was just Aislinn, yes. In a heartbeat. Without question.

But no matter what they said to each other in the soft darkness, she wasn't just Aislinn.

She couldn't say she would accept the mate-bond if it was offered to her, but she also couldn't bear to decide that she'd deny it, either. The thought of giving him up was a dagger between her ribs, a sharpness that only abated if she turned her thoughts away.

Hakon wouldn't be like Brenden and Sir Alaisdair. She wouldn't look apathetically on their fizzling romance nor look forward to his leaving. The loss of him would strike her hard, in her softest parts, and she may not recover.

The thought of taking another, the faceless, nameless husband her father suggested, was just as distasteful. Bitterness burned the back of her tongue just thinking about having to lay with another man, feeling another's hands on her, seeing another's face above her. Her guts twisted with anxious nausea at the idea of giving over her body to someone else.

*I don't want anyone else.*

That wasn't an answer, not really, but it was all she knew.

She didn't know if he felt a mate-bond growing between them or if he even wanted it to. She didn't know if she would or even could accept it if he did.

*I might not know until I find out either way.*

It was the cowardly way out, to stall, but Aislinn was tired. None of the bards ever mentioned how tiring it was to be brave, and Aislinn had to rally all her courage just to climb from her bed and face each day. She thought she deserved a little patience from herself.

Even if she was disappointed in herself for it, starting the cycle all over again.

Unhappier than she was before, Aislinn pulled another report from the top of the pile and buried herself in it.

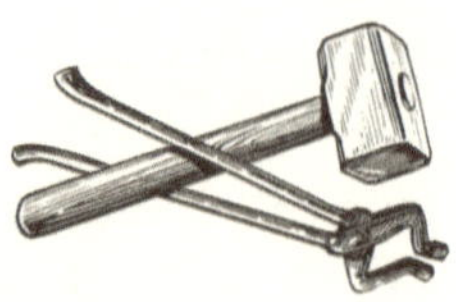

utumn began to wane into winter, and with it went any hint of good weather. Hakon beat his hammer against his anvil to a symphony of other hammers and pounding rain. It soaked the land for four days straight before their first glimpse of sunshine.

Everyone had found excuses to be outside and soak in the little sun and warmth. Then another storm rolled across the verdant hills that night, and back inside they all went.

The coming winter and transitioning to more tasks indoors weren't new to any of them, yet being confined only seemed to tighten the tension within Dundúran. Whispers echoed down the halls, and Hakon railed against his poor ear. What was said in those whispers often eluded him, and his frustration grew into fear that he missed some warning or threat to his mate.

He hardly spoke at meals anymore, his gaze flitting between anyone speaking and watching for Aislinn. More often than not, she didn't take her meals in the hall, leaving him to eat in silence and despair as he strained his ears for anything.

What he did hear didn't cause him any alarm. The staff were concerned but loyal. They spoke of Jerrod and what he'd been like. They remarked on the rain and how muddy it made the roads and perhaps that was why no messages had come. They worried over Aislinn and what this would mean for her, echoing Hakon's own fears.

The days shortened and darkened, and with each that passed, it felt as though a shroud fell over Dundúran. Smothering and dark, they all stifled beneath its weight.

Those most sensitive to it were the newest additions to the castle.

"Is this always such a grim place?" Caitlín asked one soggy afternoon as they took their break. "We hadn't imagined such a pall when we sold our forge and came here."

"This business with her brother was . . . unexpected," Hakon said.

Fearghas *hmphed*. "Not unexpected," he muttered into his cup.

"No?" said Caitlín, fishing for more.

"Anyone with eyes could see that boy would do something stupid like this. But then, the lord has never been firm with him. The heiress, either. They're spoiled, both of them. Always been fighting with each other. Now it's come to war, and we'll all pay the price."

"Lady Aislinn will handle her brother," Hakon grumbled.

"She will, huh? How? You going to fight for her when she needs us to fill out the ranks?"

"Gladly," Hakon growled.

"We won't fight," insisted Caitlín, having gone pale.

"Nobody's said anything about fighting," Edda hurried to reassure her.

"You're fools if you think it won't come to that. Sooner or later, that whelp is going to come for what he thinks is his. Won't matter who's in his way."

"It will be for nothing. The people are loyal to Liege Darrow and Lady Aislinn," Hakon said, his fingers making indents in his cup from how tightly he gripped it.

"We'll see how loyal they are when those mercenaries are raping and pillaging. That's all Jerrod's got to promise them, loot and fucking."

"Watch your mouth," Edda growled.

Fearghas shrugged. "Doesn't do anything to deny the truth."

"And neither does fearmongering," she spat back.

"Fates, Edda," Caitlín croaked, clutching at her mate's tunic, "what have we done? Why did we come here?"

Edda made soothing noises to reassure her mate as the apprentices looked on with worry from where they manned the bellows. Fearghas took a loud sip from his cup.

"Lady Aislinn will—"

"Spare us, halfling. No one doubts your . . . *loyalty*."

The fire in Hakon's belly burned hotter than the forge as he glared at the head blacksmith. Red rimmed his vision, and his beast snarled in his mind, howling for retribution for the disrespect.

"When this is said and done, all will remember who was loyal and who was not," Hakon growled.

"You threatening my position?"

"I don't need to. I do your work already."

Fearghas's face above his expansive beard reddened, a vein popping along his bare scalp. "Where's your lady now, halfling? She hasn't visited the smithy in an awfully long time."

Nostrils flaring, Hakon's muscles bunched. The festering sore inside him throbbed with the direct hit, and his pride stung to see the smug knowing in Fearghas's eyes.

It was only the click Edda made with her tongue, an orcish noise of disapproval, that stopped Hakon from hurling himself across the smithy at the stupid, hateful human.

Gritting his tusks, Hakon flung the mangled cup into the open forge fire and stalked out into the rain.

He was almost immediately soaked as he walked blindly into the courtyard. Droplets sizzled and steamed against his overheated skin. Rain splattered against him, drenching his hair and tunic and pooling in his pockets.

Hakon didn't know where he went, only that he walked. The rain bit at his exposed skin, but he hardly felt it. He only noticed how cold his hands had become when a warm nose pressed into his palm.

He looked down to see Wülf trotting alongside him.

His room would smell of wet dog for days, but he was glad of the company.

Together, they walked aimlessly through the deafening rain.

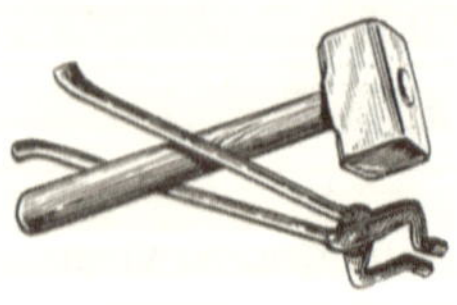

Although her eyes stung with tiredness, Aislinn headed for the guest wing of apartments rather than trudging to her own. Sorcha had insisted that Aislinn come to the rooms she and Orek shared before turning in. With how much Sorcha and Orek did for her, she couldn't say no. And, amidst the anxious drudgery that filled her days, there were worse ways to end the evening.

At the door, one of her guards knocked before opening it for Aislinn.

"Would you like us inside with you, my lady?" asked the other.

"I'll be perfectly fine. Thank you." She offered him a sleepy smile before entering the small solar.

Inside sat Sorcha and two halflings. All of them stood upon her entrance as the door clicked shut behind her.

Aislinn's heart went *pitter-patter* when Hakon grinned shyly at her. "Hullo, Aislinn."

"Hakon . . ."

"I wish it was more, but we thought you both deserved an hour," said Sorcha.

She looked at her friend in shock. Sorcha threw her a saucy wink before taking her mate by the hand and leading him into the adjoining bedroom. That door shut softly behind them, closing Aislinn and Hakon in together, alone.

Aislinn stood rooted to the spot, overwhelmed to finally be in the same room as her blacksmith. She wondered if he was angry or frustrated with her and whether this had been his idea. She wanted to know how he was and what he did to fill his days and if he missed her as desperately as she did him.

None of that made it past her lips.

Eyes stinging with tears, Aislinn made her feet move. The moment she rocked forward, he was in motion, and in the next breath, she was enfolded in his arms.

She buried her face against his chest and sighed with relief.

A big hand cradled the back of her head, fingers digging into her hair.

"Ach, *vinya*," he rumbled, his purr thickening his voice, "how I've missed you."

"I missed you so much," she murmured against his throat.

He held her for a long time, gently rocking them back and forth, a soft sway that lulled the sharper edges of her fears. Nothing had changed since entering the solar, and yet everything was different within his arms.

The heat of his chest burned away her doubts and allowed her mind to go quiet.

*He feels so good. He feels right.*

Surely this was what the mate-bond had to be. She'd never felt so close to a man before, like he was part of her. Like being separated from him was functioning without a limb. Like something was missing, and she only realized what it was to be whole when they came together.

Her stinging tiredness eased into a soft sleepiness as she ran her hands up and down his front. She burrowed beneath his heavy sheepskin coat, her knuckles rasping against the soft inner wool, to run her fingers along his tunic. His skin radiated warmth just beneath, and she wished there was time to be together, skin to skin.

"Sit with me?" he said into her hair.

She nodded, following him when he sat in one of the cushioned chairs to settle in his lap. Hakon pulled her close, tucking her to his chest and wrapping her up in his arms.

Aislinn's head fell into the crook of his shoulder, and she couldn't help another sigh of relief.

"You must rest more, *vinya*. You're running . . . what is the human phrase? Running yourself . . .?"

"Ragged," she said, smiling despite his concern. She loved his puzzlement with idioms. "I know. But there's so much to do."

"I know there is. Too much. You must let others help you. Let me help you."

"This helps," she sighed, already falling asleep. She curled her hand around the side of his neck, and the pulse in her palm matched his in his throat.

With a hum of pleasure, she kissed the underside of his chin and closed her eyes, the temptation too great.

Hakon held his sleepy mate, biting back all the things he wished to say. Her exhaustion was palpable, and within just a few minutes of sitting still, she began to doze in his arms.

"I would be beside you, always," he murmured into her hair.

"I know you would." Her words slurred with tiredness, and soon her breathing evened out.

Frustration nipped at him, but he put it aside. He'd had plans when he approached Sorcha about arranging this meeting, had so many things he wished to say and ask. How she fared, if she was eating enough, if he could help her in any way, if she longed for him with a fraction of the ferocity he did for her.

The words died in his throat, replaced with a rumbling purr that was just for her. The cadence was meant to soothe and coax, temper and tempt. He could take some satisfaction in her falling so easily into his arms. That she trusted him to sleep, when he knew she often struggled to, was its own gift.

Her sweetness surrounded him, and he contented himself with filling his senses with her. He pulled one side of his coat over her, hoping the wool would retain a little of her scent. His hands ran in gentle strokes up and down her back and flank, amazed all over again that this most beautiful of creatures was his mate.

Fearghas was wrong. Hakon would do more than fight for this woman. He'd do far, far worse.

Hakon was beginning to realize . . . he needed to change his plan again.

Wooing her to his land and hoping she would give up her position was naïve. Perhaps it might've worked, given time and without her cockroach of a brother threatening her.

Now, though, he feared he'd have to take more drastic action.

Fates, the lengths and depths he was willing to go to keep her safe. She would fight for her position and her people, and he would support her, protect her, fight for her. He'd give his life for her, for he was hers; all of him, blood and bone and devotion, it was hers.

She may not have given herself to him in the same way yet, but he would take her safety as his own. He claimed it, here and now, and vowed that it came first for him. Above all else—even her happiness.

Hakon vowed that should the situation grow as dire as Fearghas portended, he wouldn't hesitate to steal her in the old way. He'd risk his life and more—ever having her heart—if it kept her alive.

That was all that mattered to him. She was all that mattered.

She was everything.

26

Aclear, cold day dawned over Dundúran, and Aislinn was stuck inside. Despite the chill, she'd propped open the east window to catch a little fresh air as she pored over the most recent correspondence. Still nothing from Connor nor her father, and the silence was eating her alive.

This morning was a little better, though, and not just because of the sunshine. Sorcha had managed another meeting for Aislinn and Hakon, and she'd spent an hour in his arms the night before. It wasn't much, and she was more than a little embarrassed that once again she'd quickly dozed off in his lap, but it kept her going.

She was considering asking him how he'd feel about loaning her his coat, just so she could sleep wrapped in something of his, when Brenna entered with a tray of breakfast.

"It's frigid in here," Brenna exclaimed, hurrying to deposit the tray so she could bustle about the study closing windows. "You'll catch your death."

Aislinn filled her mouth with toast, not needing an argument this morning.

She ate with one hand and prepared to take notes with the other. With the windows closed, Brenna stood alongside the desk and withdrew her list.

They ran through the daily tasks, as well as any outstanding issues that still needed Aislinn's attention. Those were beginning to accumulate, so many other things needing her attention that anything that wasn't urgent got put in the growing pile on the corner of the desk. She hated the sight of it and tried to attend to at least one thing from it a day.

It wasn't enough. That was becoming starkly apparent.

Aislinn preferred to do the work herself, but even she had to admit that this was far too much for one person. *I'm running myself ragged, as Hakon would say.* She saw the concern in not just him, but Sorcha and Fia, Captain Aodhan, and even the youngest pages, who watched her as if they expected her to keel over in exhaustion.

Some days, that felt likely.

The issue that faced her was that, despite all the authorities granted her, one that hadn't was the power to dispense her authority to others. An heiress acting as regent had vast remit, but she couldn't further divide her father's authority and therefore would have to wait until his return to appoint anyone.

For now, she was on her own.

*Just a little longer. He has to return soon. Any day now.*

Brenna finished with her list, and Aislinn sighed with relief to find that nothing new or incredibly urgent awaited her that day. She would've turned back to her morning correspondence when Brenna delicately cleared her throat.

"There was one last thing, my lady."

Aislinn's brows rose to see the pinched, anxious way Brenna regarded her. "Yes?"

"You said to bring anything suspicious or out of the ordinary to you."

"Indeed. Have the maids heard something?"

Brenna shook her head. "It isn't that. I . . ." She replaced the list in her pocket and smoothed her stiff skirts. "You won't like me saying this, but I feel I must. Several have come to me after hearing the blacksmith speaking orcish with Miss Sorcha's husband."

Aislinn folded her hands on the desk. "Orcish is their native tongue."

"But it's not spoken here. They both speak Eirean. Why talk in a language no one else understands?" Brenna frowned. "What do they have to hide?"

"They likely know that everyone is feeling the strain and want to keep their conversation private. They're allowed to speak their native language, Brenna."

"Yes, but *why* do they? That's the question. What are they saying, truly?"

Aislinn bit back all the sharper things she wanted to say. Slumping back in the seat, if only to annoy Brenna with her bad posture, she finally settled on saying, "The only reason Jerrod is alive today is because Orek was talked out of popping his head off his neck like a chicken. He'd never conspire with the very man who sold Sorcha."

Brenna's lips thinned, her expression growing disgruntled, as if she hadn't thought of that.

"That may be," she said, "but the blacksmith must be carefully watched. I wouldn't be surprised if he has his own designs."

"Designs? On what?"

Brenna pinned her with a quelling frown. "On you."

The blood fell from Aislinn's face. "What?"

"Everyone sees how he looks at you, Aislinn. And worse, the way you look back." Brenna shook her head in disappointment. "With all that's happening, he may get *ideas*."

*I always look forward to his ideas.* Aislinn just bit back that statement, knowing it'd only scandalize Brenna further and possibly push her firmly into supporting Jerrod.

Aislinn had to hope that, while their flirtation was known, the extent of her relationship with Hakon was still secret. For his sake as much as hers. Tensions had grown throughout the castle as they all waited for further word; she didn't want who the heiress kept as a bedfellow to start circulating, too.

*What does that mean for Hakon and me?*

Another thing she didn't know. It would be smart to cut ties, or at least end their romance while this threat loomed. She'd forced herself to consider it more than once, but she just couldn't do it. She couldn't give him up. Even though she had so little of him now, just those stolen hours with him in Sorcha's solar sustained her like a flower finding the sun. She soaked up his support and comfort, and just that little bit got her through the ensuing days.

It was an impossible situation, the answer to which seemed to be to just . . . keep things as they were.

Still, she could do something about Brenna's notions of an orcish conspiracy.

"I have full confidence in Orek, Hakon, and Edda. I'm sure they just speak their native tongue for a bit of comfort."

Rather than mollifying the chatelain, Brenna's scowl only deepened. "So you'd have me spy on our people, your own kind, but you inherently trust the halflings?"

Aislinn's mouth fell open, words escaping her.

Was that what Brenna thought? Did others think her biased, too?

She scrambled to think of something to say, only saved by Fia rushing through the door.

It wasn't the rescue Aislinn had hoped.

"Milady," Fia said breathlessly, "Baron Bayard has just arrived."

Aislinn blinked in surprise, not sure she believed it.

"Padraic Bayard, here? So soon after the council meeting?"

Fia nodded, though Bayard's presence didn't seem like it could explain the paleness of her pretty face. "He's brought a whole company of knights with him. At least a hundred. They're all out in the courtyard."

Heart dropping into her stomach, Aislinn hurried to the window.

Just as Fia said, dozens of mounted knights stood in neat formation inside the castle courtyard. At their head on a fine black gelding sat Bayard, his ruby doublet shining in the morning light.

"Fates, what's he doing now?"

A headache sparked behind her eye as she watched him dismount and hand his steed over to a groom. A handful of castle staff and Dundúran's own knights moved around the fringes of the gathered force, nervously talking behind hands.

So many things to do—she didn't have time for this buffoon.

"I will meet him in the east solar," Aislinn sighed.

Fia curtseyed quickly before flying back out of the study.

Turning to Brenna, Aislinn said, "Have his preferred room prepared. No doubt he means to stay awhile."

Perhaps if she handed him the tax documents that needed checking and approval, he'd run right home to his vineyards.

No, she wouldn't be so lucky.


Aislinn sat in the east solar at the front of the castle, sunlight streaming in from the courtyard below, picking at her cuticles. Everything she could be doing pressed on her shoulders, and everything she wished she was doing filled her head with daydreams.

Thankfully, Bayard didn't keep her waiting long.

One of her guards opened the door to let Fia and a grinning Bayard in. "Baron Padraic Bayard to see you, milady."

"Thank you, Fia. Please send for some cider and bring my notebook."

Once Fia made her retreat, Aislinn turned her attention to the dashing baron now adorning her solar. His smile widened when he had her gaze, and he swept into a courtly bow. Aislinn bobbed her head in acknowledgement.

"Lord Padraic, I trust everything is all right?"

He held out his hand, and Aislinn reluctantly offered hers. He took it and kissed the back of her hand, cool lips lingering longer than necessary.

From above her hand, he asked, "Is wanting to be blessed with the sight of you not reason enough to visit?"

"Flattery," said Aislinn. "Please, have a seat."

Taking her seat once again put a little needed distance between them, although Bayard leaned forward to rest his elbows on his knees, as if he might spring out of his chair at any moment to fall on his knees before her.

She knew the lord to be a prideful man, a little vain and pompous, but otherwise fairly innocuous besides his frustrating habit of visiting often and for days. Looking upon him now, though, there was a certain set to his shoulders. He'd dressed in his usual finery, but there was a more militaristic cut to it, all hard lines without any frills or extravagance. His boots, while polished to a high shine and no doubt expensive, were of the type a soldier might wear, and he'd forgone his usual leather or velvet trou for a more practical pair of dyed wool. For Padraic Bayard, this was downright frugal.

"What brings you to Dundúran, my lord? And so soon after the council meeting. You have me worried."

"You've no reason to worry, my Lady Aislinn. Or at least, I aim to ensure you've no reason." His smile widened, and he somehow leaned even further toward her.

Aislinn could only blink, unsure what he was playing at. One of the many reasons she found Bayard tiring was his insistence on word and courtly games. He was fond of innuendo and implication, a master wielder of half-truth and veiled flattery. He could talk circles around her and still say nothing at all.

She had little patience for it on a good day—and today certainly wasn't that.

"I'm afraid I don't follow."

Bayard nodded, adopting a serious mien. "The news you shared about Lord Jerrod at the council meeting made me fear for your safety. Here all alone, I want to ensure that you are protected."

"I have my garrison, and we expect my father to return with the rest of the company soon. Dundúran has weathered attacks before. I'm perfectly safe here."

"I certainly hope that's true, and I don't doubt the capability of your people. It's only, I wanted to ensure your safety myself. I've set my own garrison at Endelín to additional patrols and have them making inquiries in the villages."

"Thank you for your preparedness."

"I'm fortunate that the vineyards of Endelín have had so many fruitful harvests over the past years. It means that my coffers are full, and I'm able to keep a large garrison."

Aislinn bit her cheek, trying to figure out where this winding path led. He'd already paid his dues and was one of the few vassals who didn't complain about the increase. Everyone knew how bountiful the verdant valleys of Endelín were; they'd long been the most fruitful vineyards in all of Eirea. The Bayard family was proud of their land and house and ensured any who'd listen knew of the size and quality of their harvests.

"I'm glad to hear it," was all she could think to say.

"I say this to you first, for I don't wish for my news to worry you."

*Fates, we haven't even started approaching the point.*

Aislinn managed a weak smile, but before Bayard could continue, Fia entered with their cider. She expertly poured them each a cup before taking position to Aislinn's right, ready with a notebook to jot down anything pertinent.

*Assuming, of course, that he has anything actually worthwhile to say.*

Taking an elegant sip of his drink, Bayard declared, "Excellent. Some of the finest cider comes from the mills of Dundúran. Perhaps after you might care for a sample of Endelín? I've selected another excellent vintage, a younger and sweeter wine this time."

"You are most generous. Perhaps with dinner—it's a little too early in the day for me."

"Of course."

Aislinn sipped her own cider, the warm tang of apples filling her belly and offering her a bit more patience.

"You were saying, Lord Padraic?"

His expression turned grave, and his chestnut curls spilled across his forehead as he reached into the pocket of his long doublet.

"Forgive the dramatics, my lady. I come with grim news." From his pocket he pulled a folded letter of rough paper, the type that would be freely available in most taverns and inns. "I have received word from your brother."

The cup nearly slipped out of Aislinn's hand. "You've had news of Jerrod."

"He's written to me himself." He turned the letter in his hand with his fingers, drawing attention to it but not offering it to her. "He boasts that he's gathered a force of hundreds. He says that I and other nobles would be handsomely rewarded for supporting his claim—and not retaliated against if we at least stay out of his fight. Your brother means to turn your nobles against you, my lady."

Aislinn went numb.

Fia acted fast, plucking the teetering cup from her hand.

"You're sure?" Aislinn asked him through stiff lips.

"I'm afraid so. I know Jerrod's handwriting, and it carries his voice. This all seems like something he would do, no disrespect to your family."

Aislinn was too cold with shock to decide what degree of insult that was. Instead, her gaze fixed on that letter.

He fiddled with it another moment before continuing. "This is why I fear for you, my lady. I'm sure your people are to be trusted, but until your father's return, you're vulnerable here alone. That is why I offer myself and my company to your disposal. I won't leave until I know that you and Dundúran are safe."

Aislinn's mouth fell open, but she'd nothing to say. Denial, refusal, indignation fought valiantly up her throat, but nothing came out.

Something passed over Bayard's face that she'd never seen from him before. A slyness, a cunning that made her skin crawl. It was . . . malicious the way he looked at her then, even as he eased from his chair to kneel before her, the picture of honorable nobility.

"I am loyal to you, Lady Aislinn. You have my arm and my devotion. Is it not proof that I bring you this news rather than support Jerrod?"

"Your loyalty is deeply appreciated, my lord."

"Thank you, heiress." Reaching out a hand, he rested it over hers in her lap, running his thumb along the inside of her knee. "I hope, though, for more than your appreciation."

Finally, he handed the letter, not to Aislinn but to Fia.

"In times like these, loyalties should be rewarded, should they not?"

Something inside Aislinn shriveled, and she wished she could recoil from the man. He leaned forward even further, pressing his chest to her legs.

*Wrong,* shouted everything inside her, louder than carillon bells, *wrong wrong wrong. He's—*

"You have my loyalty and my protection, Lady Aislinn. If needed, I'm prepared to use my own fortune to hire our own mercenary force to combat your brother. In return, I would ask you to consider my proposal. It would be the utmost honor to have your hand in marriage."

Her stomach turned, the sip of cider burning like acid. It took effort not to wrench her hands away—even more not to laugh in his face.

*How dare he?*

*How could he even think—!*

She watched him watch her closely, that handsome face hardened into something ugly. He had her cornered and he knew it. If that's what it took to finally obtain her, he would leverage the threat of Jerrod against her.

It was a gamble, to be sure, but a good one. On the one hand, Aislinn needed his continued loyalty. Endelín was a rich estate—and

Dundúran's closest neighbor. She couldn't afford to fight off an attack from Bayard and Jerrod, certainly not without a full company of knights.

Yet should she refuse, his company was already within the walls of the castle. He would side with Jerrod and reap his reward.

Good gods, Padraic Bayard had invaded Dundúran Castle with the aim of making her his bride.

Aislinn bit her cheek until it bled.

"Are you negotiating for my hand, my lord?"

"I'm making veiled threats, in fact." Smiling, he stood to his full height. "My men have orders that should they not have sight of me, or should I be harmed or detained in any way, they have permission to begin looting the city."

Bayard tried to kiss her hand again, but Aislinn snatched it back. Damn propriety.

Standing herself, Aislinn spat, "This is low, Bayard. Even for a snake like you."

He merely shrugged. "Perhaps. But think of your people before you say anything too insulting."

Tears stung her eyes, and panic clutched her throat. A fit loomed at the fringes of her mind, accelerating her pulse until she heard it thrumming in her ears. She'd long since lost feeling in her fingers and clutched them into fists to hide how they shook.

She had to get rid of him before he saw her like that. She wouldn't allow him to have that to use against her.

Aislinn wouldn't let her fits be her downfall.

Through tight lips, Aislinn said, "I will consider your offer. Nothing can be officially decided until my father returns, though."

"You're a brilliant woman, Lady Aislinn. I'm sure you can make a decision before then." Executing another perfect bow, he turned for the doors. "I insist that I stay until you decide. You and Dundúran need the protection."

He left Aislinn shaking in his wake, her rage almost as visceral as her terror.

Fia caught her when her knees gave out, helping ease her back into the chair. "Oh, milady, what will we do?"

With a trembling hand, Aislinn opened the letter from Jerrod.

She hoped against hope that it was fake. A conceit to color his ruse. Such a scheme certainly wasn't beneath Bayard—nothing was.

But as she read the message, written in Jerrod's familiar sloppy scrawl, her heart sank. The writing was his, the words were his.

The information was sparse; he could be overstating his numbers to tempt or terrify the nobles to his side. The promise was clear, however—join and be rewarded, stay out and be left alone. Retribution for supporting Aislinn was implied with every boastful word.

And it wasn't just Jerrod's message to Bayard that proved it was all true.

Over the coming days, more of her vassals sent alarmed letters, telling her of similar proposals from Jerrod.

The pile on the desk in her father's study grew ever higher.

But the letters she waited for never came. Nothing from Connor or her father.

Aislinn had never felt so alone, surrounded by guards and staff and barracks full of Bayard's knights.

Her corner was growing smaller, and . . . no ideas came to her. No brilliant solution presented itself. Her mind skipped over the problems again and again and . . . nothing.

She could make Bayard wait for a few days, but then what?

Aislinn had to hope that by then, that elusive solution would come to her.

Otherwise . . .

She couldn't stomach the thought.

# 27

"Can I expect to see you at luncheon?" asked Bayard from the study door.

With all his airy smiles and good humor, few would suspect he was blackmailing Aislinn. Since outlining his ploy, Bayard had been nothing but courtesy and charm, as if to prove that he could be tolerable as a husband.

Aislinn knew otherwise.

"I'm afraid not," she said, dipping her quill in the inkpot, "there's far too much to do."

"I've hardly seen you since yesterday."

Aislinn bit her cheek. "If you find yourself bored, I suggest you return to Endelín. Such rich vineyards surely require your undivided attention."

"Alas, I have excellent handlers. My time is nothing but yours." Bowing, he threw her a wink. "Dinner, then."

Aislinn grumbled after him, the letter she'd been composing stagnating in her mind and the thought lost. This letter had to be perfect—one didn't always write to the king asking for aid.

She'd prevaricated for as long as she could. As an heiress to a rich demesne, seen as a usurper by some, she wasn't assured of the half-Pyrrossi King Marius's support. When Queen Ygraine was well enough to rule, she left her liege lords to their own business, involving herself only when asked or when royal intervention was needed. King Marius, however, took a heavier hand.

Merrick Darrow had long been trying to avoid drawing the royal eye. With Queen Ygraine ailing again and King Marius handling the reins of government, Aislinn's father feared incurring meddling that had otherwise passed over the Darrowlands.

Now, she might invite exactly what her father tried to evade. Yet, without word from him, Aislinn had little other recourse.

At the very least, she had to tell the king that a mercenary force was likely to cross the King's Wood and parts of Gleanná's own demesne to reach the Darrowlands. Mercenaries often kept encampments on the border, selling their services to the margraves or waiting for another war to break out between Caledon and Eirea. She couldn't abide Jerrod inadvertently starting a war.

Where she found herself stuck was asking the king to intercept the mercenaries. Throwing herself on the mercy of King Marius didn't inspire enthusiasm, but then, her options were running low.

Aislinn understood it would incur the king's interest and possible meddling. She also knew that meddling might include a marriage prospect, as her father had warned.

She didn't think the king could propose anyone as odious as Bayard, but then, there were plenty of awful people—it didn't matter that they were dressed in finery and ate delicacies.

It didn't truly matter who the king proposed if he decided to saddle her with a husband—the man wouldn't be the one she wanted. This was why Aislinn couldn't form the second half of the letter, her heart tearing itself in two at the thought of opening the possibility.

The corners were closing in, and a way out, an outcome where anything went her way, seemed almost infeasible if not impossible.

She didn't want to give up Hakon nor give in to Bayard.

But every day without her father and their company tolled in her mind, announcing the follies of her hopes.

Captain Aodhan rapped his knuckles on the open door, offering her a welcome distraction. When he made to bow, Aislinn gestured at the door, silently asking him to close it behind him.

With the door shut and closing them in alone, Aislinn allowed her shoulders to relax. It wasn't that she distrusted the guards or thought a gaggle of chambermaids stood listening around the corner—there was just something comforting about the closed door.

None of what she said was allowed outside the room.

"My lady," the captain greeted.

"Thank you for coming. Do you have any news for me?"

"Nothing pressing. Baron Bayard's men have been billeted in the west barracks. I kept them apart from our own garrison, as you requested."

"Good." She didn't know if it would help, but it felt safer to keep Bayard's knights sequestered however they could. "They are taking direction well?"

Aodhan's lips thinned. "Some have already begun carousing in the city. Baron Bayard keeps a . . . less strict handle on his men."

That's what Aislinn was afraid of. Bayard's men in town, ready at a moment's notice to wreak havoc. The castle staff were already under strain with the possible threat of Jerrod, and now unfamiliar knights were in residence. The townsfolk were likely to soon wonder what was amiss. Bayard visited Dundúran often, but never with a company.

"Have you determined their loyalty to Bayard?"

After getting her emotions under control yesterday, Aislinn had quickly sent for Captain Aodhan and told him of Bayard's plot. She'd never seen such a black look on the captain's face, and she'd thought for a moment he meant to storm from the study and challenge the baron to a duel for her honor.

Aodhan was honorable down to his marrow, and such underhanded tactics, threatening ladies, were beyond the pale. Aislinn took some consolation in his outrage, that she wasn't being just a spoiled girl for railing against Bayard's machinations. Aislinn set Captain Aodhan to sussing out if there were knights they could turn or ways to undermine Bayard's authority, as well as keeping a discreet eye on the baron.

"Not yet, my lady. That will take time. Their captain does, however, seem to be a cavalier sort more interested in coin than duty." He spat the assessment, and Aislinn knew for Aodhan, the description was akin to the deepest insult.

"We might have to exploit that. If enough can be bribed, whatever is left may not pose much of a threat."

"I've ensured my best information gatherers are close to their company. For now, it will be best to play hostess. Let them train in the courtyard and drink in the taverns. The more comfortable they are, the more mistakes they will make. Can Lord Padraic be strung along?"

"That's the question. I believe so. But still, have someone near him always, in case he needs to be detained. That will at least allow us to get ahead of his coup."

Captain Aodhan nodded; they were in agreement, even if neither liked the plan.

"I hate to see you threatened like this, my lady. If it was within my power, the baron would be exploring the accommodations of the dungeon."

"Thank you, captain. I'd like nothing better. But for now, for the safety of the people, we'll play his game. We just have to play it better."

Placing his fist over his heart, Aodhan said, "I will not fail you, my lady. You are safe within your own castle, and your people are loyal. They won't soon forget this treachery."

Hand over her own heart, Aislinn replied, "Thank you, captain. Your faith and loyalty mean a great deal to me." She would've buckled long ago without good people around her like Captain Aodhan.

The captain bowed, and with a few more words, departed.

He left Aislinn with a heavy but determined heart.

They had a plan. She wouldn't have to give in to Bayard—she would beat him at his own game. She only had to stall for time, rally the other vassals, and when her father returned, she'd enjoy seeing Bayard whine from a prison cell.

That was the plan, at least. And plans had a way of going awry.

Later that afternoon, Aislinn finally got her message from her father.

Fia came flying into the room, her cheeks nearly as red as her hair and her chest heaving for breath. Catching herself on the desk, she practically threw the letter at Aislinn, proclaiming, "It has your father's seal!"

Heart jumping to her throat, Aislinn tore at the rough paper.

The message, the very words, didn't make sense, not on her first read.

Her second brought a little clarity—and horror.

The third . . .

The third broke her heart.

> *Kit,*
>
> *I write to you from a sickbed on the Pyrrossi border. We followed intelligence from Kinvar that those who took Sorcha were hiding out in a border village. We tracked them down and hung them. Before we could source supplies for the return journey, we were waylaid near a town called Salona.*
>
> *There were signs that the town had cases of sweating sickness, but our spirits were high and we ignored them.*
>
> *Fates, how stupid I've been.*
>
> *Half the company has contracted the disease. Most have survived after a few days of serious illness, but recovery is long and arduous. We have isolated ourselves and are tak-*

*ing care of our own, but none will be able to travel north
for at least another fortnight.*

*I'm so sorry, kit. In my confinement to bed, I realize
how much of this is all my folly. I should have gone after
Jerrod. I should have waited to undertake this mission in
spring—if at all. I should—*

*There are so many things I should have done.*

*Do whatever you must to make safe the city. Write to
the king and queen. Summon an army. Do what I cannot.*

*You were always the best of us, kit. Your mother and
me. I thank the fates that it is you who protects our people.*

*Should I survive this, I will make every haste to return
to Dundúran—and every effort to earn your forgiveness.*

*All my love,
Your Father*

A tear splattered onto the page, smearing her father's words, and
she quickly put the letter down.

The soggy words stared at her without remorse, their message
stark.

Aislinn was alone.

"Milady . . .?"

She looked up to see Fia watching her with obvious concern, the
color drained from her freckled cheeks.

"I need paper. The good paper. And more wax. And find Captain
Aodhan. And Sorcha. And and and—" *And Hakon. I want Hakon.*

Fia grabbed her hands and squeezed. "It'll be all right, milady. It's
all right. Whatever it is, just—we'll make it right. Let me find Miss
Sorcha. Just stay there, I'll be right back—!" And she flew from the
room on her errands, feet hardly touching the floorboards.

Aislinn did as she was told, staying right there. She didn't think
she could move, the enormity of her father's letter pressing her into

her seat.

The shock delayed her threatening fit, but she thought she was past a fit, onto something she'd never known.

Hopelessness.

The gaping maw of it opened wide inside her, sucking down everything good and pleasant.

Her father and reinforcements weren't coming.

Her father could be dead even now.

Fat tears spilled down Aislinn's face, but she couldn't move her hands to wipe them away. Frozen in place, her breathing came shallow and reedy, and her fingers went numb.

Fates, what was she to do?

Bayard couldn't know. No one, beyond those she trusted most, could know.

She had to write the king and queen. It didn't matter what the king might do, so long as he sent aid, Aislinn would pay the price. She had to write to all her vassals, command them to send reinforcements, and test their loyalty in a way she'd been hoping to avoid. She had to make safe the city, one already infested with Bayard's men.

She had to—had to—there was so much she had to—

All she could do was bury her head in her hands and weep.

# 28

His plan was insanity—pure madness—and had more holes than a sieve, but it was all he had, and Hakon was desperate. The old sagas told of the insane, reckless, dangerous things orcs did when suffering with unrequited mate-bonds, and he understood them all.

Hoisting the rope higher on his shoulder, he slipped around the east side of the castle, craning his neck to spot the third-floor balcony of Aislinn's solar. The night was a dark one, the moon merely a sliver, leaving the shadows deep and inky despite the puddles of light from the tall torches lit throughout the courtyard.

He couldn't be too careful. In fact, it'd be smarter to give this whole asinine scheme up entirely. But he needed to see his mate.

It was more than the angry beast rumbling in his chest.

It was more than the aching loneliness carving his heart in two.

Something was happening. Something had changed.

Dundúran Castle was already mired in tension before Baron Bayard and his men arrived. Now, with almost double the knights in the barracks but half unfamiliar and loyal to the baron, a sense of fear had begun to permeate the very stones. Maids kept their heads down and hurried from task to task, not stopping long enough to be harassed by the visiting knights. The stables were overwhelmed, and the kitchens ran at all hours, the ovens never allowed to cool.

No one could quite understand it. Bayard's knights felt more like an occupying army than the reinforcements Captain Aodhan and Aislinn both claimed them to be. The strain was evident in both of them, covert, unhappy looks passing between them.

As far as any staff knew, no word had come about Lord Merrick or Jerrod and his mercenaries, so why the sudden presence of Bayard—with so many armed knights?

Hakon couldn't shake the feeling that danger was closing in around Aislinn, and he wouldn't stand for it. He had to see her.

Kneeling on the cobblestones, he gave the hand sign for Wülf to sit. The mutt did, looking up at him dutifully as Hakon relayed more signs, instructing him to return to their room and wait.

Hakon intended for the block he'd tied to Wülf to make as much noise as possible along the way.

Giving the signal to go, Hakon stood. Wülf grumbled, rising to his feet and shaking out his coat. With a canine huff, the dog started out through the dark, the block clattering behind him.

Hakon just needed a few moments of distraction. And to charm a good bone from Hugh as a reward.

Letting loose the rope, he swung the grappling hook he'd filched from the armory, gaining momentum until it swung in a wide loop. He let it fly, hand hovering over the slithering rope.

The hook caught between two rails of the balcony. With a testing tug, Hakon secured the rope around himself, made a loop for his foot, and heaved himself up.

Hand over hand, he climbed.

His beast rumbled with impatience and hope, thinking soon, *soon* they'd see her.

He climbed faster when the stones of the railing whined under his weight.

Sweat beaded down his neck as hand over hand, leg up, hand over hand, he made the third level.

Hoisting himself over the rail, Hakon pulled the rope up behind him and listened.

The east courtyard below was silent. No alarm had been raised. He didn't even hear the block Wülf dragged behind him.

Flaring his nostrils, he dragged in as many scents as he could before turning to the set of arched doors leading into her solar. From what he could smell, it was only Aislinn in her room. It pleased a visceral, instinctual part of him that it was only female scents that came from his mate's rooms, and the only one other than his mate's was Fia's, and it wasn't fresh.

He tried the knob and—it was locked.

Biting down on his frustration, he peered through the leaded panes into the solar.

The room was dim, the fine fabrics of the drapes and rugs and tapestries absorbing the meager light that flickered from a half-dozen candles across the room. It was enough, though, for his orcish eyes to see Aislinn bent over a writing desk, hurriedly scratching at a piece of parchment.

Just the sight of her soothed his unruly beast a little.

With a knuckle, Hakon rapped on the windowpane gently.

Aislinn jumped in her seat, startled eyes looking about the room. He rapped again, drawing her gaze and—

His heart sank into his stomach.

He caught the glint of tears in those wide eyes.

She blinked at him in surprise, and he realized his big hulking form must look threatening, a dark mass come from the shadows to tap at her door.

"Aislinn," he murmured, not sure she could hear, but her name tasted right on his tongue. "Please open the door."

She stood slowly, taking a few cautious steps before hurrying to the doors. The lock *clicked* open, and Hakon hastened inside, shutting and locking the doors behind him.

For a long moment, they just stared at each other.

Her solar wasn't warm but wasn't cool either, the fire in the hearth banked for the night. Candles flickered about the room and one lantern burned low. Despite the late hour, she was still in her gown for the day, her hair still set with pins.

*Something's wrong.* He could smell it in her scent, the salt from her tears burning his tongue, and could see it in her posture, as if a small breeze would topple her.

When she finally opened those perfect lips to speak, it was to tell him, "You can't be here."

Hakon tossed the rope to the floor and closed the distance to her. Taking her face between his hands, he said, "I had to see you."

"If someone sees . . ." Fresh tears gathered at her lashes, making Hakon go cold. "Bayard can't know."

"Fuck Bayard," he growled. "What's he got to do with this? What's happened, *vinya?*"

She shook her head, still held between his hands, as tears spilled down her face. To his horror, her lip trembled, then her face crumpled. A sob wracked her, and Hakon hurried her back to her chair at the desk before she could slump to the floor.

He knelt before her, his soul shredded to see her tears. "Please, *vinya,*" he begged, "please don't cry." Hakon could withstand many things, but not her tears.

She shook her head again, burying her face in her hands.

He placed his hands gently in her lap, fingers aching to knead and soothe away her sadness, but he tried to keep still.

Her hands fell on his, damp from her tears, and for a horrible moment, he thought she meant to push him away.

Aislinn slipped forward off her seat into his arms. Hakon rocked back, taking her weight, and wrapped her up in his arms—just where she belonged.

A purr rattled to life in his chest as he tucked her tight to him, the vibration the only thing that kept him from shattering. Tears prickled at his own eyes to see her misery, and he gritted his tusks against his gums to keep in the roar of despair that clamored in his throat.

How dare anything make his mate cry?

Aislinn buried her face against his throat. He murmured soothing sounds into her hair, those tears branding him as they ran down his chest. Fates, he couldn't bear this.

But he did. For her, he bore her tears and hurts. He held her for a long while, offering his silent support.

When the tears began to slow and the sobs lost their strength, Hakon shifted her in his arms, holding her in one and wiping away her tears with a thumb.

"Ach, *vinya,* you break my heart," he said.

"I'm sorry," she sniffed, "there's just so much . . ."

"Will you tell me?"

Her throat bobbed on a swallow, and more tears spilled over her lashes, but she took a long, fortifying breath. Then, in halting words, she told him. Of Bayard's true reason for staying in Dundúran. Of her father's plight in the south. How even now she was drafting letters to the king and queen, as well as all her nobles to raise an army.

"I never thought—how has it come to this?"

Hakon couldn't answer, too consumed with rage.

Bayard was blackmailing her. *Threatening* her. Trying to claim that which wasn't his.

His purr deepened into a violent growl.

"Hakon . . .?"

"Where does he sleep, *vinya?* I will deal with this now."

Eyes wide, she clutched at his tunic. "No! You can't threaten him."

"I'm not going to threaten him." He was going to tear Bayard's head from his neck with his bare hands.

"No," she said again, more firmly. "I'm trying to solve this without violence. If his men suspect anything, they might . . ." She shook her head. "I just need time."

"He threatens you," Hakon hissed. "This is unacceptable. He should be in your dungeon."

Aislinn chuckled once without humor. "You sound like Captain Aodhan."

Good. Someone else had sense.

"Aislinn—"

"No." She tried to frown up at him, but it quickly dissolved back into watery despair. "Don't fight me, too."

"Never." He dropped his head to press kisses to her damp face. Her tears stung his lips, but he didn't care. "I am for you, *vinya*. Always. Tell me how to help you."

She cupped his face in her hand, her touch so achingly soft. "You can't."

"I don't accept that."

"There's nothing you can do. You're . . ." *Just a blacksmith.*

Hakon stiffened.

Straightening in his lap, Aislinn looked up at him in regret. "There's nothing to do but wait," she amended. "I need time."

"You would bargain with your hand. With your *life*."

"Yes."

His lip curled in disdain. "It's too high a price."

He knew she agreed from the way her mouth thinned, but she said nothing.

Hakon's throat closed around all the demands he wanted to make. That she let him kill Bayard. That she come to him as she had before. That she be his and only his, politics be damned.

That she let him steal her into the night, never to look back.

They sat in their silent impasse, neither finding words.

His heart began to thump, the tie he felt to her, to the bond growing between them, tightening with tension. Distance had grown between them, the chasm wider with every moment, and he didn't know how to reach her.

What they had was new, fragile, and for the first time, he truly feared that it might not survive the winter.

But then, in the silence, more tears spilled from her eyes. Hopelessness pulled at her face as she murmured, "What if my father dies?"

Her lips peeled back across her teeth in a show of despair, and Hakon wouldn't allow it. He pulled her back into his arms, denying the distance.

This Hakon understood. Grief and how it chewed you up inside. Made all the worse by grieving for someone who wasn't yet gone. Hakon had watched his grandfather's passing inch closer, and no amount of pleading or denying had stalled it. For all his love and strength and wish for it not to be so, death had come. It always did, in its time.

He knew, though, that those weren't comforting words to hear. It wasn't what he'd wanted to hear in his grandfather's last hours, and it wasn't what he told his mate, either.

"He's strong," Hakon said instead, "it isn't his fate."

Tears garbled her words as she curled into him.

Hakon stood, cradling her close. She protested when he began to snuff the candles, insisting she needed to finish the letters.

"They'll keep."

The solar slowly plunged into darkness, Hakon keeping only the lantern lit as he carried it and her into her adjoining bedchamber.

The room was dominated by an ornately carved four-post bed. Heavy green curtains embroidered with pastoral scenes had been pulled back and tied to the posts, and a small mountain of pillows sat neatly at the head.

He set the lantern on the bedside table and her on the bed. Kneeling, he unlaced her boots and carefully pulled each foot free. She watched him with heavy-lidded eyes as his hands delved under her skirts to find and untie her stockings. The warm silk glided against his fingers as he pulled them down the curves of her legs.

"Morning will come, and you are strong enough to meet it."

Her face fell, and he feared more tears. Instead, she reached down to take his face in her hands. Her forehead met his, and in the warm darkness, they shared breath.

His heart ached for her and for all that was unsaid and unknown.

"I would do anything for you, *vinya*," he couldn't help whispering. She had to know—had to see that all he was and would ever be was hers. Her birthright, the politics, none of it truly mattered. He wouldn't give her up—he couldn't.

Even if it meant stealing her away. He wouldn't let her burdens pile one atop the other until she buckled. If she wouldn't let him help her here, he would take matters into his own hands, for she was all that mattered. Her life, her safety. She may hate him for it, but she would be free.

With a sigh, she pressed a soft kiss to his lips. "Can you take my mind off everything, at least for a night?"

He knew what she asked, and he couldn't stop the disappointment. *Ask more of me,* he wanted to demand. *Take what's yours.*

Hakon would make her understand. But for now, this he could easily give.

He took her lips in a claiming kiss, one that was not fast but not slow. He coaxed, he tempted, his hands running up her legs to tug her to her feet.

He spun her round to untie the laces of her stays. Her gown loosened, and he couldn't resist dropping kisses on the curve of her neck and shoulder as the fabric fell away. She tilted her head, giving him more access, and he trailed kisses up her neck to her ear, where he murmured, "I will give you everything, *vinya*. All you have to do is ask."

She shuddered under his hands, and he made quick work of the rest of her garments. When she stood naked before him, he had to stop and run his hands along the curves of her waist, feeling her perfection for himself.

Fates, she was too beautiful for words.

Her eyes were still damp, her expression so vulnerable it nearly broke him. He couldn't fall on her like the beast he felt like, not tonight.

Taking a step back, he toed off his boots and began pulling off his own layers as she turned down the bed.

He came for her again naked and didn't miss the almost shy way she looked him up and down. It'd been too long since he felt her skin against his, and he hissed with pleasure when she fitted herself against him.

He ran his hands along her back in light caresses, gentling himself for her.

When she would've climbed into the bed, he stopped her. She looked on with surprise as he laid himself on his back, cock bobbing against his belly in anticipation. But that would have to wait.

"Hold onto the headboard."

Her brows arched. She climbed in after him, throwing her leg over his waist to straddle him. He filled his hands with her backside and pulled her up his body.

"I want you on my tongue, *vinya*. Let me taste you."

A shuddering breath escaped her, and she stared at him a moment longer, as if to confirm that he was serious. He held her gaze as she slowly crawled her way up his body, hands kneading at her flanks. Her spun-gold hair fell around him in a sweet curtain as her face hovered above his.

When she bent for a kiss, he gave her a quick one before swatting her backside. "Other lips."

She gasped at his vulgarity before finally straightening. Hands on the headboard for balance, she placed her knees on either side of his head.

He wrapped his arms around her thighs, pulling her down to him. A hungry growl rumbled in his chest as her scent overwhelmed him. He could feel her heat on his lips and he hadn't even begun.

Smiling, he captured her gaze, relishing how she trembled with anticipation, her hair hanging about her face as she watched him.

He started with a swipe of his tongue from cunt to clitoris.

Aislinn gasped, nearly sitting upright, but he pinned her with his arms. His purr buzzed on his lips as he closed them around her clitoris, making her jerk, but he held her again, forcing her to take all he meant to give.

Hakon feasted.

His mouth moved in greedy strokes and slurps on her cunt, sucking and nipping at her as he gulped down her slick. She tasted primal, like spring rain and fresh earth and lightning strikes. He bathed himself in her, tongue flicking and circling and spearing inside to drink from the source.

Her middle quaked and her arms shook with the effort of holding herself up, but Hakon wouldn't relent. He gorged himself on her cunt, his hunger growing with every stroke of his tongue. His cock leaked spend along his belly, his bollocks pulsing with need, but he was too enamored of her to stop.

She filled her fist with his hair and tugged, urging him on. He purred loudly in pleasure, praising her with the noise and setting it against her clitoris.

*Take your pleasure, take what's yours.*

"Hakon—!" she gasped.

Her back arched, glorious hair thrown back as she came. The tendons of her neck stood out starkly against her throat, her mouth opening wide around a silent scream. Her hips rocked against his face until he was raw, chasing down every shred of pleasure, and it was *glorious*.

He held her up by the waist, feeling how her muscles shivered and contracted as she rode her peak. Fates, nothing compared to this. Not glory, not wealth. He could spend all his days just like this and be the happiest male who ever lived.

He felt the last of her pulsing orgasm with his tongue buried inside her.

Her arm dropped from the headboard, and she slumped back onto his chest.

Hakon lifted her to lay her out on the bed. The sight she made was a feast itself, and he indulged for a long while just devouring her with his gaze as he ran his hands up and down her quivering body.

Aislinn watched him with a small smile teasing at her lips, carding her fingers through his hair as he kissed up her body. She welcomed him into the cradle of her body, parting her thighs and reaching up to take his face in her hands, guiding it down to hers for a long, drugging kiss. The type of kiss that made a male forget his name and all vows of honor.

As his tongue tangled with hers, Hakon caught one of her hands and pulled it above her head. The other joined it, and he held hers in one of his. Pulling away from her kiss, he kept her gaze as he drew one of her legs around his hip.

"You've ruined me, *vinya,*" he said as he teased his cockhead against her entrance.

Aislinn moaned and arched in welcome.

He slid through her slick then inside with ease. Pushing inside her was like coming home, the hot give of her body so exquisite, it bordered on pain. It'd been too long since he'd had his mate, and sweat beaded down his spine with the effort it took not to shove inside and rut her mindlessly.

His control hung by a thread as he began to move, the sight of her laid out beneath him, hands above her head, breasts swaying in rhythm, pink cunt spread wide around him, nearly undid him.

What did was the way she looked at him, eyes gone soft and sultry, a smile teasing those plush lips. He wanted to kiss her everywhere every day in front of everyone. He wanted all to know she was his and he was hers. He wanted there to be no secrets, no distance, no obstacles. He needed her to be his with a savagery that stole his breath.

Nothing would stand in his way.

This brilliant, glorious female would be his in every way.

"Run away with me," he rumbled. The words slipped out, but he felt no regret.

*Choose me.*

Those lips parted, and her cunt clenched around him so perfectly. Hakon growled, unable to withstand it any longer.

He fell upon her, claiming her mouth as his hips thrust her into the bed. Her nipples pressed into his chest, hard points against his pebbling skin. Her hips rolled to meet his, an insatiable pace that lacked rhythm or finesse. They chased down their pleasure together, desperate and wild.

Hakon's crackled down his spine, and he burst.

He poured himself into his mate, his hopes and fears and desire. She writhed beneath him, meeting his every stroke, pulling everything from him and demanding more.

He gave it. He would always give her everything.

Bodies quaking, the tension snapped, and he was lost to the searing pleasure.

The mate-bond sang, thrumming like a second heartbeat.

Hakon gasped, easing down into his mate's arms as his body went lax. He kept most of his weight off of her, but the feeling of her beneath him, her body still trembling with aftershocks, was too wonderful.

He mumbled her name, pressing a lazy kiss to the side of her neck.

Her hand smoothed over his hair, and she turned her face to his ear.

"I can't," she whispered.

# 29

Hakon woke with an aching heart. Peeling an eye open, he squinted against the burgeoning daylight streaming into the bedchamber from the far wall of arched windows.

The bed was the most comfortable he'd ever slept in, the fabrics softer than any he'd ever felt.

He only cared about the sleeping form of his mate beside him, her back tucked to his front. She slept soundly, her face easy. None of her myriad of worries lined her face, and Hakon couldn't help running his finger along her cheek and pushing her hair behind her ear for an unobstructed view.

He'd woken up with his mate in his arms before, but always in the murky darkness of predawn. There was something about lying with her here, in her bedchamber, *her* bed, sunlight bathing them, that had his foolish heart daydreaming.

*It should always be like this.*

They shouldn't ever have to sleep apart.

Yet . . .

*I can't,* she'd said. *I can't.*

She couldn't run away with him. Or wouldn't.

The blow still stung, even as he molded his body around hers and breathed deeply from her sweet-smelling hair.

He hadn't truly expected her acquiescence; everything he knew about her told him she would stand and fight. Yet to hear it still set his heart to aching bittersweetly. In the old days, when an orc had made off with their desired mate into the mountains, it hadn't always been consensual—a main reason why the tradition had fallen out of favor.

Hakon feared it might end up being so with his own mate. If Aislinn wouldn't come willingly, would he dare take her anyway?

They would be hunted. Captain Aodhan himself would track them. Aislinn may even resist him and try to get away. Chief Kennum in Kaldebrak may very well refuse to allow him back with a human captive, and a noble one at that. Siggy would surely beat him over the head.

He understood all this and yet—if it came to it, if it was her safety over her position, he would do it. For her.

Hakon let his eyes slide closed and put away such thoughts. The situation hadn't grown so dire yet, and he had no qualms with wringing Bayard's neck before making off with Aislinn. Whichever solution was better for her, Hakon was determined to see it through.

The lazy morning sun lulled him back into a doze, his body lax and spent from a night of lovemaking and his mind content to plan how best to separate Bayard's head from his shoulders. His thumb ran in slow circles over her ribs, and his fingers toyed with the ends of her hair.

Inside that room, it was easy to pretend. Despite her rejection, lying there with her only filled his heart with imaginings of what could be.

Lost in his fantasies, he didn't hear the door to the solar open.

He did, however, hear Fia's shriek of alarm and quick attempt to muffle it behind her hand.

Aislinn lurched upright, and Hakon moved to block her with his body.

They all held perfectly still, staring, waiting—

The door opened again, one of the guards calling, "Is everything all right?"

"Yes," Fia called back. "Just a spider."

The guard chuckled and closed the door again.

When she turned back to the bed, Fia threw a scowl Hakon's way, and he returned it, even as his ears burned. Marching over to the bed, Fia planted her hands on her hips and stared down her nose at them.

"You just couldn't keep away," she huffed, her accusation for both Aislinn and Hakon.

A growl rumbled beneath Hakon's sternum, not liking being scolded, especially over finding a way to be with Aislinn.

Fia pointed a finger at him. "Don't you growl at me. You both know how risky this is, what with everyone jumping at their shadows and Bayard acting like he's already lord of the castle."

Hakon growled in earnest, muttering an orcish curse under his breath.

Aislinn's head dropped into a pillow to muffle her groan.

"Up with you now," said Fia. "I was going to let you sleep in, but the mayor is here asking for you. It seems that Bayard's men are getting comfortable in town and harassing several taverns."

Aislinn groaned again. "Sorry excuse for knights," she mumbled. Pulling back the sheets, she climbed out of bed.

Hakon watched on with a mix of curiosity and fury.

Anger for the knights behaving poorly toward the people of Dundúran—and even more for their baron who used them as a threat against Aislinn. Yet it was tempered with a sweet wonder as he watched his mate quickly ready for her day.

Neither she nor Fia shooed him from the room as he slowly got up himself and began to dress. He watched them through his lashes as Fia pulled a fresh shift, stockings, and stays from one of three large armoires in the room. Aislinn selected a plain green gown, telling Fia she didn't want to fuss with anything fancy but instead get to the great hall.

Fia laced her stays and gown as Aislinn plaited her hair. It all happened in concert, a perfectly timed domestic harmony. Witnessing it softened something in Hakon.

This was what mornings should be like for them always.

He wanted to see this part of his mate, the private, domestic side when there were no duties to do or people to please. She and Fia chattered easily, and he felt honored to be privy to their inner world. It felt like something of an acceptance, that he now too got to inhabit this most private realm, and it took the sting out of her denial last night.

When she finished, Aislinn walked over to where he sat in a chair, lacing his boots. Taking his face in her hands, she bent to bestow a kiss on his lips.

Heaviness hung between them—he worried what he should say and what she would say to him. She wouldn't have allowed him to stay, to watch her dress, if she meant to be rid of him.

"I'll go now. You stay in here with Fia until the corridor is clear."

"All right." He reached to press her hand more firmly against his cheek. "Be safe, *vinya.*"

She gave him a smile, though it didn't reach her eyes. With another kiss, she left her rooms, the guards closing the door behind her.

Hakon and Fia waited in silence for a long moment. When all was quiet, she waved him toward the bed.

"At least be helpful while you're here, if you would."

He stood and rounded the bed, helping her strip it of the coverlet, blankets, and sheets. It only seemed fair to help after the mess he'd made of it pleasuring Aislinn last night—about which he had no regrets.

He eyed Fia under his lashes and thought, no, she wouldn't let him take one of the sheets to have Aislinn's scent.

The bed bare, Fia fetched a fresh set of sheets and blankets from a deep trunk.

"Did she sleep well?" the maid asked as she handed him one end of a sheet.

"Yes."

"Good. She hasn't been sleeping much."

"I worry for her."

"I do, too." Fia frowned at the blanket she unfolded. "This business with Bayard is the last thing she needed."

"Is she . . ." He didn't know how to ask without sounding pathetic.

Fia looked up, taking his measure, before answering his unspoken question, "She's no intention of accepting him. They wouldn't suit at all, not that Bayard cares. She's playing for time." She peered at him from under her lashes. "She needs someone very different from the baron. Someone who can put her and the Darrowlands first."

His beast snarled at the insinuation that he didn't know how to care for his mate, but Hakon bit it back. That wasn't what Fia said, even if what she had was almost as hard to swallow.

"Does he pose a real danger to her? Should he not be imprisoned for treason?" Hakon couldn't imagine Chief Kennum or even Lord Merrick standing for such insolence, but then, Bayard wouldn't have moved against them. He saw an opportunity with Aislinn vulnerable and meant to exploit it.

Hakon would ensure the baron lived to regret it.

"I can't imagine him doing her any harm," said Fia. "He needs her. Doesn't mean he can't sit around and be as insufferable as possible, of course."

Hakon appreciated her growl of disapproval.

"And his men?"

"A threat to what my lady holds most dear." Fia stopped fluffing the pillow to regard him seriously. "She's always put her people first, and they love her for it. They will defend her and her claim to the end."

Ears heating, Hakon dared to admit to her, "She is first in my heart."

Fia nodded slowly. "Good. She deserves nothing less."

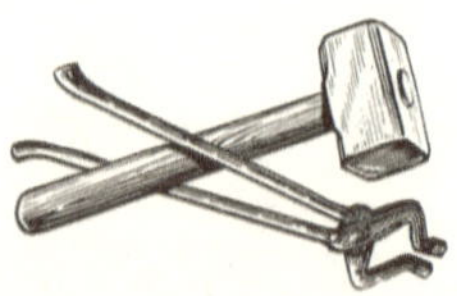

"You have my promise, Mayor Doherty, that all knights will behave with utmost decorum," Aislinn said to the aggrieved mayor of Dundúran. As an elected magistrate of the people, it was his duty to bring issues concerning the townsfolk to the Darrows, particularly for sudden or urgent problems.

Doherty, a kindly man with a bald head and portly gut and far too many grandchildren, as he put it, scowled at Bayard. The baron stood off to the side, aloof and imperious. For the entire meeting with Doherty, he'd looked as though he bit into something sour.

Aislinn was beyond annoyance—hearing of how dozens of Bayard's knights were carousing nightly, harassing women, scaring livestock, and even drunkenly rolling barrels into the river had her gall rising. Fates, how did Endelín function if Bayard allowed his company to behave like spoiled youths?

*Perhaps he didn't.* Perhaps they'd been told to be as unpleasant as possible while in Dundúran.

The thought soured Aislinn impossibly further toward the baron—and didn't fill her with confidence that Captain Aodhan would find a way to turn enough of them against Bayard.

"Please send me a report of everyone whose property was damaged. Baron Bayard will happily compensate them."

Bayard choked, glaring at her before smoothing his expression. "Yes, compensated in full," he said.

Doherty sighed. "Very well. I'd rather this not be necessary at all. The people are worried enough with so many unfamiliar swordsmen about."

"I mean only to ensure the safety of our heiress," said Bayard. Aislinn had to wonder if he knew his smile was so oily or if he was attempting something else.

Doherty made an unconvinced sound, turning back to Aislinn. He took her hand in his dry, wrinkled one and patted it. "Is there any news from your father?"

Aislinn felt the prickle of Bayard's interest along her neck.

"No, nothing yet," she lied. "But then, the roads are muddy."

Doherty nodded. "Let us hope his mission is successful and for his swift return." Casting another moody look at Bayard, the mayor bowed his head. "Thank you for seeing me this morning, my lady."

"You are always welcome, Mayor Doherty. My warmest wishes to your wife and all two-hundred grandchildren."

"Ha!" the old man laughed. "Try at least five hundred!"

Aislinn smiled, waving farewell as the mayor took his walking stick and marched from the great hall. Her heart rested a little more content knowing her people were resilient; they could weather whatever was to come. She hated lying to Mayor Doherty and the people of Dundúran, but there didn't seem to be a compelling enough reason to cause them worry.

When she knew more, she'd tell them herself.

For now, she had to handle the problems she could.

Turning on Bayard, she leveled him with a frown. It was a wonder what a good night's sleep after being thoroughly made love to by her blacksmith could do for her. Aislinn felt downright feisty, sizing up the baron as she decided how best to scold him.

"Keep your company in line, Bayard. They aren't on leave, and they have no right to terrorize the people."

"Have you really heard nothing from our dear Liege Darrow?"

He caught Aislinn off-guard with the sudden question.

Pursing her lips, she said, "If I had, I'd tell the staff."

"Would you, though?" Bayard smiled that slick smile and began to stroll in a loose circle around her. "Maybe you would, if his return was imminent. But then, what if he wasn't returning? What if he'd been delayed? Would you tell them then?"

"Are you concerned you may soon have to face my father and explain what you've done?" she asked instead of answering, one of her mother's favorite tactics. "You should be."

"I'm not, in fact."

Coming to a halt, that frivolous smile played at his lips, but his eyes had gone dark enough to put a tremble of fear in Aislinn's belly. She reminded herself they weren't alone; her guards were near.

"What I am is impatient. You're stalling, hoping for word of your father that may or may not have come."

"You're welcome to leave at any time, my lord. I'm certainly not keeping you here."

"I'm not going anywhere. Not without an answer."

"Then I'm afraid you'll have to find more patience. I have more important things to see to."

Bayard caught her by the arm before she could leave. "My patience won't last forever, my lady. I suggest you make up your mind."

"And I order you to let me go," she said loudly.

The guards moved closer, and Bayard released her.

"Go ahead and play your hand," she warned him. "The people of Dundúran will never forget. You won't take the city, they won't submit to you."

"Perhaps. But then who would repel your brother when he comes?"

"I don't need you and your company to deal with Jerrod."

"Then why not have me thrown in the dungeon? If you're so sure of your victory."

"Because life isn't cheap to me," she spat. "Your company are still my people. I am heiress of the Darrowlands. One day to be Liege Darrow. Everyone, including vassals, are my people. I won't have them fighting each other and spilling their blood for something as foolish as your ambitions."

His smile was ugly. "This is why you will never succeed as Liege Darrow. Politics and ambition are what make demesnes strong. The Darrowlands will wither under your soft hand."

"What makes a land strong is her people. I pity the people of Endelín if their baron truly doesn't know that."

Bayard chuckled mirthlessly. "Worry about your own people, my lady. And remember, my patience wears thin."

With a sweeping bow, he left her, determined to have the last word. Aislinn watched him go, anger boiling in her belly and fear banding around her heart.

As much as she abhorred violence and sought to handle the situation without it, perhaps she really should just let Hakon rip Bayard's head off. It was certainly an efficient solution to the problem.

# 30

Aislinn only grew surer of that thought as that day passed and the next. Bayard seemed disinclined to endear himself to anyone, her or the staff or the people of Dundúran.

Oh, he was cordial and charming where he could be, filling the castle cellars with wine no one asked for. However, his retinue was a source of tension within the castle, both for Dundúran's own knights and the staff. He held them to no standard of conduct other than that he always have guards of his own to follow him about as he meandered the castle and made a general nuisance of himself.

As the kitchen staff served that night's meal in the dining hall, Aislinn eyed the elaborate plate Bayard had insisted upon, wondering if Hugh had spat in it. From the evil way Tilly smiled when she lifted the lid of the tureen, Aislinn thought it likely.

"Are you sure you won't at least try it?" Bayard asked, swirling the creamed potatoes and sauce.

Tilly subtly shook her head as she placed Aislinn's simpler fare in front of her.

"No, thank you," she said, content with her lightly seasoned chicken and bread.

Bayard sniffed over her meal. "You eat the same as the staff."

"Not always. Hugh is good enough to make my meals specially. The staff are much more adventurous than me, I'd never condemn them to my boring palette."

"Shouldn't they be grateful for whatever is put in front of them?"

Aislinn slid her gaze over Bayard and arched her brows. "I could say the same of you, baron, as a guest. Alas, another way we don't suit at all."

Bayard smiled in that wolfish way she was coming to dread. "But I so enjoy our debates."

"I think that's the only thing you would enjoy from a union between us. I'm certain we'd make each other miserable."

Hand over his heart, Bayard said, "You wound me, my Lady Aislinn, that you think I wouldn't want to romance my bride."

"Blackmailing and threats aren't romance."

"Not to you, perhaps." He sighed. "They are a means to an end, I'm afraid. All I need is an answer, and I shall be the picture of a besotted groom."

"Whoever I marry wouldn't become Liege Darrow but lord consort. While you would move from Endelín to Dundúran, I fail to see any significant improvements to your life. From what you've said, Endelín is paradise."

"There is much to be said for being lord consort of a demesne as powerful as the Darrowlands. And perhaps I'm further sighted than you."

"How so?"

"Perhaps I'm wise enough to lift my head and see which way the winds are blowing." He sipped from his wine, leaving Aislinn to try not to frown as she parsed out his meaning. "The Eirean way of doing things is on its way out. The king has a far more Pyrrossi way of ruling."

Aislinn sat back in her chair, finally understanding just how long of a game Bayard was willing to play. "You hope to marry me and convince the king to give over the Darrowlands to you, because I'm a woman."

He said nothing to confirm it, but Bayard did lift his cup to salute her.

"It isn't the worst plan I've ever heard, but it's certainly not the best."

His smile faltered, though he clung to his air of charm valiantly. "No plan is absolutely perfect."

"All of it hinges on forcing me to wed. I think perhaps you misjudged me, baron." His smile fell a little further, hinting that she was right. "I think you allowed your ambitions to color your perception. I've no intention of cowering at the first threat."

He leaned forward, for the rest of the room presenting a smile, but Aislinn saw an animal baring its teeth. "Is that your answer, then? You refuse me?"

"I will wed you when it is the only option available to me," she said.

"And what do you think is available to you? We both know your father isn't coming. He'd have been here by now or at least sent word. You're alone."

"I've written the king," she said, enjoying the look of surprise that overtook his face.

"And do you suppose that will endear you to him? An heiress who can't protect her demesne."

"I suspect he'll be grateful for the intelligence that mercenaries intend to cross his lands not at the behest of Caledon, thus avoiding war. And," she leaned forward herself to ensure he heard her, "I wrote the queen as well."

All pretense of charm fell from his face. "What good will the queen do you?"

"She is our sovereign, and I know her to be a caring woman. She will help."

"The queen is ailing. She won't be any help to you."

"I suppose you think so, with your low opinion of women rulers. But the king is a regent who rules only by the favor of the queen. You would not even be that, baron." She smiled when she saw the confusion in his eyes. "I would ensure you were consort in name only. You would have no power, no say. You couldn't force me to your bed and I wouldn't go. You would be powerless, childless, and friendless. Is that truly the life you want?"

Setting down her spoon and napkin, Aislinn folded her hands on the table. She'd gone a little heady, thinking she might win an argument with the unctuous baron, but caution still gripped her stomach tight.

"Give this up, Bayard. Should you somehow succeed, I will endeavor to make your life misery after humiliation. So leave Dundúran, and we'll forget this ever happened."

His hand struck out to grasp her by the wrist. "You would do well not to test me, my lady."

"You would do better not to test *me,* baron." Pulling her hand away, Aislinn glared. "I have written the other nobles and will raise an army to meet my brother. I don't need your knights."

"Are you sure they'll come?" he spat, voicing the very fear that consumed her. Aislinn paled, and he smiled to see it.

The far door to the great hall burst open. She might not have looked away from the snake before her had the door not banged with such force against the stone, and had it not been Connor Brádaigh who strode through.

He hastened up the hall, ignoring how the great room hushed at his sudden appearance.

Aislinn's stomach dropped to see the state of him—dirty, matted, with a nasty cut across his face. Sorcha and Orek jumped up from their spots at the near table, but he didn't stop, marching for Aislinn.

She hurried down from the high table to meet him, Bayard forgotten.

He stopped only when he stood before her, a man weary to the bone, kept going only by sheer determination.

"My lady," he said, "forgive the delay."

"Connor, what's happened?" Sorcha demanded, trying to turn his face so she could inspect his cut.

He ignored his sister, his expression grave. Aislinn already knew what he'd say when he continued, "I was found by the mercenaries and held prisoner, meant for ransom. I escaped when we crossed into the Crown Forest."

"Then . . ."

Connor nodded. "Jerrod is coming. They're four, maybe five days behind me at most."

Knowing what he would say still didn't prepare her for its impact. It hit Aislinn deep in the chest, where she'd pushed all her hurts and pains.

Jerrod was coming to attack her and their home. Her own brother.

Everything she'd thought, everything she'd done—wrong.

Panic stampeded through her, crushing her windpipe. Her next breath brought her no air, and in the next she was gasping. The worries and fears and decisions pressed all around her, caving in her chest.

Her knees wobbled before buckling. Someone caught her before she went down—someone else said her name.

*No, no, not here.*

Not now. Not in front of everyone.

Tears gushed, clogging her nose, and her vision went bright with bursts of blue and green.

No no no no—

Hakon stood from his place at the table, dinner forgotten. He'd hardly touched it, watching the volleying between Aislinn and Bayard while trying to read lips.

Before Connor Brádaigh walked into the hall, hardly recognizable.

Pulse throbbing so hard it nearly choked him, Hakon watched as a small group gathered around Aislinn and Connor. Words were said he didn't catch. And Aislinn nearly went down.

Brenna caught her and began to lead her out of the hall.

A gasp swirled through the staff.

Fia too jumped to her feet, hopping over the bench.

"Fia," he begged before she could leave.

She looked at him with wide, scared eyes before nodding once.

He followed on her heels as they made for the far side of the hall, passing a growing group of knights and an agitated Bayard, who was being kept back.

Captain Aodhan waved Fia through but stopped Hakon.

"He can come," said Fia.

Hakon barely waited for the captain's approval, pushing past into the corridor. A door to the right was open, leading into a storeroom. Extra chairs and tables sat draped in cloth, a fine layer of dust blanketing it all.

Just inside, Connor, Sorcha, and Orek had gathered in a semicircle around Brenna, who held Aislinn by the shoulders. Fia rushed forward, only to stop and join the others watching as Aislinn sobbed and gasped and wailed—and Brenna shook her.

"Be calm!" cried the chatelain. "Aislinn, look at me! Calm yourself!"

But Aislinn was lost to her tears, her head thrashing violently back and forth as fat tears rolled down her cheeks.

Brenna shook harder. "Stop it! Stop now!"

Hakon stepped through the others, forcing Connor and Sorcha out of his way. He pulled Brenna back by her shoulder, not roughly but firmly enough to make the older woman move. She sputtered as he separated her from Aislinn, clawing at his hand.

"How dare you?" she howled.

"You don't touch her," Hakon growled back.

He pulled Aislinn deeper into the room and into his arms. With a shuddering gasp, she collapsed against him, taking great fistfuls of his tunic. Her body wracked with sobs, he stood with her for agonizingly long minutes, her cries echoing in the silent storeroom.

The others looked on with mixed expressions, concern and disbelief coloring their faces. Brenna scowled at him, trying to hover nearby, but whenever she got too close, he bared his tusks at her. Even Sorcha, her hands up in placation, he rebuffed.

*Her fault. She laid this weight upon Aislinn's shoulders.*

"Hakon, enough," Orek warned him in orcish.

"You saw what she did to her. You saw her lay hands on my mate," Hakon hissed.

*Take her and run. They don't understand. They can't keep her safe.*

A red haze gathered along the fringes of his vision.

His hold tightened as her tears wetted his shirt. The sounds of her despair gutted him, and he walked the knife's edge of his control. One sudden movement, one wrong word and he would lose himself to the berserker rage.

Giving up on Hakon, Brenna instead tried to edge closer to Aislinn and penetrate her tears. "Stop this now," she said, more softly this time. "Tell the orc to let go of you. Here, dry your tears." And she pulled a kerchief from her pocket to hand to Aislinn.

But his mate didn't see, her face buried in his chest.

"We've all had enough of your comfort, chatelain."

Brenna's lips thinned. "How dare you? She is the heiress, and you— you're a blacksmith. Let her go this moment."

He did no such thing.

When Brenna opened her mouth to spit more fire, Fia laid a gentle hand on her arm.

The room dissolved again into silence, which suited Hakon just fine. Keeping an eye on the others, he turned more of his attention to his mate, offering what comfort he could. A soft purr, just for her, not loud enough to hear, rumbled in his chest.

Dropping his head nearer hers, he whispered, "It's all right, *vinya*. I have you."

He didn't know what had drawn the sudden fit—didn't really care, either. He could guess.

She'd been playing for time, but it'd just run out.

After long moments of soothing strokes up and down her back and whispered promises in the warm well of air they shared, Aislinn's sobs began to abate. She took great gulps of air to stop the shuddering, and soon he heard her exhales take on a pattern as she blew air through her mouth. He joined her, matching his breath with hers, and together they breathed.

She stopped trembling.

Aislinn picked up her head from his chest and looked at him with puffy, reddened eyes. He swiped his thumb along her cheek, catching the last of her tears.

"Jerrod is coming," she murmured.

Hakon could only nod.

*So be it.*

Her face crumpled with the truth Connor had brought, but she didn't let herself fall back into tears.

"I have to tell them."

Hakon's grip tightened. "Send someone else," he begged her. She needed rest and comfort, a night of soft blankets and deep sleep to meet the troubles of tomorrow.

She shook her head sadly. "It has to come from me."

He wanted to argue, wanted to clutch her to him and refuse to let her go, but when she moved to step back, his arms fell away.

*Get her alone. Need to get her alone, and then run—as fast and as far as we can.*

Her sad eyes broke his heart—and hardened it, too, for what he had to do.

Gritting his tusks, he watched her leave the storeroom and turn back to the dining hall. Connor and the women followed, leaving Hakon with only Orek.

Hakon went to follow too but expected the hand that smacked into his chest to stop him. He turned his head to glare at Orek.

"Don't you ever growl at my mate like that again," said the other male in orcish.

"She made Aislinn heiress. She put this burden on her. None of this would've happened if it wasn't for Sorcha."

Orek bared his small tusks at him. "Sorcha had the choice thrust upon her. Aislinn was heiress in everything but name. With her brother gone, who else would take command? She was always meant for this."

Hakon's nostrils flared in a huff, and he pushed past Orek out into the corridor. He heard his mate's voice and followed it back to the dining hall. Finding a spot just inside the door, he watched as she spoke to the gathered staff from the steps of the high table.

"It's as I feared. My brother and a force of mercenaries is imminent. We have four days, perhaps a little more."

The hall erupted in nervous whispers, the staff looking from Aislinn to one another and back again. Their fear filled the hall to the rafters, the tension of the past weeks solidifying into a hard knot of trepidation.

"Now isn't the time to panic. Preparations must be made. Your superiors will have your assignments in the morning, but for now, please try to get some rest."

Hakon watched on as she answered questions from the worried staff. Pride swelled in his chest, but it was nothing to his own concern for her. His beast was frantic inside him, seeing her all alone, fielding the volley of questions and fears, and Bayard lurking like a vulture just waiting for a kill.

A growl caught in his throat.

She was good to her people, and they loved her for it, but who would protect Aislinn? How could any of them ensure her safety?

They couldn't. Only Hakon, her mate, could.

A heavy hand landed on his shoulder, and Orek managed to turn him a half-step. His frown was thunderous and disapproving.

"I see the look in your eyes," Orek said in orcish. "If you know her at all, then you know she'll never forgive you for it."

"I don't care," Hakon snarled.

"Look around you. *Look*. She isn't just your mate. She is so much to so many. You cannot take her away from that—nor take it away from her."

Hakon pulled his shoulder out of Orek's grip. "You'd do the same if it was your mate."

"No, I wouldn't. I *didn't*." Scrubbing a hand across his face, Orek sighed. "I thought about it. I wanted to. But I couldn't take her away from her family, her people. I knew, if I was to be her mate, I had to be one of her people. Her clan."

The crust around Hakon's heart cracked, but he shook his head against it. "It's not the same."

"I don't envy you, but you must decide, my friend. Do you want a mate, or do you want Aislinn?"

# 31

Aislinn sat at her father's desk, her untouched breakfast before her, as Connor recounted his harrowing ordeal with the mercenaries again and Fia took notes.

Caught just before they broke camp in the Strait, his life had been spared only by his name. Jerrod himself had confirmed Connor's identity, saying the Brádaighs would pay a ransom for his return. To Dirk, the brutal leader of the largest band of mercenaries, this meant that Connor could be roughed up a bit.

Aislinn winced every time she glanced at the wicked cut bisecting Connor's left cheek, now stitched and covered in honey and ointment.

"And how does Jerrod seem?"

Connor sighed. "They kept us apart. I think Dirk feared there might still be some loyalty between us." He laughed once without humor. "Honestly, my lady, he seemed half-mad. You must prepare yourself, for it isn't the brother you knew coming."

"No, it's not." Aislinn wondered if the brother she'd known ever truly existed at all.

Her gaze fell to her hands, a familiar guilt gnawing alongside all her worries. What more could she and her father have done? Was Jerrod always meant for this destructive path?

She'd kept herself up late into the night wondering these things. No answer she settled on gave her any comfort or consolation, and she feared she would just have to swallow the truth that her brother was rotten. Whether born that way or allowing it to fester inside him over his life, Jerrod's heart was black with hate and resentment. He'd chosen this course, and Aislinn had chosen hers.

When she looked back up at Connor, she found him eyeing the tray of food. He'd cleaned his own plate, but the hollowness of his cheeks spoke of a desperate kind of hunger, one Aislinn was grateful never to have known. Keeping only a piece of toast, she pushed the tray toward him.

Connor thanked her, not minding that the porridge and sausage had nearly gone cold as he tucked in.

"You're confident of their numbers?"

Connor nodded. "More than five hundred, less than six. I'd hoped they'd fight amongst themselves, but the prize of Dundúran seems enough to get them to work together. For now, at least."

Aislinn picked at her cuticles as she watched him eat. Five hundred she could match; six hundred perhaps not. And that didn't figure in whether or not her company would have to fight off Bayard's. She couldn't afford to weaken her garrison—not to mention what it would do to morale, of both the knights and the townspeople.

She had announced the developments in the market square earlier that morning, unable to stomach food before knowing her people were aware. Horrified faces surrounded her, shouting questions and demanding answers. Aislinn did what she could, allaying the worst fears by assuring them that every preparation would be made.

Anyone was welcome to shelter within the castle walls until Jerrod was dealt with. Supplies would be offered to fortify houses and businesses, and her knights would be leading lessons for anyone who wished to learn basic combat and defense. She assured them it wouldn't come to that, but she knew, perhaps better than most, that worry and anxiety needed something to do.

When she left the square, she was full of pride for her people. They were resilient and resourceful. After their initial panic, they rallied, and already, preparations were underway to make safe the city and castle. From her window, she could see some had pitched tents within the courtyard already, and a steady stream of supplies flowed from the castle armory and storerooms.

All would be well—as well as it could be, at least, were it not for the annoyance of Bayard's knights.

Her belly burned with rage at the situation Bayard created, leveraging the lives of her people against each other. Their impasse had grown tiresome at best, but Captain Aodhan hadn't brought her any encouraging news. For whatever reason, Bayard's knights were holding fast to him.

She didn't need his company to fight—just to not get in the way. She'd received word back from her nearest vassals, all promising forces. Margrave Holt and several others said they'd come themselves to defend Dundúran.

No word yet from Gleanná, but then, that would take more time.

Her heart lurched painfully, and Aislinn focused on her breathing. She kept her face turned toward Connor as he talked, but she didn't truly hear him as she battled back her panic.

With effort, she imagined big arms wrapping around her. A warm chest to bury herself against and hide away.

She focused on the memory of how Hakon held her, talked her down, and it was enough to stave off the panic. Her breathing evened out, and she clenched her hands together on the desk to hide how they trembled.

Aislinn came back into the study calmer but was left with an ache deep inside. She didn't want the memory of Hakon. She didn't want him hidden away behind closed doors, nor Brenna scolding them for touching. She didn't want a tryst by night.

She wanted everything. She wanted him.

Hakon felt right in a way that few things or people did. Like an idea that translated perfectly to paper or a recipe that went right the very first time. Little felt truly *right* to Aislinn, and she spent most of her days content with tolerable. Hakon was far more than that, and in the same way reading, drafting, and inventing were parts of her, she thought he could be, too.

After all this was over, she would ask him about the mate-bond, if there was a chance one might form between them. If she could face and defeat her brother and his mercenary force, what was a little question compared to that?

Nothing. Well, perhaps something, but only a little. And that little could unlock everything.

A knock brought her round, and she looked up from her musings to see a page hurrying into the study. He stopped in the center of the room to bow before scurrying closer.

"Milady, it's Baron Bayard," said the page, "he's demanding an audience in the great hall."

She and Fia exchanged frowns before Aislinn rolled her eyes. "He's gotten entirely too comfortable." Pushing up from her seat, she joked, "Perhaps he means to announce his departure."

"We can only hope, milady," Fia agreed.

Together, the three of them and Aislinn's guards left the study to make the quick walk to the great hall, the page scampering off to other duties. Aislinn used the short march to hone that rage in her belly. The dueling with Bayard was tiresome, but she couldn't let her defenses lapse because of it.

They soon made the great hall, a herald announcing her arrival. The dozen or so people in the hall—a few staff, several town elders, Mayor Doherty, two magistrates, a handful of guards, and Bayard of course—turned to watch her mount the four shallow steps up the dais.

Aislinn stood beside her father's seat and folded her hands behind her back.

"Baron," she said coolly.

Bayard stepped forward and bowed.

"I'm not a dog you can summon," she admonished quietly.

"And yet here you are," he whispered back.

A growl, suspiciously orcish sounding, caught in her throat.

"I'm told you wished an audience with me?"

"Indeed. I find I am impatient for your answer, Lady Aislinn, and my poor lover's heart can't be made to wait any longer with the threat of battle looming." Dropping into an even deeper bow, Bayard spread his arms wide. "I declare my right to call a Choosing."

Surprise sounded through the hall.

Aislinn's was silent, her stomach dropping to her toes.

A Choosing was an ancient Eirean custom, unpopular nowadays but still sacred. At a Choosing, the suitor who called for it, as well as any other in attendance, could lay out their suitability, declaring why they were the best choice as they knelt before the intended.

The intended, often a noblewoman or princess, would then have to choose from the suitors. At least, in ancient times, she'd been forced to choose. Later Choosings allowed her to choose no one. However, once the suits were denied, they could never be made again. It forced chieftains to commit to an alliance or not, intractable children to marry, and scheming mamas not to string suitors along. There were also ballads and folk tales of how otherwise doomed lovers had used the tradition to plot their union.

If the potential bride chose a suitor, she sat upon their knee, and that was that. They were handfasted in promise to each other that very day.

Choosings were old-fashioned but legally binding. As a suitor with a provable history of pressing his suit, Bayard was allowed to call for a Choosing.

All eyes fell upon her, wide with morbid curiosity.

There was only one thing she could say. "I acknowledge your right and accept. But I invoke my right to a day to consider. And give any other suitors time to appear."

A tick jumped in Bayard's cheek, but he nodded in agreement. "Of course, my lady. We must do this right."

She nodded back, sealing their pact. "Very well."

Aislinn descended the steps numbly, mind whirring.

Fia rushed to her side. "Milady—"

"I must speak with Captain Aodhan. Now."

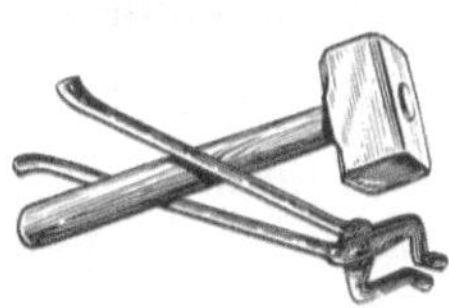

Hakon waited as long as he was able, gleaning what he could from the whispers and gossip. The news was all over the castle within the hour, how the baron had called for a Choosing and Lady Aislinn had actually agreed. Preparations were underway amid all the current chaos of a castle soon to be under siege, and Hakon could hardly fathom the turn of events.

*She's run out of time—and so have I.*

A forge left to burn became too hot, and so Hakon was all morning.

Finally, late in the afternoon, when he could stand it no longer, he went in search of her.

Hakon found her in her father's study. He bit back his annoyance at the guard who stopped him and called inside, "My lady? The blacksmith wishes an audience."

"Yes, let him in."

Hakon pushed past the knights, relieved to find Aislinn alone.

She nodded behind him. "You may close the door."

He did, the *click* of the latch signaling they were alone. As alone as they ever were.

When he turned back to her, it was to see the beginnings of a smile on her face as she rose to greet him. He wanted to rush to her, to taste that smile, to gorge himself on the precious moments he had.

Instead, he rumbled, "What is a Choosing?"

Her face fell, and Hakon's beast growled inside him. Fates, she was going to tell him something he didn't want to hear.

As Hakon stood in the center of the room and Aislinn paced, she explained this Choosing to him. Suitors, claims, finality. He understood it on its face, even if he didn't see why it was so binding.

Bayard was forcing her to choose on the eve of battle, and if he didn't receive the answer he wanted, he intended to decimate her forces before Jerrod arrived to finish it. That was the sum of it, even as she told him every detail she knew about Choosings, from their beginnings to their current legal precedent, as was her way.

He let her talk, hoping at least the sound of her sweet voice would calm him, but it didn't. All day, since hearing of this Choosing, his body had buzzed as if some force compelled him to *move*. He thought her presence might help, but if anything, learning the scope of the Choosing only made it worse.

The buzz became an itch, a compunction. He bit back the need to throw her over his shoulder this moment and leap from the window, making off with his mate.

When she came to a stop in her pacing and her words, Hakon asked the question that scratched at him all day.

"Will you choose him?"

Aislinn shook her head. "I don't want to. I'm working with Captain Aodhan on a plan to mitigate his reaction, but . . ." Tears gathered along her lashes. "I fear the outcome. Hakon, I . . . I'm frightened."

He was there in a moment, taking her face between his hands. His green skin stood in such contrast to her warm golden colors. He loved her colors. He loved how she wrapped her hands around his wrists and looked up at him with such trust, such vulnerability. Without speaking, she asked for his comfort.

Fuck Bayard. Fuck all of this.

Nothing should be allowed to frighten her. She deserved all that was right and good in this world, and Hakon railed against all that wasn't.

"*Vinya,*" he murmured, "come away with me. We'll go somewhere new, somewhere safe. I will take care of you, always."

She gave him the most beautifully sad smile he'd ever seen, her tears slipping into the cracks of his hardened heart to erode away his resolve.

"I wish I could. But, Hakon, I can't." She squeezed his wrists. "Good or ill, this is my life. I can't run away."

He knew her answer before she said it, but he needed to hear it one more time from her lips.

Closing his eyes, he dropped his head to hers and breathed her in.

Fates, how naïve he'd been when he left Kaldebrak. Thinking that finding and taking a mate would be simple, straightforward. Nothing in this life was ever so easy—and nothing in his life would ever be more worth it.

He was worse than naïve, he was a fool. A fool for her.

Hakon loved her. More than was wise and more than he ever thought possible. He'd hoped the stories were true but hadn't been ready to be proven right. The truth had a way of doing that, rewriting hopes and amending plans.

The little life he'd built in his head was a good dream, and when he pressed a kiss to her soft lips, he mourned the loss of it. Grief didn't have to be tangible or reasonable, and he'd spent so long running from it. He allowed it its space, his kiss tinged with a sadness for the life that could have been.

He would have made her happy in that meadow. He would have built them a good life, full of happy days and warm nights.

That wasn't to be. And for the first time, Hakon knew that was all right.

Pulling her close, he held her tight to his chest as he told her, "I choose you, Aislinn. Today, tomorrow, for always." And he sealed that promise with a kiss, hoping it would be enough.

When he finally lifted his head, she met him with a curious gaze growing to concern.

He couldn't tell her his plan, for she might try to stop him. Her heart was too good, and he wanted it for himself. So Hakon would do what he should've done a long time ago.

With a final kiss, he bid her farewell and left the study.

It was a short walk to the rooms Orek and Sorcha shared. A swift knock brought his friend to the door, a look of bafflement on his face.

"I need your help," said Hakon.

And quickly. His time was short, and there was much to do.

# 32

The morning of the Choosing, Aislinn woke well before dawn. She'd hardly slept at all, her big bed feeling entirely too large and lonely. The weight of the world rested just outside her bed curtains, and she hid from them under the covers for as long as she could.

Fia and Sorcha came to prepare her, her maid bearing a tray of light breakfast and both of them a solemn expression.

They spoke little, for what was there to say?

Aislinn did ask after two things as Fia curled her hair around a cloth headdress and pearl hair pins.

"Captain Aodhan is in place?"

"Everything is ready," Fia assured her. She rubbed Aislinn's arm in solace when she caught her troubled expression in the mirror.

"And . . . Hakon?"

Fia's attempt at a smile fell. She shook her head. "No one has seen him. I'm sorry, my lady."

Aislinn's gaze skittered away to the window, wondering where he could be. She'd thought yesterday in the study . . .

*I choose you, Aislinn. Today, tomorrow, for always.*

His words had seared into her soul, giving her such *hope*.

Only, he was gone. Nowhere to be found when she'd asked for

him later that same evening, hoping to find out what he'd meant by his words.

Sorcha said Orek had gone with him, wherever it was he went, a fact Aislinn clung to. Hakon couldn't truly be gone if Orek went with him, surely. He couldn't be leaving her for good.

Tears pricked her eyes, and Aislinn hurried to wipe them away.

Sorcha took her hand. "It's going to be all right. He'll be found. Just focus on today."

She nodded. Survive today for the real test.

By midmorning, Aislinn looked a proper noblewoman. Fia stepped back to let her observe herself dispassionately in the mirror. The silk brocade and pearl-studded headdress and gold chain of office on her shoulders felt more like a costume than herself.

Sorcha came up behind her in the mirror. "You look so beautiful."

"I don't feel beautiful," Aislinn admitted.

Sorcha wrapped her arms around her, careful of the chain of office. "I know. But you look every bit the heiress you are. Like you aren't to be trifled with."

That did spark a small grin. "Oh?"

Sorcha nodded. "Standing up there on the dais, you'll be a sight to see. I hope Bayard quakes in his expensive boots."

Aislinn kissed her friend's cheek. "Thank you for being with me."

"We're beside you, every step," Sorcha assured her.

"Everything is ready," Fia added. "He won't be a worry to you anymore."

That was certainly something to look forward to. Laying her plans with Captain Aodhan yesterday had offered some distraction from her worries. Aislinn was determined not to give Bayard his way, but the consequences of that had to be planned for.

She would reject him and expose his treachery to the dozen or so nobles who'd arrived in time to witness the Choosing. Detaining him and his guards in the great hall would be key, as they had to be secured before anyone could inform Bayard's company. The next few hours had to go perfectly, without surprises.

If they did, Aislinn would be rid of the threat of Bayard. Survive today to fight tomorrow.

Heartened by her friends' words, Aislinn nodded and led the way from her rooms. Outside, her guards waited to flank her, and all of them began their quiet procession to the great hall.

The walk seemed to take far longer than it usually did, and it wasn't all due to her heavy skirts. Aislinn's pulse thrummed at her dry throat, and she clutched the wooden rose Hakon had whittled her in her pocket for comfort.

The great hall was already full when the herald announced her arrival, and the soft shift of fabrics as people turned to watch her ascend the few steps murmured through the large space. When she gained the top of the dais, she stood beside her father's seat and folded her hands behind her back.

Her next breath wobbled as Aislinn looked out at all the curious faces staring back at her.

It was more than Aislinn's calling an army that saw the great hall so full. Most must be curious to see what would happen at the first Choosing in decades.

"Well," she said, ensuring her voice carried, "shall I get to choosing?"

A nervous rumble of laughter went through the crowd.

Aislinn focused on her breathing and holding her wan smile. She spied Sorcha and Fia from the corner of her eye offering looks of sympathy and support, and it was enough to calm her nerves. But oh, she wished she didn't stand up here alone. She wished she didn't have to entertain such a silly scheme. She wished her own choice, her heart's choice, was there in the hall himself.

But then, perhaps it was better if Hakon wasn't there to witness the Choosing. Aislinn remembered her jealousy at the maids fawning over him and could only imagine what a Choosing would be like for him.

That assumed, of course, that his feelings for her went anywhere near as deep as hers did for him.

*He has to care for me.* She'd been wrong about men, about a lot of things, before, but she didn't think she was wrong about Hakon.

Maybe seeing him burn with jealousy would be her answer.

Or maybe she just wished to see his face, to draw strength and comfort knowing he was there.

It didn't matter now, though. She'd never know, because he wasn't there.

Her gaze fell on Bayard as he strode forward, exuding confidence and wealth. His dove-gray doublet was studded with silver thread, his velvet trou molding to his lithe legs, and a fur-trimmed capelet embroidered with his family crest draped from his shoulders. His brown curls were glossy and all in perfect placement, and a ring glinted on every finger.

He smiled at her, exposing the dimples that bracketed his mouth, and if Aislinn knew nothing of him, he might seem charming and handsome. A perfectly genteel suitor come to press his suit.

Bowing to her, Bayard gracefully knelt onto one knee.

"I am Baron Padraic Bayard, here to offer myself for the hand of Lady Aislinn Darrow. I am the only son of my house, lord of Endelín, and am a cousin thrice removed to Queen Ygraine herself on my mother's side. There are no richer vineyards than those of Endelín, no home so beautiful as mine, and . . ."

Aislinn stood as still as she could as Bayard laid out the many fine things he could offer her. Wealth, status, comfort.

Except, she already had all those things.

There was only one man she'd met in her whole life who could offer her not only what she truly wanted but needed, too. Comfort, support, friendship. She wanted a man who made her life richer from his very presence, who filled her life with love and acceptance.

She didn't need fine fabrics and glittering jewels—just the whittled rose she treasured and the heart of the man she loved.

*Oh, fates, I love him.*

In the maelstrom of Jerrod's imminent return, she hadn't been able to put words to all the feelings she held for Hakon. In her heart of hearts, she feared naming it would make it too real, and with all the threats looming over her and Dundúran, it seemed foolish to try her luck anymore. There was a chance she could lose her father, her title, her very life—she wasn't ready to lose her heart, too.

Then again, perhaps it'd been lost long ago, when he smiled at her under the floppy hat she made him wear, or when he taught her his hand-talk.

*Good gods, I've loved him since I knew him.*

". . . my stables are stocked with no less than fifty of the finest horses, and my cellars overrun with good harvests . . ."

Aislinn could hardly stomach listening to Bayard rattle off his noble attributes, and she wasn't the only one grateful when someone coughed loudly.

"Get on with it, lad," Earl Starley muttered.

A tick in Bayard's cheek jumped, but he smiled to smooth it over. "I offer all this, as well as my title, my protection, and my loyalty."

His last words hung in the air, and as he gazed up at Aislinn, his meaning was perfectly clear.

Silence reigned for a long moment as Bayard continued to kneel.

"Are there any other suits?" Aislinn forced herself to ask.

Bayard looked over his shoulder, a good-natured, boyish smile on his face that fell when Baron Burgoyne strode forward.

Aislinn looked on in surprise as the baron got to one knee—with some effort. His fiery red hair had begun to gray at the temples, as he was closer in age to Merrick Darrow than Aislinn. Burgoyne was a pleasant man with a loud sense of humor, and his eyes twinkled as he grinned up at her.

Winking up from where he knelt, Burgoyne announced, "I hope you'll forgive me, my lady, but I had to give into temptation. And," he leaned forward, whispering loudly, "I figured you'd appreciate a choice other than this prick."

The crowd sniggered, and Bayard gave up all pretense of pleasantry. Frowning darkly at his new rival, Bayard hissed, "And what would you be able to do with a young bride, Burgoyne?"

"Far more than you, lad," Burgoyne whispered back.

The crowd laughed and tittered, and Aislinn couldn't help blushing. She didn't mind the levity so much, but she *hated* that everyone's thoughts were now on who would bed her better.

As Burgoyne began to list his own attributes, Aislinn glanced to the side at Sorcha. Her friend shared her grimace.

Next, Aislinn looked for Captain Aodhan and easily found him near the main double doors to the great hall. He gave her a subtle nod, eyes pointing her toward where several of her own knights were slowly making their way through the crowd to surround Bayard and the five guards he'd brought with him.

The sight gave her confidence, enough to listen patiently as Burgoyne made his own show of the Choosing, bringing the crowd to fits of giggles, mostly at Bayard's expense.

Aislinn wished she could indulge in the humor, but her insides twisted with nerves as his speech wound down. In a moment, it'd be time to choose.

When Burgoyne finished, his booming voice left an echo in the great hall. The air lost its levity as the crowd seemed to lean forward, waiting with bated breath to hear her decision. They held perfectly still, except in the back, where bodies were moving out of the way of one figure, taller than the rest.

Aislinn couldn't look long, turning her attention to the two suitors knelt before her.

*It's time.*

Her throat closed around the words, but she forced herself to say, "If there are no more suitors—"

"There is one more."

A gasp rang out, followed by another and another, a wave of noise that parted the crowd.

Aislinn's heart stuttered to a stop.

Hakon walked with an even gait through the parting crowd. The hall held its breath as he made his way forward, coming to stand alongside the kneeling lords. Keeping her gaze enthralled with his, he knelt before the dais.

"I am Hakon Green-Fist, here to offer myself for the hand of Lady Aislinn Darrow."

The crowd erupted in noise, bafflement and surprise trumpeting to the rafters.

Above it all came Bayard's incensed voice. "He cannot suit! He's a blacksmith! An *orc!*"

"Any suitor may make their suit," Aislinn said through lips she didn't feel, unable to move her gaze from the man she loved kneeling before her.

He looked . . . so handsome. His hair had been trimmed, and an iron torque sat round his neck, polished to a high shine. The leather coat he wore fit snugly to his great chest, embellished with silver and iron at the shoulders and cuffs. A belt circled his thick waist, the buckle studded with gems and worked into intricate whorls. Boots of fine leather encased his calves, tooled with motifs and hemmed in metal.

He looked every bit an orcish prince come down from his mountain to claim the human maiden.

He took Aislinn's breath away.

*He's here.*

"I am not noble, nor full-human. What I am is in love with you, my lady. You already have my heart, and no matter what happens today, whatever you decide, you will always have it and my loyalty."

Aislinn's hands trembled where she clasped them behind her, and tears began to fall from her eyes before she could stop them. She didn't dare move, though, for fear that this would all be a dream, that he would stop and take his beautiful words back.

"Before you choose, know that I'm not the only one who pledges their loyalty to you. My kin at the otherly camp will stand and fight for you. You've offered us a home, a haven, and we'll fight to defend it. All of us will fight like ten men."

Murmurs went through the crowd, and Aislinn's lips parted in surprise.

She hadn't thought to ask the otherly folk to fight. Allarion had pledged his sword, but the others . . . they'd come to the Darrowlands looking for peace.

That they would agree to this . . .

Aislinn searched Hakon's dear face, and her stomach sank with suspicion.

"What have you done?" she murmured, her fears coalescing when his expression turned grim.

"My land now belongs to them. They are landholders, just as many gathered here, and owe you their fealty. They will fight."

He traded his land. The land with the meadow and the outcropping, where he would build his own forge. Where he wanted to take her and lay her down and make love in the flowers in spring.

He gave it up. For her.

More tears came, dripping from her cheeks, but Aislinn couldn't stop.

His stoic face broke for the first time, and he leaned forward to whisper, "Please don't cry, *vinya*. It breaks me to see you cry."

Aislinn shook her head, finally pulling a kerchief from her pocket.

She soaked the little cloth through as Hakon continued.

"I am a master blacksmith, and I will work night and day to ensure your soldiers are fitted for battle. When the day comes, I will take up arms and fight with them. No matter what you decide today, I will fight for you, my lady. My kin, too."

Aislinn released a wobbly breath.

"My loyalty, my strength, my heart, all of it is already yours, whatever you decide. In return, I ask only for you. I do not want title nor position, only to stand beside you. To be your mate, your husband,

and the father of your children should you choose to have them. That is all I ask, for that is all I need in this world. Just you, *vinya*."

Her vision blurred through her tears. Aislinn stood on the dais alone, but it felt much higher, as if she teetered upon the edge of a precipice. She had the sensation of falling, although she did not move, her heart lodged in her throat.

He offered a solution to the threat of Jerrod, of Bayard, of a life alone.

He offered everything she wanted—himself.

There would be consequences. Oh, yes, their path wouldn't be straight or smooth. But they would walk it together, and that was all Aislinn needed.

She moved before she realized it, stepping down from the dais to the three suitors knelt there.

Aislinn had eyes only for one, coming to stand before her blacksmith.

Her mate.

She sat upon his knee—choosing him for all to see.

Aislinn wound her trembling arms around his neck, not quite believing he or his words were real. She pressed her forehead to his, needing to feel the burn of his skin against her own, and gasped at the tangible tether that looped around her heart, pulling her to him.

She could imagine and feel and taste the life he promised.

"I love you," she whispered against his lips.

"I love you, too, *vinya*," he rumbled, that purr she'd come to realize was just for her springing to life in his chest. "More than the mountain is tall and the cave is deep." She felt his grin against her mouth. "That's an orcish idiom."

The joy spilled from her in a laugh, and then she was kissing him, sealing them together. His arms came around to hold her tight, and she clung to him, feeling how his heart thundered in his chest to match her own. The rightness of him eclipsed all else—for once, Aislinn's mind went quiet and her senses dulled, and all she could do in that moment was savor him.

"Does this mean you'll have me?" he asked softly in the little cave of breath they made between them.

"Fates yes, but only if you'll have me in return. And tell me where you've been."

"Gladly, but later, perhaps."

"Yes, later."

"They're all watching us, aren't they?"

"Very much so. We'll be the talk of the castle for quite some time." Leaning back, Aislinn regarded him seriously. "Are you sure?" she murmured.

He drew her hands down from his face to his heart. "With everything I am."

Lit up brighter than a lantern, Aislinn smiled and stole one last kiss before regaining her feet. He followed her up, claiming her hand as they turned to face the shocked, whispering crowd.

Nearest them stood a chuckling Burgoyne, who'd long since gained his feet. He winked at Aislinn in good humor, relieving her that he didn't take offense.

Bayard, on the other hand . . .

"Unhand me!" the baron yelped from near the main doors.

Aislinn took a few of the dais steps so she could see over the heads of the crowd. When she met Captain Aodhan's gaze, she nodded.

Her knights moved as one, taking hold of all of Bayard's guards and shutting the doors to the great hall to prevent any from escaping.

The crowd buzzed, their surprise giving way to nervousness. They moved in a rolling wave away from the doors, closer to the dais, as a struggling Bayard and his knights were brought forward.

"What is the meaning of this?" demanded Baron Morraugh, pushing his way to the front of the crowd. "Do you mean to take us hostage?"

"Of course not, Baron Morraugh. Please forgive the dramatics," said Aislinn. Raising a hand, she called for calm. She didn't receive it, but the crowd did direct their attention to her.

"Since arriving in Dundúran some time ago, Baron Bayard has threatened me and my townsfolk with violence should I not agree to wed him."

Gasps and whispers met her accusation, and many eyes turned toward the baron, who stood squirming to try and get away from Captain Aodhan's firm hand.

"His knights have harassed the people of Dundúran, and Bayard told me in no uncertain terms that if he didn't get his way, he would set them on the commonfolk, as well as side with my brother."

Aislinn turned to behold Bayard, an ugly sort of pleasure filling her to see his useless outrage. He was a rat caught in a trap who knew time was up.

"Calling this Choosing was an attempt to force my hand. I never intended to accept him, but we must stop word from reaching his company."

Bayard sneered. "You reject me for a blacksmith?" He spat on the ground. "Orc-slut."

Hakon lurched forward, but Aislinn staid him. The crowd grumbled unhappily at the insult.

Captain Aodhan's grip on the baron's shoulder tightened until the man squeaked and began to buckle. "What shall we do with the baron, my lady?" he asked.

"I think the dungeon would best suit his ambitions."

"Indeed, my lady."

"He is a peer of the realm," argued Morraugh.

"And he will receive a fair trial when my father returns," said Aislinn. "Until then, Baron Bayard is held under the charge of treason." She nodded at Captain Aodhan. "Take him."

Grinning a bit evilly, Captain Aodhan led his knights with their prisoners out of the great hall.

With them gone, Aislinn waved for the doors to be reopened in a show of trust.

Morraugh glanced at the open doors before squinting up at Aislinn. "And what of this business with the orc? Are we really to believe you're choosing him?"

Aislinn looked to the halfling beside her and found him gazing back. He stood stoically again, and she had the feeling that he would stand aside if she asked him to.

She'd never ask that of him, today or ever.

"Yes, I have," she said. Standing several steps up, she was almost of a height with him, perfect to hug his arm to her chest. "He is patient and kind and good to me. He makes me happy."

A small smile broke across Hakon's face, and his eyes were so full of love for her, Aislinn could only smile back with unbridled joy. He meant so much to her, far more than her simple words, but he deserved to be told in private. What they felt was between them, and she didn't owe Morraugh or anyone else more.

Still, Morraugh and several other older lords sputtered.

Thinking quickly, Aislinn said, "Choosings traditionally end in a handfasting. As the seniormost noble here, it would be an honor if you would perform the rite, Baron Morraugh."

The old man gaped at her in surprise, his beard twitching.

In truth, it would be an honor for Morraugh to preside over the betrothal of the heiress, but she let him think what he would.

After a moment, Morraugh nodded. "I am at your service, my lady."

Ushering him up with a hand, Aislinn had Morraugh mount the dais as she and Hakon faced each other on the bottom step. She looked up at her handsome halfling in wonder, unbelieving that her luck had changed so quickly.

Morraugh cleared his throat. "We'll need something to bind your hands."

Sorcha was suddenly at her elbow, handing over a red ribbon. She winked when Aislinn looked at her in surprise. "I was hoping this was how today would go."

Aislinn grinned, starbursts of joy sparkling through her as Morraugh began.

"Do you, Lady Aislinn, mean to have this man to wed and to love?"

"Yes, I do."

"And do you, Hakon Green-Fist, mean to have this woman to wed and to love?"

"For always."

Baron Morraugh wound the ribbon around their joined hands, tying them together. "As senior peer of the realm, I recognize your promise to each other and wish you well. May your hearts be true and your nuptials swift."

And with those words, Aislinn was betrothed to her halfling.

Applause went up from the crowd, but Aislinn hardly heard. Standing on her toes, she met Hakon's kiss, hoping the small gesture was enough to show just how much she loved him.

They spent a good hour receiving well-wishes and congratulations, one Aislinn hardly remembered later in her daze of disbelief and happiness. All the while, she clung to her halfling, unwilling to let him go or out of her sight for fear it was all just a dream.

When the line to speak to them eventually thinned and people drifted into smaller groups to discuss the morning's events in detail, Aislinn finally felt like she could breathe. Her people's acceptance still shocked her, though perhaps she hadn't given them enough credit before.

She was sure not all would support her and Hakon, but for today, this was enough.

"That leaves only what to do about Bayard's knights," she said, her bubble of happiness threatening to pop.

Hakon turned to face her, taking her hands in his. He kissed each knuckle before asking, "Do you trust me?"

Aislinn's brows rose. The answer perhaps wouldn't have been so simple even a few days ago. She trusted him with her body, her mind, even her heart, but trusting matters of state to others was something else entirely.

Now, though, as she gazed upon her betrothed, the answer was indeed simple.

"Yes."

He nodded. "Then allow me to handle it? Aodhan and I will have it dealt with by tomorrow."

"All right," she agreed. "But don't be long. I'll be waiting up for you."

A roguish smile overtook his handsome face, and his eyes went hungry as he leaned down for a kiss. "Good," he rumbled, "because tonight, I intend to make love to my mate."

# 33

Hakon walked with Captain Aodhan to the barracks that evening, restless and ready to have this over with. Everything he'd ever wanted was within his grasp, his beautiful, brilliant mate waiting for him, and he was determined to end the night as a fully mated male. The quicker they could finish this, the better.

*"Just be careful,"* Aislinn had told him anxiously. *"I worry."*

*"Of course."* He'd tipped up her face with a knuckle under her chin. *"Your people and all the plans you've made are one of your best designs. Everything is working as it should. You just have to let it work."*

Her eyes had gone wide in understanding, and Hakon couldn't resist tasting her wonder in a kiss. *"I'll be back soon. I have many promises to keep."*

"Easy, consort," Captain Aodhan said when Hakon tried again to hasten their pace. "Let everyone get into place."

Hakon grumbled but did as the captain said, letting the man catch him up. Shaking out his shoulders, he rounded the barracks with Aodhan, keeping to the shadows to watch Bayard's knights filing in for the night.

They had been allowed to carry on as normal that afternoon and evening, drinking in town and making general nuisances of themselves. Everyone coming and going from the castle was strictly controlled, and word never reached them that Bayard now inhabited a dungeon cell. A few made inquiries, wondering when Bayard would return from the Choosing, but all the Dundúran guards had strict instructions to prevaricate.

The moon hung high in the sky by the time the last of the knights straggled into the barracks, and the slow minutes itched at Hakon's skin.

When the last knight finally staggered inside, Hakon's blood began to pump fast.

With a signal from Aodhan, the doors were quickly shut and barred from the outside.

"Are you ready?"

"More than," Hakon confirmed.

He followed Aodhan through a side door that was promptly locked behind them. Touching his wrist, the silky fabric of the handfasting ribbon gave him enough calm not to barrel through the captain and make short work of all this.

*Fates, I'm going to marry her.*

His fortunes had changed so fast, his heart had whiplash from the force and suddenness. He'd never doubted his resolve, only the circumstances that kept them apart. He could hardly comprehend it, but he would never, ever question or take it for granted.

*She chose me.*

Hakon would rise to that honor, starting tonight.

It was time to meet Bayard's underhandedness with a show of force.

He and Captain Aodhan entered the main block of the west barrack, full of cots and confused knights. Bayard's company had gathered loosely in the center, some looking on in a drunken daze, many already down to their underclothes. Dundúran's knights and guards marshalled around the perimeter of the room, their helms drawn down and hands on their weapon hilts.

Hakon and Aodhan approached, the Dundúran knights closing ranks behind them.

A tall, fairly young knight with dark hair and a pug nose that'd been broken more than once stalked forward to meet them. Hakon knew him to be the captain of Bayard's company, and he'd asked after the baron several times throughout the day.

"What's this, Aodhan?" the other captain spat, mouth twisted with outrage. "Piss poor to attack us in our drawers."

"I'm not attacking you, Garth, and I don't intend to. Provided you mind your manners, of course."

Garth sneered. "Where's the baron?"

"Exactly where he belongs," said Hakon, stepping forward.

Garth turned his glower on him, but Hakon merely looked back, unimpressed.

"Lady Aislinn has rejected your lord, and he's been taken into custody on the charge of treason," Aodhan informed Garth, though he projected his voice so all in the barrack heard. "I'm willing to be gracious and assume none of you knew the extent of your lord's treachery, threatening violence against our heiress and the people of Dundúran. No knight worth their spurs would be part of such a plot."

The company's silence was telling, and Hakon's beast growled with disgust.

"As he is without an heir and in custody, your oaths belong now to your heiress," said Aodhan.

"You can honor your oaths," Hakon said, "or you can join your lord in a cell."

Murmurs, angry and anxious, burst through the company.

With a snarl, Garth advanced on Hakon. "And who're you to make such demands, halfling?"

Hakon squared his shoulders, looming over the man by half a head. "She's my *mate*. Do you want to find out what it means to cross an orc's mate, human?"

*By the old gods, no words ever tasted or sounded so good.*

A sort of horrified understanding overcame the captain's face, and he recoiled in disgust. "She chose *you?*"

"She did. And you'd be wise to choose her, knight."

Garth snorted in derision, but it took only a glance over the man's shoulder to see his company weighing their options. Hakon seriously doubted any would truly wish to join Bayard in the dungeon; the baron didn't seem the sort to garner loyalty out of respect.

Instead, Hakon spoke their language. Bribery may not have been necessary, but he was willing to participate if it meant getting back to Aislinn that much sooner.

Hakon held an uncut gem up to Garth's face, letting the deep purple catch the light. Garth's eyes betrayed him, pupils dilating as he fixed on the sudden sparkle.

"You won't go without compensation. You owe Lady Aislinn your loyalty, but she is fair and ensures all her knights are paid well."

Garth's gaze reluctantly flicked to Hakon then Captain Aodhan. The other captain gauged them for a long moment, but his gaze drew unfailingly back to the gem.

From behind him, one of the other knights cried, "Long live Lady Aislinn!"

"Long live the heiress!"

"To the lady!"

A chorus of pledges rang out, filling the barracks with ardent promises of loyalty to Aislinn.

Hakon contained his smugness when Garth reached out and snatched up the gem. "Have it your way. We'll fight for her."

"Your show of loyalty is heartwarming," Hakon drawled.

Garth scowled, even as he pocketed the gem.

"Keep your knights contained and ready," Captain Aodhan warned. "We expect the mercenary force in a few days. Until then, your company is confined to the barracks and courtyard."

The other captain's lips thinned, but begrudgingly he nodded in agreement.

Captain Aodhan nodded back. "Excellent. I always knew you were a smart man, Garth."

Hakon would've reveled in the triumph of the night—if he didn't have an even greater, more precious triumph waiting for him.

Aodhan escorted him through the castle, although Hakon wasn't entirely sure why until the captain said, "I'm pleased for you, Hakon. But I'm more pleased for our heiress."

Hakon looked at the captain in surprise.

"Lady Aislinn is a good woman. Everyone in the Darrowlands knows it. She needs someone who will love and protect her as fiercely as she deserves. I have hope that's you."

"I won't fail her."

He would give everything to and for her, including his life—both his mortal life and the life he thought he would have. It was nothing to an orc to sacrifice and die for their bonded mate; Hakon had lived for a long time with that truth before meeting Aislinn. Giving up his ideas and dreams of what a good life was, though, had been harder to accept.

As had the difficult truth Orek tried to make him see. Hakon spent so much of his life hoping and wishing for a mate of his own that the idea of one nearly eclipsed the real woman. He'd built up and clung to the idea of a mate and a life with this imaginary woman so tightly that he'd nearly lost her.

He had to love Aislinn as Aislinn, not just his mate.

He'd come to these realizations almost too late, and the thought of how close he'd been to losing her entirely sent a shiver down his spine.

Leaving her yesterday had been difficult, as was asking Orek for help. Neither would have compared to losing her, though, so Hakon swallowed his pride and chose his mate, chose Aislinn, above all else.

Those hours leading up to the Choosing had been a blur of movement. He and Orek had bounced down the country lanes as fast as they could in a spare cart, arriving at Scarborough in a cloud of dust. Allarion and Bellarand hadn't seemed surprised to see them, and the fae agreed to come to the aid of Aislinn and Dundúran. For his help, though, he asked one promise of Hakon. He agreed without thought or care, already halfway down the lane back to the Brádaigh estate.

Over dinner in the otherly camp, he'd traded his land away—this time with some thought and care. He mourned the life that would never be, but in the end, Aislinn was worth every sacrifice. And, he was proud that the land would help establish his friends within the Darrowlands.

Half belonged to the manticore pack, who drove a hard bargain for their aid. Orek had been disappointed and disgusted, but Hakon understood. All the males hoped to find their own mates and begin their own pride. They needed land for homes—and to impress the families of possible brides.

The other half went to establishing a true village for those still in the camp—the small harpy flock and the dozen halflings who had yet to purchase farms of their own now had a permanent place, no longer dependent on the charity of the Brádaighs.

Hakon, however, had thrown himself on the charity of Aoife Brádaigh. He'd been scrubbed and trimmed and fitted. The morning of the Choosing, Orek bundled him into a cart as Calum and Blaire helped him don the finery they'd cobbled together. It felt as though he'd just slid his arms into the sleeves of the coat when he'd walked into the great hall, his eyes only for the woman he'd come to claim.

Fates, he couldn't believe he'd done all that in so little time. He owed Orek and the Brádaighs a great deal.

But that was for tomorrow.

He and Aodhan arrived at Aislinn's door in the wee hours, but Hakon knew he'd find her awake.

Turning to the captain, Hakon extended his hand.

The captain took and shook it, bowing his head in respect. "It gives me peace of mind to know that now, any threat to her has to go through you first."

"I'm a much larger target," Hakon laughed.

Bidding the captain farewell, Hakon nodded at the guards flanking Aislinn's door. They bowed their heads and opened it for him without question.

Hakon walked through the threshold into her solar for the first time, his chest so full of satisfaction and triumph, it made his ribs ache.

He was sure their union would be met with ugliness. No doubt today offered them a respite from the sheer shock of it—an heiress choosing a halfling—as the news spread. Not everyone would welcome him nor Aislinn's choice, and they had to prepare themselves for the backlash.

That was for tomorrow, too.

Shutting the door behind him, Hakon beheld a scene more perfect than even his dreams.

Aislinn sat curled up in a plush armchair by the hearth, the book in her lap forgotten as she watched him enter. Wülf slept on a velvet cushion at her feet, and the toes of one foot stuck out from the hem of her dressing gown to scratch him.

She looked so soft and content, a smile overtaking her lovely face. Her hair hung unbound in a riot of mismatched curls from the pins and braids, and her freshly scrubbed face glowed in the firelight from the hearth. Putting the book aside, she bound from her seat and into his arms.

Hakon caught her up and lifted her off her feet, making her giggle.

"You're here."

"I'm here."

She shone brighter than the summer sun as she smiled at him, her face full of the same wonder that overwhelmed Hakon.

*So many of my days will end just like this—with her, in this room.*

The realization nearly brought him to his knees with gratitude.

"Did everything go all right?"

"It did." And he'd tell her all about it—later. Tonight, she had no need for worries or fears.

He scooped her up, earning more giggling as he strode through to the bedchamber. When he set her down near the bed, her hands made hasty work of all his buttons and knots, but he should've known better than to think she could be wholly distracted.

As they undressed the other, she demanded to know where he'd been, and he told her all about his travels and bargains.

"That land was yours," she said with a sadness that tore at his heart.

"Yes. Mine to do with as I wished. It did as I'd hoped—it secured a chance for us."

"More than a chance." Taking his face in her hands, her look grew shy. "Does this mean I'm your mate?"

Hakon couldn't help his wince. He hated seeing her uncertainty and knowing he could have spared her this worry.

"It means that I'm yours. Your man, your mate. When an orc finds the person they wish to bond with, little in this world can stop it. The bond I felt to you grew even before I knew it was there."

Taking her hands, he placed them over his heart. "This is yours. Should you claim me as your mate, I would be the luckiest male alive."

Her gaze was terribly serious as she looked up at him then. She'd already chosen him in front of a hall full of her people, but this felt even more important. She'd chosen him in her way, but in the soft darkness of her bedchamber, half-naked and desperate for her, he asked her to claim him in his.

"I'm yours," she whispered. "For longer than I knew it myself, I've been yours. I love you, Hakon. I would be your mate."

Hakon shuddered with the impact, the bond cinching tight just behind his ribs. He'd never imagined it could manifest like that, nor that he would feel the echo of her heart alongside his. He could wait no longer. Stripping away the last of their clothing, he placed her in the center of the bed.

Fates, what a vision she made, all warm golden skin, her leonine curls strewn across the blankets. She gazed up at him with such love, such acceptance—his heart could hardly hold his love for her. It was too vast, too heavy.

He had to show her.

Crawling over her, he purred when she welcomed him into the cradle of her body. He claimed her lips in a searing kiss, the first of many, a whole lifetime of kisses that told her without words that he was hers. Wholly. Irrevocably.

He covered her body with his, claiming her in kisses and caresses. Nowhere was spared, he had to have all of her, if only to prove to himself that this was real.

When he reached down to feel how her cunt burned for him, his purr deepened.

"My good mate," he rumbled, "how you burn for me. Do you want to feel how I burn for you?"

Her needy moan was his answer, and he guided her hand to take hold of his straining cock. Together, they fed him inside her waiting body, and together they moaned and cried out as he pushed deep. She clasped him tight, her grip a promise that she'd never let him go.

Seating himself to the hilt, Hakon came home.

# 34

Aislinn arched into a delicious stretch, spreading her toes and rolling her shoulders. Her skin slid against even warmer skin, and the memories of yesterday filled her heart with such gladness. Rolling onto her other side, she beheld her sleeping betrothed.

She'd never seen Hakon asleep before. In all the nights they'd spent together, they'd either woken at the same time or he was the one to wake her so she could slip back to her rooms.

He seemed so at ease, the hard lines of his face softened by sleep. His pointed ears lay flat against the closely shaven sides of his head, but the longer hair at the crown flopped across his forehead in an almost boyish swoop. His lips were parted just slightly, revealing the tip of a tusk, and too tempting for her to resist.

The heavy arm thrown across her waist tightened and pulled her in as she kissed him awake. She should probably let him sleep, but she couldn't bear her joy alone.

He came awake slowly, his mouth moving lazily as she tangled their legs.

*What a way to greet the new day.*

She loved it. Most of her mornings had been spent alone. There was plenty she enjoyed about that, as well as having a bed to herself.

However, there was far more to enjoy with this arrangement, and she could see herself quickly growing used to him here, in her bed, in her rooms, in her life.

*He's mine. Well and truly mine.*

The thought was almost too fantastic to believe. She couldn't think on yesterday without a touch of wonder. Aislinn didn't know how things had gone so well, nor if an old god smiled upon her finally, but she wouldn't take the opportunities for granted.

Bayard in the dungeon, Hakon in her bed.

Everyone was just where they should be.

Aislinn was running her hands all over her man's fine chest when he finally pulled back. Those gentle brown eyes opened, his gaze so tender it nearly made her squirm.

"Good morning, my mate," he murmured.

"Good morning, husband-to-be."

That earned her a grin, his eyes crinkling and that devastating dimple appearing in his cheek.

He lifted his big hand to draw her hair back from her face, and he cupped her cheek for a long while, holding her gaze and sharing breath. Aislinn knew he wished to say something, but she didn't rush him, content to lay in his arms.

When he finally asked, his brows drawn low with worry, it nearly broke Aislinn's heart. "Are you sure?" he whispered. "Outside this room . . . not everyone will welcome us."

"I'm not afraid," she whispered back. "Those who dislike it will learn to accept us or hold their tongues. I'm sure of you, Hakon. Unless you . . ."

Her stomach swooped to think that he might have second thoughts. Romantic gestures and pillow talk were all one thing, but living beside her, an Eirean heiress, was entirely another. It wasn't a life suited to many, and it would present many challenges.

He dispelled her fears quickly, shaking his head. "Naught will separate me from you now." Pulling her hand up his chest, he placed it above the steady drum of his heart. "The bond has taken—I'm yours for always, past the gods calling us home. I just wanted to know that you're sure."

"More than sure."

His answering smile was small but more magnificent for it. People might mistake him for unassuming, that his quiet nature meant a quiet mind or mild spirit. Just the opposite. Aislinn saw just how brightly his inner fire burned, a hot core of iron that could bend but not break.

They would forge a life for themselves, the two of them.

"I love you, my darling," she murmured against his lips, happy tears welling against her lashes.

"Ach, *vinya,* you start the day by spoiling me." Pulling her atop him, his hands caressed every curve as his mouth claimed hers. "There aren't words enough to say how much I love you," he told her between kisses, "nor for how glorious, how brilliant, how—"

The door to the solar opened. Wülf bounded up from his bed by the fire, barking.

Aislinn slid back into the blankets as Brenna bustled into the bedchamber, her eyes rounding with shock to see Hakon.

"Abed together?" she admonished. "You aren't even married yet."

Holding the blankets to her chest, Aislinn sat up, frowning.

Arm folded above him and hand beneath his head, the picture of male repose, Hakon was quicker with his rebuke. "We're bonded in the orcish way," he told Brenna calmly.

"We aren't in orcish territory, and *you,*" Brenna pointed an accusing finger at Aislinn, "aren't an orcess."

No, she wasn't. What Aislinn was, was spitting mad. Embarrassment colored her cheeks, but she refused to feel guilty or ashamed for being caught with her own betrothed. She and Hakon had lain together dozens of times now, and it was on the tip of her tongue to lash Brenna with that fact.

Throwing her arms up in exasperation, Brenna proceeded to one of the armoires to fetch Aislinn clothes.

"If you insist on doing this, you should at least do it right," Brenna lectured as she pulled underthings from a drawer. "Households aren't combined until *after* the marriage."

"I only have two trunks. It will be easy to combine households."

Brenna scowled over her shoulder at Hakon for his joke, but he only grinned.

Drawing a long breath, Aislinn placed a hand on his arm.

*Enough.*

"Brenna, you cannot come barging in without knocking anymore. This is my room, my refuge, and now it's Hakon's, too. You must announce yourself like anyone else."

That got the chatelain's attention. Turning round to face the bed, Brenna frowned incredulously at Aislinn.

"I'm not just *anyone,* my lady."

"No. But if you're so worried for Hakon and me to adhere to protocol and appearances, you should lead by example."

Brenna blinked, and Aislinn knew she was right. Although Aislinn had no plans to send Hakon from her bed, she did understand that some transgressions couldn't be tolerated anymore, not if their new life together was to have a successful start.

Steeling herself, Aislinn stood from the bed, taking a blanket with her to wrap around herself. Both Brenna and Hakon had seen her naked plenty of times, but having a little covering helped her feel more secure when she told her mother's oldest friend her decision.

"Things are changing, Brenna. I . . . Dundúran cannot go on like it has. Once Jerrod has been defeated, I intend to implement reforms. The first of which is," she drew herself up tall and met Brenna's stare, "I want you to begin training a successor. When they're ready, you will receive your full annuity and more in recognition of your service to my family."

Silence hung heavy between them, and Aislinn could see she'd truly surprised the chatelain.

Brenna's power and opinion were so solid, so assured, they'd ruled

Aislinn for a long time. She'd needed that rigidity in the dark days after her mother's death, as well as Brenna's competence as she herself learned how to govern Dundúran Castle.

But Aislinn wasn't a girl anymore, nor was she a weakling in need of a firm hand.

There were many times Aislinn thought herself broken, that her mind was just too strange. After her mother's death, she was made to feel ashamed of herself, and that shame carried the echo of Brenna's voice.

It'd taken her too long to realize that her own way of thinking, of doing things—it wasn't a weakness but a strength.

"You can't mean i-it." Brenna's voice cracked, and her hand flew to her mouth to hold in a sob.

Clenching her teeth against her own answering sob, Aislinn nodded. "I do. You've served ably, and I've leaned on you many times. I'm grateful for all of it, Brenna. But you've shown you don't approve of how I will rule the Darrowlands."

She reached out to squeeze Brenna's arm, but the chatelain stepped back, out of her reach.

"It's time you live for yourself, Brenna."

Aislinn hoped, with time, the woman would come to see it as the opportunity it was rather than the punishment it must feel like. The annuity set aside for staff of Brenna's caliber and tenure was sizeable, and she could do anything she liked with it. Aislinn would ensure Brenna had whatever she needed for this new part of her life.

But she wouldn't change her mind. She could no longer trust Brenna, and in these important, vulnerable early days of her rule, Aislinn needed people she could trust.

Eyes glittering with ferocious tears, Brenna exacted her final strike. "You break my heart. First your brother, and now you." She shook her head with disbelief. "After all I've done . . ."

*You've done so much.*

Aislinn swallowed past a sticky throat. "I can dress myself this morning, and we will take breakfast in the dining hall. Please, take a moment for yourself."

Lips pinched, Brenna bobbed before turning on her heels and marching from the room.

She left an uncomfortable silence behind in the bedchamber, as well as a shard of guilt lodged in Aislinn's chest. She rubbed at it, but the sharp pain wouldn't leave her.

A rustling from the bed drew her attention, and she watched as Hakon rose and came to her. Kissing her brow, he enfolded her in his arms.

"Should we worry over her?" he asked gently.

Aislinn knew what he asked. It would've been smarter to tell Brenna her decision *after* Jerrod was dealt with, as she couldn't wholly guarantee the chatelain wouldn't do something foolish out of hurt or spite. Yet, as she told Hakon, "I'm having her movements monitored. She may love my brother better, but there's little she can do now."

"Perhaps, but still, best let Captain Aodhan know."

"I will. I just . . ." Aislinn lifted her head to look at him, so he could see her conviction when she said, "I didn't like her invading our space. She has often wielded shame like a weapon, but we have nothing to be ashamed of. It is she who should be ashamed of her bigotry."

One side of Hakon's mouth kicked up in a grin. "Indeed. My fierce mate. You are a force to be reckoned with."

She didn't feel like it, but the words were a solace to her aching heart. Difficult decisions and changes were coming, but she could make it through. She had him.

Sighing, Aislinn let herself melt back into his warmth and comfort. She would need it in the coming days more than ever.


The following days were a dichotomy of painful waiting and breathless activity as Dundúran prepared.

More townsfolk made camp in the courtyard, and the castle kitchens and stores were open day and night to feed them. Businesses were boarded up; mills, tanneries, and breweries were closed; and the market stalls shuttered their doors. Many took up the offer to learn self-defense from the garrison, and more lent their labor to the city and castle smithies.

Forges bellowed smoke alongside the kitchens, baking steel and iron into arrowheads and shields. Some folk spent their days peeling carrots and potatoes, others sharpening poles into wooden stakes.

It filled Aislinn with pride to see her people come together. They didn't complain, even with the impending threat. They rallied, and their steadfastness reaffirmed her own resolve.

They also accepted the large halfling at her side.

To be sure, there were murmurs of doubt, even hostility, toward their union. However, they were murmurs only, and as the strenuous days passed, the sight of Hakon by her side lost its novelty.

Aislinn leaned on her blacksmith, and she hoped the people saw how he never wavered. He set his own back into fortifying the garrison and castle, working alongside the other Dundúran smiths when he wasn't accompanying Aislinn. He gave his sweat and blood to defending Dundúran, its heiress, and its people—and those people saw.

His care, for her and for her people, filled those parts of Aislinn that she hid away, the hurting and cracked parts. His calm, steady presence lent her confidence and reassurance, and even in those rare times when he wasn't beside her, she had only to think of him and touch her whittled rose to keep the worst of her fears at bay.

When those fears grew too great, he was there, offering his hand to hold or chest to cry into. Rather than fight them, she allowed her fears their time, pouring out what she had in order to carry on.

With his help, she appointed and delegated, and the castle ran the better for it. The time it freed left her available to meet and strategize with those vassals who began to arrive with their companies.

As she walked the ramparts of the castle, hope coursed thick through her veins to see the growing army camp south of the city.

Some earls could spare ten knights, some margraves came themselves with fifty. Each addition was welcomed by Aislinn and the people of Dundúran, and as the days passed and their numbers grew, the threat of Jerrod and his mercenaries didn't seem so dire.

There was no word from her father, nor the king or queen, but that was all right. With Hakon beside her and the people of the Darrowlands united around her, she knew there would be but one outcome.

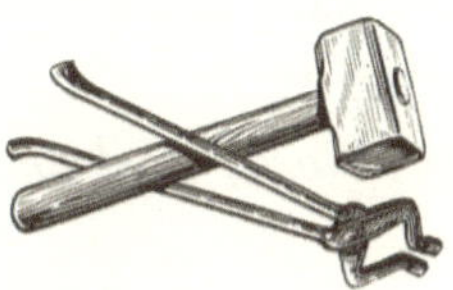

"You must hold still, *vinya.*"

"Sorry." His mate smiled down at him contritely, but within a few moments, her attention had flitted back out the window. She rocked back and forth in her distraction, her mind no doubt in five different places, none of them in the smithy with him.

Hakon bit back his grin and held onto her hips to still her.

The apprentices and other blacksmiths looked on with mixed reactions, mostly annoyance that he was taking up time and space for his project, but he wouldn't be deterred.

Last night, scouts had returned with word. Jerrod and his forces were drawing closer, would be here tomorrow. The city was a buzzing hive of activity, those townsfolk who hadn't already done so moving into the castle for shelter or fleeing to the east. The people had dealt with the stress of an impending attack admirably, and now that they knew when the mercenary force would arrive, a strange sort of calm had settled over Dundúran.

Its heiress included.

Hakon had offered all the calm and encouragement he could over the past days, but now he wasn't sure he had any left for himself. Especially not when she'd emerged from her meeting with her vassals with the strategy to meet Jerrod in the field.

*"I want to spare the city and people as much as possible,"* she'd told him as they lay in bed last night.

*"I understand, but that doesn't mean you yourself must lead it."*

Everything inside him roared and raged at the thought of his mate, untrained in the fighting arts, sent out to meet her brother and his mercenaries. He loathed the idea and said as much, multiple times and vehemently.

Aislinn was set in her decision, though. No matter how he argued or cajoled or withheld her orgasm.

*"My mind is made. I have to do this. And you must finish what you start, or else I'll be cranky with you."*

He'd heeded her threat, but even as his mate broke apart on his tongue, he still rumbled with a trepidation so deep, it nearly paralyzed him.

So, he'd extracted promises from her and gotten to work before dawn.

*"I'll meet Jerrod in the field. He may yet be reasoned with."*

*"Fine, but you'll do it armored."*

He hadn't time to make her a proper cuirass, instead using an unclaimed set in the armory. He cut away excess metal, and when she arrived late that morning as promised for her fitting, he marked the plate with charcoal to determine where else he had to adjust for the best fit he could give her.

A close-fitting cuirass was better than a loose one, but he knew in the back of his mind that it likely mattered little. Still, she'd promised to wear it as some modicum of defense when she otherwise refused to stay within the safety of the castle walls.

She'd also promised that she wouldn't fight but instead fall back to the safety of guards specifically assigned to her when Jerrod turned to violence, as Hakon knew he would. It was the most he could hope for, and he tried to content himself that she would be surrounded by hundreds willing to give their lives for hers.

If he was honest, though, the thought of her so close to danger was driving him to madness. His beast paced inside him, restless and unhappy. Hakon's unease crawled just beneath his skin, and he'd no patience for the other smiths when they told him the cuirass was good enough, to leave it.

Nothing could be just *good enough* for his mate.

She had to be protected, safe. As safe as he could make her.

Although he wasn't a master fighter himself, he would stand with her. He would be her shield, and if all else failed, all other defenses breached, at least she would have some plate and mail protecting her. They could stop a stray arrow and a glancing blow—he had to pray that was the worst she'd face.

His innards clenched painfully at the thought of even that.

*She shouldn't be in battle. She should be in our bed, safe and content. She should—*

A soft hand lifted his chin and routed his stampeding thoughts.

He looked up to see her gentle gaze upon him.

"I can hear you thinking," she said. Leaning down, she whispered against his lips, "It's going to be all right. I know it."

Hakon pulled in a long breath tinged with her sweet scent. He received her soft kiss, trying to let it calm him.

Fates, she was too good for him, for all of this. She deserved only good things, and after tomorrow, Hakon would ensure that's all she received.

The threat to his mate ended tomorrow. Jerrod, his mercenaries, any who would question Aislinn's position as heiress, they would meet his war hammer or fall to their knees. Nothing would be allowed to threaten or endanger or sadden her again. Instead, the Darrowlands, Eirea herself, would see just what Aislinn Darrow could do.

Tomorrow would be the end—and the beginning.

# 35

The day Aislinn had been dreading began with a drizzling fog that left droplets clinging to hair and noses. Her column of knights, soldiers, and warriors sniffled as they marched, their breath puffing in front of them.

Despite the drizzle, Aislinn's chest burned with determination. Even though her darling betrothed had made a fuss even as they marched from the castle gates, Aislinn led the procession out of the city to the western meadows herself, ready to put an end to all of Jerrod's scheming.

The ground at least wasn't too soggy yet, and the mud wasn't too thick, making their trek easier. She sought the good in anything she could, determined not to let the worry gnawing at her stomach get the better of her.

Her horse's ears flicked back and forth, reminding Aislinn to relax her thighs and take a breath. Riding out mounted was a concession she'd made to Hakon and Captain Aodhan's concerns. When Orek heard she would ride, he'd insisted Sorcha did, too, so her friend rode to her left while Hakon strode to her right, easily keeping pace with her horse.

Behind them marched the might of the Darrowlands, over six-hundred armed human fighters, as well as about a dozen half-orcs, a pack of five manticores, four harpies, one fae and his unicorn steed, and one dragon in his human shape. Allarion and the otherlies had met them at the city gates, solemn but sure.

Their presence meant the world to Aislinn, and she'd thanked each of them.

Captain Aodhan had wondered aloud if Theron, the dragon, might not shift to his larger form and bring the matter to an end with an undeniable show of force. The idea had shot excitement through Aislinn's veins, but Theron declined, stating he couldn't risk taking his larger form and rumor getting back to his brothers that he was now in Eirea. Hakon had looked as though he wanted to argue, but Aislinn accepted Theron's wishes, thanking him for offering what aid he could.

From her left, Captain Aodhan came riding on his own mount. "Here is suitable, my lady," he told her before breaking off again to begin organizing their forces.

Aislinn and her party stopped in the middle of the meadow as the Darrowlands soldiers formed ranks on either side. Within a few short moments, they spanned the entire meadow, blocking the road and cutting off any easy passage toward the city.

As her troops formed up behind her, Aislinn tried not to fidget. The hauberk and cuirass encasing her torso were heavy and unfamiliar, and she had an incessant itch on her shoulder she couldn't get to. She was glad of the protection the armor offered, but she felt strange inside it, as though it was finally acknowledging the threat that came for her today.

Nerves jittering in her stomach, Aislinn looked to Hakon, her steadfast halfling. He was already looking up at her, his face grim but determined. He wore a complement of boiled leather armor—gorget, cuirass, greaves, and vambraces—with a sash of Darrow blue from shoulder to hip. A war hammer sat strapped to his back, and an array of knives, daggers, and a short sword hung from his belt.

He looked positively dangerous, but his touch was gentle when she reached out her hand for his. They both wore gloves, and Aislinn missed the feel of his skin on hers, yet his warmth seeped through the leather.

Then the ground beneath them began to tremble.

Aislinn's horse shifted nervously beneath her, and she had to pull her hand away to soothe the animal.

Over the next rise, a figure appeared. Then another, another, a whole line of them, from one side of the meadow to the other.

Heart jumping into her throat, Aislinn watched as a mounted force descended into the meadow on its opposite side.

A hand covered hers, and Aislinn squeezed it. She shared a look with Sorcha, glad of her friend's support but also wishing she wasn't here, in danger. Aislinn wished none of them were, that none of this was necessary, but the time for wishing was far past.

Her heart raced as she watched the mercenaries draw closer, more and more of them coming over the hill. She thought perhaps they were comparable in number to her forces, but more of them were mounted than her own. Their journey from the Strait had to be swift, before Gleanná could summon a force great enough to stop them.

The rumble of troops grew louder, the ground quaking, and birds leapt from the trees into the skies, cawing in fright. Her horse's ears swiveled back and forth, and the creature nuzzled Sorcha's horse for comfort.

Her army stood stalwart behind her, watching the enemy draw near in silence.

When the last mercenaries had made it over the rise, Aislinn was fairly confident that their forces were evenly matched in number. She had to trust that her fighters were of better caliber and put her faith in the tactical mind of Captain Aodhan.

First, though . . .

A rider broke off from the main mercenary force, trotting out into the middle of the open meadow. Aislinn didn't need to hear the voice that called out to know it was her brother.

"Sister, I would have a word!"

Hakon snorted in disgust beside her, and she had to agree. Her brother hadn't changed and never would, always demanding without ever giving.

But if Aislinn could end this without bloodshed, she would.

She gathered her reins, prepared to meet her brother.

Hakon snatched her saddle pommel, his face a rictus of terror. "No," he growled.

"I will hear terms, as is customary. Both parties are safe during a parley."

"I don't fucking trust him."

"I don't either." She squeezed his hand before pulling it off her pommel. "But I'll see what he has to say for himself. Please, you must stay here." She couldn't bear it if he was hurt in another of her brother's treacheries.

Aislinn nodded to Allarion and Orek standing beside Hakon. Each man took hold of one of Hakon's arms, keeping him in place when Aislinn gently nudged her horse forward.

His outrage shook the meadow. "Aislinn," he roared, "*Aislinn!*"

"I have to do this," she murmured to herself.

She rode forth at a steady pace, blinking back tears to hear how Hakon fought the other men to be free and go with her. She vowed this would be the last time she ever denied him a place beside her. For the rest of their lives, wherever she went, he would go—never to be apart.

This, though—Jerrod was her brother, her responsibility. Her mistake.

Jerrod sat waiting, and if she hadn't already known it was him, she might have mistaken him for someone else. Drawing closer didn't offer more recognition, only underscored how very much her brother had transformed.

His hair and beard were unkempt, almost scraggly. His gray eyes, their mother's eyes, his most striking feature, were sunken and hollow but somehow overbright. He'd always had a finely carved face, with high cheekbones and a cut jaw, but his contours were too sharp, too concave. He bore the look of a starving wolf in the ravages of winter, hungry and desperate.

The sight of him struck her with a fear she'd never known.

For all that she and her people had planned, she hadn't counted on the very sight of him upsetting her so greatly. That he could look at her like she was a bug to be trampled beneath his boot.

*He won't talk terms.*

She could see it even now.

Still, she decided to listen when he began to talk. Jerrod always was fond of talking—or perhaps, more accurately, of hearing his own voice.

"You're brave to meet me, sister. I thought you'd be behind the highest walls of Dundúran."

"And you're foolish to bring mercenaries here, brother. It seems we actually know very little of each other."

Jerrod's lips thinned. "I take it that since you're here to greet me and not father that he isn't here. On another campaign south, I suppose?"

"Perhaps father is here, lying in wait."

Jerrod made a show of chuckling. "You always were a poor liar, Aislinn. I know father isn't here."

"You wouldn't be brave enough to try this otherwise."

His face hardened. "My qualm isn't with father, not truly. It's with you."

"And what have I done now, Jerrod?" she sighed. They'd had this argument before, many times. Usually he was drunk or had been the night before, but this argument all the same. It was somehow even more pitiable to have it when there was an army at his back.

"You took everything from me. *I* am father's heir. *I* am to be Liege Darrow."

"I took nothing, Jerrod. Father stripped you of your position because of what you did. If you actually wanted to be Liege Darrow, you should've thought of that before behaving like a spoiled child."

Color rose in Jerrod's cheeks, and his eyes darkened in a way Aislinn knew well. But set in that haggard face, a bolt of fright skittered down her spine.

"You could've refused it! You could've defended me, your brother! But no, you side with anyone else and turn me away."

"I sided with Sorcha, my friend, whom you wronged in the worst way. What you did to her was reprehensible and beyond forgiveness."

"And what about you? Forsaking your own kin for a commoner? Admit it, this is what you've always wanted. Clinging to mother's skirts then to father's."

"Jerrod, how many times must I say that our parents loved us equally?"

Her brother snorted with derision. She couldn't help but agree, although she'd never admit it. But then, Jerrod had made himself so difficult to love. Willful, arrogant, and often prickly, he thought he deserved love and loyalty without question or recompense.

"And what have you ever done for me, Jerrod?" she blurted, tired of this already. "You say I have no love for you, that I stole from you— what have you done for me, then?"

He reared back as if slapped, his astonishment so profound that Aislinn was offended. The thought probably hadn't ever crossed his mind, not in a long while, anyway.

"The position you so passionately argue for now meant nothing to you. You never performed your duties. You never cared about the people or the running of the demesne. I saw to the castle. I attended the meetings and hosted the banquets. I did everything, Jerrod. I've been heiress long before I was named it."

For a moment, her brother had no response other than to stare at her. Aislinn relished his stupor, her righteous anger making her brave.

"Dundúran, the Darrowlands, they're *mine*. My responsibility, my life. I won't let you march mercenaries into my city. I won't let you threaten my people and destroy their lives." Using her reins, she drew their horses parallel so Jerrod had to look at her when she declared, "The Darrowlands and its people are irreplaceable, but your pride is cheap. Go, Jerrod. Go far away and never come back."

His breath steamed from his parted lips, and he glowered at her with such malice, such loathing that Aislinn knew, in that moment, that only one of them would survive the day.

Her heart broke as her brother glared at her with all the hate and rage he'd felt throughout his life. He looked a boy to her, the boy she'd once known and pitied, but that wasn't the man glaring at her now. The boy she'd known and pitied had long since perished.

The sound of heavy hoof-falls broke the dark spell weaving between them, and Aislinn looked up with alarm as a big mercenary cantered for them.

An outraged cry rang out from her own troops, but Aislinn held her head up to meet the man.

He was large, his shoulders and chest wide like a blacksmith's, and his hands scarred from many fights. His nose had clearly been broken and reset badly at least once, and a scar bisected his tanned cheek.

"Dirk, I presume." He looked just as Connor had described him.

The mercenary smiled cheekily at her, revealing a missing front tooth.

"Milady," he said, bobbing his head. "We've come to take your castle." His look darkened with menace when he turned it on Jerrod. "What's taking so long?"

Aislinn watched in surprise as Jerrod curled in on himself, his shoulders rolling forward as if to make himself smaller. He wouldn't meet the other man's gaze and turned his face to the side.

"She won't meet terms," Jerrod said, almost meekly compared to how he'd spoken to Aislinn.

"You haven't given me any yet."

Dirk growled with annoyance and slapped Jerrod's shoulder hard.

Her brother nearly lost his seat, his knuckles going white as he clutched the pommel to steady himself.

"We want the city and everything in it. That's what we were promised."

Aislinn observed her brother and the mercenary, gaze flicking between them. Dirk stared back at her, all swaggering confidence, and with every movement, Jerrod cowered away.

"I'm surprised you'd take promises as payment," said Aislinn, her mind whirring. It was abundantly clear with Dirk present now that Jerrod wasn't the person to speak with. Somewhere in his foolish dealings, he'd lost control of the situation.

Jerrod's eyes flicked up to her, and Aislinn understood the desperation there. Once more, she saw not a man but a boy in trouble, caught in a situation far over his head.

But Aislinn couldn't and wouldn't save him again.

"We'll take more than just promises. A city like Dundúran, it's too big of a prize."

"You won't hold it for long. The crown would never let mercenaries keep the demesne seat. I won't let you, either."

Another set of hooves pounded the earth, and Aislinn's horse shifted to make room for Captain Aodhan's mount.

"We wouldn't be breaking the terms of parley, would we?" sniped the captain.

"Fuck off, knight. I'm dealing with the lady."

"Now you're dealing with the lady and her captain."

Dirk's look darkened again.

"What would it take to make you and your men go away?" she asked, drawing his attention back to her.

The mercenary smiled an oily smile. "Far more than you can pay, I reckon."

"A number, please."

"All your larder, all your coin—" he licked his bottom lip as his eyes trailed down her body "—and your pretty cunt spread for me."

"How dare you?" Captain Aodhan roared.

Dirk laughed, spreading a grimy feeling over Aislinn at the thought of letting him anywhere near her.

"No," she said simply. "My terms are these—leave now. Leave with your lives and make for the border, before the crown has you all hanged."

That earned her only a snort from the mercenary. "Don't think we'll be doing that, milady."

"I warn you, my forces match your own, if not outnumber them. And they aren't all human."

That got their attention. The mirth fell from Dirk's face, and Jerrod's gaze snapped over her shoulder, his eyes narrowing to try picking out the otherly fighters.

In the silence, she thought she could just hear Hakon, still struggling to get to her.

"Do you see that orc? The one fighting to be free? He's my betrothed, and he means to rend you all limb from limb. I don't mean to let him, of course. Unless we can't come to an agreement."

Jerrod paled, and both men looked at her with disgust.

"Orc-slut," Jerrod hissed. "The both of you."

Aislinn sneered back. "Better than a sniveling coward."

"There's a fae and a unicorn, too," Captain Aodhan announced loudly, enough that the mercenaries in the front lines could hear. "And a dragon. Do you really want to fight against all of that for a little lordling who couldn't hold his own seat?"

Jerrod shifted in his saddle, his gaze gone nervous as he looked from Aislinn's troops to Dirk and back again. Dirk himself glowered, reluctantly looking around Aodhan to see what he could.

"Fuck it," he growled, "just kill her here!"

With a boot, he kicked Aodhan's horse in the neck, sending it recoiling to the side. With his paw of a hand, he reached for Aislinn, quicker than a whip, his fist closing round her forearm. He pulled her nearly out of the saddle, her feet slipping free of the stirrups.

Shouts rang out from either side, and the whiz of arrows flew through the air. Horses screamed as the arrows lodged in the soft ground near them. Both sides charged forward, shaking the earth with the pounding of hundreds of feet.

Aislinn clawed at the arm that held her, heart thudding with fear when she saw Dirk go for a knife at his belt. She had her own, but it felt so far away, so impossible to reach and react faster than this blackguard.

"Aislinn, *down!*"

She heard Hakon's thunderous roar through the cacophony.

*Just need a moment—buy yourself a moment!*

Grabbing Dirk's arm, she threw herself from the saddle as dead weight.

The mercenary yelped, his horse bucking and leaping with fright. It crashed into Jerrod's mount, and together, the three of them tumbled to the ground.

# 36

The ground punched the air from Aislinn's lungs, and she lay in a daze on her side for a long moment, fighting to keep her vision from drowning in bright green bursts. Her head sloshed when she tried to move it, and her wrist pained her—though not enough to be broken.

With a groan, she rolled onto her front.

The sounds of male moans brought her round, and Aislinn looked up to see Dirk and Jerrod prone but both beginning to rouse.

Her arm free of Dirk's hold, Aislinn tucked her limbs under her, lifted onto all fours, and began to crawl.

The clang of battle reverberated around her, the Dundúran and mercenary forces clashing in dueling waves of metal. Her head throbbed and her wrist complained, but she made herself keep moving. She dodged as the three horses pranced around them and whinnied, nowhere to go in the throng of bodies pressing close.

Aislinn ducked and rolled out of the way of a hoof. The horses were frightened and agitated, making a wall of flesh between her and the battle on the other side.

She heard Captain Aodhan calling her name, telling her to regain her mount, but there was no chance of that. Her horse bucked and kicked, trying to make a path through the melee without success.

A hand snatched her ankle and tugged, pulling Aislinn down.

With a yelp, she rolled onto her back, hand grasping at her belt for her dagger.

Jerrod loomed above her, his eyes darker than coals. He wrenched her by the ankle again, yanking her that much closer. In his other fist gleamed a wicked knife, pointed down and ready to strike.

Aislinn kicked and wriggled, throwing her weight into escaping. Her hand fumbled at the hilt of her own dagger, fingers cold and trembling.

Her foot connected with Jerrod's chest, and with an *oomph* he reared back.

Aislinn drew her dagger and staggered to gain her feet.

Soldiers and horses cried out as the battle raged around them, the shriek of steel disorienting her. She wanted nothing more than to hunker down and clap her hands over her ears, but the need to survive stung her skin, urging her up, *away*.

A body smacked into hers, and she went toppling to the ground. Her dagger flew from her hand, and it was all she could do to catch herself and not get a mouthful of dirt.

Instinct rolled her to her back, and she clawed at Jerrod's face above her. He hissed with pain as her nails left angry red welts in their wake. He lashed out blindly with his knife, slashing the air as she struggled.

Her foot connected just below his ribs, in the soft, vulnerable side, and she kicked again, again, forcing him away.

That knife whipped through the air at the same time as her leg. Her trou and skin gave as the knife sliced across her outer thigh, and Aislinn screamed.

The bite of pain and gush of blood made her head swim, and her arms shook and nearly collapsed.

Jerrod stared at her wound, her cascading blood, his eyes full of shock. Then they shuttered, as if he meant to put away any vestigial love or care he had for her. Upper lip pulled back in a snarl, he clutched his knife and held it high.

A cry of pain, of outrage burst from her lungs as Jerrod screamed with triumph.

*Not like this—I can't die today!*

Everything inside her cried out, and she threw her hands in front of her to catch the descending point of his blade.

Something drowned out every other sound—like the crash of a mountain slide, the rolling boom of thunder, the crack of an icy glacier. The resonance of it erupted through every vein, clapping against her ears with the strength of a stampede.

A battle cry, a savage promise, it came at them, Jerrod and her, without mercy.

Aislinn saw only a blur of green breaking through the battling bodies, recognizing Hakon only by the cut of his dark hair. Tusks exposed in a snarling grimace, nose wrinkled back like an angry wildcat's, he burst through the crush of fighting.

He came faster than she could see, his war hammer swinging over his head.

Jerrod had time only to look up before the hammer came smashing against his head.

The sound of his skull cracking apart filled Aislinn's ears, and she screamed and fell to the ground as her brother's body, without the top half of its head, slumped to the side.

Her stomach revolted, and Aislinn held onto her breakfast with sheer will. She trembled, willing herself not to look at Jerrod.

Huge, booted calves filled her vision, and she peeked up to see Hakon standing above her, the long handle of the hammer in one hand and a knife in the other. He stood with feet planted wide apart, and when mercenaries rushed him, he hardly moved at the impact.

Aislinn made herself small and low to the ground as Hakon stood over her, defending her. With Jerrod down and the horses scattered, the main battle pressed in around them. Mercenaries came at Hakon from all sides, trying to catch her by the boot.

Hakon swung his hammer in a wide arc, keeping them back. He roared at them, fiercer than a lion and twice as terrifying, the tendons of his thick neck popping.

"A hundred gold pieces to the one who brings me her head!" she heard Dirk shout.

More mercenaries rushed them, forcing Hakon closer. He stepped over her, keeping her body between his boots, and she curled up on the trampled ground, hands over her face.

"My lady!" she heard someone shout, and then the *thump* of something landing close to her.

She looked to see a shield laying nearby.

Using Hakon's leg as leverage, she reached out and snatched the shield, dragging it over her. Just large enough to cover her, she kept it at her back as Hakon guarded her front, moving as the mercenaries jostled and thrust, trying to get past him.

All she could see was legs up to the knee, feet dancing in circles as Hakon roared and pounded and struck. Blood splattered her and the shield, louder than a downpour on a metal roof. Bodies fell around them as Hakon unleashed his fury.

*Berserker rage.*

She'd heard of it, that the same instinct to mate within orcs and dragons could lead to mindless, ferocious violence.

Her lungs collapsed around a wobbling breath.

Her blacksmith, her Hakon, so sweet and gentle—a berserker.

Another headless body slumped to the ground in her vision, and Aislinn couldn't help squeezing her eyes shut. Her stomach roiled as her heart pounded, bile burning the back of her throat.

*Hang on, just hang on. It will be over. It has to be over.*

She told herself this, and yet the sounds of bodies breaking never seemed to stop. She could hear how Hakon panted, his great body heaving for air, but he wouldn't cease, his hammer striking against anything that ventured too close. She could feel how his legs trembled with exertion, but he gave no quarter, beating back each wave of attackers.

"Fucking shit! It's one damn orc—a small one at that!"

"This one's not normal!"

"Something's wrong with it!"

"Berserker rage! He's a fucking berserker!"

"With me!"

Aislinn felt Hakon stagger for the first time as multiple bodies rushed him. A growl, low and menacing, hit her ears, followed by the clang of steel. His calves flexed, digging his heels into the dirt, and Aislinn shifted the shield as he moved, trying not to trip him.

A grunt echoed above her, and she felt him shudder. Blood dripped down the leg of his trou, and Aislinn's heart jumped to her throat.

*No!*

She clutched at his calf, his blood dribbling over her hand, as she searched frantically for an abandoned weapon. Anything!

*Don't just lay here! Help him!*

But there was nothing she could grab without straying from his protection.

As if he could feel her thinking about crawling out from under him, Hakon used his heel to push her back under the shield.

Another grunt, another shudder.

"Hakon!"

But the sound of her voice only made him roar, and she felt how he threw his whole body into his next strike.

The mercenary line buckled, and at least three bodies collapsed to the ground. Aislinn thought she recognized Dirk's dark head, turned at a wrong angle on his shoulders.

Hakon loosed a resounding roar, and all the legs around them took a hesitant step back.

"They're down!" she heard Captain Aodhan call. "Mercenaries, your leaders are dead!"

"Dirk's down!" the mercenaries cried through the ranks.

"Fucking shit, I'm not dying today."

"This orc is deranged."

The legs wavered, and something close to a silence fell around them. Then the feet were tripping over themselves, the circle around her and Hakon falling away.

The ground quaked beneath her with the surviving mercenaries retreating, and she peeked over the top of the shield to see them scattering into the trees, pursued by her forces.

Aislinn sucked in a quavering breath, not quite ready to believe it was almost over.

She stayed curled on the ground, unmoving, waiting for some sign from Hakon.

But her halfling didn't move either, standing his ground above her, even as his trou soaked with blood.

"Hakon . . ." she tried, but if he heard her, he didn't acknowledge it.

Aislinn waited, holding her breath and straining her ears. Each time she tried to rise or edge out from under the shield, Hakon pushed her back. He wouldn't relinquish his hammer or move away, making her think the threat wasn't gone.

It was a long, painful wait. Her palm was warm and sticky with his blood, but her calls to him went unheeded.

More legs gathered around them but kept their distance.

"Aislinn!" she heard Sorcha call.

"I'm here," she called back. "I'm all right!"

"Glad to hear it. The mercenaries are in full retreat. But . . ."

Orek delivered the dire news. "Hakon is in a berserker rage."

"He won't let us near," said Sorcha, and Aislinn heard the deep worry in her voice.

"Talk to him, my lady," said Captain Aodhan, "try to calm him. We must see to his wounds."

Aislinn's heart sank.

"You're the only one he'll listen to now," called Orek.

# 37

Hakon saw red.

The cry of his mate in pain seared his very soul, burning away all thought and reason. He charged forward, through the insignificant bodies of men and horses that blocked his way.

*Get to her. Protect her. Mate.*

His hammer and knife were extensions of his arm. It didn't matter that he was less of a fighter than Orek or Allarion or Aodhan—his very heart lay in that meadow, and he would get to her. No matter what.

The ground was slick beneath his feet, and horses and mercenaries screamed as they met the blunt face of his hammer. He swung it high above his head, clearing a path as he charged. On his left, Bellarand galloped, gleefully skewering humans on his wicked horn, as Allarion's sword cut through flesh. On his right, the dozen halflings charged, battering the mercenaries with sheer force.

He broke through the circle of bodies ringing Aislinn, her brother, and the mercenary leader.

The smell of fresh blood invaded his senses, and he saw it. Her blood, running down her leg from a wide slash.

Hakon *howled*.

His hammer swung wide and smashed into the head of the male

stupid enough to hurt *his mate*. Brain and blood and skull splattered the ground, satisfying his bloodlust.

The beast inside was all Hakon knew—he was instinct only, the will to defend his mate his only care. He stood over her, protecting her with his very body.

He could hardly discern the writhing mass of bodies that circled them. They jabbed and thrust, trying for an opening. Hakon gave them none.

He treated each that dared to his hammer. Necks cracked, faces split, and blood watered the ground around them. Still they came, one after the other or two-by-two, all eager, apparently, to die.

His mind separated from his body, and he couldn't feel the agony of his abused muscles. He was her shield, the dam holding back the river, and he would not break. They crashed against him, trying to overwhelm him with their numbers, but he would not submit.

They were nothing—and he protected everything.

The mercenaries shouted to one another, the worried cries of prey in flight. Hakon heard but didn't understand, the beast uncaring of language. It knew only *instinct* and *fight* and *protect*.

More gathered and tried to rush him again. Their wave crashed against him, but he was the cliffside and would not give. He met every thrust, every strike.

A grunt of pain escaped him when a slash carved across his chest. The hot gush of blood merely made him angrier.

With a resounding roar, he swung his hammer again, uncaring if it opened him to attack. He felt the crack of bone against his hammer, and a big human went down, his neck broken.

Another blade found his side in a glancing blow, the sting of it making him snarl with outrage.

But something had changed. He smelled it on the humans still dancing around them.

His mate's small hand grasped his calf, and he felt her moving beneath him. He pushed her back with his heel.

*Stay. Mine. Mate.*

Another came for him, and Hakon caught the attack with his knife, sending the human away with a shove before another took their place.

More came. More shouted. More died.

Hakon felt nothing but his rage, his mind gone to the swing of his hammer. He smelled only blood, heard only screams. Somewhere, deep down, beneath the beast and instinct and fear for Aislinn, his heart shuddered.

The bodies began to thin.

The ranks of the attackers broke.

Shouts rang out, a voice he recognized. It made the mercenaries hesitate, turn back, retreat.

Hakon roared at their fleeing forms, daring them to try.

*Fight me! Fear me!*

He would kill all of them, every single one for threatening his mate and their home. The offense could not stand; they had to pay for their insolence with their blood.

Hakon felt his mate moving beneath him, and he flexed his feet, tightening his hold on her.

He wouldn't let her go. She was his, his to protect and feed and fuck. He'd defeat every male here if he must, for she was his mate. *His.*

Bodies gathered round them again, though they kept further back this time. He might have recognized the voices now, but nothing penetrated the red haze that encrusted his mind.

Hakon bared his tusks and raised his hammer.

*Aislinn.*

They said his mate's name.

Aislinn.

Her hands moved over his calves, and he felt her wriggling out from under him. Despite trying to keep her low to the ground, she gained her feet, forcing him to watch both her and their enemies.

Growling in frustration, he crushed her to his chest with the arm of his knife-wielding hand. She groaned under the pressure, but for a moment he didn't care. She wasn't allowed to leave him. He'd hold onto her unto death.

Her hands searched his chest, and a noise of despair left her throat.

She spoke to him, her face turned up to his. He recognized the pleading in her voice, that she said his name.

The rage shuddered but did not give.

There were still enemies about. He could smell other male orcs and the blood. He needed their blood to make his mate safe.

He shook, and for the first time, he was aware of the agony in his body. His arms trembled with the effort of holding his weapons aloft. His wounds stung as blood seeped from the sliced skin.

"Hakon, please."

Her voice called to him, and with a quaking breath, his gaze finally fell to hers.

She reached up to take his face in her hands. Although she wore gloves, he could feel her softness. She exuded it, her eyes wide and luminous and desperate.

"It's all right," she crooned. "We're safe. We've done it."

Hakon shook his head.

The males—the blood—

"I'm safe," she whispered to him. She rose to her toes to kiss his chin. "You kept me safe."

Of course he did. She was his mate, his *vinya*. He would give his life to her, in battle, in service, in all ways.

He'd promised her as much.

Tears slid down her face, something he couldn't abide. Never.

"Come back to me. Please don't leave me alone."

The words reached deep inside him to wrench at his heart. The organ lurched within his chest, a painful pang that reminded him—

He was Hakon Green-Fist, betrothed to Lady Aislinn Darrow. He went nowhere without her.

"Aislinn."

She smiled through her weeping. "That's right. Hakon. Hakon."

The red seeped from his vision, a world of green and blue and the brilliant gold of his mate's hair coming into focus.

Hakon blinked, peering over her head to see their friends and allies gathered round them, looking on with worry. Whatever mercenaries remained were dead, the meadow strewn with their corpses.

*It's done. It's over.*

His arms gave, weapons falling away. He wrapped them around her, breathing her scent.

*She's safe.*

"I'll never leave you, *vinya*," he promised her.

Aislinn nodded and collapsed into his arms. Hakon bore them to the ground, his legs giving out. On his knees, he held his mate, not quite believing but so damn grateful.

# 38

To a riot of applause, Aislinn rose from her father's seat upon the dais in Dundúran's great hall. The great room nearly burst to the rafters with people and noise, hundreds of hands clapping, hundreds of faces smiling, hundreds of bellies full of wine and meat.

After a grueling day, it was time for celebration. The wine cellars and kitchen stores had been thrown open, and the castle courtyard and city streets glowed into the night with people reveling in the day's victories.

It'd taken the afternoon to make sense of the meadow. Efforts to bury the dead mercenaries would go on for days yet, and she had mounted parties patrolling the surrounding land and villages. With luck, the fleeing mercenaries would be driven right into the waiting crown forces and justice.

Their own dead had been brought back for proper rites, and Aislinn went herself to those families in Dundúran who'd lost kin. Some vassals had insisted her cut be seen to first, and that she should change, but Aislinn went as she was, bloodied and battle-weary. She wept with the families, offering them her deepest sympathy and the sword of their fallen kin.

The pain of losing over twenty good knights wouldn't soon go away. It hurt her heart more than the ache in her leg as she walked from one side of the castle to the other, seeing to everything that needed it. The activity took her mind from the horror of the day, and she was glad of the respite.

Eventually, though, Hakon's patience came to its end. He insisted she be seen to and promised he would allow a healer to look at him if she did so first. Sitting in her solar as the physician cleansed and stitched, the day had fallen upon Aislinn, an avalanche of emotion crashing through her.

She'd wept into Hakon's shoulder, trying to hold her left leg still for the physician. He murmured soothing things to her, things she would believe someday. For tonight, she was heartsick, and he seemed to understand.

When the stitching was complete and her eyes finally empty of tears, she'd leaned back to see the grim set of his face. There was no true triumph in bloodshed, and much had been spilled to secure her position as heiress. She wouldn't soon forget her dead knights, nor the sight of her brother's broken head.

As Fia helped her change into a clean kirtle and brushed her hair free of dirt and debris, Hakon finally allowed the healers to see to him. Aislinn couldn't help hovering, worrying over the nasty slice across his beautiful chest and the gash to his side.

The physician assured them, but mostly Aislinn, that the wounds weren't deep and would heal well. Hakon seemed not to mind them, but Aislinn found watching him being stitched more upsetting than having it done to her own flesh.

*"Orcs heal quickly,"* Hakon promised her. He sat calmly with a bare chest as the physician did their work, never flinching or groaning.

Aislinn could only chew nervously on her cheek and, when the physician was finished, assure herself of his health. She ran her hands over his warm exposed skin, careful to avoid his bandages.

Somehow, fresh tears threatened to spill. Pulling her into his arms, Hakon cupped her head against his chest and purred softly for her.

Her new tears came but at least without sobs, and she soaked up his warm comfort for a long moment, breathing deep of his rich, masculine scent.

His hand ran down the length of her hair in slow, soothing caresses, and after a time, she regained her composure.

She helped clean him of the grime and blood of the day, Aislinn herself scrubbing his hands. She sought every speck of blood and dirt with a militancy, not satisfied until he was wholly green again. He calmly let her, understanding that she needed this, needed to see that they were both washed clean of the day and its horrors.

When he was clean and freshly clothed, he'd offered her his hand and accompanied her back out to see to more.

Aislinn looked to him from her place upon the dais and winked. He grinned back at her from where he stood to the side of the dais, his eyes ringed with fatigue, but standing stalwart nevertheless. She didn't know how she could have faced this day alone; through seeing the families of the dead and the healer and speaking with every person in Dundúran, it seemed, he was there beside her.

*Thank fates for that. Thank every god, old and new, that we saw sense.*

Her gratitude for him, for having him at her side, was depthless.

With a nod from him, Aislinn raised her hands, drawing the attention of the gathered crowd.

"My good people," she said, her voice carrying to the rafters, "the day is ours!"

A loud cheer went up, shaking the very stones of the castle.

"Today may have been the darkest the Darrowlands has seen since the wars of succession, but it was also our finest. We showed the kingdom that this is not a land to be bullied or threatened. You have defended Dundúran, you have defended *me,* and I won't forget your sacrifice. Thank you. Thank all of you."

If it was possible, the cheering and clapping grew louder, into a din even the gods must hear. The giddy relief emanated from everyone gathered there in the hall, and it was a balm to Aislinn's heart. Her people had weathered much in her name, and she would keep her word. She'd never forget what they sacrificed for her nor what it meant to be their liege lord.

Waving, Aislinn stepped off the dais and into the waiting arms of her halfling.

More cheers went up when Hakon pressed a kiss to her hair.

"To Lady Aislinn!" they cried.

"To Lord Hakon!"

"Long may she reign!"

"Liege Darrow! Long may she reign!"

Aislinn's cheeks hurt from smiling so wide. "Tonight we celebrate!" she announced, earning another resounding round of cheers.

Slipping his arm around her waist, Hakon led her to the side of the hall, and together they accepted well-wishes. Mayor Doherty came with several of his many grandchildren, patting her hand and then Hakon's. Captain Aodhan and Hugh, arm-in-arm and both a little too deep in their cups to care that everyone saw them together when they'd been keeping their affair secret for years, clapped Hakon's arms. Sorcha kissed their cheeks, and Orek bowed over their hands. Connor bowed before them, Baron Morraugh said a word to either of them, and Baron Burgoyne laughed and told a joke while his wine sloshed over the rim of his cup.

It was Allarion they saw last, the fae seeming to materialize from the crowd itself to stand before them. His cloak had been thrown back over his shoulders, revealing intricately engraved armor the color of midnight. He bowed low, his face as merry as Aislinn had ever seen it—which was to say, the smallest smile graced his lips and his brows weren't so low over his eyes.

"My lady, my lord," he said. "Good tidings come with your victory."

"It's the first and last battle I ever hope to see," said Aislinn.

"Indeed. Then you are already a finer ruler than most. It shall be a relief to make my home in a place governed by laws and compassion rather than bloodlust."

He smiled enigmatically, as if he knew he only piqued Aislinn's curiosity. So little was known about the fae court in Fallorian, and Allarion's presence here in Dundúran only raised more questions.

Even more strangely, Allarion turned to Hakon and said, "You will remember your promise."

"Yes," said Hakon, his demeanor grave.

Satisfied, Allarion bowed once more and disappeared back into the crowd as eerily as he'd arrived.

Aislinn turned to her halfling. "What did you promise?"

"Nothing. Yet." Hakon pulled a face. "I promised him one promise for his help today."

"Hm. He told me he would fight, as a vassal of the Darrowlands, no promise necessary."

"Well, then. A fae living up to their kind's reputation for cleverness." He pulled her deeper into his side, leaning down to say quietly, "Don't worry yourself over it. Whatever he asks, I'm sure it won't be nefarious."

She made a noncommittal noise. "Well, you may have promised him, but I didn't. We'll allow him leave within the law."

Hakon grinned. "Just so, my lady."

Aislinn smiled fondly back, her eyes roving the dear lines and shapes of him. Fates, she'd never tire of looking at him. The exhaustion of the day was clear in the lines across his face, but he stood tall, his shoulders back, and wouldn't stray from her side. She would have to get him another gold hoop or two for his ears. If they were for accomplishments, he'd certainly earned them.

His hand came to cover hers on his arm, and when she looked into his eyes, she realized that he'd mistaken her silence for something dire.

Something had clung to him all afternoon, and she sensed it was finally ready to be divulged. She watched as his throat bobbed, and she waited patiently as he quietly found his words.

"Did I frighten you today?"

Aislinn laid her head against his arm. "Yes."

He stiffened beneath her cheek, and she hurried to explain. "I didn't know you could be lost to the berserker rage. I've never seen anything like it."

"I didn't know I was capable of it," he admitted. "But I saw you go down and . . ."

"You were incredible. They're already telling stories about you." It was early yet, but already the people of Dundúran looked differently upon Hakon. He'd defended her ferociously, and they had taken note. He'd proven himself to them in some way, and Aislinn swelled with pride to see them coming to understand what she already knew.

"It was . . . necessary."

"I know." Squeezing his hand, she said, "I'm sorry you were put in that position at all. I was so scared, and you saved me. I'm glad of it. But to see you not yourself . . ." Her breath went wobbly in her chest. "I worried I might lose you to it."

"I felt lost. For a time. But even then, I knew I was yours. That I had to protect you."

She smiled sadly. "Let's not do it again, though. All right?"

"I can't promise that. I'll protect you to my last breath, *vinya.*"

"I know, my darling. I know. But before that last breath, I want us to live a very long, very happy life."

That eased most of the tension from his face, and he finally smiled for her again. "Anything for you, mate."

"Good. Now, let's extricate ourselves and go to bed. I want you to hold me."

A saucy purr burst from his chest, sending her laughing as they made their farewells. It took some time and delicate diplomacy to make their escape from the great hall. Even corridors of the castle burst with merriment, and they were stopped every few paces by someone else.

It was slow progress back to their apartments, but as they neared the residential wing, revelers began to dwindle. Except . . .

Aislinn's pace slowed as she listened and heard . . . singing.

She shared a curious look with Hakon.

Leading him back, they entered the otherwise empty east solar. Its tall windows on the far side glowed with light from the courtyard, drawing her toward them. The singing grew louder as they approached, and Hakon opened the glass door onto the balcony.

She stepped out into the night to the sound of thousands of voices singing.

The courtyard glowed as brightly as the day with hundreds of torches and a dozen bonfires, the city illuminated with a warm yellow glow. A crowd of thousands had gathered there, spilling out the castle walls into the city beyond. Windows had been thrown open despite the chill, and the smell of warm cider and roasting meat scented the air.

It took a moment, but the people nearest the balcony soon saw her. Cheers rang out, and people called her name.

Aislinn stepped further onto the balcony, pulling Hakon along with her. Filled with a delight so potent it almost hurt, she waved at the singing crowd, drawing more cheers.

Pulling her into his side, Hakon leaned down to kiss her hair. "They love you, Lady Darrow," he whispered against her temple, "but not nearly as much as I do."

Happy tears escaped her, and she laughed, her body unable to contain all her joy and relief.

As more in the crowd turned toward the balcony, the cheering grew in volume, until it felt and sounded as if the whole world shook with their voices.

Aislinn didn't know who began it, but she recognized the first lines of an old Darrowlands ballad, one even older than Eirea as a united country. It was their song, an anthem just for them. Of their rolling heartland and fertile forests and winding rivers. Of how their people never knelt nor broke.

She sang with her people, loudly and off-key and with her whole body. Her lungs ached and her spirit sang along.

Tonight, the Darrowlands came together in celebration.

Tonight, Aislinn felt a happiness wider and deeper than she ever had before. One born of hope and prospect and dreams.

Tonight, her people were safe, her mate was beside her, and she was free.

# 39

*Four Months Later*

Aislinn carded her fingers through Hakon's hair, biting her lip as she peered down at him between her thighs. He always made such a delicious sight there, his brown eyes hot and hungry in his flushed green face, his big shoulders wedged between her legs or her knees thrown over them.

A moan escaped her as his tongue made wicked circles around her clitoris, teasing and playful. She'd woken up this very special day to his hands on her body and his tongue running patterns over her skin. He settled himself down the bed between her thighs and looked content as a cat to stay there all morning.

Any other day, she may have let him. Waking up this way was her favorite, and he well knew it. In their months together, Aislinn had learned to indulge in late mornings. There was little she liked more than listening to the rain patter outside as her halfling licked her to a shattering orgasm.

Today, though—they were to be married today.

As if he could sense her reminder, a grin played at his lips, the corners of which she could just spy over her mons. He pressed his face more firmly into her flesh, lapping at her mercilessly. One of his hands circled over her thigh to spread her wide, and a fingertip began to play at her clitoris as his tongue thrust inside her.

Arching off the bed, Aislinn slung a leg over his shoulder to pull him closer. He rewarded her with a deep purr, setting his lips to her clitoris so she could feel his pleasure.

"Play with your breasts. Let me see you," he rumbled, eyes dancing.

Sucking in a breath, Aislinn palmed her breasts, plumping them and running her thumbs over her nipples as he went back to giving her a most thorough tongue-lashing.

Her lids dipped closed as she fell into the sensations, her hips rolling to meet his tongue. He kissed her cunt like his life depended on it, tongue spearing inside and arching up to catch that special place on the upper wall.

Aislinn shuddered, sparks bursting through her blood. Fates, if he meant to do this all day, she might just agree to delay the wedding a day.

Her release took her by surprise, coursing through her with waves of pure pleasure from her curling toes to her thrown back head.

She was more surprised by the firm knock that sounded on the bedchamber door. Aislinn yelped, aftershocks of her orgasm quaking up her middle.

"My lady? Are you awake?" Fia's voice came from the cracked open door to the solar.

Her friend had quickly become wise to their antics and learned to knock first before seeing anything untoward. Although, Aislinn didn't think Fia minded too much—when she'd walked in and caught an eyeful of Hakon's rounded backside one morning, she'd thrown Aislinn an appreciative wink before clapping her hands over her eyes.

Aislinn looked down at Hakon—only to find her betrothed grinning widely, with no intention of stopping.

"We're awake," Aislinn called back, heart pounding, "but—"

She clenched her fingers in his hair to get him to slow his infernal tongue.

"—indecent."

She didn't think she imagined Fia's snort of amusement.

"I'll come back with a bit of breakfast, shall I?"

"Yes, please! Thank you!"

Fia's laughter echoed from the solar as she left to give them a little more time.

Although she'd been elevated to Aislinn's seneschal and Aislinn now had a new handmaid appointed to her, Fia wouldn't hear of anyone else helping her on her wedding day.

Aislinn had thought maybe Fia would be a good candidate to replace Brenna, but she'd taken to the offer of seneschal with more enthusiasm. In truth, it fit her talents and sharp mind better. Fia's aid was invaluable in the running of the castle and administration of the demesne, and Aislinn was grateful for her competence and companionship.

Aislinn's second choice to replace Brenna had recently taken over as chatelain, and soon after, Dunduran bid farewell to Brenna. It was with mixed feelings that Aislinn said goodbye, and she'd be lying if she said she didn't feel the sting of Brenna not wanting to stay for the wedding acutely. There was nothing else to do except give over Brenna's annuity and wish her well, though.

Brenna hadn't been the only one to leave. Fearghas too had requested his annuity and left not long after receiving it. From what Aislinn understood from Hakon, who still spent some of his time at the forge, the smithy was a much more harmonious place with Edda and Caitlín in charge. A handful of other staff had left, but far fewer than Aislinn feared, and it hadn't taken long to fill their positions.

She and Fia were making good progress in finding suitable candidates to fill the several high-level ministerial roles. Already their new master of coin saved Aislinn many a headache over the accounts, and a new master of grain for the southern demesne would begin their duties in summer.

Their efforts were aided by the return of her father.

Merrick Darrow returned to Dundúran in midwinter, having lost almost half of the company and at least a stone in weight. His gaunt face shocked Aislinn, but that hadn't stopped her from embracing him with all her strength. Over the winter, he and the surviving knights were diligently nursed back to health, although many still had a dullness to their eyes, Merrick included.

It hurt Aislinn to see her father so reduced, and most of the duties of Liege Darrow remained with her as he slowly recovered. He took the news of Jerrod's death with stoicism, although Aislinn more than once found him weeping silently into his hands. She decided not to tell him it was Hakon who'd delivered the killing blow—Hakon himself hardly remembered, and it didn't seem important anymore.

Jerrod was dead. It was time what was left of their family moved past his sins.

Despite her anxiety over what her father would make of her betrothal to their halfling blacksmith, Merrick took the news with good humor. He welcomed him, and over the ensuing months, Hakon proved himself the son Merrick had always hoped to have. Aislinn watched on, glowing with pride as her father and her betrothed spoke animatedly at dinners or when Hakon bowed his head and listened carefully to Merrick's advice.

All in all, it went far smoother than she could have dreamed.

She did, though, receive a stiffly worded letter from King Marius, informing her of the *crown cleaning up her little mess* and congratulating her upcoming nuptials, even if *the choice of groom was thoroughly surprising* and wouldn't she rather consider one of his strapping royal nephews. She might've lost sleep over the message had Queen Ygraine not sent her own, her tone much warmer and congratulatory. She welcomed Aislinn's reign in the Darrowlands and applauded her on her good choice of spouse—as word of Hakon's suit in the Choosing had spread quickly throughout Eirea.

*Friendship and love make the strongest foundation.*

"Come back to me." Hakon pressed a kiss to her inner thigh. "I'm not done with you, and now I must start all over."

Aislinn groaned as his tongue speared back inside her, demanding her undivided attention and denying her a chance to come down from her first peak.

She loved it when he got a bit bossy. After days spent making decisions and issuing orders, it was a delicious relief to be taken care of. She fell into pleasure each night by his command, and she longed to hear his soft, demanding words. Just a few wicked whispers from him could have her quickening with desire, no matter where they were.

Plucking at her breasts again, Aislinn squeezed his head with her thighs, trying to hasten him. He knew her game, though, and took her flanks in his hands to control her pace. His fingers strayed under her backside, and he lifted her hips up to meet his gorging mouth.

Aislinn threw her head back on the pillows, another release rushing toward its peak. Her hips rolled and rolled with her building orgasm, her world reduced to the slick slide of his tongue against her. He rumbled with satisfaction, a vibration that shook her to the marrow and made her see starbursts.

He held her as she thrashed and writhed, that pleased grin on his face.

When her body finally went lax, he carefully set her legs down, kissing each thigh with reverence. His eyes were dark with hunger and intent as he crawled over her. He planted his hands on either side of her head, and Aislinn wrapped a hand around his thick wrist.

"Fates, you're more beautiful than a sunrise," he growled, head dipping to capture her lips with his.

She tasted herself on him, and a fresh spark of lust began to burn in her belly. She spread her thighs for him, and he nestled his hips against hers, his cock burning against her mons.

Aislinn gasped at the heat of him.

"Put me inside you, *vinya.*"

His eyes trained on her with an intensity that made her shudder with desire. She loved it when he looked at her like that, like she was the center of his world.

Keeping his gaze, she reached down to take him in hand. He burned her palm, spend already leaking down the shaft. She slicked her hand up and down in gentle, firm pumps, watching as he twitched and grew hungrier.

"Just ensuring you'll meet me at the ceremony."

A deep growl rumbled through his wide chest. "Nothing will keep me away. You're mine, Aislinn Darrow."

Aislinn knew it, she just enjoyed hearing it.

She guided his cockhead to her entrance, biting her lip to feel how their bodies sealed together. He wasted no time, pushing deep inside. His hips pressed forward, not stopping until he was fully seated inside her.

Aislinn's mouth fell open with the deep stretch, delighting in how her body gave way for him. With his size, it was never a truly easy entry, but she loved the burn and stretch, loved how he opened her wide and made room for himself, demanding his place inside her body and heart and life.

He pulled back only to thrust inside again with a powerful *smack*.

Dropping his head, he rumbled in her ear, "You're going to feel me all day. Through every speech and ceremony, you'll feel me here, deep inside you, and know whose mate you are."

"Yes!" she gasped.

He thrust again, making her breasts bounce.

"Say it."

"Yours! I'm yours!"

He purred with pleasure, and his mouth claimed her in a hungry kiss, his tongue thrusting into her mouth as surely as his cock into her greedy cunt.

Their bodies met again and again in a litany of wet slaps, the sound and smell of sex filling the room. Noises escaped her lips, mewls and groans and pleas for more, harder, *yes*. She demanded everything and she received it, her halfling taking her with a relentlessness that left her breathless. His body was always in motion, rolling like the tide against her.

Slick and spend leaked from where they joined, easing his way. His thrusts grew quicker, his rhythm breaking apart. A tendon in his neck stuck out in stark relief, his arm muscles bunching as he held himself above her and pistoned his hips in mindless, decadent mating.

Aislinn clutched at his great chest, digging her fingers into the meat of muscle. His heart pounded beneath her hands, and his purr vibrated across her palms.

"Hakon!"

"Come for me, *vinya*. Let me have this until I can strip you from your wedding gown tonight."

The image and the promise of it pushed her over the edge into perfect pleasure. She writhed with it, milking his cock and drawing him impossibly deeper. Her fingers clung to him like talons as she came apart at the seams, vision going blurry and heart pounding so hard, it surely would break from her chest.

Folding his arms around her, he dropped his chest to hers and pounded inside. He didn't spare her from the onslaught of his need, and she wrapped her legs around his hips, taking, wanting it all. He moaned her name into her neck as he came, lashing her with ropes of hot, sticky spend.

Aislinn groaned, cunt clenching him tight with aftershocks as he gave her his release.

When he was spent, he slumped into her, and she gladly took his weight. She enjoyed the crush of his great body, liked feeling totally and utterly surrounded. He was her protection, her buffer—and she didn't think she could go without him ever again.

As their bodies cooled and came down from the heights of pleasure, Aislinn gently ran her fingertips along the side of his head and pressed a kiss to the other.

"I love you, Hakon."

With a rumbling purr, he picked up his head to gaze at her, his eyes gone soft.

"I love you, Aislinn, my heart, my everything."

"Are you ready to marry me today?"

"Nothing will stop me."

Many hours and layers of fabric and hair pins later, Aislinn stood just inside the doors to Dundúran Castle with her father. The people of the Darrowlands had gathered in the castle courtyard, spilling out into the city itself, having come to see the wedding of the heiress and black-smith.

Her stomach knotted with nerves, but they didn't overwhelm her. The emotions were all good—and she knew, in a few short moments, she'd be with her halfling.

From outside, they heard a great boom of applause start up.

"Almost time," said Merrick.

Aislinn drew alongside her father, tucking her hand into the crook of his elbow. He covered it with his own.

"He's not what I imagined for you, kit," Merrick admitted quietly, "but he's everything I'd hoped."

She smiled up at her father, effervescent with joy. They had gone through so much together. Even before Jerrod disgraced himself, it often felt like it was just the two of them. It was why, for so long, she thought her father could do no wrong. That he was perfect and she had to hold herself, and Jerrod, to his standard.

Aislinn understood now that her father was a man—one who made mistakes. She loved him the more for it, even if there was a part of her that had yet to forgive him for his last campaign. He'd promised her never again, and every day he held to that promise. It would take time and trust to heal the heartbreak, but she had more than enough love for her father to see it through.

It helped that they were now a family of three. Hakon was the partner she could have only dreamed about. To be sure, they had their days of disagreements. He hadn't taken immediately to the work of future lord consort, and it'd required effort to find a balance between supporting her and continuing his work. He was truly talented at the forge and didn't wish to give it up.

Now, he focused on teaching the apprentices. Two more had been added to the castle smithy, and it was his duty to ensure they were taught properly, allowing the other smiths more time to see to other business.

He also worked with Captain Aodhan and the garrison on shoring up the Darrowlands' defenses to ensure nothing like Jerrod's coup happened again. He forged good relations with the guild-masters, particularly the smiths and stonemasons. He acted as an envoy with the growing otherly village founded on the land he'd bought, bringing their news and issues directly to Aislinn.

All of it, though, had taken time and sacrifice. He was perhaps even more uncomfortable than her in courtly functions. He'd needed thorough teaching about manners, customs, and tact, and Aislinn wasn't the best tutor, as she hardly understood them herself. There were times during banquets that she used his hand-talk under the table to help him understand the conversations around them.

In their first fortnight betrothed, Aislinn had waited for him to decide she wasn't worth it. She lived in dread, awaiting the moment he gave her up. Yet, it never happened, and Aislinn realized she'd given him far too little credit. Hakon was nothing if not determined, and he was learning. He never backed down from a challenge.

It was why she knew, with absolute certainty, that he was out there already, awaiting her with his family.

His aunt Sighíl had been fetched by one of Hakon's halfling friends, and she and her family had arrived just in time for the wedding. Aislinn immediately liked Siggy, even if the orcess talked so loudly she was tempted to cover her ears as they spoke. Her mates were good-natured, and her twin girls were darlings, making fast friends with the younger Brádaigh siblings.

In fact, she thought she could hear Siggy herself cheering the loudest just outside.

"I'm ready," she told her father.

Merrick smiled. "Yes, you are."

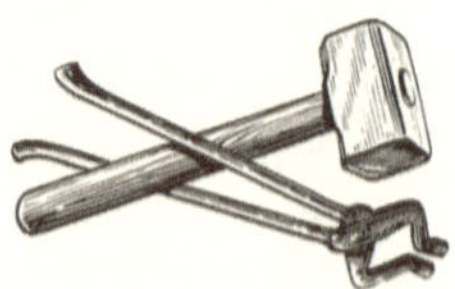

Hakon stood in the shade of a tall wooden trellis erected on the castle steps, purple cones of wisteria hanging down to perfume the air. The spring sunshine was bright, the sky a clear azure, and a gentle breeze blew through the courtyard.

Thousands of eyes watched him, and he tried to ignore the prickle along his back. He'd done his best to look the part, let valets shave and clip and scrub within an inch of his life. Days had gone into making and fitting his doublet of Darrow blue, its thick brocade catching the light; Siggy had insisted on using another day to affix all the *needed*—her word—additions like metal cuffs and silver buttons.

Siggy had brought a trove of gifts, and he spent a good hour that morning standing still as she bedecked him with a fortune of her finest creations. Around his throat she clipped an exquisite gorget, tooled with hammer and arrow motifs. On the gorget she'd mounted a thick golden torque, customarily worn by mated orcs, inset with the deepest blue sapphires. She'd replaced his *plain*—her word—steel buckle with one of silver filigree, studded with more motifs and sapphires.

And for his ears, she presented him with new golden hoops, one set with sapphires of the Darrow blue.

"*Are these gifts or advertisements?*" he'd half-joked.

Siggy just smiled toothily. "*It can mean more than one thing.*"

When she stepped back, satisfied with her work, Hakon felt a stone heavier and like he was marching back into battle, the finery his armor.

Standing there under the expectant gazes of all the Darrowlands, though, it truly was like armor—and he was glad of it. Even if his skin was green and his ears pointed, he didn't want to be a halfling blacksmith in their eyes—he wanted to look like he belonged beside his mate.

Horns sounded from the front of the castle, and Hakon's heart leapt to his throat.

He caught Siggy's eyes from where she stood at the front of the crowd with Viggo, Halstern, and their twins. She grinned widely around her tusks, clapping and cheering, and threw him a wink.

*"Do you think* gadaron *and* gamanan *would be pleased?"* he'd asked her in a quiet moment.

Siggy had snorted with laughter. *"To hear of you marrying a human noblewoman? They'd be shining brighter than the moon over it."*

*"But would they be* happy?"

Siggy looked up from the gorget clasp. *"They* are *happy,* vittarah. *Can't you feel it? It's in the sunlight, on the breeze. It's in your mate's smile and will be in the eyes of your little ones. That is their love for you."*

The truth of their love beat bittersweetly beside his heart, a bond not unlike the mate-bond he felt to Aislinn but for his dear grandparents. He could feel their happiness, their approval, and he knew they would have adored Aislinn. *Gamanan* would have loved her openness and humor, and *gadaron* would have admired her quick mind.

Aislinn would have fit into his family as well as he felt he fit into hers. It gave him some comfort, a balm for the soreness of not having his grandparents here with him.

Siggy lifted her hands above her head to clap and nodded over his shoulder.

Hakon sucked in a breath. *I'm ready.*

He turned toward the castle, the crowd behind him growing deafening as Lord Merrick emerged with Aislinn.

She was resplendent.

A gown of Darrow blue hung from her shoulders, revealing her delicate collarbones and throat, around which dangled teardrops of sapphire and aquamarines. Layers of blue silk draped from her hips like a fall of water, rippling as she walked. Gold and silver thread caught the light, making her sparkle and glitter. Her hair had been brushed and braided to a high sheen, shining like pure gold. Pearls glinted in the curls, and her crescent headdress was studded with them.

Her wide smile was the most beautiful of it all, and that only grew when she caught sight of him waiting for them.

Hakon's heart thudded painfully in his chest, the mate-bond pulling tightly, as if to draw them together faster.

*Fates, she's beautiful.* She looked every bit the noblewoman—more, she looked like the proud heiress of a great demesne, the leader of a strong people. *And she's mine.*

Love and pride heated his blood, and he reached greedily for her as she approached with her father.

Aislinn joined him under the trellis, folding her hands with his. Her smile outshone the sun overhead, and his nerves burned away in the presence of her radiance.

He hardly heard Lord Merrick as he began to speak. A hush fell over the crowd, everyone leaning closer to hear.

"As liege lord of this land, it is the greatest of honors to bind my daughter, Lady Aislinn Darrow—" he smiled fondly at her, his voice cracking "—with Hakon Green-Fist. We celebrate their union today, tomorrow, and for always."

The people clapped and cheered, calling their names.

"Have you, Aislinn Darrow, come here today of your own free will?"

"Ardently, yes," she answered, squeezing Hakon's hands.

"And do you mean to take this man as your husband, to pledge yourself to him, to bind yourself to him, and to give him all the rest of your days?"

"Yes," she said for all to hear. But for him, she added, "They're already yours."

Hakon fought with all his might not to grab her and crush her to his chest and never let go. This woman—she was everything to him. Hopes and dreams paled in comparison to her.

Lord Merrick turned to Hakon, a twinkle in his eyes. "Have you, Hakon Green-Fist, come here today of your own free will?"

"Nothing would keep me away."

"And do you mean to take this woman as your wife, to pledge yourself to her, to bind yourself to her, and to give her all the rest of your days?"

"Yes. I've been hers since I first saw her."

The crowd cooed and laughed and cheered.

"And will you, Hakon Green-Fist, swear fealty to the Darrowlands, to its Liege Merrick Darrow, and its heiress Aislinn Darrow?"

"Yes."

"Will you give your life for her, serve her, and uphold her rule?"

"With everything I am."

Nodding his approval, Lord Merrick pulled a blue strip of velvet from his pocket. Hakon and Aislinn lifted their joined hands, and her father carefully wrapped the cloth around them before tying off the ends in a small knot.

"Tied together, bound together, joined together."

The words imprinted upon his soul, and the breath rushed out of Hakon. Relief, terror, love, they all invaded his senses until all he could see was her.

*She's mine.*

"I declare them husband and wife—and your future Liege and Lord Consort. What say you?"

"We welcome them!" cried the people of the Darrowlands.

"Then before your people, make your vows and seal it."

Hakon pulled his mate close, resting their bound hands against his chest, over the heart that drummed a tender beat. He slid his free hand around her waist, needing to feel her. He was aware of the thousands of eyes upon them, but holding her kept him centered.

"You were my friend first," Aislinn said, tears gathering at her lashes. "You've always seen me for who I am. Your patience, your kindness, everything you are is a gift. One I will cherish all the rest of my days. Not everyone is lucky enough to marry their friend, but today, I'm a very lucky woman."

The people gushed and cheered, but Hakon hardly heard. His ears rang not from the crowd but the promise of her vow.

"I came to the Darrowlands seeking a new life. A home and a family. I thought I knew what I wanted—and then I saw you. Against reason, I hoped for the impossible. I couldn't give you up, and I never will. You are more than I ever dreamed or hoped—you're everything. And I will spend my life giving that to you in return."

Dropping his head to hers, he murmured against her lips, "You own me, *vinya.*"

He took her mouth and sealed their promises with a kiss. Around them, the crowd cried with gaiety, calling their names and well-wishes. The courtyard hummed and shook with their clapping and stomping, and Hakon could feel their deep love of Aislinn.

He understood them—he was just as lucky as the Darrowlands to have her.

# Epilogue I

*Six Months Later*

Aislinn clapped her hands over her ears and laughed as Siggy led her rowdy family in another loud song. The home was uproarious over Aislinn's successful deal with Chief Kennum, and Siggy was in the mood to celebrate.

Siggy needed little excuse to celebrate.

Since their first meeting shortly before for the wedding, Aislinn had taken a quick, strong liking to the loud orcess. They were opposites in nearly every way, yet they got on spectacularly.

Siggy was always singing songs, old ballads and sea shanties and new rhymes of her own making. They kept her twins, a darling set of little girls about eight years old, endlessly entertained. Her mates, Halstern and Viggo, pretended to grumble and roll their eyes, but Halstern often hummed along and Viggo bounced his leg to the tune.

Aislinn exchanged looks with Hakon, the two of them breaking out into laughter as Siggy swung her arms and sang at the top of her lungs.

The whole of Kaldebrak would surely hear. Perhaps that was the point.

It was a grand way to cap off her successful meeting with Chieftain Kennum and their last night in the mountain city.

The visit to Kaldebrak had been months in the making. Siggy said she hadn't forgotten the promise Hakon made her, that he'd bring his new mate home, and refused to leave Dundúran after the wedding without another promise from the both of them that they would visit within the year.

Aislinn might not have truly considered it, but she wanted to see an orcish city and more of the world outside her demesne. Her father agreed, and messages began to flow between Dundúran and Kaldebrak, negotiating an official visit.

It took time, and permission had to be sought from the crown. King Marius had written back an emphatic no, but Queen Ygraine had given her consent for Aislinn to treat with Kaldebrak on behalf of the Darrowlands. Aislinn glowed just thinking of the queen's letter and the confidence Queen Ygraine placed in her. The two had struck up a friendship over correspondence, and she couldn't wait to write the queen of her successes.

There had also been plenty of other business to see to while they waited for royal approval. Most importantly was the trial of Padraic Bayard. The matter had been referred up to the crown courts, as the Darrows couldn't be impartial judges. Crown magistrates assessed the matter and oversaw the trial.

Bayard looked much changed after his months in a dungeon. Gone was his swagger and haughtiness. He begged for his life, but after hearing Aislinn's account and testimony from multiple knights formerly in Bayard's employ, the magistrates handed down a sentence of treason. Bayard was beheaded four days later. Aislinn and her father had attended, although she'd turned her gaze away even before the sword fell upon his neck.

Bayard left behind no apparent heirs, although several had already emerged to claim the rich estate. Endelín was currently under the Darrows' purview until a new baron could be decided upon.

With that matter settled, she and Hakon had finally left in midsummer, accompanied by twenty knights led by Captain Aodhan himself.

The journey was slow, and Aislinn soon learned she perhaps wasn't the best traveler. She'd never been so sore or tired, and the worst part was trying to read while in the carriage specially fitted for the trip made her nauseous.

Hakon did his best to distract her, making games for them to play and thinking of topics to get her talking. She enjoyed getting to walk with him or ride alongside him, seeing the dramatic landscapes of southern Eirea.

As agreed, they left behind the company of knights except for Aodhan and another guard when they reached the outskirts of Green-Fist territory. Although Chief Kennum had graciously offered his hospitality, Siggy wouldn't hear of them staying anywhere else.

They were stuffed inside her home, warm and cozy, and Aislinn loved it. The accommodations were few, but she slept tucked tight to her darling mate, ate hearty orcish food, and soaked in the glorious warmth of Siggy's home. The stone house was full to the brim with love, evident in every ceramic dish and mantelpiece bauble.

The fortnight in Kaldebrak had been some of the best days of Aislinn's life, as she strolled the streets with Hakon. He proudly showed off his human mate, and their first few days had been crowded with curious guests. They couldn't walk anywhere very long without being stopped. Aislinn was quickly picking up the language with so many people eager to talk with her.

When her novelty eventually faded, they were able to traverse the wide cobblestone streets of Kaldebrak in peace. Hakon showed her all his favorite places, the great market square with its ornate black marble fountain; the first vein, an ancient hole dug through the mountain that was supposedly the very first mine in Kaldebrak; the hot springs deep within the mountain, as well as the lava flows deeper down; and the summit, where you could look out across the Griegen Mountains for miles unobstructed on a clear day, with a wondrous view of the *vinya* roses that sprouted along the slopes. They were in bloom in midsummer, blanketing the mountains in red and pink.

After she'd explored his city, Chief Kennum had hosted her and Hakon for several days, in which they began talks to open trading between their lands. Aislinn was well aware of the wealth of Kaldebrak and had worried what the Darrowlands could offer in return. Hakon helped her prepare her proposal, using his knowledge of both places to predict what the chieftain might be most interested in.

Although it wasn't said in so many words—at least not ones Aislinn understood—the threat of war loomed for the great orcish stronghold. In the time Hakon had been away, Kennum had aligned himself with the ambitious southern chieftain known as Vallek Far-Sight. Other clans were holding out, however, and a Pyrossi force was reportedly gathering along the border.

In their talks, Aislinn secured exclusive trade agreements between Kaldebrak and the Darrowlands, opening a flow of gems, iron, and finished silverworks for salt, wine, dried fish, and grain.

*"The most important thing in war is to keep your warriors fed,"* Kennum had told her. *"And their tankards full."*

Being with Hakon had somewhat prepared her for the chieftain of Kaldebrak, but she was still taken aback by the size of him. Easily two heads taller than Hakon and wider, despite his years and graying mane, Kennum took up all the space he was in. His hand had absolutely swallowed Aislinn's when they shook in greeting, but he'd touched her with the utmost gentleness.

It'd been amusing to see her brave, burly mate's ears glowing red in the presence of his chieftain, and the respect Hakon clearly had for the older orc endeared him to Aislinn more than anything else.

With their visit almost over and their business complete, it was time to celebrate one last time.

Siggy had spared no expense or effort, her stone table laden with a honey-glazed turkey, a mountain of roasted root vegetables, sauces and creams, sweet breads, and rich stuffings. Aislinn had endeavored to be a good guest and tried everything put in front of her. A few textures didn't agree with her, but on the whole, she was pleasantly surprised to find that orcish food was delicious.

Leaning over, Siggy captured Aislinn with a brawny arm, hugging her to her side. "Ach, don't leave me tomorrow, niece! I can't bear it!"

"We'll plan another visit for next year," Aislinn promised. This had been a grand adventure, sore backside or not, and she could hardly wait for another journey outside the Darrowlands.

"And you're always welcome to visit Dundúran," added Hakon.

The twins jumped up in their seats, excited at the idea of traveling there again. They'd made fast friends with the Brádaigh siblings and had a grand time running about the castle.

"Keeley said we can visit the horses this time!" said Ingrid.

"And we'll get to see Auntie Aislinn's bridge!" said Sigrid.

Aislinn glowed with pride from the crook of Siggy's arm. The bridge was nearly complete, and she had to pinch herself every time she saw it. Witnessing her vision come to life, seeing all the hard work the guilders poured into it . . . the sight nearly brought her to tears every time she beheld it. Aislinn looked forward to officially opening it for use before the autumn harvests began.

"Some of the children have taken to jumping off the top and floating downriver to the other bridge," she reported. It'd scared her at first, but it looked like a refreshing relief from the summer heat.

She looked up when she realized Siggy, Halstern, and Viggo had gone completely silent, their eyes widening.

The twins shrieked in excitement, bouncing out of their seats.

"I want to jump off Auntie Aislinn's bridge!" they sang as they ran round the table.

Halstern groaned as Siggy and Viggo chased the girls around the table, trying to get them back in their seats.

Aislinn blushed, realizing the trouble she'd made. A hand took hers, and she looked up to share Hakon's wide grin.

When the twins began clambering up furniture to practice their jumps, all three parents rushing after them with flailing arms, Hakon threw his head back and laughed.

Aislinn tried to apologize through her laughter, but she doubted anyone heard.

Dinner descended into madness, as it often did, and Aislinn loved it.

She loved even more when her husband pulled her into his lap and wrapped her up in his arms.

He shook with laughter, his eyes watering as he craned his neck to watch the twins' antics. Wülf and some of his siblings joined the fray, barking and prancing.

"I think the neighbors will be happy to be rid of us," Aislinn whispered to him.

"No doubt," he chuckled. Turning his face to hers, he stole a quick kiss, which made the twins squeal in delight. "To be honest, I'll be happy to have you to myself again soon."

"Well, yourself and twenty knights itching to get home."

Drawing the longer hair at the crown of his head off his forehead, Aislinn smiled fondly at her mate. Fates, he was a handsome man. None of this would have been possible without him, and Aislinn couldn't imagine her life any other way now.

She didn't know how she'd survived before. Well, she did, but life was no longer about just coping or surviving. Life was for living, and she did it alongside her mate.

Touching her forehead to his so no little impressionable ears heard, Aislinn whispered, "Although, perhaps my big strong mate might want to steal me away in the old way? For a day or two?"

That got her a purr, his pupils dilating as his gaze turned hungry. His hand slid to her backside under the table and squeezed.

"Orek's told me about a cave, perfect for stealing away with a mate."

Aislinn kissed him, tasting his smile, her heart far too full for her chest.

"I can't wait."

# Epilogue II

*Two Years Later*

Hakon lay still in their bed, his little baby daughter cooing softly on his chest. Roslinn had deigned to doze once she'd been placed there, lulled by his steady breathing and heartbeat. He held her little rump in his hand, ensuring she wouldn't kick herself off and tumble into the blankets. Again.

His other hand rested on Aislinn's thigh, where he rubbed softly with his thumb. She lay beside him, head resting on his shoulder, carding her fingers through their daughter's wispy blonde hair.

The moment was perfect.

Some went through life without a single perfect moment, but Hakon had been blessed with many. He had his mate to thank for that. She took his breath away with her brilliance and kindness. She'd made a place for him in her life beside her, bent the demesne and kingdom itself to her will to keep him. Over their years together, she'd taught him, consoled him, loved him.

And now, she'd given him the most precious of gifts.

Roslinn had arrived almost three weeks ago now. She came screaming into the world, her lungs working just fine. The sound had been the most beautiful he'd ever heard after a long day of labor for Aislinn.

They hadn't always thought they would have a child. Hakon was content to have just Aislinn, no matter the noises her father and the vassals made about an heir. But a year ago, his mate had felt herself ready.

*"Maybe just the once,"* she told him, and he agreed wholeheartedly.

The first months of pregnancy hadn't affected Aislinn much, and those symptoms she did develop didn't slow her down. At least, she tried not to let them. When she grew too round to manage stairs, she had him carry her up and down, for *"This is all your fault,"* as she liked to remind him. He just chuckled and kissed her hair and took her where she needed to go.

When she was too heavy with Rosie to walk much at all, she'd had work sent to their rooms. It distracted her from the discomfort, but the latter half of the pregnancy had worn on her. Confined to their new apartments, she'd stayed abed more than she wished.

They'd moved into the larger suite meant for the liege and their family soon after deciding to try conceiving. The larger bedchamber and solar suited them, as did the small nursery off the solar. Aislinn set up a sedan beside her desk to work from, and she probably would have kept her books while in labor if he hadn't earmarked her page and carried her to the bed.

What ensued then had been the longest day of Hakon's life. Aislinn paced the room for hours, hair matted with sweat, her skin pale. For a long while, the baby just wouldn't come.

Her fear grew with every hour, and more than one midwife had to reassure her that this wouldn't be like her mother's pregnancy. She was doing just fine. The baby was in the correct position, just taking their time.

No one spoke it, but the fear grew that the baby, a quarter orcish, may be too big to bear for Aislinn.

Hakon had stayed with her despite the sour looks from the midwives, helping lift her in and out of bed. He held her up when she tried to bear down standing up, and with each unsuccessful attempt, his panic swelled and his beast whined, more scared than he'd ever been.

Finally, deep into the night, little Rosie had decided to greet them. As he held his exhausted mate, their daughter had been placed in Aislinn's arms. Hakon held everything in the world then, everything that mattered. It was his first perfect moment with Rosie.

Fates, three weeks with a newborn had changed Hakon in ways he'd never imagined. For the first week, he'd been absolutely terrified to touch Rosie, fearing his big hands would crush her. How could they not—she was so small, so delicate, so perfect.

Her skin was the palest green, like new shoots and springtime. She had her mother's flaxen hair but Hakon's dark eyes and pointed ears. Her limbs were chubby with health, and every time she squeezed his finger with her little hand, Hakon rumbled with a love so pure and deep, it took his breath away.

She was so far not much like either of them, instead sassy and loud. *"Siggy will love her,"* Aislinn joked. She certainly seemed to know she was an important child with title and position, for if a newborn could be imperious, Rosie was. But Hakon could tell already she'd be as smart as her mother. His little daughter wouldn't be one to cross.

Snuggling closer, Aislinn asked him, not for the first time, "Are you sure one is enough?"

Hakon was content to wait a long while for a second child, if they ever even tried for another at all, not wanting to see his mate go through such an ordeal again. Although Rosie hadn't been as large as everyone feared, she was still larger than a human baby, and Aislinn's body would take a long while to recover.

"I have more than I ever could have dreamed, *vinya*. You, Rosie, our life—my heart aches with how full you've made it."

She pressed a kiss into his cheek. "You always know just what to say."

Turning his face to hers, he received another kiss this time to his lips. "It's the truth."

Aislinn hummed happily, lingering for more kisses. He was happy to give them, and they passed long moments just like that, slow kisses as their daughter slept peacefully.

When she pulled away, she touched her forehead to his. "Do we have to go?" she whispered.

"Yes," he said, "we promised your father."

Aislinn heaved a sigh, resigned. Hakon bit back his smile at the noise, and carefully, he sat up. "Come on, *vittarah*," he told his daughter when she began to squirm, "it's time to meet your people."

Handing off Rosie for her noontime meal before they left their chambers, Hakon changed into more courtly attire. Both he and his mate were used to informal, comfortable clothes—that hadn't changed with their marriage or Rosie. Still, special occasions called for special attire.

He still wasn't entirely used to pulling on the fine clothes that sat in an armoire full of clothing just for him. Made of the finest fabrics and leathers, embroidered with silk and silver threads, they were clothes for a prince. Or a lord consort. It'd taken a long while to get used to his reflection in the mirror when he wore the clothes, but for all the strangeness, it made him proud to stand beside his mate looking so. Like he deserved to be there. Like he belonged.

Dressing Rosie and Aislinn was a much longer affair. Rosie squirmed and laughed as they tried to fit her little arms through the sleeves of her small frock, and she delighted in kicking her tiny slippers from her feet.

"This child is going to enjoy running through the castle barefoot, just you watch," Aislinn grumbled as she tried again to finish dressing Rosie.

"You mean like you do?" he teased from behind her, where he stood lacing her stays.

That earned him a scowl over her shoulder. "Don't you take her side."

Hakon just chuckled.

When Rosie was as dressed as she'd allow and Aislinn was comfortable in one of her looser maternity gowns with her golden waves brushed and shining, Hakon took a moment to admire his little family. It pleased something deep and instinctual to see them all in matching Darrow blue. They were together, a unit, part of the same whole.

His mate handed him Rosie, but he handed her right back. "You carry her," he said, "and I'll carry you." Ducking down, he rose with his mate in his arms, her long skirts draped over his arms and Rosie secure in hers.

Aislinn blushed. "I can walk. For the most part."

"You walked this morning," he reminded her.

She'd made a valiant show of going to the dining hall for breakfast. The staff had risen from their seats to applaud her, and cheers had rung out so long that Hugh had to come up from the kitchen to scold everyone to eat before the food got cold.

"That's true." Aislinn laid her head against his shoulder as they walked. "And I find this is the superior form of transport."

Hakon laughed. "It's my most treasured duty, my lady."

"I may have you carry me around forever."

"Careful, I might start to think you're serious and do it."

Aislinn giggled into his neck, which made Rosie start gurgling happily.

They were all laughing by the time they made the great hall. The guards at the posterior door grinned at the sight before opening it for them. "My lady, my lord," they said, smiling when Rosie stared at them.

As they entered, the heavy metal-tipped cane of the herald dropped to the ground three times before the man announced, "Their Graces Lady Aislinn, Lord Consort Hakon, and Lady Roslinn."

The hall buzzed with excitement, and Hakon looked out at all the curious faces gathered. It was far more than Merrick had told him were likely to attend, but then, many would want this first glimpse of the new Darrow heir.

Hakon had been adamant that introducing Rosie to the people would come only when Aislinn was healthy enough and not a moment sooner. He'd been horrified to learn that noble mothers and children were often brought out a day or so after the birth, and in no uncertain terms, he'd told Merrick that that wouldn't happen with Aislinn and Rosie.

His father-in-law had deferred without argument, and he'd thankfully kept at bay the vassals who'd wanted to offer their well-wishes and see the new heiress apparent.

Hakon felt the way Aislinn stiffened with surprise to see so many faces. Rosie felt the change too and made a noise of uncertainty.

"They're all excited to see you," Hakon whispered.

"If only it was mutual," she whispered back.

Hakon pressed a quick kiss to her temple as he ascended the dais.

Merrick already stood beside his seat, and he smiled warmly to see them. The man had aged greatly in the past years, his ordeal with the sweating sickness stealing his vitality. Aislinn had nursed him back to health with sheer will, and although more frail, he'd taken to his more reduced role amiably. The coming of his first grandchild also seemed to invigorate him, and he was always looking for an opportunity to steal Rosie away for a few hours.

Merrick extended his hand, and Hakon placed Aislinn carefully in her father's seat. She looked up at him with wide, anxious eyes, her unease thrumming through their bond.

"They are here for you and Rosie," Hakon assured her.

Standing again, he took his usual place beside the seat.

Merrick leaned down to kiss his daughter and granddaughter. Rosie laughed up at him, grabbing for his beard, which she always loved to play with.

The gathered crowd held their breath as Merrick and Hakon stood on either side of Aislinn and Rosie. Hakon recognized many faces—Mayor Doherty and many other town elders; all the guild-masters had come; Morraugh, Starley, Burgoyne, Holt, and many more vassals; Allarion and his bride, manticores, half-orcs, and harpies and their human mates. And at the front stood Orek and Sorcha, surrounded by their family, their own new baby boy tucked safely in Sorcha's arms.

Sharing their pregnancies had only strengthened the friendship between Aislinn and Sorcha, as well as Hakon and Orek. Sorcha's son Fionn had arrived just two weeks before Rosie, and Hakon suspected they would be fast friends as they grew.

The crowd was full of halflings of all kinds, the Darrowlands home now to dozens of otherly folk and their human mates. A village of them grew on and expanded from the land Hakon had traded to the manticores, and all were fiercely loyal to the liege and heiress who'd provided them with a chance.

Hakon looked upon Aislinn, his heart swelling with pride at the sight of her holding their daughter. Her expression was still pensive, but her shoulders were back, her spine straight. Rosie gazed out at the crowd curiously, assessing her people.

In the first days after Rosie's birth, Aislinn had cried with her worries over the life Rosie would lead. Would the people of the Darrowlands truly accept their green-skinned daughter as heiress and eventually liege?

"I, Merrick Darrow, Liege Lord of these lands, have the honor of presenting my firstborn grandchild. I recognize her as Roslinn Darrow, blood of my blood, heiress apparent of the Darrowlands."

The crowd gazed in wonder at Aislinn and Rosie as Merrick paused to let his declaration resound.

"Who here will pledge their fealty to my daughter, blood of my blood?" Aislinn asked, her clear voice ringing to the rafters of the great hall.

Without hesitation, Hakon knelt. "I do swear."

Like the tide rolling across the shore, one by one, every knee in the great hall bent.

In those dark hours, when exhaustion and worry for their daughter hung heavily around Aislinn's neck, Hakon had pulled her close.

*"They have loved your father. They love you. And they will love Rosie, too—for your father, for you, and for herself."*

And as Hakon gazed out at the great hall, at the Darrowlands kneeling before his mate and little green daughter, he knew what he'd said was true. The Darrowlands loved them.

But not half as much as he did.

# Glossary of People, Places, Pronunciations, Medieval Things, & Orcish Words

**Allarion** (ah-lar-ee-on)—a lone fae warrior living in the Darrow-lands, rider of Bellarand

**Aislinn Darrow** (ash-lihn)—heiress of the Darrowlands, daughter of Merrick Darrow, sister of Jerrod, our heroine

**Andreen** (ahn-dreen)—harpy living in the Darrowlands

**Aodhan** (ay-dawn, like Aiden)—captain of the guard for Dundúran Castle

**Aoife Brádaigh** (ee-fuh brah-day, almost like Brady)—Sorcha's mother, wife of Ciaran Byrne, famed horse trainer

**Balar** (bah-lar)—manticore living in the Darrowlands

**Balmirra** (bahl-meer-ruh)—ancient orcish stronghold

*baron*—in the book, a noble rank above earl and margrave but below liege lord

**Bellarand** (bell-uh-rand)—black unicorn, grumpy, lets Allarion ride him

**Blaire Brádaigh** (blare brah-day)—sixth Brádaigh child, Sorcha's sister

**Brenna** (bren-uh)—chatelain of Dundúran Castle

**Brigitt**—maid in Dundúran Castle

**Briseis** (brih-zay-iss)—half-dragon living in the Darrowlands, sister of Theron

**Caitlín**—blacksmith at Dundúran Castle, mated to Edda

**Caledon** (kal-ih-don)—northernmost kingdom of humans that split from Eirea hundreds of years ago

**Calum Brádaigh** (kal-uhm brah-day)—fifth Brádaigh child, Sorcha's brother

*chatelain* (shat-uh-lane)—a woman who oversees the running of a castle

**Ciaran Byrne** (keer-ahn burn)—Sorcha's father, husband of Aoife, famed knight

**Claire**—maid in Dundúran Castle

**Connor Brádaigh**—second Brádaigh child, Sorcha's brother

**Cormac**—Hakon's deceased human father

*daron (gadaron)*—orcish for *father (grandfather)*

**Darrah** (dar-uh)—Orek's pet raccoon, likes carrots, name means *little acorn*

*demesne* (duh-mane)—similar in meaning and pronunciation to domain; historically, the land attached to a noble manor; in the book, means the regional lands overseen by liege lords (e.g., the Darrowlands)

**Dirk**—mercenary leader

**Dundúran** (dun-dure-un)—capital city of the Darrowlands; can mean the city or the castle itself

*earl*—in the book, a noble rank below liege lord and baron but above margrave

**Edda**—orcess blacksmith at Dundúran Castle, mated to Caitlín

**Eirea** (eer-ee-uh)—central kingdom of humans, still recovering from brutal wars of succession

**Endelín** (en-dih-leen)—nearest noble estate to Dundúran, richest vineyards in the Darrowlands

**Eoin Burgoyne** (oh-in burr-goyn, like Owen)—baron, vassal of the Darrows

**Fearghas** (fur-gus)—head blacksmith at Dundúran Castle

**Fia** (fee-uh)—Aislinn's maid and friend

**Garth**—captain of Bayard's knights

**Gleanná** (glay-ah-nah)—capital of Eirea

*gorget* (gore-zhet)—piece of neck armor that covers the throat

**Granach** (gran-ack)—large village near Dundúran, close to the Brádaigh estate

**Griegen Mountains** (gree-gun)—mineral-rich mountain range in the southwest, occupied by orcs

*guild*—an association of craftsmen or merchants that oversee the stages of production of their craft/product (e.g., stonemasons, bricklayers)

**Hakon Green-Fist** (hay-kon)—half-orc blacksmith at Dundúran Castle, our hero

**Halstern**—mate of Siggy and Viggo

**Hugh**—head cook at Dundúran Castle

**Ingrid**—Hakon's deceased orcess mother

**Jerrod Darrow** (like Jared)—Aislinn's brother, disgraced former heir of the Darrowlands, son of Merrick Darrow

**Kaldebrak** (call-dih-brack)—orcish stronghold in the northern Griegen Mountains, where Hakon is from

**Keeley Brádaigh** (kee-lee brah-day)—seventh and youngest Brádaigh child, Sorcha's sister

**Kennum Green-Fist** (ken-um)—orc chieftain of Kaldebrak

*kirtle*—a dress or outer layer of one, usually worn over petticoats or a chemise but under an outer layer like a gown or coat

**Liam**—potter at Dundúran Castle

*liege lord*—historically, a superior lord/authority to others; in the book, the highest rank of noble below the royal family, rules and oversees the entire demesne

**Lisbet Canvarraugh**—noblewoman, regent to her daughter, vassal of the Darrows

*lord/lady*—in the book, honorific of any noble person of any rank, usually attached to the person's given name

**Maeve Brádaigh**—fourth Brádaigh child, Sorcha's sister

*manan (gamanan)*—orcish for *mother (grandmother)*

*margrave*—historically, a noble rank that oversaw the lands along the borders of a kingdom; in the book, the lowest noble rank after liege lord, baron, and earl

**Maritza** (mar-ihtz-uh)—harpy living in the Darrowlands

**Marius Caellus** (mar-ee-us kay-luhs)—King Consort of Eirea, half-Pyrrossi

**Merrick Darrow**—Lord of the Darrowlands, father of Aislinn and Jerrod

**Morwen**—head gardener at Dundúran Castle

**Nareeda** (nah-ree-duh)—harpy living in the Darrowlands

**Niall Brádaigh**—third Brádaigh child, Sorcha's brother

**Orek Stone-Skin** (ohr-eck)—half-orc hunter living in the Darrow-lands, mated to Sorcha

**Owen**—potter at Dundúran Castle

**Padraic Bayard** (paw-rick bay-ard, almost like Patrick)—baron, vassal of the Darrows, Lord of Endelín, suitor to Aislinn

**Pyrros** (peer-ohs)—southern kingdom of humans, has conquered other lands, countries, and tribes to the south

**Róisín Darrow** (ro-sheen)—Aislinn's deceased mother

**Sean Starley**—earl, vassal of the Darrows

*seneschal* (sen-uh-shull)—historically, the overseer of a manor or a high-ranking official; in the book, the direct assistant to a lord/lady

**Sighíl** (**Siggy**; sig-heel)—Hakon's aunt, mated to Halstern and Viggo

*silphium*—a now-extinct type of plant used by ancient civilizations for a myriad of purposes, including as perfume, medicine, and contraception; it was so highly prized and used that it was cultivated to extinction by the end of the Roman Empire

**Stanley Morraugh** (mor-ah)—baron, vassal of the Darrows

**Sofie Brádaigh**—Sorcha's aunt, Aoife's sister, a healer and midwife

**Sorcha Brádaigh** (sor-sha brah-day)—horse trainer, mated to Orek, friend to Aislinn, eldest of many siblings

**The Strait**—an isthmus of land that connects Caledon with Eirea, often contested between the two kingdoms

*sweating sickness*—a mysterious deadly disease that afflicted medieval Europe; scientists today are unsure what the diseases was or what caused it; symptoms came on suddenly, starting with coldness, exhaustion, and headaches, followed by a fever and sweating

**Theron** (ther-ohn)—dragon living in the Darrowlands, half-brother of Briseis

**Thom Doherty**—mayor of the city of Dundúran

**Tilly**—cook at Dundúran Castle

**Vallek Far-Sight** (val-eck)—orc chieftain of Balmirra

**Varon**—half-orc living in the Darrowlands

*vassal*—historically, a landholder who owed allegiance to a higher lord/authority in exchange for that land; in the book, all the noble landholders who owe fealty to the Darrows as liege lord

**Viggo**—mate of Siggy and Halstern

*vinya*—orcish for *rose,* specifically the type that grows on the slopes of Kaldebrak

*vittarah*—orcish for *little hammer*

**Wülf**—Hakon's wolfhound, likes kitchen scraps

*yeoman* (yo-man)—historically, a free but not noble man who owned a landed estate; in the book, all non-noble landholders

**Ygraine Monaghan** (ee-grane mon-uh-han)—Queen of Eirea

**Ysera** (ee-sehr-uh)—harpy living in the Darrowlands

# Author's Note

Hello! Thank you so much for reading *Ironling!* I hope you enjoyed Aislinn and Hakon's story and this return to the Monstrous World!

Sequels are always scary. I hope you enjoyed this story as much as *Halfling*. The characters and setting were fairly different on purpose, I didn't just want to write *Halfling* all over again. Aislinn and Hakon needed to be their own people, and it was so much fun putting them in a crowded, fully staffed castle. How will they find time together? Are they really as sneaky as they think? (Of course not, everyone knew lol and you know they had bets going behind the scenes.)

I thoroughly enjoyed the opportunity to world-build in this book, as well. Getting the continent map by Daniel's Maps was a dream come true, and I love it so much! There's still lots to fill in as I explore the world, particularly outside the Darrowlands, so stay tuned for more to be discovered. I have lots of plans and ideas for this world—what promise will Allarion ask of Hakon? Why do they call him Vallek Far-Sight? Why won't Theron shift into his larger form? Will the manticores lure a bride to their meadow, and will the harpies find a man who's man enough for them? TBA!

I was also grateful for the opportunity to explore characters with different abilities and neurodiversity. Aislinn's neurodivergence is based on several things, mainly the condition formerly known as Asperger's, as well as anxiety disorder and panic attacks. Neurodivergence is a broad category, and I hope I did justice to Aislinn's experience. I wanted it to be authentic without pegging her in precise holes.

I also hope that I handled Hakon's partial deafness with care and authenticity. As I was researching blacksmithing, I was intrigued by the fact that so many did lose their hearing, which is understandable given the profession. It got me thinking about what kinds of challenges that would present for a blacksmith who's a long way from home, as well as the workarounds a creative mind would come up with.

Writing both of these characters, and their love story, was such a joy. This summer (of 2024) absolutely clotheslined me due to family health issues and several other Big Life things, so it was a treat to get to escape into Aislinn and Hakon's romance. I loved all the stolen moments in the rose garden and making Hakon so Clark Kent-coded.

I hope you enjoyed this exploration of the Darrowlands, as well as all the cameos of Orek and Sorcha (and Darrah)!

I'm excited to continue developing this world and peeking into other otherlies' lives. What's going on with the fae?? We find out next time on Desperate Househusbands: Eirea. *Sweetling* is out now!

Thank you so much for reading! If you enjoyed this story, I'd so appreciate it if you'd consider leaving a review. Reviews are so important in helping spread the word about a book and getting it in front of more eyeballs. Thanks again!

Come say hi on social media or check out my website, www.sewendelauthor.com, for more on my stories and to explore awesome merch!

Thanks so much!

# Acknowledgements

I'd also like to take a moment to thank some of the people who made this book possible!

A huge thank you to Mita and Abigail, my writing besties and the best beta readers out there! And thank you to Meg and Isis for their help in sensitivity reading to ensure that the experiences of the characters felt authentic. I'm  grateful for their insights and guidance.

Thank you to Leah, my awesome PA, who helped me go from hobbyist to big girl author with my own website and everything.

I'm also so grateful to my amazing ARC team, y'all are amazing!

And I have to mention too the amazing artists who helped bring Aislinn and Hakon to life. A huge thank you to Beth Gilbert, the stunningly talented artist who illustrated the cover. I also want to thank Lucia, Ali, Sasha, and more, you're all so amazing and I'm so grateful for the care you've taken with my book babies!

# About the Author

S. E. is a California native who grew up with animals; her ginger tabby is her current writing partner and lets her know when it's time to take a break (by laying on her keyboard). She graduated from the University of California, Davis with a master's in creative writing and uses all her available time to build worlds, characters, and their stories. She enjoys animal rescue shows, almost everything in Trader Joe's, and all the beautiful landscapes of California.

# Other Works

*A Time of War and Demons* (House of the Rising Sun, Book 1), fantasy romance novel

*Aerie* (Broken Wings Duet, Book 1), fantasy romance novel
*Haven* (Broken Wings Duet, Book 2), fantasy romance novel

*Stone Hearts* (War of the Underhill, Book 0), historical monster/fantasy romance novella
*Heartsong* (War of the Underhill, Book 1), monster/paranormal romance novel, February 2026
*Heartsworn* (War of the Underhill, Book 2), monster/paranormal romance novel, October 2026

*Halfling* (Monstrous World, Book 1), monster/fantasy romance novel
*Ironling* (Monstrous World, Book 2), monster/fantasy romance novel
*Sweetling* (Monstrous World, Book 3), fae/fantasy romance novel
*Faeling* (Monstrous World, Book 4), monster/fae/fantasy romance novel
*Changelings* (Monstrous World, Book 5), monster/fantasy romance novella collection, Autumn 2025 + Spring 2026
*Foundling* (Monstrous World, Book 6), monster/fae/fantasy romance, Summer 2026

# Stay in Touch

If you'd like to stay in touch, come on over to socials and say hi! I'm around on most platforms as se.wendel.author, and I'm most active on Instagram. Come check it out to find out about what I'm working on, get some reading recommendations, and get spammed with pictures of my cat. What's not to love?

You can also check out all my books, commissioned art, and book merch shop on my author website (www.sewendelauthor.com)! Lots of good stuff over there!

I've also started up a monthly newsletter. The first is out now and you can subscribe on my website to keep up with me and my news.